THE PRINCE'S
FORBIDDEN BRIDE

REBECCA WINTERS

A FORTUNE'S
TEXAS REUNION

ALLISON LEIGH

MILLS & BOON

First Published in Great Britain 2019
by Mills & Boon, an imprint of HarperCollinsPublishers,
1 London Bridge Street, London, SE1 9GF

The Prince's Forbidden Bride © 2019 Rebecca Winters
A Fortune's Texas Reunion © 2019 Harlequin Books S.A.

Special thanks and acknowledgement to Allison Leigh for her contribution to the Fortunes of Texas: The Lost Fortunes continuity.

ISBN: 978-0-263-27243-7

0619

Printed and bound in Spain
by CPI, Barcelona

THE PRINCE'S FORBIDDEN BRIDE

REBECCA WINTERS

How lucky was I to be born to my darling, talented
mother, who was beautiful inside and out?

She filled my life with joy
and made me so happy to be alive!

I love you, Mom.

PROLOGUE

A TRUMPET SOUNDED, followed by the voice of the announcer.

"This year's winner in the sixteen-year-olds' jumping and dressage, in the junior division of the Emerian *concorso*, is Princess Donetta Rossiano of the country of Domodossola. Congratulations to this unparalleled equestrian and her horse, Blaze!"

Everyone in the crowd clapped with enthusiasm.

"She has been the reigning international champion in these events since her first appearance at the Windsor *concorso*, when she was ten years old and accompanied by her father, King Victor of Domodossola. Today she's accompanied by her trainer, her father's cousin, Prince Lorenzo, a world-famous equestrian in his own right."

There was more clapping.

"And now Her Royal Highness, Queen Anne of Emeria, will present the winner's cup."

Donetta was overjoyed to have won, but she was even more excited to receive her prize from the queen. The elegant young monarch was so lucky to be born in a country where she *could* be queen.

Being the eldest of three daughters, Donetta had always dreamed of being queen of Domodossola one day. Somehow she would make it happen. Even if the law didn't allow women to rule, she was determined to find a way to get it changed.

Prince Lorenzo stood next to her. "You deserved to win the overall championship because you're the best! I knew you would do it. Too bad your family couldn't be here. They would be very proud."

"Thanks, Lorenzo, but I'm glad you're here. You're the expert who taught me how to ride. You deserve a prize, too." Lorenzo had won many awards in *concorsos* throughout his youth.

Donetta was secretly thrilled he'd come. Lorenzo, who also served as her chaperone on these trips, always gave her the freedom to have fun at the different *concorsos* without following her around, something she needed badly today.

"If Princess Donetta will please come forward to the dais."

"Go claim your well-deserved prize," Lorenzo whispered.

A round of applause accompanied her walk to the table, where pictures were taken of her with the queen. When Queen Anne handed Donetta the cup, she whispered, "You're the most outstanding female rider I've ever seen, Princess Donetta. I expect to hear of more exciting victories on that remarkable horse."

"Thank you, Your Majesty. This is a great privilege for me."

Donetta could only imagine doing this same thing for a young rider one day when *she* was queen.

She carried the engraved silver cup back to her spot in line with Lorenzo, treasuring the moment.

Another trumpet sounded, followed by the next announcement.

"This year's male winner in the sixteen-year-old division is a name we've been applauding since he first rode his horse at the Windsor *concorso* at the age of ten. Prince Enrico of the country of Vallefiore, riding his horse, Rajah! If you'll come forward to the dais, Queen Anne will present your international winner's cup."

The prince stood next to his first cousin Prince Giovanni. Giovanni had lost his parents in a plane crash, and after introducing him to Donetta, Enrico explained that his parents had taken over raising Giovanni. He lived at the palace with Enrico and his family. The two were like brothers and did everything together. Donetta had liked Giovanni immediately.

As her gaze riveted on Enrico, he flashed her a glance that said he was equally excited to see her and be with her again. They had plans when this was over. If her fifteen-year-old sister Fausta were here, she would say he was so dreamy he looked like a movie star.

He was *more* than dreamy.

Six years ago the prince had caught Donetta's ten-year-old eye when she'd first watched him perform at Windsor in his division. Even at the age of ten, he'd been a little taller and stronger than the other male contestants of his age. With his olive skin and dark hair, he'd definitely been the best looking.

Back then she'd noticed everything about him, from his penetrating black-fringed eyes to his outstanding performance on his splendid black horse, Malik. She'd envied the way the two were so tuned in to each other; it was as if they were one.

To Donetta's surprise, Enrico had sought her out after the prizes had been awarded. He'd complimented her on the way she rode and she'd returned the praise. From then on, whenever they saw each other at the dozen *concorsos* held every year in various countries, they would try to spend time together. No one else existed for them. They would discuss the finer points of each other's performances and talk about their lives.

Because of Enrico's striking looks and intelligence, Donetta never noticed the other male contestants. Whenever she learned he was on the list of competitors for his age group, her eyes always sought his and he'd find her once the competition was over.

They'd walk off away from the others. Often they hid out on the grounds to talk and laugh. From that first *concorso*, she lived for each meeting.

Today, as Donetta watched him accept his silver cup, she realized he was becoming a man, one whose looks and charisma had a visceral effect on her.

Donetta examined her heart and realized she had an infatuation for Enrico that wasn't about to go away.

Now that his presentation was over, the groups disbanded and she handed her silver cup to Lorenzo, who would be staying to talk to the officials.

He smiled at her. "I'll see you at the entrance in an hour?"

"That's perfect. Thank you!"

In a quiet voice he said, "I know why you've always been so excited to ride in every *concorso* possible, and I've kept a blind eye. Have fun, but be careful and remember—you've been promised to Prince Arnaud. Need I remind you that the Rossianos and the Montedoros have been in a feud over trade rights for two hundred years. If your parents ever find out about you and Prince Enrico..."

"Don't worry. I'm always careful and I know you won't tell." None of his warnings bothered her a bit. She was excited to be with Enrico. They loved being together whenever they could, especially knowing it was forbidden by their two families.

Now was her chance to get away and be alone with him. She started walking her horse toward the stable, knowing he would catch up.

"Donetta?"

She trembled as that seductive voice did unexpected things to her, but she didn't want people to know she was waiting for him. It was always better if he was the one who approached her. Her legs felt less substantial as she turned to him.

"Enrico!" She was so excited to see him she could hardly stand it.

"Congratulations! You gave a superb performance!"

"I wanted to tell you the same thing, but we can't talk here. How about we both mount our horses and take a ride away from the track?"

Donetta wanted to be with him all day. Right now she was too eager to spend time with him to worry about an ancient feud, or her parents' plan that she marry Arnaud one day. Enrico's parents had promised him to Princess Valentina of Vallefiore one day, but like Donetta, he didn't give it any thought.

They walked to the stable. She found her horse's stall, where her groomsman had brought Blaze after her last event. "I'll meet you here after you've retrieved Rajah. We'll have to ride bareback."

A smile broke out on his handsome face. "Do me one favor? Don't wear your helmet." His eyes played over her features, sending a thrill of excitement through her body.

She chuckled. "Why?"

"Because for once I'd like to see your hair completely uncovered." On that unexpected note he strode away from her on his long, powerful legs. No guy could look better in riding breeches than he did. At six-two, he was becoming a man.

His comment had caused her to tremble. She removed her Devon riding jacket and helmet. After shaking her head to loosen her hair, she walked over to Blaze and offered him a treat and gave him a hug.

"You were brilliant today. I love you. How would you like to take me for a ride without the saddle? We're going on a walk with Rajah."

She removed the trappings and her devoted horse nudged her. "Ah…that feels good, doesn't it?"

Donetta reached for the reins and mounted him. No more competition today. No more rules. Just pure fun with the most gorgeous guy she'd ever known. For him to have asked her to go riding with him on this special day made her happier than she'd ever been in her life.

As they backed out, she saw Enrico without his helmet, coming on his stallion. Normally they didn't allow stallions to enter the competitions, but it seemed they'd made an exception for the prince in this competition. He had total control over his animal.

Enrico, too, had shed his jacket and had loosened his white show shirt at the throat. When they walked out into the sun, the rays glistened on his luxuriant black hair.

Donetta's willingness to ride bareback was one of the reasons Enrico found it so exhilarating to be with the princess. Her spirit of adventure made her different from all the other princesses his family forced him to spend time with.

None of them could ride the way she did or be more entertaining. As his best friend and first cousin Prince Giovanni had been saying since they'd been coming to the *concorsos* together, Princess Donetta was poetry in motion, on or off her mare.

Her five-foot-seven-inch height gave her a regal elegance that had nothing to do with her title. In her navy-and-beige riding kit she looked spectacular, especially with her silvery gold hair cascading down her shoulders and back, shining like one of the waterfalls secreted in the mountains of Vallefiore.

She'd been very pretty, but now with those shimmering light green eyes that reminded him of the South

Seas he'd seen in his travels, she'd turned into a raving beauty. Whenever he saw her in a crowd—always surrounded by more males than females—he couldn't take his eyes off her.

"You rode a new horse today, Enrico. Why did you name him Rajah?"

Her question brought him back to the present. "To befit his kingly Arabian ancestry. His breed runs wild on the plains in my country and his instincts are phenomenal."

"I'd love to see a sight like that. He's absolutely gorgeous. With him you'll continue to win every competition from now on."

"I'm sure you will, too. No other rider comes close to you."

She beamed as he led them on a path away from the track to the park in the distance. When they reached the trees, they dismounted. "I brought a picnic for us."

"You're kidding!"

Enrico pulled a blanket out of his saddlebag and spread it on the ground. Then he produced several sacks of sandwiches, fruit and drinks.

"This is fabulous, Enrico." She sat down with him to eat.

"Much as I want to spend the entire weekend with you, that isn't possible. I'd give anything if we were eighteen. Then I'd be able to take you to an early dinner and dancing in some trendy café. But we're not old enough to go out to a place like that yet."

"No. My parents would never allow it. What about you?"

"I could steal away with you now if I could, but since that isn't possible, we'll have to wait until we're eighteen. Then we'll do whatever we want. You're the only girl I want to be with."

"I think about you all the time."

He darted her a penetrating glance. "You don't know the half of it. As soon as we turn eighteen, we'll go out after every *concorso*. That's a promise. In the meantime we'll have to make do with picnics."

"Next time it will be my turn to bring the food. I'll manage it somehow." She glanced at her watch and moaned. "I'd better go back. Lorenzo gave me an hour."

"What would happen if you're two hours late?"

"I don't dare test him and find out."

"I was just teasing, but it doesn't mean I can't dream."

"I know. I feel the same way."

He got to his feet and cleaned up the mess. After putting everything back in the saddlebag, they returned to the stable.

Frustrated that they had to part, Enrico dismounted in front of Blaze's stall. "I'll help you down." He held out his arms. "I won't let you fall."

Donetta glanced at him again with that enticing smile. "I'm sure I can trust you." She reached for him. The second he felt her in his arms, he pulled her against him before lowering her to the ground. Every beautiful part of her fit perfectly, increasing his desire for her.

"I'm going to miss seeing you, let alone our talks, Donetta." Unable to help himself, he lowered his head to kiss her mouth, knowing he wouldn't be able to be with her until the next *concorso*. She tasted so good he couldn't stop and began kissing her long and hard, sweeping them away until both were breathless. This kiss would have to last.

Sometime later he unwillingly released her. "Until next time. Have a safe flight home, *bellissima*," he murmured before reaching for his horse's reins to walk away.

Two years later, there'd been twenty more horse competitions where Donetta had met with Enrico. They'd enjoyed picnics and kissed each other until they were breathless. Now that they had both turned eighteen, Donetta was dying to be with Enrico again because they could really be together now for hours and hours.

After she won the overall championship for eighteen-year-olds at the *concorso* in Vienna, she'd worked it out with Lorenzo to look the other way while she and Enrico went out to dinner. She promised to be back at their hotel by 11:00 p.m., and Giovanni had hired a limo for them.

Donetta almost died with happiness when Enrico took her to a club where they could have dinner and dance. He never let her out of his arms, kissing her cheek and neck.

"You don't know how long I've waited for this, Donetta."

"Oh, yes, I do! Thank heaven there's another *concorso* next month, otherwise I'm not going to be able to handle the separation."

He kissed her lips before dancing them back to their

table. It was already getting to be eleven o'clock, but she didn't care. She wanted to stay out all night with him.

"Donetta," he said after they sat down. "There's something I have to tell you, but I'm dreading it."

Some nuance in his voice told her she wasn't going to like it. "What's wrong?"

"Today was my last time to ride in a *concorso.*"

She blinked. "What are you talking about? We can ride in competitions until we're a lot older. I don't understand."

He gripped her hand across the table. "Next week I'm leaving for England to attend university at Cambridge. Giovanni will be going with me. I won't be riding in any competitions from now on. There's no time. During the next four years I'll be spending most of my time studying. There'll be a few visits to see my family."

Donetta had been so drunk with happiness the import of his statement took a minute to sink in. "I see," she said in a quiet voice. "What will you study?"

"Business, law enforcement, finance, economics, agriculture."

"I'm envious."

"Aren't you going to be attending college, too?"

"Yes. Next month, but it won't be in England. My parents insist I get my education at Domodossola University. They don't want me going far away."

"I wish you could come to Cambridge, where we could spend all our free time together after our classes are over, to study and do *other* things..." His words caught at her heart. "Will you be competing in more *concorsos* while you're at university?"

By now they'd been served dessert, but she couldn't touch hers. "Maybe some of them."

"After the performance you put on today, I have no doubt you'll continue to win everything. I heard what the head of the Austrian federation said to you after your win. Your ability on a horse is breathtaking."

"Thank you," she said, trying to smile, but her heart was heavy.

"It's killing me that I won't see you again."

Enrico squeezed her hand harder. "I know I've upset you. Now you have some idea of what the separation's going to do to me."

Tears flooded her eyes. "The thought of not seeing you again... I can't handle it. Your presence has always made the competitions more exciting for me. Everyone asks, is Prince Enrico going to win again? They think I know. And I do," she said with a teasing smile.

"Now you're really flattering me. I'll watch for your name in the competitions coming up on the lists in the next few years and try to get away to see you."

"Oh, please come!"

"I don't want to lose you, Donetta. In the meantime let's write to each other. I'll send you letters through your equestrian foundation and ask Giovanni to mail them."

She brightened. "I'll do the same through your organization and put Prince Giovanni's name on the envelope so he'll send them on to you. No one will be able to monitor them. Our families will be incensed if they find out that a Montedoro and a Rossiano have been carrying on a forbidden relationship all these years."

"You're right. That old ridiculous animosity over trade rights between our two countries is still a sore spot with my family. But I refuse to worry about that right now."

"I've never worried about it," Donetta said with stunning honesty. Neither of them had talked about the people they were promised to. Both sets of parents would be enraged about what had been going on behind the scenes.

"Much as I don't want to, I'd better get you back to the hotel. Lorenzo will be looking for you, and Giovanni will be waiting for me at the airport. We're flying home on the royal jet tonight."

That revelation brought more pain to her heart as they left the club in the limo.

"Come closer, Donetta. I don't want to waste one second of the precious time we have left." He pulled her into his arms and kissed the daylights out of her until the limo pulled up in front of the hotel.

He finally let her go. "I'll write to you as soon as I'm in England. Stay safe and send me some pictures."

"I'll be waiting for your letters and pictures, too."

They embraced one more time before he helped her out of the limo. She ran inside the hotel, where Lorenzo was waiting for her.

He looked at his watch. "You're only a half hour late. I can forgive you for that."

She hugged him hard. "Thank you for being my friend."

"Why the tears?"

"I've had some disappointing news, but today was the best day of my life."

* * *

Dear Donetta,

When you told me you were participating in the concorso at Aix-en-Provence in France, I bought this book for your twenty-first birthday. It tells the history of the white Camargue horses of that region. I believe you'll find it fascinating.

I plan to fly in for your competition and will be staying at the Hotel Cezanne, where you are staying. I'll ring your room.

We'll spend as much time together as we can while I'm there. I'm longing to see you again. All the letters and photos have kept me going, but it's been a century since I kissed you.
Enrico

After reading the book from cover to cover, Donetta kissed Enrico's letter. It traveled to her purse, her pocket and her pillow. She had it with her when she entered the hotel. This time her staff stayed at a different hotel. So did Lorenzo, who'd flown here with her but had come only to watch her perform, not keep tabs on her.

Once she was in her room, her pulse raced and wouldn't subside, because she knew she'd be seeing Enrico shortly. She had brought several outfits with her, not knowing what to wear. After much indecision she chose to wear a filmy short-sleeved dress in champagne color and bone-colored sandals.

To please him Donetta left her hair long and flowing from a side part. After applying pink, frosted lipstick, she put on hoop earrings of the same light green color as her eyes. She wanted him to take one look at her and never let her go.

When the room phone rang, she literally jumped before picking up.

"H-Hello?" she stammered.

"Thank heaven your voice hasn't changed."

His had grown even deeper. "Neither has yours."

"Are you ready?"

"Yes," she answered, almost out of breath.

"Meet me in the lobby in five minutes. I've rented a car. We're going to take off and find a charming spot away from the world where we can be alone."

Donetta came close to fainting when she saw the man of her dreams standing near the entrance, wearing a tan suit and sports shirt. No man came close to her picture of Enrico, who was the personification of every woman's dream of a dark-haired prince. At almost twenty-two, he was truly breathtaking and sensuously male.

"Bellissima," he murmured. His black eyes played over her hungrily before he grasped her hand. They walked to the parking area and got in his car. He drove them out of the city to the suburbs and pulled up to a place called the Patio.

"Before we get out, I have to do this."

"Enrico—" she cried as he reached for her and his mouth closed over hers. It didn't seem possible that she was in his arms again and they were giving each other kiss for kiss, unable to get enough.

Evening turned into night as they tried to make up for the years when they hadn't been able to be together. The letters and photos hadn't been enough.

"If you're dying for dinner, we'll get out of the car, but I don't want to let you go."

She shook her head. "I'm only dying for you. After your letter and gift, which I love, I haven't been able to concentrate on anything. All I want is to be with you."

"We're safer here than back at the hotel, where everyone knows us. But this is no way for us to have a relationship. One more year of schooling for both of us and then we can make plans to be together. What if we take a trip after we graduate? How about two weeks to the South Seas or a Caribbean island?"

"I'd give anything to go away with you. Anything!"

"Then we'll do it. You're so beautiful, Donetta, I think I'm hallucinating. Kiss me again."

After another half hour they ended up driving to a store for fruit and some quiche. "I need to get us back to the hotel. You're performing in the morning and need your sleep."

"No, I don't. I only need you."

The car was their sanctuary. They didn't go into the hotel until after one. "I'd come to your room, but then you'd never get rid of me and we'd be the target of every eye. I'll be at the stands in the morning to watch you on Blaze."

They rode the elevator to the second floor, where he had to get out, but they clung to each other.

"Enrico? How soon do you have to get back to Cambridge?"

"Tomorrow night."

"Why don't we just drive away right now until you have to be at the airport. I'll skip the competition."

He pressed his forehead against hers. "You can't do that. I can't let you. But we'll be together all day tomorrow." Enrico let her go and stepped out into the hall. He looked back. "Meet me in the lobby at seven and we'll go somewhere for breakfast before you have to report to the stands."

"Don't go, Enrico. I'm afraid."

He frowned. "Why do you say that?"

"Because I'm too happy."

"You don't know the meaning of the word yet. *Buona notte e sogni d' oro*, Donetta."

Golden dreams. She'd been living in one since they'd met in the lobby. "*Buona notte*, Enrico."

The elevator door closed and carried her to the third floor. When she reached her room, the phone was ringing. She rushed to answer it. "Enrico?"

"Good. You're home safe and sound for tonight. I'll be dreaming of you."

"I dream of you every night," she confessed.

"One of these days we won't have to do that anymore."

He clicked off.

She was slower to hang up. If he meant what she thought he'd meant, he wasn't just talking about a two-week vacation. Filled with elation, she whirled around the room before settling down long enough to undress and get to bed.

CHAPTER ONE

THERE WAS NO sight more beautiful to Crown Prince Enrico da Francesca di Montedoro than the island country of Vallefiore. In the early morning light, the sun's first rays appeared like fingers over the magnificent vertiginous mountains and sparkling waterfalls.

From his vantage point atop the highest peak, he could see his country was surrounded by the deep blue waters of the Ionian Sea splashing against rocky shoreline cliffs and hidden grottoes.

He'd always likened his country to a dazzling blue-green jewel whose lakes and villages made up its many facets, including the plains where the wild Sanfratellano horses ran free.

His eyes followed the lay of the land over rolling hills and orchards to palm-studded sand. Everything could grow here in its subtropical climate. But as his father, King Nuncio, had told Enrico when he was a boy, without more fresh water to irrigate, it couldn't flourish as it should.

From that day on, Enrico had a dream that one day he'd find a way to bring much-needed water to all parts of the eleven-thousand-square-mile island. Now, at the age of twenty-seven, he and his cousin Giovanni, always his best friend and now his personal assistant, were slowly fulfilling that dream.

Today he'd come to the topmost point of the new water treatment plant to talk to the foreman, Giuseppe, and work out a few small problems. They talked for several hours and discussed the results of the huge project he and Giovanni had developed. At this point other countries wanted to adopt it.

After saying goodbye to the foreman, he climbed back in his Land Rover, surrounded by his bodyguards. He headed down the mountain for the palace in Saracene an hour away. The capital city was located on Lake Saracene, the large, brilliant light green body of water resembling those in the tropics.

Donetta possessed eyes that same color. He remembered the last time he'd looked into them before kissing her senseless. Those two days in Aix-en-Provence had been heaven. She'd once again won another competition, filling him with pride. He'd come close to kidnapping her for good before he came to his senses.

Consumed with ideas for the two of them after graduation, he'd returned to Cambridge more anxious than ever to finish his studies and fulfill his desire to be with her on a permanent basis.

But right before his graduation, his world had come close to falling apart when he'd learned the tragic news that his father had been diagnosed with Alzheimer's and his mother needed him. He had to fly home immediately and forgo his graduation ceremony.

What made the situation worse was his mother's insistence that the palace keep the world in the dark over the king's diagnosis. She didn't want the citizenry to learn that the disease had taken over completely and he could no longer function. This meant Enrico was forced to settle into his duties as crown prince the second the jet touched down.

Enrico was put under further pressure when his mother arranged for Valentina to be a visitor to the palace. The queen was demanding he marry her. Both sets of parents had been good friends for years and she expected Enrico to propose immediately. At the time of the marriage, an official coronation would make Enrico king. Only then would it be revealed that King Nuncio was ill.

Enrico had no intention of marrying Valentina, but the visits had been captured in the news, creating the excitement of a coming royal wedding for the country. To end this nightmare, he'd told his mother there would be no wedding in the foreseeable future while he was attempting to run the affairs of the kingdom.

His desire to take Donetta on a two-week trip had been thwarted by circumstances beyond his control. In his next letter to her, he told her the vacation would have to be put off and he wouldn't be writing any letters for a while.

Without giving away the secret about his father, he explained his work for the country had become too involved. When the time came, he would get in touch with her again.

He'd received a response that said she understood

how busy he must be and hoped to see him again soon. "I miss you, Enrico." He could hear her voice that tugged on his heart. That was the last letter from her.

Now it was five years later and he still couldn't stop thinking about her and wishing they could meet again. Did she still miss him? How would they really feel about each other after such a long absence?

At the age of eighteen Enrico had already made up his mind over the woman he wanted in his life. In his wildest fantasy he'd even dreamed of Donetta becoming his bride, despite knowing such a marriage would raise a furor with their families.

Because of the two-hundred-year-old dispute that had made their countries enemies, Enrico had never told anyone about her except his cousin. But not even Giovanni knew the extent of Enrico's feelings.

Enrico needed to find out how much of their relationship had been driven by rebellion, and how much had been based on a genuine and deep love for the each other. Ever since he'd competed on one of his special horses in an international *concorso ippico* held in England, he'd admired Princess Donetta Rossiano's ability in the dressage event.

For a ten-year-old she was a marvel, much better than any of the guys on all the teams represented from around the world. He'd approached to tell her so and was struck by the shimmering green color of her eyes, which had grown fiercer as she'd matured.

She, in turn, had complimented him and had admired his horse. As they'd talked, she'd asked lots of questions about the breed he'd chosen, revealing her exceptional intelligence.

Enjoying her company, he'd spent time with her at the various tracks after each *concorso*. He liked being with her when she trained before an event. Drawn to her like crazy, he'd laughed and flirted. Her discipline and composure made Donetta stand out from the others. He'd been fascinated.

Over the years Enrico had watched the beautiful princess from Domodossola with the long, flowing silvery gold hair compete in dozens of *concorsos* just as he had. By the age of twenty-one she was all grown up, with a keen intellect and opinions on subjects that kept him riveted. On top of everything else she was the best jumper and by far the most stunning young woman he'd ever seen or known.

There was no woman like her and he *had* to see her again. Although she no longer competed in *concorsos*, she now ran the equestrian organization for her country's entrants.

A month ago Giovanni had suggested Enrico travel with him to Madrid, Spain, to watch their country's participants and horses perform in the day's events. Though Donetta might not be there, Enrico made the decision to go anyway.

It was late in the day when he finally caught sight of her near the stable. At least he thought it was Donetta, but wasn't sure until she turned around to talk to someone. To his shock she'd cut her long, diaphanous hair. It had been styled to form a feather cut that framed her beautiful face.

One look and he knew his attraction for the five-foot-seven blonde beauty had only intensified over the years. His pulse rate accelerated. When she saw him, her fabulous green eyes darkened with emotion.

"Enrico—"

"It's been five years, Donetta." Thank heaven there was no ring on her finger.

She smiled, but the element of excitement was missing in her eyes. "Now we're all grown up."

Yes, they were. Her womanly figure took his breath away.

"Your Sanfratellano horses are still making winners out of your riders."

He cocked his dark head. "It appears your country is celebrating another champion, too, but she didn't ride like you did at the *concorso* in Aix. I'll never forget our time together." Nor the way she'd filled his arms during those two days in France. "How long are you going to be in Madrid?"

"I should have left five minutes ago. The limo is waiting to take me to the airport as we speak."

Her answer came as a huge disappointment. "You have to leave right now? When I saw your country's name on the list for this competition, I came specifically to see you."

By the way she held herself taut, he knew this meeting had shaken her as much as it had him. "Knowing how busy you've been helping your father run the country, I'm surprised you could get away."

He sucked in his breath. "I deserved that, Donetta. If

we could go out to dinner and have some private time together, I need to apologize to you for so many things."

She shook her head. "I didn't say that to be mean-spirited. You don't owe me anything, Enrico. We were young, we had our fling behind our parents' backs. Those years were magical for me, but we both knew our real destiny was still out there waiting for us. But I have to admit I was shocked when you stopped writing. It hurt more than you know to realize that day had come for you."

"There were reasons," he whispered.

"You think I don't know that?" She let out an audible sigh. "I'm glad to see you again. It's such a surprise. You look wonderful."

"So do you, *bellissima*. I'd give anything if you didn't have to go yet."

"I'm sorry, but my staff is waiting for me and we're on a tight schedule. I'm grateful you came. Seeing you has given me closure. *Addio per sempre*, Enrico."

Goodbye for good? If she thought that, she had another think coming.

He watched her walk away on those long, slender legs until he couldn't see her anymore. Damn if she wasn't more gorgeous than any woman had a right to be.

Enrico had admired Donetta through a boy's eyes, but now he was a twenty-seven-year-old man and recognized those feelings for her had taken root at an early age. They'd never gone away.

No matter how bad his father's Alzheimer's had become, it was time to do something about the way he still felt about Donetta. But Madrid hadn't been the place to reconnect. She'd dropped an impenetrable shield around herself, with good reason.

He needed time and privacy so she couldn't dismiss him, because that was exactly what she'd done. It was his fault. By ending the letter writing at the time, he'd left her to believe he'd gone on to follow the path his parents had outlined for him. Enrico couldn't blame her for anything and needed to start over again with her.

On the flight back to Vallefiore with Giovanni, Enrico broke his silence over coffee and confided his long-held secret to his cousin. "I fell for Donetta when she was only ten years old. I would have married her after college if Papà hadn't already been so ill and needed me."

His cousin nodded. "I suspected *that* was the reason for all the letter writing. But the queen would never allow such a marriage. As if the bitter enmity between our two countries weren't reason enough, I'm afraid she's going to have a coronary when you don't marry Valentina."

"It's *my* life. I want Donetta. Always have. Seeing her again has let me know she's the one for me."

"Have you said as much to her?"

"Not in so many words."

Giovanni sat forward. "Why not?"

"I intend to the next time I see her."

"Next time? Did she ever admit she was in love with you?"

"No. If she had, I would have run away with her." He'd hoped to hear those words when they'd been in Spain, but they hadn't come, probably because Donetta was wary of him. Deep down it had bothered him. "Why are you asking me all these questions?"

"Because I'm afraid I have bad news for you about her."

"What do you mean? I've kept track of her and I know she's not married yet." Enrico had always followed news about her and her family. Today he had the proof she wasn't attached to any man. Not yet...

"That's true, but you're still out of luck."

"Stop speaking in riddles."

Giovanni's eyes were as black as Enrico's. "You could never have married her."

"What are you saying?"

"I hate to tell you this, but I have it on the best authority that Princess Donetta has turned down every proposal ever received because she never plans to marry!"

Enrico shook his head. "Come on, Giovanni. It's me you're talking to."

"Don't I know it, so you *have* to take me seriously. Get this—she's living for the day when Domodossola's laws of succession change to allow women to rule. She wants to be queen."

"That could never happen."

"You and I know that. Nevertheless, up to this point in time she has wanted to reign and reign *alone*. No husband. That's why she's our age and still single!"

With that explanation, Enrico burst into laughter. That didn't sound like the Donetta who'd shared her feelings with him on paper. What he'd just heard was ridiculous, and yet it wasn't beyond possible that she did want to change her country's rules established over centuries. Besides her brains and beauty, she was the most unique woman he'd ever known.

The woman did have strong opinions that excited him, but he had no idea she was so ambitious.

"Tell me, Giovanni. How do you know all this?"

"Because I have a secret, too. As you know, your father put me in charge of the Sanfratellano Horses Federation when I was only twenty. He wanted our country to have a presence at all the international *concorsos*."

Enrico nodded. "I told him you should be the head since you knew the most about them. It made me very happy when you accepted the position."

Giovanni had been the right person to head their lucrative horse breeding business unique to the island. The Montedoro family had been renowned for over a thousand years for their fabulous Sanfratellano horses, which boasted a distinguished pedigree. They brought buyers to their stable from all over the world.

"I was happy about it, too. Once college was behind us, I got busy planning the schedule for our country's participation in more competitions when I wasn't helping you. As you know, I traveled to the various *concorsos* on the list and met Princess Fausta Rossiano in Paris last fall at a competition."

"Donetta's sister was there?"

"Yes. She came with their aunt and Donetta, who was in charge of her country's entrants. From what I've been told, the two sisters are thick as thieves. They look a lot alike. I guess our Montedoro genes are tuned into a certain type of woman. Fausta is a knockout, too."

"I agree," Enrico said.

"Naturally I wanted to get to know her better. But her best friend, Mia Giancarlo, whose father is an international banker I've worked with, gave me some private info about the two sisters that was fascinating."

"Go on."

"Mia told me that Fausta won't date any royals and would refuse to go out with me. It seems she has turned down many royal proposals because—get this—she plans to marry a commoner!"

"Are you putting me on?" Enrico demanded.

"I swear not. That's when Mia told me that Donetta has refused to marry for the reasons I just explained. It seems the only normal sister is the youngest one, Princess Lanza. She's now married to Prince Stefano of Umbriano,"

"That's right." A whistle escaped Enrico's lips.

But Enrico wouldn't allow this gossip to thwart him. In his gut he knew Donetta had loved him. He was determined to pursue her at any cost. Giovanni had given him enough information to offer her something she wouldn't be able to turn down.

"I'm going to create a situation where we can be legitimately together so I can propose. The truth is, I can't get her out of my head. I've been a fool to pretend to be doing my duty when all these years she's been the one."

"I guess if anyone can try to persuade her, it's you. But you're forgetting your mother. She'll forbid it."

"I'll remind Mamma that she had her opportunity to reject or accept my father's proposal when the time came. Now it's my turn."

"Good luck with that."

It was evening when they arrived at the palace grounds and parked outside the west wing. Their bodyguards followed in another car. He and Giovanni shared a suite of offices where he could get busy plotting before they went to their own apartments to sleep.

"I've come up with a solution to get her here, Giovanni. Don't go to bed yet. Our country has never hosted a *concorso*. What do you say we plan the most spectacular event ever put on in any country? I realize it will take time and effort, but it will be worth it."

A long silence ensued while his cousin eyed him through narrowed lids. "You crafty devil."

"How are you feeling on this beautiful July day, Papà?" Twenty-seven-year-old Donetta had served herself breakfast at the huntboard in the small dining room of the palace and sat down at the table with her parents and sister Fausta.

"I'm fine."

"Are you?" She flashed her mother a glance for verification. Her father had a heart condition he'd finally admitted to after their youngest sister Lanza had gotten married to Prince Stefano of Umbriano on New Year's Day.

"He's upset that Stefano had to fly to Argentina over mining business yesterday," Fausta explained. "Papà doesn't know how long he'll be gone, and this time Lanza went with him."

Lanza had been their father's pet forever, but since marrying Stefano, she went everywhere she could with her husband. Lanza's childhood crush on Stefano had turned into a love he reciprocated. They were crazy about each other, but their father missed her and didn't seem as happy these days.

"He *had* to go," Donetta reasoned. "What's really troubling you?"

Her father, King Victor of the country of Domodossola, looked down and frowned. "Since their wedding, Stefano has been much busier running his mining interests than I thought he'd be."

Donetta could have told him as much. Her father had hoped his new son-in-law would take over a lot of the responsibilities of governing, but Prince Stefano was a gold mining engineer. He'd brought much-needed funds to his country of Umbriano in the Alps, and now to their Kingdom of Domodossola on the French-Swiss-Italian border.

Marrying her younger sister Lanza hadn't changed what he did for a living, even though he tried to give their father as much of his time as he could when he was home.

"So why don't you lean on me while he's gone?" Donetta knew her plea would fall on deaf ears, but she said it anyway.

Her dream had always been to rule Domodossola on her own when her father no longer could, but the law of succession didn't allow a woman to rule. She'd been forced to give that dream up a long time ago.

"I can manage the latest contracts on the timber we're shipping to Umbriano." Among her college courses she'd taken finance and accounting.

He shook his head. "You're sweet, but I've got Giulio working on them." Except that their financial advisor was eighty-two and had started making mistakes.

She finished her coffee. "In that case, I'll ask you to excuse me while I go to my office."

"Don't leave yet," her father said unexpectedly. "Your mother and I have something vital to discuss with you."

She lowered her head. That could mean only one thing. *Marriage.* What else? How many times in her life had they brought it up to her!

"We've received half a dozen invitations from Prince Arnaud's family, asking that you'll spend time with them. Just last week another request came from the royal family pleading with all of us to visit their estate at Haute Vienne. It's time. You can't avoid it any longer!"

"Please take this seriously, Donetta," her mother begged her. "When they came to Lanza's wedding in January, Prince Arnaud spoke to your father and me in private. Since being with you in Paris while Fausta was there, traveling with your Zia Ottavia, he's most anxious for the betrothal to take place. The man is entranced by you, darling. You have to do something about it!"

"I'm not ready yet, Mamma." She'd found Arnaud attractive and realized that she appealed to him. But in her heart of hearts she knew that Arnaud wasn't in love with her any more than she was with him. If he weren't a royal, he would be free to choose the woman he desired.

"You said that to us a year ago, darling. Arnaud has been very patient," her mother declared. "He told me he's never wanted to marry anyone else since he met you."

"It's true," Fausta interjected. "Arnaud couldn't take his eyes off you."

Maybe so, but Fausta knew where Donetta's true heart lay and was angry at Enrico for dropping her sister.

The one man who'd stayed away five years.

Donetta loved Fausta for being so loyal and listening to her while she'd suffered over that first year after the letters stopped coming. At first she'd imagined Enrico's family had learned about the letters and his liaison with a Rossiano. In their fury, they'd demanded he break things off immediately.

Whatever the explanation, that had been the blackest, bleakest time in her life and only in the last year had she managed to pull out of the pain. There had been recent rumors that Enrico would be getting engaged to Valentina. What chance did Donetta have at this point? It had taken her a long time to realize that in the end Enrico had stopped loving her. What a stupid, foolish fool she'd been to keep him alive in her heart all this time!

As she'd told him in Madrid a month ago when he'd shown up out of the blue, they'd had their fun living in a dream. But that period when they'd ignored the fact that they were both promised to other people was long since over. Seeing him again had given her the closure she'd needed even if he wasn't wearing a wedding ring yet.

"I find Arnaud very handsome and know he's successful," her mother continued reciting his virtues, breaking into Donetta's tortured thoughts. "We all know how well thought of he is in his country and what a wonderful husband he will make you. Your Zia Otta-via thinks he's perfect for you."

Her aunt's opinion held a lot of sway with her mother.

Suddenly her father sat forward. "It's past time you got married, Donetta." His no-nonsense voice shook as he said it. With his heart condition, Donetta worried when he got this upset. "To think our youngest is al-ready married, yet our oldest is still single. It isn't right. This silliness about you not being ready for marriage has gone too far and has to stop."

"Please consider what we're saying." Her mother got up from the chair and put a hand on her shoulder. "Arn-aud will be coming to Domodossola tomorrow. He says it's on business, but we all know the real reason. He's so eager to see you. Will you allow him to call on you tomorrow evening? I'll plan a special dinner."

Her mother never knew when to give up. She took a deep breath. "Do you really like him, Papà?"

He stared at her without blinking. "Of course I do! I've been planning on your marriage for a long time. We've known and liked his parents for many years, too. I'm very impressed with his sincerity. You've had many suitors, but I honestly believe he'll make you a wonder-ful companion you can love and trust."

Her mother hugged her. "All we ask is that you give him the chance to spend more time with you."

"Amen," her father asserted.

Resigned that her parents weren't going to stop pres-suring her, Donetta got up from the table. "Since it's so important to you, go ahead and invite him to dinner, but I can't promise anything."

"I believe something wonderful will come of it," her father reminded her.

She decided to change the subject. "While we're all still here, I wanted to give you some good news. The Carrera charity raised enough funds to pay the work crew's final bill for renovating the Santa Duomo Maria Church that was damaged during the last earthquake. Piero e Figli have done a remarkable job."

"Their work has always been excellent," her mother murmured. "That's my favorite church in the city."

"Mine, too, Mamma. The frescoes are priceless. I just hope more funds keep coming in to start work on some of the other buildings since we can't dip into the treasury."

"Absolutely not." So spoke her father whose voice sounded stronger since her capitulation.

"Then I'll see all of you at dinner tonight."

Fausta shook her head. "I'll be eating in town with Mia."

Her best friend, Mia, a nurse at the Hospital of the Three Crosses, was on Fausta's fund-raising committee. But Fausta was spending more and more time in town with her. Donetta figured there was a compelling reason why she hadn't been around much lately. Fausta continued to meet new men along with Mia, and Donetta had promised to keep it a secret from their parents.

In turmoil over Enrico's disappearance from her life and now her parents' insistence that she marry Arnaud, Donetta gave her parents a kiss and left the dining room.

Dispirited, she headed to the south wing of the fifteenth-century palace, where all the offices were located. She had her own office next to the room where their legislature met. But she was often away from the palace doing fund-raising and goodwill tours.

When she was gone, she relied on her secretary, Talia, to run the daily business, bring in the mail and do odd jobs in her absence. Talia, a married brunette in her thirties with two children, nodded to her as she entered the room.

"You've received something important in the mail this morning. It's stamped top priority and it's from the country of Vallefiore, Your Highness."

CHAPTER TWO

JUST HEARING THE name Vallefiore brought Donetta close to a faint. Since seeing her last month, had Enrico decided to write to her anyway? Why? After his cruel silence over the years, did he think she'd welcome a letter at this late date?

But her curiosity got the best of her and her hand trembled as she reached for the envelope. It took a moment before the pounding of her heart calmed down. After sitting in her swivel chair, she noticed it had been addressed to Princess Donetta Rossiano of the Domodossola National Equestrian Association. Donetta had been in charge of it since she'd stopped performing at twenty-one.

Inside was an official invitation from Prince Giovanni di Montedoro, head of the Vallefiore National Equestrian Association.

Not Enrico?

Her heart fell.

Prince Giovanni was always at the *concorsos* with their federation, but until last month she'd never seen Enrico with him since their competitive days. This invitation was announcing an international *concorso* covering the last two days of August, a month from now.

She, along with other invited royals, was to be a special guest of King Nuncio and Queen Teodora, and sit in their box for the events, followed by dinner and a spectacular fireworks presentation by the lake.

Donetta was absolutely amazed. Their country had never sponsored a *concorso* before. Once again her heart pounded unnaturally hard as she took in the information. Entrants from ten to twenty-one years of age would be competing in the capital city of Saracene, the location of the royal palace.

Her thoughts went back to her first competition in England at the age of ten. Donetta had won all the events in her age group on her British thoroughbred, Luna, a young mare her father had purchased for her. Luna's pedigree dated back to Eclipse, the famous race horse from the Windsor Great Park era. How she'd loved that horse and Enrico's!

She'd found out Enrico rode a fabulous Sanfratellano horse from his country, a breed that had existed in some form for centuries. In the Middle Ages the Arabian breed became popular among the Norman nobility, having been preferred by the Saracens who ruled Sicily and other nearby islands like Vallefiore until the eleventh century.

Enrico rode a high-spirited horse from that breed, which in past times could bear the weight of a fully armored knight. In the mountainous islands of the Ionian Sea region, he'd told her, a battle horse's strength was often more important than a lighter horse's speed.

Receiving this invitation from Enrico just after leaving the dining room where her parents had begged her to give Arnaud a chance to settle on an official engagement pained her terribly. Did Enrico want to apologize to her this badly? She didn't get it.

Memories ran through her mind. That day when he'd helped her down from her horse because they'd been riding bareback, he'd pulled her into his arms and kissed her so thoroughly she'd never wanted him to stop.

It had been the thrill of her young life and his image had been burned into her heart and memory. But apparently that moment hadn't meant the same thing to him. Kiss the lovesick girl and sow his wild oats before settling down with Valentina, was that it?

Maybe he'd fallen for someone else he'd met at the university. Or possibly some beauty he'd come across during his travels. Or maybe the answer lay in the simple fact that his youthful, heated feelings for her had abated and he hadn't wanted to take that two-week vacation with her after all.

Donetta would always have questions that would eat her alive if she didn't learn the truth. Maybe she'd get the answers if she attended this *concorso*.

"Talia? Will you please send a message to Prince Giovanni that our equestrian association plans to accept. There's no time like today to start contacting the association staff and participants from around the country to make travel and lodging arrangements."

"Yes, Your Highness."

Donetta's thoughts were running wild. While she was in Vallefiore, she would purchase a Sanfratellano horse for herself and have it shipped home. Besides the king and queen, some of the Montedoro royal family would probably be present at the events. She knew they had two married daughters. Would Enrico also be there to explain his behavior?

He was twenty-seven now. She was surprised he hadn't married Valentina yet. Donetta had always thought he was the most attractive man in the world. No male of her acquaintance ever sat a horse as magnificently. She appreciated beauty in any form.

Before seeing him in Spain she'd lodged some unkind thoughts about him. He'd fallen off the pedestal she'd put him on. But she'd had to scratch her negative thoughts when he'd said he'd come to Spain expressly to see her and apologize.

To make things harder for her, he'd dressed in chinos and a silky brown sports shirt, leaving her breathless. How on earth was she ever going to get him out of her system?

She decided it was a good thing Arnaud would be coming to dinner tomorrow evening to help her deal with what she'd only been able to consider as Enrico's rejection of her.

Her mom was right that Arnaud was handsome in that certain French way. It was long past time she put thoughts of Enrico away for good and accepted the inevitability of marrying Arnaud, who'd been actively pursuing her.

"Talia? I have some shopping to do, but I'll check back with you later." Donetta decided to buy a new dress and shoes. It had been a while.

Apparently her effort didn't go unappreciated. At dinner the next night, Arnaud whispered, "I've never seen you look so *incroyable*. That lovely green dress matches your eyes. I can't stop looking at you, *ma belle*."

"Thank you, Arnaud. You're quite a sight yourself."

He did look pretty amazing in his evening clothes. They wandered out on the terrace off the large dining room after dessert and talked several hours. "You have to know why I'm here. Will you marry me, Donetta?"

She lifted her head. The time for truth had come. "Can you look me in the eye and tell me you're in love with me? You know what I mean. The kind of heart-wrenching love that leaves you breathless and aching inside until nothing else matters in this world?"

He searched her eyes for a long moment before he said, "Why do I get the feeling you've known a love like that?"

She fought not to look away while her guilty heart pounded with sickening speed. "*I* get the feeling you haven't known a love like that yet, or you would have married her without your parents' consent."

The silence convicted both of them.

"Thank you for being honest with me, Arnaud. I do love you for that. Maybe we can make a go of an arranged marriage and children based on a mutual liking and fondness for each other."

"Donetta—"

"Let me finish. I know you like me, and I care for you. But this is the problem of being born to royal parents. They are pressuring you to marry and they've picked me. My parents want me to marry you and have wanted it for a long time. This has been planned and wished for on both sides for years. Though I've liked you better than any of the men who've made proposals, it isn't love."

Up to the point that Enrico's letters had stopped coming, Donetta had remained resolute in her determination that the two of them had been in love. To her consternation, she feared she'd been deluding herself.

"It can grow into love," Arnaud murmured, breaking into her painful thoughts. "I want you to come to Haute Vienne next weekend. There's so much to show you, and we'll talk. Hopefully you'll fall in love with my home and like me better. Let's find out if we can see our way clear to announce our engagement."

Donetta had to admit she was touched. He *was* sincere and truly a wonderful man. If she broke her own rule and decided to marry since her desire to be queen of Domodossola was hopeless, Arnaud would be the perfect choice for a husband and father of her children. Forget Enrico.

He gripped her hand tighter. "Donetta? Will you come next weekend?"

She closed her eyes. Why not? "Yes, I'll be happy to come. Thank you for inviting me."

"Ma chère," he said in an unsteady voice and pulled her into his arms to kiss her.

She responded to him, waiting for the magic she'd felt when Enrico had hungrily kissed her. But there was no comparison and never could be. She wasn't in love with Arnaud, nor he with her.

Donetta was now a grown woman who'd become somewhat distrustful and cynical after seeing Enrico's picture in the media with other women. She'd also heard rumors of a possible marriage with Valentina.

As for Donetta, she'd been a starry-eyed twenty-one-year-old whose heart had been full of Enrico. But she shouldn't expect to be in that insane condition ever again.

A month later, Enrico rode out early on Friday morning to the Vallefiore National Airport in one limo, Giovanni in another. His staff from the palace were meeting the planes flying in with the contestants and their horses from Domodossola and other countries. They would take them to their lodgings so that Enrico and his cousin were free to meet the royal jet.

He hadn't slept all night in his excitement to see Donetta again. The August *concorso* hadn't come soon enough for him. After installing her at the palace, he wouldn't leave her side during the day's events. Tonight after dinner and fireworks for everyone along the lake's waterfront, he would whisk her away for an overnight campout on the island in his Land Rover.

Enrico had done all the packing and preparations ahead of time. Her associates would take care of Domodossola's participation in the competition, while he enjoyed all day today and tomorrow with her in private.

As the jet taxied to a stop, Giovanni got out of his limo and greeted the two male staff deplaning first. Donetta would be next.

In his official capacity as crown prince, Enrico exited the limo in his white royal summer suit with the blue sash from shoulder to waist. He watched at the bottom of the stairs as she started to descend. But when she saw him, she faltered for an instant before coming all the way.

Between her pale pink three-piece skirt suit and her hair, he was dazzled. Talk about a vision. His hope that she'd come had been realized.

"Donetta? May I be the first to welcome you to my country."

"Thank you, Enrico." She smiled. "I didn't expect to see you again. On behalf of my country, we're happy to be here for this *concorso*."

He reached for her hand to kiss the back of it. "If you'll come with me, we'll drive to the palace, where you can freshen up before the first events in dressage begin at ten a.m."

"My secretary said that my staff and I were booked at the Montedoro Lake Front Hotel."

"I hope you don't mind, but I had you installed at the palace. This is the first time I've been able to show you around. In truth I've wanted this opportunity since I finished my university studies, but my father's poor health changed my world.

"I couldn't tell you about it in my letters because I'd made a promise to my mother to keep silent. She feared word would get out about him. I'm sure it has, but there's been no mention of it in the press yet. She has wanted him protected for as long as possible. Seeing you again, I know I can trust you not to say anything to your staff."

They walked to the limo where the chauffeur helped both of them inside and shut the door. He sat next to her as they drove off.

"I had no idea your father was ill. What's wrong with him?"

He glanced at her lovely profile. "He was diagnosed with Alzheimer's right before my graduation."

"Oh, no—"

"No one except our personal staff knew the truth at the time. Since my return, I've been running the country more and more. Sadly, his condition is now severe."

A small gasp escaped her throat. "Is he bedridden?"

"No. His caregiver gets him dressed and sees that he's fed. Mostly he sits in a wheelchair near Mamma. He has a total lack of awareness and can't take care of his daily activities. Besides agitation, he occasionally has a hallucination and even wanders at times. His paranoia is worse and he doesn't know the family."

Donetta turned to him. "How horrible. I'm so sorry, Enrico."

Her sincerity tugged on his emotions. "My mother and sisters can hardly bear it. He's Mamma's whole life."

"So she's been totally dependent on you since you came home?"

He nodded.

Donetta bowed her head. "The people in my country don't know about my father's heart trouble, either. Our family is worried about him, but at least he knows us and still has help from Stefano in running things. How do you handle it?"

"A day at a time. After seeing you in Madrid, I talked it over with my cousin Giovanni to host a *concorso* here. I'd hoped you'd come so I could explain certain things to you. I've needed to take a few days off for some real enjoyment."

She smoothed her suit skirt. "I'll admit I was surprised when my office received your invitation."

"I, for one, am very glad you decided to accept it. When we were younger, you asked me a lot of questions about the Sanfratellano horses. I thought I'd take you to some places where they run wild and you can see them for yourself."

"I'd love it!" She'd said it without hesitation.

"After this evening's fireworks we'll drive to that part of the island and camp out so you can watch them at first light."

"In tents?" He felt her excitement, which was contagious.

"Or in sleeping bags under the stars. I'll bring food for us. What do you think?"

"You've made it impossible for me to turn you down."

That was the idea.

Donetta's eyes widened as they came in sight of the fabulous Montedoro palace, which was reflective of the Mudejar and Renaissance décors of former times. An enchanting garden and pools lined in beautiful *azulejos* tiles took her breath away. The Moors and Romans had left traces of their cultures behind.

Enrico accompanied her up the steps into the south

wing and walked her to her apartment on the second floor, where her luggage had been placed. He left her at the door. "There's a tray of food for you if you're hungry. I'll be back for you in twenty minutes and we'll leave for the stand at the exhibition grounds."

"Thank you, Enrico."

When he left, she rested against the closed door, trying to get a grip on her emotions. Hearing some of the details of his life since college had told her how wrong she'd been in her thinking about him, and it had left her shaken.

She looked up at the intricate fretwork ceiling reminiscent of those at the Alhambra in Spain, where she'd been recently. Awestruck by such beauty, she wandered over to the arched Moorish windows that overlooked a pool in the inner courtyard. This was Enrico's home.

Seeing such a gorgeous man standing at the foot of the stairs outside her plane a little while ago, dressed in royal whites, had almost given her a heart attack. When she'd decided to come to Vallefiore, she hadn't been sure she would even see him.

From the moment she'd caught sight of his black hair and tall, fit physique, nothing had unfolded the way she'd imagined. For one thing, she'd learned he was acting king now. All the power and authority rested on his shoulders, but if anyone could handle it, he could.

To think he'd spent the last five years supporting his father and family at a time of great sorrow for all of them had changed her thinking.

Confused and conflicted by some of her earlier negative thoughts about him not being sincere, she freshened up and then walked into the Moorish-inspired sitting room to eat. There was juice, coffee, mint tea, rolls and pastries, sugared almonds, anything you could want.

Enrico had gone all out for her. Why would he do this now and stage a *concorso* to see her? Did he think she was so angry that only an invitation like this could bring her here? But to go to so much trouble didn't make sense. In truth, she didn't understand his motives.

A knock on the outer door caused her to jump. She finished her last bite of roll, reached for her purse and hurried to let him in.

His black eyes played over her in the same way they'd done before, when they'd stayed in the rental car, wanting to hold on to each other the night before having to say goodbye. It had sent heat through her body then, too. "Are you ready, or do you need more time?"

Donetta couldn't get over how devastatingly attractive he was. It was hard to breathe. "I'd like to go so we won't be late for the entrants in the ten-year-olds' division. I'll never forget my first performance and how nervous I was."

"I watched your outstanding performance and would never have guessed you had a nervous bone in your body."

"A lot you know." His flattery was getting to her.

He helped her down the magnificent staircase to the doors of the south entrance. The bright sun was warming the air by the second as they walked to the limo and climbed in. After a short ride they came to a huge park.

A canopied stand filled with invited spectators from the royal family had been erected midway to another canopy where tables with tablecloths and flower centerpieces had been set up for lunch.

Once the limo stopped, Enrico escorted her up the few steps to the dais reserved for the royal family. In one glance Donetta saw that he had a stunning brunette mother and brunette sisters who sat with their husbands. Naturally, his father was missing.

Enrico cupped her elbow. "Donetta? May I present my mother, Queen Teodora?"

"Your Majesty." Donetta curtsied to her.

"Mamma. Please meet Princess Donetta Rossiano of Domodossola."

His mother put out a hand to shake Donetta's. "I'm pleased to meet you, my dear. I've heard you're a great equestrian and a beauty. Now at least I can see you live up to your reputation for the latter."

But there was frost in her voice. Something was definitely wrong. Was she incensed that Donetta, from an enemy country, had been invited and had come to the *concorso* when the queen was expecting her son to marry Valentina?

Donetta smiled into his mother's dark brown eyes, but the queen didn't smile back. With that last comment, Donetta had got the feeling his mother was in shock. It went beyond the natural aversion from the queen over the feud that had separated their two countries for so many years.

"Thank you. I want you to know I'm the one who's honored to meet you, Your Majesty. My parents have asked me to convey their greetings to you and King Nuncio. I'm sorry to hear he isn't feeling well today."

The queen ignored Donetta's comment. "We hope to host the first of many *concorsos* in the future."

"Mamma?" Enrico interjected. Obviously he'd noticed his mother's deliberate snub. "If you'll excuse us, I want Donetta to meet Lia and Catarina and their husbands."

"The performance is about to start, Enrico."

Donetta got the impression he'd infuriated his mother.

"There's still time."

He cupped Donetta's elbow and introduced her to his sisters, one of whom was pregnant, and their husbands. The four of them were gracious and smiled, making her feel better. Then he helped her take her place next to him while he sat by the queen.

His cousin Prince Giovanni took over the microphone to announce the opening of the *concorso*, and the competition began.

Watching the young entrants for the next two hours took Donetta back in time. But as each age division performed, she realized no participant displayed Enrico's outstanding horsemanship. Year after year, he'd been the master she'd hero-worshipped.

But leaving for university had prevented him from entering any more horse competitions for his country. Once Donetta had finished college, her father had asked her to run their country's horse federation.

When there was a break in events, Enrico leaned closer. "Your country's participants are exceptional, but no one rides the way you did," he said in a low voice.

"I was thinking the same thing about you."

"That's nice to hear. Walk with me to the other canopy, where we'll be served lunch before the jumping competitions start. If you need to freshen up, there are restrooms behind the canopy."

"That's good to know, but I'm fine right now, thank you."

Everyone in the stand followed them to the tables. Donetta expected Enrico to help his mother, but she noticed one of her sons-in-law had already started to escort the queen. Donetta was being given special treatment and knew his mother had to be close to apoplectic that she'd dared come to Vallefiore.

Once Enrico had helped her to sit at an individual table and took a chair opposite her, she couldn't stay silent any longer. "Enrico? When there are officials from other countries represented here, why are you showing me this exceptional kind of interest? Your attention to me is like a slap in the face to your mother."

She had to wait for his answer because the palace staff had already started to serve them lunch and iced tea before they could have privacy. There was only a certain amount of time to eat in order to stay with the day's agenda.

"Because years ago you and I were attracted to each other and planned to take a vacation together. Unfortunately that didn't work out. But you have to know I've always wanted you to be my guest. To my chagrin, life happened when I had other plans. Up to now, problems have been the story of my life." His frank speaking melted her heart.

No one knew that better than Donetta, whose royal

responsibilities were forcing her to consider marriage to Arnaud. Her last visit to Haute Vienne hadn't helped her make up her mind. She still hadn't been able to tell him she'd marry him. But she'd promised that after this trip to Vallefiore, she would give him an answer one way or the other.

Enrico's dark eyes bored into hers, sending a thrill through her body. "The damn fraud case that caused our two countries to cease all business was never proven and should have ended years ago. Under my reign I intend to have it investigated and solve the mystery so I can reopen negotiations with your father."

Was the feud the reason he'd cut off relations with her? "That would be so wonderful, Enrico."

"I agree. Even more important, it's a miracle you're here at all. I couldn't have been more excited when Giovanni told me you had accepted our invitation."

Everything he was saying to her now had resurrected her old feelings of desire for him while she enjoyed the exquisite seafood salad. "I have to admit I was excited to come to the country that produced your magnificent horse Rajah and hopefully see you again in your own surroundings. We used to talk a lot about each other's lives."

"Being with you was always the highlight of my trips to those competitions," he confessed.

She had to suppress a moan. "I felt the same way." Clearly, they'd both been crazy about each other despite knowing it was wrong, but destiny had kept them apart.

"Donetta?" His voice broke in on her tumultuous

thoughts. "It's time to go back to the stand. Are you ready?"

"I am. The lunch was delicious. Thank you." She stood up and followed him over to their seats behind Giovanni, who was ready to announce the afternoon's activities. All the while she felt the queen's hostile brown gaze on her.

The jumping trials were her favorite discipline to watch, but her mind was so full of Enrico and their conversation she had a hard time concentrating. At the end of the day Giovanni made the announcement that the crown prince himself would give out the awards.

Donetta's gaze stayed glued on the gorgeous acting king as he stood before the awestruck winners and honored each of them with their cups. One young man from Domodossola won a first place in the sixteen-year-olds' division. Though she was excited for him, it was Enrico who filled her vision.

Her heart thudded when she realized she wouldn't be flying back home until tomorrow evening. For once she didn't have to say goodbye to Enrico. He'd planned for them to spend the night and next day together.

In the past she'd always walked to the stables to talk to her country's participants and see their horses first-hand, but not today. Enrico wanted to get going and not waste time.

Luckily, Donetta always brought several changes of casual outfits. Since Enrico was taking her camping, she had a choice of pants and blouses to wear and decided on her tan pants and hunter green blouse.

After talking to Giovanni and congratulating him

on supervising such an outstanding *concorso*, Donetta climbed into the limo with Enrico and they were driven back to the palace, where she could change out of her suit.

He walked her to the door of her suite. "I'll come by for you in an hour. Does that give you enough time?"

"An hour is perfect. Enrico?"

"Yes?"

"Before you go, I just wanted to say that because you're the crown prince, you gave all of today's winners a great thrill presenting them with their cups. That one young girl from Spain looked so excited to meet you she reminded me of myself when Queen Anne handed me my trophy. This day will stand out in all their minds."

His black eyes gleamed, leaving her breathless. "As long as it has been memorable for you, that's all I ask."

The second he left, she closed the door and removed her pink suit, but her body was trembling. She took a shower and washed her hair. It didn't take long to dry and style.

Ten minutes later Donetta heard the knock on the door. She gathered her suitcase and purse and hurried to open it, coming face-to-face with Enrico. He had to be the most dashing male on the planet. She swallowed hard as she took in his rock-solid physique.

No longer in his whites, he wore khaki pants and a matching short-sleeved khaki shirt open at the neck. His black eyes and hair, combined with such a burnished complexion, made her joints go weak.

She felt his eyes wander over her, causing her pulse to race. "You should always wear green," he said in his deep voice. "Have you forgotten anything? We won't be coming back until tomorrow. I hope you won't mind that we miss dinner and the fireworks. I have other plans for us." Her pulse flew off the charts. "Does your pilot know you won't be flying home until late in the day?"

"I'll let him know. Enrico? What about your mother? Is she aware you're with me tonight? I didn't come to Vallefiore to cause more discord between our two countries."

"I have no doubts she knows what we're doing. She has her spies. If I'm not wrong, she's supervising the help putting my father to bed and complaining to him about any number of things she can't change. She believes he understands, even if he doesn't talk. Sadly, I don't think he does, but it helps her to let off steam."

Donetta moaned. "She must be upset that you're entertaining a Rossiano."

"Could be, but I don't care."

Neither did she. Being with him like this tonight was all she could think about.

CHAPTER THREE

ENRICO HELPED DONETTA into the Land Rover. Surrounded by heavy security, he drove them toward the mountains in the distance. They still had two hours of daylight left. Time for her to take in the scenery while he set up camp for them.

It wasn't long before she exclaimed, "The landscape is so green and fertile! Do you get a lot more rain here than I had supposed?"

He chuckled. "I'm glad you've noticed. It means my work since returning from England hasn't been in vain."

"What do you mean?"

"It's not rain but irrigation. Let me explain. Since agriculture forms the basis of Vallefiore's economy, Giovanni and I have studied the agricultural challenges of our country. Between us we developed a system of piping and pumps to cover the huge island with fresh water converted from sea water.

"This innovation has brought whole new possibilities for more jobs for our young people, more money for infrastructure, increased production of our pipe manufacturing plants as well as a profusion of farm implements.

"Our farmers are growing three times as much produce, which means enriching the economy and exports. We're building timber assets now in demand internationally and contributing to the country's prosperity."

"I'm so impressed I don't know where to start."

Enrico chuckled. "Even though there's much work to be done yet, we're satisfied about the progress made so far. But the agricultural problems are only part of my responsibilities and worries. My other important work stretches further to oversee national security in order to establish law and order. We have a lot of problems right now."

"What kind?"

"Well, I've stopped the construction of most new renewable energy projects. I'm trying to ensure that the corruptive elements of society are rooted out of the industry before allowing fresh projects to go forward.

"Though my father has worked on the problem, he hadn't been aggressive enough. I've seen that their influence in the country has to be wiped out by vetting those businesses affected and jailing the heads, no matter the consequences. Between that and our water needs, I've been busy."

Her eyes widened. "You've managed to put in pipelines all over this huge island to pump in the sea water and make it potable?"

Enrico nodded. "We've a long way to go to cover the whole island, but in the last three years we've seen some success and are encouraged by what is happening."

Her smile lit up a spot inside him he didn't know was

there. "It's a miracle what you've done so far. I can't tell you how in awe I am."

"Enough to forgive me for ending the letter writing? I didn't mean for it to be permanent, but when I reached home, between the concerns of the government and the needs of my mother, I barely had time to put one foot in front of the other."

"Of course I forgive you."

"Then you're a saint."

"Hardly. Look what you've done for your country so far! To think what could be done for some of the countries of East Africa suffering from drought."

"I think about it all the time."

Talking to Donetta had always stimulated him, but never more than now. While they were talking, he'd driven them into the mountains. "Before dark there's a sight I want you to see. It's around this next curve." A minute later he pulled his Land Rover to the side of the road.

When a cry escaped her lips, it was the most satisfying sound he'd heard in a long time. With the sun getting ready to set, its last reflection was captured by the spectacular waterfall, the longest one on the island.

"The locals call it Percorso al Cielo."

"The pathway to heaven," she murmured. "How absolutely beautiful."

He glanced at her. "When I first saw you perform on your horse, the hair cascading a silvery gold almost to your waist beneath your helmet reminded me of this waterfall. When I saw you last month, I was surprised to see you looked a lot different from my boyhood memory of you."

She turned to him. "Do you know your hair was one of the first things I noticed about you when you were just ten?"

He smiled. "I hope to keep it for a while."

"I can't imagine you losing it."

"That day will come."

"Maybe when you're eighty."

"I like your vote of confidence." They laughed as he drove back on the road.

"Where are we going?"

"To our campsite to eat and get ready for bed. It's about ten minutes from here, on a bluff that overlooks part of the plain."

"I can't wait to see the wild horses."

"When you've had your fill tomorrow, we'll come back and swim in the pool beneath the waterfall."

Her eyes met his. "That sounds like heaven, but I didn't bring a swimming suit."

"No problem. We keep spares at the palace for visitors. I brought one for you in my knapsack."

Before long they reached the bluff. He found a spot beyond the trees to park the car next to the pit he'd dug years ago and always used when he cooked out. "Do you want me to set up a tent tonight?"

"Oh, no. It's a warm evening and I love sleeping out in the open." Donetta was a woman after his own heart, which was pounding unhealthily fast. "Let me help you."

She opened the door of the Land Rover and walked

around to the rear to get the sleeping bags. They worked in harmony. Enrico set up a small camping table and chairs, aware the bodyguards were somewhere around. Then he got out a cooler along with his flashlight and a liter of water.

While she made coffee and cut the bread to make fried bruschetta with the ingredients he'd brought, Enrico got a fire going and put down the grill to cook their steaks, potatoes and the bread for the bruschetta. Soon they sat on the chairs to eat their food with the greatest enjoyment. Enrico hadn't had this much fun in his whole life.

He slanted her a glance. "How did you learn to be such an excellent cook?"

"The palace chef took my sisters and me under her wing. She once said, 'Princess or pauper, you need to learn how to prepare food. You never know when it will come in handy.' When I get back to the palace I'm going to thank her for all those lessons."

"I'll send her my own letter," he declared. "I've never eaten fried bruschetta. It's ambrosia and I don't ever want to eat it any other way."

She smiled at him in the firelight, which brought out her classic features and the high cheekbones that emphasized her beauty. "I think it tastes so good because we're out of doors. I'm sure I've told you before that my sisters and I loved to play in the woods outside the palace. Occasionally we'd rescue a creature like a wounded bird. My sister Fausta was good at giving first aid and nursed several rabbits back to health.

"Do you know when my sister Lanza was on her honeymoon, they found a little red fox in the snow? They took care of it and she wanted to keep it, but in the end they put it in a wildlife shelter."

Enrico ate the last of the bruschetta. "Sounds like you and your sisters had a lot of fun growing up. My sisters and I did, too."

"I remember some of the antics you told me about in your letters."

"Giovanni often joined us. We hiked a lot and played in the lake in front of the palace. Some nights we slept out on the sand so we could fish from our sleeping bags."

She chuckled. "What fun! Luckily for your sisters, you were there to protect them, so your parents probably weren't alarmed. But Papà worried about us and wouldn't let us stay outside at night. If I could have, I would have built my own secret hideout deep in the forest by the lake and slept in it every night. I should have been born a boy."

Laughter burst out of Enrico. Everything she said enamored him. "I can't picture it."

"Boys have a lot more fun and can do everything."

"So can girls."

"Not when you're royal and born in my country."

Their conversation had taken a sudden turn that brought veracity to Giovanni's inside information about her ambition to rule on her own. Translating what she'd said, he understood that Donetta couldn't grow up to be queen.

Enrico got to his feet to start the cleanup. He'd let the fire die down until it was time to go to sleep. "Your father let you become one of the finest equestrians in your country. As I recall, he bought you your first horse that came from a champion."

She nodded. "You're right about that and I love him for it."

"Just think. Without him, we would never have met."

They stared at each other for an overly long moment. "I'm sure that's true." In the next breath Donetta did her part to help him. After he suggested she go behind one of the trees for privacy, he laid out their sleeping bags with pillows side by side, adding an extra blanket for her if she wanted it.

Once he'd locked up the food and cooler in the car, he doused the embers and waited in his bag for her return. He would sleep in his clothes and put on a fresh outfit in the morning.

It looked like she'd decided to do the same thing as she walked toward him. The three-quarter moon had just come up over the mountain and the light illuminated her hair.

"Your bed is waiting for you."

Donetta laughed gently and climbed inside. "This has been a magical day, Enrico."

"It should have happened after I got back from England. A lot of life has gone on in the meantime." He turned toward her, rising up on one elbow. "Donetta— what's happened to your understanding with Arnaud? I'm asking because if it is still on and I were he, I'd be ripped apart with jealousy."

She lay on her back, staring up into the heavens. "We

were together recently. He's asked me to marry him, but I haven't given him an answer yet."

"Does he know about our past?"

"No."

"Are you going to tell him?"

"I'll have to if I decide to accept his proposal."

Such stark honesty caused Enrico to suck in his breath. "Why did you agree to come camping with me?"

She turned on her side toward him. "Why do you think? Though your invitation here has come years too late for my liking, I couldn't resist accepting, if only to find out if I'd been harboring a false memory."

"In what way false?"

He heard a troubled sigh escape. "Had I been foolish to think you'd cared for me all those years?"

The high-pitched sound of a jackdaw rent the air. "You *know* I cared."

"But we didn't go away on that vacation. I understand why, but it has been a long time. Too long," she whispered.

Her mournful response resonated in his heart. Suddenly she rolled on her side away from him before he could reach out to kiss her. She needed convincing.

"Tomorrow I'll waken you early to see a sight you'll never forget. *Buona notte*, Donetta."

"*Dormi bene*, Enrico."

Sleep well? Between his desire for her and the need to protect her even with the security hidden beyond the trees, he doubted he'd sleep at all. But to his surprise he did succumb at last and didn't stir until his watch alarm went off at six thirty.

He looked over at Donetta, who was still sound asleep. Taking care to be quiet, he got out of his bag and freshened up before preparing coffee for them. In the cooler were ham-filled rolls and plums to serve for breakfast. For snacks he'd brought his favorite sugared almonds.

With everything ready, he walked over to her sleeping bag and hunkered down. The sun was just coming up over the mountains. "Donetta?" He gave her a little nudge and she rolled over. When she opened those fabulous green eyes of hers, he got lost in them. "Good morning. It's time to get up."

"*Buon giorno.* I can't believe I slept so well. I hope *you* did."

He nodded. "It has to be this air."

"I agree. It's heavenly here. Excuse me for a minute while I freshen up."

She got out of her bag and slid on her sandals, then hurried behind the trees for privacy. When she reappeared, she looked good enough to eat with that glorious hair slightly disheveled and no makeup, which she didn't need anyway. He motioned her over to the camp table, where he handed her a mug of coffee.

"Umm. You've even fixed breakfast for us. You'll make someone a marvelous wife one day," she teased before sitting down to eat.

Amused, Enrico walked over to the car and brought back a pair of binoculars that he put on the table. "These are extra powerful and will come in handy for you."

"Thanks. You've thought of everything. I'll never be able to repay you for all you've done."

He was pleased to see she was hungry and ate everything. "I've been waiting for this a long time. Your being here is payment enough. When the invitation for the competition went out, I'd hoped your country would accept, but I wasn't at all sure that *you* would come as well."

"I told the queen it was an honor for us. I wouldn't have missed it."

As he bit into another roll, they felt vibrations beneath their feet. "The horses are coming. Quick, Donetta. Follow me to the blanket I spread out. We'll lie on it to watch."

In another half minute they lay side by side on their stomachs. He handed her the binoculars. The thundering grew louder, and suddenly, the plain below was filled with black, brown and bay horses galloping for what Enrico believed was the sheer joy of being alive.

"Oh—" Donetta cried out in awe. "Look how gorgeous they are! It's unbelievable."

He knew exactly how she felt to see such majesty loose and free in the wilds. "I marvel every time."

The herd followed their leader, a magnificent black stallion. "Look how he changes directions and they all keep up with him. They're having their own kind of fun, aren't they?"

"They do it for hours."

"Who says horses don't enjoy themselves."

"I think they probably have more fun than some people do," he concurred. Donetta had his same kind of love for horses and saw what he saw, bonding them in a unique way.

She studied them through the binoculars for a long time. "The leader looks like Rajah!"

"They're all from the same bloodline."

Another hour passed while they shared the binoculars and she let out sigh after sigh. "They're all so beautiful."

"Have you decided you have a favorite color?"

"Yes. The ones with satin coats that look like melted dark chocolate in the sun. They're sleek and breathtaking, don't you think?" She suddenly turned to look at him. Their faces were only inches apart.

"Almost as breathtaking as you." Without worrying about the bodyguards, he put his arm around her shoulders and pulled her to him. Her mouth was even more luscious than he'd remembered. He wanted her more than any woman he'd ever been with in his life.

"Enrico—"

The way she said his name and kissed him back told him she'd been hungering for this, too. Unable to stop, he crushed her to him and began to devour her in earnest.

No longer aware of their surroundings, they were on fire for each other. They lost track of time, trying to assuage their needs. He was on the verge of telling her he was in love with her when the ringing of her phone penetrated the silence.

"Oh, no—"

Donetta groaned and pulled out of his arms. "I forgot to phone Arnaud and let him know when I'd be back." She struggled to her feet and hurried over to her sleeping bag to get it.

Enrico stayed put to give her privacy while he looked out over the plain. By now the horses had disappeared for the day, along with a moment he would treasure forever. But that moment wouldn't be the last because more than ever Enrico was determined to marry her and intended to carry out his original plan before she left Vallefiore.

Donetta grabbed her phone. Seeing Arnaud's name on the caller ID filled her with fresh guilt. She was shaking so much she sank down on her sleeping bag so she wouldn't fall. She'd promised to phone him but had forgotten.

Watching the wild horses running in the early morning had been a breathtaking moment with Enrico that she would never forget. Right now, she was so confused that she couldn't face talking to Arnaud. She would have to call him later.

The second she made that decision, she phoned the pilot and the plan was made for her and her group to fly home at four thirty. With that done, she clicked off and noticed Enrico had packed everything in the Land Rover but her sleeping bag.

She got to her feet and carried it and the pillow to the car. He put it in the back while she climbed in the front seat. Her watch said twelve thirty—too late to make other plans for the day.

"Are you ready for a swim in the pool beneath the waterfall?"

Donetta shook her head. "I'd love to, but after talking to the pilot, I don't think we have the time." She didn't dare be alone with Enrico or she'd never want to go home. "When we get back to the palace, I need to contact my staff and make certain everyone is on the other plane by four thirty."

"I'll admit I'm disappointed, but I understand." He started the car and they left for the city. "Because of time constraints, we'll stop at the village we passed at the base of the mountains and eat lunch. There's a café with the best *crocchè* and *involtini di pesca spada* you've ever tasted. But if you don't care for swordfish, they serve stuffed sardines with pine nuts that are delicious."

"It all sounds wonderful. This whole outing has been out of this world."

Before coming to Vallefiore, Donetta had planned on buying a horse from Enrico's country. That was impossible now. To get any more involved with Enrico would be a grave mistake on every level. He hadn't told her he loved her, let alone asked her to marry him. She'd hoped, prayed it would happen. But since those words had never passed his lips, this had to be the last time she would ever see him.

"Donetta? Why did you honestly come to Vallefiore?"

"Because you were my teenage crush I never got over. Our relationship has been like reading a book I never finished and never knew how it ended until this morning when you kissed me and I kissed you back.

"I'm not sorry for sleeping out with you and kissing you. I wanted it. But we both know that book is now closed, never to be opened again."

She now knew why he'd gotten her to fly here. He'd wanted to explain why their relationship hadn't been able to work out. Now it was her turn to explain something to him. "I plan to be Arnaud's wife soon and he has to know I will always be faithful to him."

"You'll marry him even though you're not in love with him?"

His honesty took her aback. "I never said that."

"You didn't have to."

Enrico didn't mince words. He'd apologized for what had gone wrong years ago, but he wasn't in love with her.

Donetta cleared her throat. "I'm hoping love will come and hopefully children."

"What about pleasing yourself?" Donetta didn't expect that question and started to feel uncomfortable. "If you could have your heart's desire, what would it be?"

She stifled a moan. "I've given up on that dream."

"You had a dream?"

"Don't ask. It no longer matters."

Donetta had made two fatal mistakes. Both were the result of losing sight of her goal to be queen in her own right and never taking a husband. But that logic had been fatally flawed from the beginning since it had ruled out children. Just now, when she'd mentioned them in the context of having a family, she knew she wanted children more than anything.

Looking back, she saw that her reason for coming to Vallefiore had been wrong because she'd been hurt by her perception of Enrico's rejection and had wanted answers as to why he didn't love her. Though he'd told her he'd been busy taking on the burdens of his father, if he'd truly loved her, she was convinced he would have found a way to see her long before now.

He'd always taken first place in every international competition from ten to eighteen. After lying in his arms this morning as his kisses brought her rapture, she realized he still held that place in her heart. But he couldn't tell her he was in love with her. It just wasn't meant to be.

If she didn't marry Arnaud, she knew she'd stay single for the rest of her life. That meant she'd never have children. One thing she did know was this: if nothing else, children would bring both her and Arnaud happiness.

The time would come when Arnaud would be king of Haute Vienne, with Donetta at his side. By tomorrow night, both sets of parents would be overjoyed to find out she and Arnaud had made official plans to marry, particularly when her father was ill. He wanted to see her settled.

You're going to get your wish, Papà.

CHAPTER FOUR

DONETTA WAS SO deep in thought she didn't realize that Enrico had turned into the parking area of a charming café.

"You've been so quiet. I hope everything's all right," he said as he helped her out of the car.

"I'm fine, thank you."

They ate lunch on the terrace with its many flowering pots and trees. Clients and waiters alike recognized the crown prince, but they kept their distance with his security men keeping watch. That didn't prevent every woman in sight from staring at him with longing in their eyes, wishing they were with him instead of Donetta.

Once they'd finished their delicious meal, he helped her back into the Land Rover and they continued on to the palace in Saracene. He drove them to the entrance and helped her to the suite with her suitcase.

"I have to go, but I'll be back in fifteen minutes to take you to the airport." He was out the door in an instant.

This was goodbye. Somehow she had to pull herself together and get ready for the flight. After a quick shower, she dressed in her pink suit and did her makeup in record time.

Too soon she heard the knock on the door. She grabbed her purse and suitcase before answering it. Enrico had also changed and stood there in a tan summer suit with a white shirt open at the neck. No man in this world looked as marvelous as he did.

"Let's go." He reached for her suitcase and they left the palace for the limo parked outside the steps. They sat opposite each other en route to the airport.

"While we're alone, there's something I'd like to talk to you about."

"Of course." She dreaded leaving him and couldn't imagine what was on his mind.

"This is just between us. The fact is, I too am hoping to get married in the near future."

She'd never been so shocked in her life, or in so much pain. So there *had* been another woman! But Donetta couldn't be upset with him for kissing her when she'd willingly succumbed to him.

Donetta kneaded her hands, not able to look at him. "Only hoping?"

"This princess isn't free to marry me."

Her head reared. "Why not?"

"Because she's supposed to marry another man. But I happen to know she's not in love with him."

What? "Does she know you want to marry her?"

"No."

"Why not?"

"What I have to ask of her will demand a lot since our marriage will be in name only."

Donetta was aghast. "That's no marriage, Enrico. You're not making sense."

He leaned forward. "I need a queen who'll be willing to rule while I do my own work. I believe the princess I want will feel the same way I do and is capable of fulfilling that role."

She was so stunned by his remark she had trouble forming words. "But being the ruler is *your* work. I don't understand what you mean."

"I want a companion who can handle being queen."

"But she *will* be when you marry her. My mother has been a great help to my father and I'm sure yours has been there for your father, too."

Enrico shook his head. "It's not the same thing. I expect her to reign equally with me so I can be left to do my work getting rid of the corruption while she runs the ordinary business of the kingdom."

Donetta stirred restlessly because her heart was thudding too hard for her to remain still. "Will the laws of your country allow such a thing?"

"They will if I'm the king. On my wedding day I'll be crowned and my word will be law."

She was astounded. "Have you discussed this with your mother? How does she feel about this?"

"You already know the answer to that. Valentina and I were promised to each other years ago by our families. But I'm not in love with her, and for all her sweetness, Valentina isn't up to the job of managing the kingdom at this delicate time. Since I know she has feelings for me, I don't want to hurt her."

"Your mother will be crushed, Enrico."

"You're right. Fortunately, the woman I want to marry would be able to deal with the grief my mother will give her. I'm afraid Mamma has very strict attitudes about everything and won't approve. She believes the place of the king's bride is at his side, in a wifely capacity."

No one could relate better than Donetta to the hurt and offense caused by what some might say was a sexist remark. "She's not alone in her thinking, Enrico. My own mother feels the same way."

"That's why I wanted to talk to you about this. No one would have more insight than you. The truth is, I never wanted to be king, but we don't always get what we want in this life and I've had to accept it as my lot."

Donetta had no idea he'd felt that way. The subject hadn't come up during their many conversations or in their letter writing. "Never?"

He shook his head.

"You remind me of my brother-in-law, Stefano. He didn't want the royal life, either. For ten years he was exempted by official decree, until his brother died. At that point Alberto had been engaged to my sister Lanza. In the end Stefano married her, but he had to be reinstated as crown prince first."

"He must have loved your sister a great deal to be willing to become royal again."

"Not in the beginning, but their marriage has turned into a loving one."

"Then that should give you hope that your marriage to Arnaud will turn into a loving one, too, Donetta."

"I'm going to try," she whispered, but she was shaken after being taken into his confidence like this.

"Do you have advice for me on how to reach out to her before it's too late? You and I have always been friends. More important, you're the one person I feel the most comfortable with talking about this. Anything you could say would—"

But before he could finish, *his* phone broke the silence. A frown marred his features after he pulled it out of his shirt pocket and checked the caller ID.

"What's wrong? Is it your father?"

"No, but I have to get back to the palace."

By now they'd reached the part of the airport reserved for private planes. The limo drew up to the royal jet from Domodossola. Giovanni had already arrived with her staff, who were boarding.

The limo driver opened the door for them. Enrico helped her out and walked her to the bottom step. "I'm afraid it's too late to continue our talk."

She still hadn't gotten over the shock. "Will you tell me something first?"

He eyed her through narrowed lids. "Ask me anything."

"Is she a princess I may have met and known? It could make a difference in what I tell you. But if you don't feel comfortable, I totally understand."

His black gaze impaled her. "I thought you knew exactly."

Donetta put a hand to her throat. "But how could I?"

"Maybe this will help. Her royal name is Louisa Regina Donetta Rossiano."

* * *

Giovanni sat across from Enrico, eyeing him with avid curiosity. "Out with it, cousin. I want to know one thing. Was the *concorso* a winner? You know what I mean."

Enrico rested his head against the back of the seat. "It was, until I found out she's planning to marry Arnaud. The gossip you heard about her never planning to marry was wrong."

"Then something has changed," Giovanni exclaimed. "You weren't there when Mia conveyed that info to me."

"Arnaud found a way to break through, because she's going to accept his proposal."

"I'm sorry, cousin. Your mother called me after the competition last evening and wanted to know what I knew about you and Princess Donetta. She was livid over the attention you were giving her. I told her Donetta was simply a guest, but when she found out you'd left the city with her in the Land Rover, she was visibly upset."

"She would be," Enrico muttered.

"When is Donetta's wedding?"

"They haven't planned anything yet."

Giovanni whistled.

"I had to spring my plan on her at the last minute."

"How did that turn out?"

"It didn't."

"Don't be cryptic. I want details," Giovanni pressed.

For the rest of the drive, Enrico filled him in. "She admitted she'd once had a crush on me, but Donetta is an honorable woman who's now planning marriage."

"It goes against everything I heard about her from Mia."

"You're right. It appears that somewhere along the way she abandoned her dream to stay single."

"Well, it would make sense when she's not going to be able to change the law to be queen."

"I should have gone after her when college was over."

"But your hands were full taking over for your father and implementing all the plans for the kingdom. It was a rough time to plan a marriage knowing how your mother felt."

"None of that matters now. I've got to put her out of my mind."

"Good luck on that." Giovanni shook his head. "With the king so much worse, I'm afraid Zia Teodora will be pushing you to marry Valentina."

"It's not going to happen. Unless I meet a woman who could matter to me more than Donetta, I have no plans for marriage."

"Enrico—"

"Like I said, I waited too long to propose to her. As for your help, I haven't thanked you for all you did to make the *concorso* a huge success. I know how hard you've worked and I'm indebted to you for being my friend all my life. Promise you won't leave when you get married."

"Do you know something I don't?"

Enrico looked out at the lake. Its light green color would be the constant reminder of Donetta's incredible eyes. This morning he'd held her in his arms. Her breathtaking response as a prelude before he made love to her for the first time had transformed him. He'd never be the same.

"I can guarantee you'll be married long before I ever consider it."

By some miracle Donetta made it up the steps inside the jet without fainting. For the ninety-minute flight to Domodossola, she sat there trembling, not speaking to anyone. Thank heaven she wouldn't be seeing Arnaud tonight. She needed time to process everything Enrico had just told her.

No sooner had Donetta entered the palace through her private entrance and gone to her bedroom on the second floor than Fausta knocked on the door.

"Donetta?"

She couldn't wipe the tears from her face fast enough. "Come in."

Her sister took one look at her and sat down on the bed beside her. "I *knew* something was wrong when you came flying past my room. I thought you were out with Arnaud."

Donetta got up to get some tissues from the end table. "He's taking me for dinner tomorrow evening."

"Did you have an argument? Is that why you're crying?"

"Oh, Fausta, I'm crying for so many reasons I don't know where to begin."

"I've never seen you this fragmented in my life. Something tells me this is about your visit to Vallefiore. You saw Enrico, of course."

There was no hiding anything from her sister. "Yes."

Fausta got up from the bed and walked over to her. "Do you wish you hadn't gone?"

More tears trickled down Donetta's hot cheeks. "No."

"I see. Is he as gorgeous as I remember?"

She sucked in her breath. "He's so much more that I don't have words."

"He would be," Fausta theorized. "What is he now? Twenty-six? Seven?"

Donetta nodded.

"Did he take you riding?"

The question was a natural one considering their history. She sniffed. "Oddly enough, we didn't have time to do that."

"So what *did* you do?"

She stared at her sister. "After the competition, Enrico took me camping in the mountains. We cooked dinner over a fire and I made him fried bruschetta, which he devoured."

"Ehi—"

"Last night we slept out under the stars in sleeping bags. Early this morning he wakened me so we could watch wild horses run across the plain. The ground thundered beneath us. It was the most magical sight I ever saw or experienced in my life."

Fausta cocked her head. "Sister dear—if you could see your eyes—you are a woman in love. No wonder you're having a meltdown. Are you going to tell Arnaud?"

Donetta wheeled around. "I'm not sure what I'm going to do, because there's so much more you don't know."

"That doesn't sound good."

"To be honest, I'm in a complete daze." She started pacing the parquet floor and then stopped. "I'm going to tell you something that can't go beyond this room."

"As if it would."

"I'm sorry, Fausta. It's just that so many lives could be upset by what went on between me and Enrico that I'm frightened."

"If you don't hurry and tell me, I don't think my heart will be able to take it."

Donetta drew in a deep breath. "On our way to the airport, I learned Enrico has plans to get married."

"What?"

She put up her hands. "Hear me out." In the next few minutes she explained what Enrico had told her in the limo. After she'd finished telling her everything, Fausta grasped her arms.

"Oh, my gosh. Enrico was talking about *you* the whole time! He wants to marry *you* and share his throne with *you*!" She shook her gently before letting her go. "Donetta, your lifelong dream to be queen could come true if you marry him!

"Look at what happened the second he saw you in Madrid. You get an invitation to a *concorso* from him in his own country. You've just been with him and love is written all over you. The two of you were crazy about each other back in your teens. I remember the day the letters stopped coming. It broke your heart."

"That's true, Fausta. It killed me that he stopped writing to me. But that's all over now. He doesn't love me. Enrico made it clear it would be a marriage in name only."

A frown marred her brow. "I don't believe it."

"I'm afraid he's changed."

"Look at me and tell me he didn't kiss you while you were camping."

Donetta turned aside. "We did, and I encouraged it. I know he's attracted to me, but that doesn't mean he's madly in love." She shook her head. "I guess… I don't trust that he loves me. Otherwise he would have asked me to marry him after he came back from the university."

"But if it isn't love, what other reason could there be for him to reveal you're the one he wants to marry?"

"He spelled it out. His country has problems dealing with corruption. He wants a queen who will be professional and rule while he does his own work away from the palace."

"What about children?"

"Maybe he doesn't want them."

"But *you* do."

"I know. I'm so confused and shocked that he proposed."

"What are you going to do? I can see you're gutted."

"Even if I told Enrico I would marry him, neither his mother nor our parents would allow it to happen."

"But the point is, I can tell that you *want* to accept his proposal."

Donetta turned a tear-stained face to her sister. "You probably think I'm crazy to consider marrying Enrico when he's not in love with me. But Arnaud isn't in love with me, either, and—"

"And you'd rather marry the man *you* love," Fausta interrupted.

She nodded her head. "Yes. Arnaud needs to be free of me and have time to meet someone he can truly love. But if Enrico and I tell our parents, it could make Papà's illness worse and cause a terrible rift between Enrico and his mother that he has already warned me about."

"Yet he still wants you for his wife because he knows you will make a wonderful ruler. It's what you always dreamed of."

Donetta averted her eyes. "I thought I did once, but I'd rather have his love and his children."

"You really are in love to say something like that to me."

"I am."

"When are you going to give Enrico his answer?"

"First I have to tell Arnaud I can't marry him. No matter what happens between Enrico and me—maybe nothing—Arnaud needs to know it's over between us. He shouldn't be kept in the dark a minute longer."

"Agreed. Call him tonight and end it. Don't make him wait until tomorrow night. He'll appreciate your honesty. It's the only way to do this."

"You're right. What would I do if I couldn't talk to you, Fausta?" She hugged her. "I'm thinking of flying back to Vallefiore in the morning to talk to Enrico in person. My bag is still packed. Nothing this earth-shaking can be discussed over the phone. I'll contact

Giovanni. He can arrange for me and Enrico to talk in private without his mother knowing about it."

"Go for it, Donetta."

She smiled. "I wish you'd been there to see how Queen Teodora looked at me while we were watching the competition. Daggers flew at me. She's wanted Enrico to marry Valentina for years. I know in my heart she'll never give us her blessing, feud or not."

Fausta rolled her eyes. "It doesn't sound like Enrico is worried about that, and he isn't using his father's illness as an excuse to avoid marriage. He's asked you to marry him. He'll be king. Except for the feud between our countries, our parents can't be too unhappy about this. You'll be a real queen, something you've wanted all your life.

"It's almost like he has read your mind, but I know that's not possible unless you told him during one of the times you were together."

Donetta shook her head. "I would *never* have told another soul but you and Lanza about that dream of mine. Did you tell Mia?"

"Even if I did, she would never breathe a word to anyone. In my opinion a miracle has happened to you. I'll drive you to the airport early in the morning before the parents are awake and cover for you until you contact them."

If this was out of the frying pan into the fire, then so be it. "You're a wonder!"

She hugged Fausta again before her sister left the apartment. Before she did anything else, Donetta alerted her pilot. Then phoned the Montedoro Lake Front Hotel on Lake Saracene to reserve a room for her for tomorrow. She requested that a car be sent to meet her jet. Once that was done, she sat down on the side of the bed to phone Arnaud.

"*Ma belle*—I didn't expect to hear from you tonight."

"Arnaud, I'm sorry to disturb you this late, but this call couldn't wait."

After a silence he said, "You sound so serious I know I'm not going to like it."

She swallowed hard. "It's very serious because we're talking marriage and neither of us is in love the way we should be. I can't marry you, Arnaud. It wouldn't be right for either of us and you know it!"

"You're still in love with someone else."

This was the time for honesty. "Yes. One day you'll fall hard for a woman who will feel the same way about you. I think you're a wonderful man. In my own way I do love you and wish you every happiness in the future."

"I can't say you didn't warn me."

"Take care, Arnaud."

"Be happy, Donetta."

After hanging up, she pressed the phone to her chest. Instead of feeling horrible, she felt relieved that both she and Arnaud had their freedom. It had been the right thing to do.

She packed another bag with some of her favorite clothes. Whatever happened after she reached Vallefiore, she wanted to be prepared.

After climbing into bed, she set her watch alarm for 5:30 a.m. but spent a restless night. The next morning she slipped out of the palace with Fausta, who drove her to the airport.

Donetta had no idea what kind of a reception she would get as she made the phone call to Giovanni en route. The blood pounded in her ears while she waited to reach him. But she was met with fierce disappointment when she heard his voice mail.

Donetta left Enrico's cousin a message that she was on her way to Vallefiore and would be registered at the Montedoro Lake Front Hotel before long. If he could call her back at the number on this phone, she'd be grateful.

The steward served her a meal. For the rest of the flight Donetta sat there full of anxiety and excitement over what she was about to do. If they did decide to get married, she would have to remember that this was purely a business arrangement and she mustn't engage her feelings or show Enrico how she really felt.

CHAPTER FIVE

ENRICO SAT OUTSIDE the interrogation room at the police station in the village of Avezzano, Vallefiore. The angry man being questioned didn't know he was observed.

Through Enrico's undercover work and supervision, this was the latest of ten people from western Vallefiore being investigated for suspected involvement in corrupt practices. He'd already witnessed the interrogations of the mayor, his councillor and his assistant.

The four were facing charges including extortion, fraud and money laundering after Enrico had gathered evidence over the last two months. This particular investigation was linked to subcontracts awarded to build energy farms near the village. It was long past time to crack down on corruption in a major way.

At this point a total of ten people, including those from the next village of Caserta, were under investigation. Two of them were managers from a firm that had won the main contract to build one of the wind farms, installing sixty-three turbines.

The contract was worth 120 million euros, and the proceeds from them, he knew, were being channeled to offshore bank accounts. Enrico had indisputable proof they'd been illegally trying to get into the renewable energy sector for many years. Finally he'd heard enough to give the order for their arrests.

It was the only pleasure he'd known since Donetta had flown back to Domodossola yesterday. The fact that she'd gotten on the jet instead of running back to him and telling him what he needed to hear had dealt him a crushing blow.

He'd hoped his proposal would make her see she could rule with real power, but it wasn't meant to be. She was ambitious, incredibly capable, and he'd learned she had a hunger to be queen. Deep down he knew a marriage to Arnaud couldn't possibly fulfill her.

Trying to deal with his pain, he'd chosen these couple of days to drive to Avezzano and get this investigation over. If he'd stayed at the palace, the walls would have closed in on him.

Now that he'd finished his work here, he was heading for Caserta, twelve miles away. He would find an isolated area to sleep out later tonight. He alerted his bodyguards he was leaving and went out to his Land Rover.

His sister Lia phoned to give him an update on their father. Ending the call, Enrico realized that his mother had pointedly refrained from speaking to him over the last couple of days. Clearly she was still upset about his relationship with Princess Donetta. But she didn't need to worry any longer. Donetta was gone from his life.

After a few miles the phone rang again. Hopefully, his cousin wasn't calling about an emergency that took him back to Saracene.

"Chè di nuovo?"

"Where are you?" Giovanni blurted without preamble.

"I'm driving to Caserta."

"Stop the car!"

Enrico frowned but pulled to the side of the road. "What's going on?" After talking to Lia, he knew all was well back at the palace.

"You've got to turn around and come home immediately."

"Why?" He was in no mood to put out another fire.

"Because Donetta just flew in on the royal jet from Domodossola. She's registered at the Lake Front Hotel in the palm suite and—"

"Wait—" Enrico's heart had almost exploded out of his chest. "Say that again!"

"Donetta is here in Saracene!"

He gasped. "How *could* she be?"

"I don't know. She left a message on my phone, but I haven't called her back yet. What do you want me to do?"

Enrico had to think. "I'd rather talk to her myself." *Santo cielo.* He was still trying to catch his breath. "I've turned around and am on my way home. I'll be there in forty minutes. Put a guard on her. Warn him he's not to let her out of his sight if she leaves her room! Don't tell him who she is."

"You think I'm crazy? Your mother would explode. I'll take care of it right now."

"I owe you, cousin."

Driving over the speed limit, Enrico made one vital

phone call before reaching the hotel in record time. It was midafternoon when he raced inside to her suite on the second floor. One of the palace guards stood outside the door.

"Your Highness."

"Thanks for your help." His heart refused to calm down. "You can go now."

After the guard nodded and disappeared, Enrico knocked.

"Chi è?"

That was her voice. She *really* was here. "Why don't you open the door and find out?"

"Enrico—" He heard the incredulity in her voice.

When the door opened, the exquisite sight of Donetta dressed in casual pants and a silky plum-colored blouse robbed Enrico of coherent thought. Disbelieving, he leaned against the doorjamb for support. All he wanted to do was crush her in his arms, but he didn't dare do that.

"Donetta, I don't understand. Why did you come back?"

Her eyes blazed a seafoam green. "Did I wait too long to tell you I'll marry you?"

How he loved this woman! "You've just made me the happiest man on the planet." He struggled to catch his breath.

"I phoned Arnaud last night and told him I couldn't be his wife."

Grazie a Dio. His dream was coming true.

Enrico closed the door behind him and walked into the sitting room. "When you climbed those steps yesterday, I thought I'd seen the last of you. I never want to live through agony like that again. Do your parents know where you are?"

"My sister drove me to the airport early this morning. By now they're probably aware I've flown here. I've burned my bridges and am on my own."

What more could he have asked for? She'd wanted to rule with him more than marry Arnaud. Giovanni's informant had gotten that part of the gossip right.

"Your mother has no idea you've asked me to marry you, does she, Enrico?"

"No, but her spies keep her informed and by now she has no doubt heard you've come back to Vallefiore."

"I'm sure of it," Donetta murmured.

"Which means we need to get married ASAP. To hell with the feud between our two countries. I plan to bring it to an end once I'm king. We have to make arrangements fast so it'll be a fait accompli before anyone tries to stop us. The palace priest is a close friend of mine and will perform the ceremony in the palace chapel tomorrow. He'll provide the two needed witnesses."

"I hope you're sure about this, Enrico, because there's no going back."

"Why do you think I invited you to the *concorso* in the first place? My plan has been to marry you for a long time. I'll admit it threw me when you said you were planning to marry Arnaud, but it didn't change my hope to make you my queen. I couldn't let you fly back to Domodossola until you knew I wanted you to share the throne with me."

She rubbed her hands absently against her womanly

hips. "When I was younger, I wanted to change the rules of succession in Domodossola and become queen. That dream could never have happened. But after you asked me to rule equally with you, I thought about it all the way home and decided I wanted to say yes to you."

"Suddenly my life is worth living again." Enrico was overjoyed his plan had worked. There were so many things he wanted to tell her, but he needed to make immediate plans for their marriage first.

"Though we can't rewrite the past, there's nothing to prevent us from building an exciting future. Before it gets any later, and the shops close, I'm going to phone my sister Lia and ask her to buy you a wedding dress. No one will question what she's doing and she'll bring it here."

"She won't mind? Does she know anything about me?"

"Only that she saw you at the *concorso* and was introduced to you. But she's going to find out now, and she can be trusted. While I do that, why don't you order some dinner for us from the restaurant. Anything you think we'll want."

"All right."

While she reached for the room phone, he pulled out his cell to make the call. "Lia?"

"*Ehi!* Are you still worried about Papà?"

"No, I'm calling for an entirely different reason and you can't breathe a word to a soul except Marcello."

"This sounds serious."

"It is. The woman I'm going to marry has come back to Vallefiore."

"What?"

"You heard me."

"It's Princess Donetta, isn't it?"

"Yes."

"I *knew* it when I saw the two of you at the *concorso*. Neither of you were aware anyone else existed."

"You're right about that." She was the love of his life.

"Are you really getting married?" she cried for joy.

"Yes."

"I knew you'd never marry Valentina."

"I couldn't."

"It's going to hurt Mamma, but this isn't the Middle Ages and you deserve to marry the woman you love."

His eyes closed tightly for a moment. "Amen. Right now I need your help."

"You've got it."

"Donetta needs a wedding dress. We'll be getting married in the palace chapel tomorrow. Find her the right outfit in keeping with a ceremony taking place in secret. If you hurry, you can get to the shops before they close. She's staying at the Lake Front Hotel in the palm suite on the second floor. I'll be waiting for you."

"This is going to be so much fun, *fratello caro*. The princess is gorgeous."

His sister didn't know the half of it. "I can always count on you, Lia. But remember, not a word to Mamma."

"And start a war when we know a marriage between Donetta's country and ours is forbidden?" she cried. "Eventually Mamma will find out and have to live with it, but it will be *after* the fact and I couldn't be happier."

"Love you, Lia. *Grazie.*"

"*Ciao.*"

He hung up and turned to Donetta, who looked so divine he couldn't believe she was going to be his wife. "Lia will be here in a couple of hours."

"That's so kind of her. She must be shocked."

"She's thrilled I'm getting married to the woman I want to rule with me. You should have heard the joy in her voice."

"Fausta is excited for me, too."

Enrico wanted to envelop her in his arms, but he would show her how he really felt after they got married and went away. There was a knock on the door. "That'll be room service."

"I'll get it," Donetta volunteered. "I'm sure the staff knows you and your security are here, but you should still keep out of sight."

"You're right." He disappeared in the bedroom and shut the door.

Another minute and she said, "You can come out now, Enrico."

A tray of food had been set on the small round table in the sitting room. He sat on the chair opposite her. "I can't believe we're together at last, for good. Our past is behind us."

Suddenly he was starving and ate two of the hotel's signature club sandwiches before swallowing his coffee. "After the ceremony, we'll come back here while you change. Once we talk to your parents, we'll have brunch with my parents."

"It's going to be hard facing them."

"Maybe not as bad as you think. Except for the feud, they have no reason to dislike either of us once we all get acquainted."

Donetta laughed gently. "I agree, but our secret marriage will come as a blow."

"While they try to recover, we'll be on our honeymoon."

"Honeymoon?"

"Of course. We need one, don't you think?" He had plans for them.

"Where will we go?"

"Do you mind if I surprise you?"

"Of course not. I'm just thankful that Fausta is with my parents and they know exactly what has happened. But it won't take away their pain from not being at our ceremony."

"But this is what we have to do in order to be married. In the end both families will come around."

"I admire your optimism." She put down her coffee cup. "What about your mother, Enrico? When she hears our news, she'll need your father's support."

He reached for her hand and kissed the palm. "You know very well she'll take it badly. We know what her dream has been. But she'll have my sisters to comfort her and help her to understand."

She lifted anxious green eyes to him. "How are we going to deal with all this?"

"By becoming man and wife." As he said it, they both heard a knock on the door. "That'll be Lia."

"Do you need me to go in the bedroom?"

"No." He got up from the table. "If I know my sister,

she can't wait to welcome you to the family." Enrico hurried to answer the door.

Lia was loaded with packages. "It looks like you bought out the store." He kissed her cheek. "Bless you for coming to our rescue." Enrico brought everything into the sitting room and put her purchases on the couch.

Donetta came closer. "Princess Lia? How do I thank you for what you've done?"

Enrico's brown-eyed sister smiled and stepped forward to kiss Donetta's cheek. "It was my privilege. I'm so excited this day has come I can hardly believe it."

Donetta kissed her back. "I'm still reeling. Your brother and I have known each other since we were ten years old."

Lia let out a cry of surprise. "That long?"

She nodded. "We met at a *concorso* in England seventeen years ago."

Enrico smiled. "It was instant attraction."

"But you never said a word, *fratello*. No wonder you couldn't wait to go to every single one of them!" She laughed and turned to Donetta. "Maybe one day you'll tell me why you've kept it a secret, but I won't stay here any longer to find out. You two need time alone."

Donetta's eyes misted over. "Thank you from the bottom of my heart."

Lia blew a kiss to both of them and disappeared. The second she'd left the suite Donetta cried, "She's wonderful!"

"She and Catarina will always be on our side."

"I have news for you, Enrico. I know my sisters will love you. In fact I need to phone Fausta before another minute goes by, to thank her and find out how my parents are coping."

"You do that while I call Giovanni."

She hurried into the bedroom and sat down on the side of the bed to call Fausta.

"Donetta—thank goodness you've called at last!"

"I'm so relieved to talk to you. If the parents know everything already, I'm afraid to ask if I gave Papà a heart attack."

"I think Mamma took it harder than he did."

"Was it horrible, Fausta?"

"The second I came back from the airport Mamma called me to come to their sitting room. They knew something serious was going on. After I explained that you'd always been in love with Enrico and he'd wanted to marry you but thought it was hopeless, she sobbed and Papà's eyes watered.

"He thought for a minute and then said, 'I'll be damned. I didn't think there was a man alive who could win my daughter's love to the point she would do anything to be with him.'"

"He said that?" Donetta cried in shock and surprise.

"Cross my heart. If you want my opinion, I don't think he was that upset when I told him everything. He knows you weren't in love with Arnaud."

Donetta wiped the moisture off her face. She realized her father had pressed her to marry Arnaud because he didn't want her to go through life alone. Deep down she knew that and loved him for it. "Oh, Fausta—"

"Whatever they talked about after that was in private. But when I told Mamma about your history with Enrico, she was amazed when I told her that I saw for myself that the two of you were in love."

"I'm sure that came as a shock."

"Papà seems in surprisingly good spirits. Especially when I told him what you said about Enrico planning to have the problem of the old feud investigated and put to rest. He and Mamma have been in their apartment ever since. Honestly, I think everything is going to be all right."

"Only because you were there to intervene for me. I love you so much, Fausta."

"I love you, too, and I was talking to Lanza earlier about everything. She said that after what she and Stefano went through when Alberto died before they found happiness together, they both agree it won't be long before Arnaud is going to be thankful for what you did.

"He's been spared a life of unhappiness. Stefano will tell you himself that what you did today was a courageous act he admired, even if it caused pain at the time."

Her phone was dripping wet. "Thank you for telling me that."

"Both Lanza and I are overjoyed you're going to marry Enrico."

"Your support means everything to me. I know you're both going to be crazy about him when you get acquainted with him. Fausta? If there's an opportunity, will you let the parents know we'll be phoning them in the morning, unless you think tonight would be better."

"I think tomorrow will be fine," Fausta answered. "It'll give Mamma time to warm to the idea that when

Enrico is crowned king of Vallefiore, you'll be the queen. Know what I mean?"

Donetta knew exactly what she meant. She'd become a real queen in her own right once she married Enrico. But all she wanted was her husband's love.

A knock on the door brought her to her feet. "I'll talk to you soon. *Buona notte.*"

She dashed to the door and threw it open. Enrico's black eyes searched hers. "How did it go?"

"Much better than I could have hoped for."

"*Grazie a Dio.* I want to stay with you all night, but Mamma has her own news sources. Giovanni told me word has reached her that the royal jet from Domodossola flew in and you are staying here at the hotel. I wouldn't be surprised if she had already put her own construction on everything."

She sucked in her breath. "Anything is possible."

"For that reason I'm going to go back to the palace for the night, but I'll be here first thing in the morning. We'll grab a quick breakfast and head for the chapel. When it's over, we'll come back here to change clothes and talk to your parents. Afterward we'll brunch with my parents before we leave on our honeymoon."

Enrico reached for her and gave her a warm kiss on her lips, his first demonstration of affection, but it wasn't like that morning when they'd watched the wild horses.

"You know I don't want to leave when there's so much to talk about. That's why our wedding needs to happen tomorrow. I don't want to give my mother time to come up with a reason to delay our wedding. Knowing her feelings, she would try."

Donetta nodded and followed him to the door of her suite. "I'll see you in the morning. Come early," she begged.

"You don't need to tell me that." He kissed her cheek before striding swiftly down the hall on those long, powerful legs.

She couldn't wait for morning to come. Realizing she was getting married in about eight hours, she took out the wedding dress to inspect it. The Italian-designed gown had a simplicity Donetta loved. She held it up to her in front of the floor-length mirror of her hotel bedroom.

The dreamy white A-line gown in chiffon and alençon lace featured cap sleeves under lacy short sleeves and a scalloped scoop neckline. Bands of lace appliques adorned the skirt that swept the floor. On her head she would wear a shoulder length alençon lace mantilla.

Lia had picked a dress without a long train. It was the perfect choice. Donetta hadn't wanted anything extravagant like Lanza's gown. She wasn't getting married in the cathedral with the whole country her audience. There'd be no press release, no fanfare, no family in attendance.

Once she'd hung the dress in the closet, she undid all the packages including the hose and white shoes. Lia had excellent taste. Donetta loved everything the princess had bought for her.

After getting ready for bed she climbed under the covers, recalling her father's words. *I'll be damned. I didn't think there was a man alive who could win my daughter's love to the point she would do anything to be with him.*

That was exactly what Donetta had done, because Enrico was her heart's desire, even if he didn't love her back in the same way.

Tears trickled out of the corners of her eyes.

You can't have everything you want, Donetta. But half a loaf is better than marrying the wrong man.

When Enrico knocked on Donetta's door at eight in the morning, he was stunned by the sight of her in the white wedding dress that fit her so well it could have been made for her. He kissed her cheek. She smelled like roses. Beneath her lace mantilla, those light green eyes seemed illuminated. Frosted pink lipstick glistened on her beautiful mouth.

"Whether you know it or not, you're the most gorgeous princess on the planet."

"Thank you," she answered, sounding slightly breathless.

"Are you ready to become my bride?"

The smile he remembered from years ago answered his question. "What do *you* think? You're very handsome in that white dress suit and blue sash. The personification of a perfect prince."

"*Grazie*, but no one cares about the groom. This is your day. I intend to be the best husband I can be to you."

"I'll do everything in my power to be the queen you're hoping for."

"You'll be exceptional. Shall we leave for the chapel?"

"Yes, unless you're hungry and need to eat first. There are rolls and fruit on the table."

"I can't eat. I'm too excited to marry you. The limo is waiting out in the back to take us to the chapel."

She reached for the white satin clutch bag that Lia had thoughtfully bought to go with the gown and left the room with him. They descended the staircase and walked down a hall past some shocked guests to the rear entrance, where he helped her into the limo.

During the drive to the chapel they sat across from each other. The smoky glass prevented onlookers from seeing them seated on the inside.

He smiled at her. "Everyone recognizes the hood ornament's royal crest. By the time we drive back to the hotel, our wedding will no longer be a secret."

She nodded. "I'm tired of secrets."

"We were partners in crime and got away with it for years. Once we're married, we'll never have to worry about it again."

"Except that we're committing the worst crime of all by merging a modern-day Montague with a Capulet."

"It won't be a crime once I'm king, *bellissima*. I've already laid the groundwork to investigate what really happened two hundred years ago. When I have evidence, I'll show it to your father. It'll be my gift to him for allowing me to marry his daughter."

Donetta's eyes misted over. "I'm only sorry your father doesn't realize his son is being married this morning."

"Maybe when we have brunch with him and announce our news, he'll know somehow. One look at you and he'll wonder why it took me so long."

"I'm still worried about your mother's reaction, Enrico."

"She'll recover. We just have to give her time. Right now I'm ready to take the biggest step of my life with the woman who caught my eye all those years ago."

The limo slowed to a stop. "We've arrived outside the private entrance to the chapel. Once we walk inside, there's no going back. Any second thoughts?"

She stared into his eyes. "None."

CHAPTER SIX

DONETTA WAS STUNNED by the the palace chapel, a a beautiful creation of Moorish design. The interior glowed with lighted candles as they walked arm in arm on ancient tiled floors of fantastic colors and intricate motifs toward the priest in his black robes. In these surroundings that hinted at both the Moorish and Ottoman Empires, she felt transported to the Ottoman Empire.

Holding on to Enrico's arm, she passed under one ornately designed arch after another. Each one was covered with lacelike patterns leading to stained glass windows of mosaic artisanship set in flower shapes.

Chairs with velvet cushions were placed on either side of the aisle. The two witnesses sat on the front seats.

Like everything he did, Enrico had sidestepped the rules. He explained he'd asked the elderly priest to keep the ceremony short for secrecy until they could announce their news to both sets of parents.

The priest didn't give a long sermon about marriage. What he told them was to be honest with each other, trust and love each other. Those were vows Donetta could keep with all her heart.

She was excited beyond belief when the priest came to the last part. Enrico slid the Montedoro-crested gold wedding band on her finger. To her chagrin she had no ring for him, but that was her next priority.

"I now pronounce you, Enrico da Francesca di Montedoro, and you, Louisa Regina Donetta Rossiano, husband and wife, in the name of the Father, the Son and the Holy Spirit. Amen. You may kiss your bride, Enrico."

It was the most natural thing in the world to melt into his arms after taking her vows and lift her mouth to his the way she'd done in the mountains. Donetta had to restrain her passion from here on out since he'd said their marriage would be in name only. But he'd said he loved her and she knew he'd chosen her for his bride. Now she was married to the man she loved. No more separations. Together *forever*.

They thanked the priest and signed the marriage document before walking back out to the waiting limo. This time when they sat opposite each other, he grasped her hands. "We've done it, Signora Montedoro. It's what I've wanted for so long."

"I confess that I hoped to become your wife while you were away at university, but never thought I'd see this day, Signor Montedoro."

From his pocket he pulled out a three-carat blue-white diamond set in white gold and put the ring on her finger next to the wedding band. She gasped. "I bought this diamond after college, planning to give it to you. I didn't want to present you with one of the family jewels. You need to have your own."

"Enrico."

"After I saw you in Madrid, I had it set in white gold to match your hair."

She held up her hand. "I adore it!"

The limo pulled up to the rear entrance of the hotel. "It's vital Mamma sees evidence of our ceremony and knows how important you are to me. Hopefully, when my father looks at these rings, something will register in his brain."

"I could pray for that. He has to be an outstanding father to have raised a son like you."

"You're very sweet, Donetta. We were always in lockstep. He would welcome you with open arms if it were possible. Let's hurry inside so you can change, and then we'll make that phone call to your parents."

Within a few minutes they reached her hotel room and she changed out of her wedding finery into a silky white blouse and print skirt of white and café-au-lait. When she came out of the bedroom, she found him eating.

They walked over to the couch and sat down while she reached for her phone.

"It's going to be all right." Enrico could probably tell she was trembling.

She nodded and pushed the speed dial. "It's ringing. I've put it on speaker."

"Donetta, darling?" came her mother's voice after the first ring. "The girls told us you would be calling this morning. Your father is right here."

Donetta clutched his hand. "Enrico is with me, too. We're on speaker."

"So are we."

"I don't know where to start except to tell you both I love you and always will. What I did yesterday has hurt everyone and I don't expect forgiveness. But when I came to Vallefiore and spent time with Enrico, I knew I couldn't marry Arnaud because it was Enrico I loved."

"As I love Donetta," Enrico broke in. "We've been in love for years, but my father has been plagued with Alzheimer's since I was at university." His voice rang with the truth, thrilling her. "I had to fully support him and couldn't go after Donetta until very recently. Once we saw each other again, we knew how we felt, but she was already promised to Prince Arnaud.

"I know Prince Arnaud must be disappointed. I hope that he recovers soon. We're calling you this morning to let you know that Donetta and I were just married in the palace chapel by our family priest. Later today we'll be meeting with my mother to get her blessing. I hope we have yours."

"You have it," Donetta's father interjected in a choked voice. "Only a woman madly in love would do what you did, Donetta. We want your happiness."

By now she was in tears. "Thank you."

"Donetta?" her mother chimed in. "We love you, and welcome you to the family, Enrico."

Enrico swallowed hard. "That means more to me than you will ever know. Before long the coronation will take place and we'll want your whole family here with us."

"We'll be waiting with excitement for that day. Thank you for giving us this marvelous news."

"I love you and Papà," Donetta said before they both heard the click. She buried her face in her hands.

Enrico put his arm around her shoulders. "Your parents are remarkable, *bellissima*."

"They are." She lifted her head. "So are you. The things you said to them reassured them as nothing else could."

Enrico kissed the side of her wet face. "Let's go to the palace. We'll have brunch in the small dining room with my parents. My father will have been wheeled in, but he never talks, so Mamma will preside. I love her and can only hope she'll be as gracious as your parents. Shall we go?"

Donetta reached for her handbag and he walked her out to the waiting limo with its tinted glass. After telling the driver to take them to the palace, he slid in next to her and put his arm around her again.

"After you left, I was in the depths of despair. I drove out of the city not knowing whether to work or go crazy. I couldn't have dreamed my cousin would phone and tell me your jet had arrived in Saracene. For a moment I thought I was hallucinating, but you're here and real."

"I can hardly believe it myself. It was like a dream yesterday when I heard you say you wanted to marry me. So much has happened since then that I'm still trying to take it all in."

"After we meet with my parents, we'll have all the time we want and need to get used to the idea that we belong to each other at last."

CHAPTER SEVEN

DONETTA REALLY DID belong to him now! The boy she'd been attracted to years ago had grown up to become the man she'd just married. But this was no fairy tale. They were on their way to tell his parents. Enrico's mother wouldn't react the way Donetta's parents had done. She needed to be prepared for fireworks.

The trip to the palace didn't take long. He helped her out of the limo and escorted her up the steps to the area reserved for the business of the king. The official flag of the country hung outside the throne room. Soon, this was where she would start to govern the affairs of the country with him. The feeling was surreal.

Further down the hall he led her up a staircase to the second floor, where they came to the small dining room. According to Enrico, the man who stood outside the opened double doors was his father's caregiver. Enrico patted his arm as they entered.

The king, impeccably dressed and groomed in a gray suit and white shirt, sat in a wheelchair at the head of the oval table, with his head slightly drooped. His black hair was peppered with a lot of gray.

Enrico drew Donetta with him and leaned over. "Papà? This is my wife, Princess Donetta Rossiano of Domodossola." He turned to her. "Donetta? Please meet my father, King Nuncio."

Donetta was so moved to witness the love Enrico showed his father that she had to clear her throat to speak. "It's one of the greatest honors of my life to meet you, Your Majesty. I've heard great things about you and know they're all true because I see those same wonderful qualities in your son, whom I love."

She'd never said those words to Enrico, but they'd slipped out now.

Of course there was no response from his father, but like Enrico, she hoped that something about this moment had reached a part of him that knew what was going on.

When she lifted her head, she saw the queen in the doorway, wearing a rose-colored two-piece suit. Again Donetta was reminded that Enrico had inherited attractive traits from both parents. "Your Majesty." She curtsied to her.

"Princess Rossiano." Just like that day at the *concorso*, Donetta saw no smile in the queen's eyes. This woman was her new mother-in-law.

Enrico accompanied his mother to the table, where he seated her on her husband's left side. Then he cupped Donetta's elbow, took her around and helped her into a chair before he took his place between her and the king.

Two kitchen staff waited on them, pouring coffee and serving an elaborate brunch that included a variety of mouthwatering cut melons. Donetta made the effort to eat, but her nerves had taken away her appetite.

"Papà? Mamma? I asked the two of you to join with Donetta and me to celebrate our marriage."

An audible gasp came out of his mother. Her face lost color, but Enrico kept going. "I've loved Donetta for years and now she has done me the honor of marrying me."

He'd said the same thing to her parents, convincing her he loved her as fiercely as she loved him.

His mother's brown eyes pierced Donetta. "You were promised to Prince Arnaud." Her voice sounded totally shaken.

Knowing this moment had to come, Donetta girded up her courage. Enrico gripped her hand to give her his support. "I realized at the last moment that I couldn't marry Arnaud when I knew I loved Enrico."

"Have you always been this dishonorable to your parents?"

Enrico squeezed her hand harder to give her courage. "To have married Arnaud would have been wrong, Your Majesty. But I know I've put everyone through agony and will suffer for it for a long time. All I can hope is that the day will come when you'll be able to be happy about what has happened and accept me."

"Mamma—" Enrico broke in. "I spoke to the priest yesterday. Because of Papà's illness, he understood the urgency and agreed to marry us this morning. We had a private ceremony in the palace chapel with only two witnesses chosen by the priest."

The queen's eyes narrowed. "In other words, he dispensed with protocol and waived the banns so you could have your heart's desire."

Donetta trembled.

"We've waited too long as it is, Mamma."

"Of course you knew you would never have our permission, Enrico. Have you no decency toward Valentina and her family? They'll be shattered when they hear this news."

"Valentina knows I've never loved her. If anything she'll be relieved and now have a chance to meet a man who will love her as she deserves."

"She loves *you*!"

"Love has to be reciprocated. You know that. I could never have married her when I've been in love with Donetta for years. We should have been man and wife long ago, but circumstances prevented it before now."

"How easily you say that when you realize this marriage of yours is forbidden!"

"Only if you decide it is. Something that happened two hundred years ago should have been fixed long before now. I've already started to rectify the situation as we speak."

"Well, *I* intend to do something about it now. Since you didn't choose Princess Valentina for your bride, I won't allow the cabinet to let you be crowned king. *There'll be no coronation!*"

Donetta shuddered. The queen's words couldn't have been more cruel, but Enrico didn't act fazed. His father made no sound or motion.

"Thank you for meeting us for brunch, Mamma. I'll have to thank the chef for outdoing herself. Now Donetta and I ask to be excused so we can leave on our honeymoon. If you need anything while we're gone, Lia and Catarina will be on hand. In case of an emergency, Giovanni will let us know in an instant."

Another strange sound escaped his mother's lips. A part of Donetta felt horribly sorry for his mother. The queen was in so much pain and needed the king, who was helpless at this point.

"Before we go, may I help you push Father into the sunroom first?"

"No thank you," came his mother's comment. "I'll do it myself when I've finished my coffee."

Donetta could see where Enrico had inherited his spine. Both of them were major forces. The whole situation was a nightmare.

Enrico helped Donetta from the table. When they reached the doorway, he left her side long enough to go back and kiss both parents on the cheek. After returning, he grabbed Donetta's hand and they left the dining room.

He walked her to the main floor of the palace and down a hall to one of the entrances. "We'll take my Land Rover."

After they got in, she put a hand on his arm before he could start the engine.

"Enrico—we have to talk."

"I knew my mother would hurt you. I'm so sorry."

She shook her head. "You're the one I'm worried about. But I understand she can't help but be disappointed over what has happened."

"Except that she knew I never loved Valentina or

planned to marry her. When she realizes how happy we are, she'll come around."

"But the protocol in your country dictates the banns be read four months prior to the marriage."

He grinned. "How do you know that?"

"Because I looked it up after the *concorso* in France."

"We both had marriage on our minds even then."

She nodded. "You told me how strict she is."

"You handled her beautifully. But this is *our* marriage, not hers." He started the car that had been packed with her bags and they left the palatial estate. "Have I thanked you for being so wonderful to my father?"

"The poor dear man. There needs to be a cure for Alzheimer's," she said in a tremulous voice. "I feel so sorry for your mother, too. I've heard that the spouse feels like he or she has already lost their life's partner. She must have been grieving for a long time."

"I know she has." His voice grated.

"Your father is very handsome. Now I know where you get your looks. When we were at the *concorso*, I noticed that you and your sisters resemble your lovely mother, too. One day I hope she'll be able to forget the pain."

"I guarantee it. But right now we need to talk about a honeymoon. We'll do anything you want."

Her heart raced. "You mean you haven't already planned it?"

"Even if I have, I'm prepared to make alterations. I'll do anything for you. Tell me what you'd love to do most."

"Could we go camping and hiking in the mountains and at a lake so I can catch fish?"

He let out a whoop of delight.

"I take it you've already set everything up."

"I knew there was a reason why I wanted to marry you."

She couldn't take her eyes off him. "The first time I saw you ride your horse, I was only ten, but I knew I wanted to get to know you. Young Prince Enrico had a presence even then. No other boy ever interested me after that."

"Not even Arnaud?"

"You know he didn't. My parents pressured me the way your mother has pressured you about Valentina. When I believed I'd never see you again, I decided to say yes to him in order to have children one day. Children bring happiness."

He reached for her hand. "We're going to have more happiness than you can imagine, *bellissima*."

Enrico's favorite waterfall came into view, eliciting a satisfying cry from his exquisite bride of six hours.

But this time he drove down a semi-hidden road that led to the pool below, where he'd planned a surprise for her that had been in his mind for years. She'd wanted to camp out and she was going to get her wish.

Yesterday he'd asked Giovanni to pitch a black-and-tan-striped Moorish tent on the sandbar. With two small windows for light and ventilation, it had been set up to offer Donetta the rich luxury she deserved. His cousin had gathered helpers who'd turned the interior into a sumptuous bedroom with carpets and a bathroom with every amenity for two lovers.

Enrico had sent their luggage on ahead. A small table and chairs had been placed in one end. Giovanni had promised him coolers of food and a lighted oil lamp to greet them by the time they arrived that night.

During the day they could sunbathe all they wanted. At night they would moon-bathe to their hearts' content, but he intended to make love to his wife in the privacy of their own boudoir for hour upon hour.

"Enrico—" she gasped when they reached their destination. "Oh, that tent—the pool and waterfall—it's absolutely enchanting with the moon shining down, like something out of *Arabian Nights*."

That was the idea. With his heart beating wildly, he got out of the Land Rover and walked around to her side. After opening her door, he swept her in his arms and carried her inside their tent, which would be their home away from home for as long as they wanted.

Another cry escaped her lips as she looked around the semi-dark interior in startled disbelief. Her eyes glowed that amazing green he loved so much. "You've created paradise for us."

"I love you, Donetta."

She stared at him strangely. "What are you saying?"

"I mean I really love you."

"But I thought—"

"Did you honestly think our marriage would be in name only?" he fired. "The only reason I said it was because I was afraid if I told you how I really felt, you might feel I wasn't telling the truth after five years' absence.

"But that's history now. No more thinking, *amata*. I love you and want you. After our campout, I know you want me, too."

"I've never been able to hide anything from you. Oh, Enrico—you don't know how long I've been waiting for this, dying inside because I feared it would never happen. Love me, darling, and never stop."

She didn't need to worry about that. He carried her to the huge bed with its silk coverings and cushions, then followed her down. It was heaven to be able to plunge his hands into her silvery gold hair and kiss every inch of her.

Their mouths took over, exhibiting the fire and hunger that had been building since her arrival in Vallefiore for the *concorso*. No longer needing to hold back, they began the age-old ritual of bringing each other unimaginable pleasure.

Throughout the night and into the morning they experienced pure rapture, but now she was asleep with their legs tangled. Donetta was the most giving, loving woman a man could ask for. And she was *so* gorgeous in every way it hurt to look at her.

Even at ten years of age, he'd felt her pull on him. Every year after that she had grown more beautiful and haunted his dreams. There'd been too many years of separation. They would still be apart if she hadn't found the courage to fly back to him. He marveled that she'd been so strong.

It was that strength of character he'd admired so

much after meeting her years ago. Now she was his wife and their long wait was finally over. The knowledge that she loved him filled him with a surfeit of emotion. He couldn't help pulling her closer, causing her eyes to open.

"Good morning, *mia sposa.*"

She smiled. "How long have you been awake?"

He traced the singing line of her mouth with his finger. "Long enough to want to make love to you all over again."

"I was just dreaming about you. I need you to kiss me or I won't be able to bear it."

On a groan of pleasure he fulfilled her wishes as they tried to satisfy their insatiable desire for each other. Enrico hadn't thought it possible to live on love, but his wedding night with Donetta had transformed his vision of what it was like to be married to the right woman.

An hour later she eased out of his arms and reached for the robe she'd put at the side of the bed. "I'm going to look in the coolers and serve you breakfast in bed."

"I don't need food."

"Oh, yes, you do. Stay right there. I love that picture of you tangled in the sheets like my own drop-dead gorgeous Ali Pasha of Vallefiore. I'm your captive slave, eager to grant you your slightest desire. After watching you at brunch, I happen to know you love golden honeydew melon."

He watched her open the cooler and pull one out. After she cut it, she brought two big slices on a plate for them to eat. Enrico took a bite of one and couldn't stop. "It's almost as delicious as you are."

"I'll be right back." When she returned, she'd brought croissants filled with ham and cheese, plus two bottles of blood orange juice.

They ate and drank their fill before he moved the plates to the floor. With a wicked smile he said, "Get back in bed with me."

"You mean you're not satisfied yet?" she teased.

"Are *you*, Your Highness?"

She removed her robe and slid in bed next to him. "I guess you'll have to find out."

Enrico caught her to him, so madly in love with her he didn't know how he'd existed this long without her. It wasn't until much later when he told her he wanted to go swimming with her. "I brought a bikini for you, but whether you wear it or not is your choice." He grinned.

"I think with the amount of security guarding us, I'll play it safe. As for you…" She rolled her eyes and slipped out of bed to get ready.

He couldn't take his eyes off her. "Both our suits are in the silver suitcase, *cara*."

She opened it and tossed him the black trunks before she disappeared behind the curtain that hid the makeshift bathroom. He took advantage of the time to put them on.

When she emerged in the black bikini he'd chosen for her, he let out a wolf whistle that drove her straight out of the tent, laughing. He was right behind her and welcomed the hot sun before running into the pool of water to catch up with her. But she was fast and an excellent swimmer. Her athleticism made her exciting to be with.

They played at the base of the waterfall for an hour.

When they were both worn out with water fights, he pulled her from the pool and they lay down on the sand to soak up the sun. In time it got hot enough he started to worry about her.

"I think we should go in or you're going to get a sunburn. We can't have that. Come on." He helped her to her feet and led her into the water so they could wash off the sand.

She looped her arms around his neck. "I didn't know I could be this happy."

"Tell me about it." Enrico was so enamored of her he picked her up and carried her back to the tent. They couldn't remove their suits fast enough before falling into bed in a conflagration of need.

Darkness had fallen before Enrico had mercy on her and brought her dinner in bed. Once they'd eaten their fill of meat pies prepared in the palace kitchen, they lay on their sides feeding each other grapes and almonds until they were gone.

She smiled into his eyes. "You've spoiled me so terribly I've become a lovesick wanton and I'm afraid you'll get tired of me."

He growled against her throat. "If you can think that, then you're in for the surprise of your life." She'd fast become his addiction. He started to make love to her with an almost primitive need that led to another delirious night of ecstasy for both of them.

CHAPTER EIGHT

WHEN LIGHT ENTERED the tent, Donetta awakened first and lay there studying her painfully handsome husband. Between Enrico's black hair and olive skin, he looked like a god. This morning he had a five o'clock shadow. She rubbed her cheek against his jaw, adoring the feel of it.

He was such a manly man. As she'd always thought, he was a dishy hunk. There weren't enough adjectives to describe what his looks did to her and the way he made her feel. That first miraculous kiss he'd given her when she was sixteen had been a precursor to what had happened to her during the night.

She let out a sigh of sheer exultation and stretched, unaware Enrico had opened his eyes and was watching her intently. His lips curved upward. "What was that little sound about, *tesora*?"

"You're beholding a contented wife in every sense of the word."

"Only contented?" he asked in his deep voice.

"If I told you the whole truth, it would make you blush."

"This is getting better and better." In the next breath he gave her a long, deep kiss. When he finally lifted his head, he said, "Before I do anything else, I'm going to shave."

"You don't have to. I've been lying here enjoying the look and feel of your beard."

"I adore you for saying that, but you'll like me better without it. When I've finished, shall we go fishing this morning?"

She blinked. "You mean there are fish in the pool?"

"I make sure our lakes and streams are filled. We'll catch ourselves some mouthwatering trout and cook them on the grill outside the tent. Anglers prefer them."

"You're kidding—trout? I can't wait!"

The laughter she loved poured out of him as he got out of bed and headed for the bathroom. She scurried over to her suitcase for a pair of white shorts and a sleeveless print blouse. By the time Enrico emerged clean-shaven and dressed in shorts, she was ready.

He found some fishing poles and a tackle box, and they headed outside into a world of brilliant, hot sunshine. "I'll get the grill heating up first. Then we'll walk halfway around the pool, where the fish congregate in a deep hole."

The next hour turned into a world of enchantment for Donetta. Trying to imitate his expertise as a superior fly fisherman, she managed to catch a couple of ten-inchers. Enrico, of course, brought in several that were a foot long each.

"Few people come to this pool to fish, so they've grown large."

"This is so much fun I can't stand it!"

Thrilled with their catch, she helped him clean them on the shore. He found a stick to carry them and they walked back around to the grill. The divine smell of trout cooking filled the air. Once the fish were ready, they had a feast inside the tent along with more melon, rolls and fresh coffee, brewed from a coffee maker that Giovanni had thoughtfully provided.

"Never in my life have I been so happy, or enjoyed a meal more than this, Enrico." Her eyes filled with tears. "Thank you, darling, for this wonderful honeymoon."

"It's a long way from over, *cara*. We've only just begun. Maybe tomorrow, if I can stand to take you away from our bed for a few hours, we'll hike above the waterfall. You'll see sights you won't believe. I want you to learn to love my country."

She got up and slid her arms around his shoulders, leaning over to kiss the side of his face. "It's mine, too, now, and I already do."

He pulled her onto his lap and grew sober for a moment. "I'm sorry my mother treated you the way she did."

"Please don't worry about it. Don't you think I understand? If anything, I worry you were hurt when she told you she wouldn't allow the coronation to take place."

"I'm not hurt about that, Donetta. My father is still alive. As long as he draws breath, he's still the king. But that doesn't change my plan for you and me to rule equally. I don't need to be crowned to put my wishes into action. The truth is, I'm going to need your help even more than I had anticipated."

Donetta could tell he meant it. "You know I want to help you any way I can. What has changed?"

He hugged her to him. "I'll tell you everything, but not while we're on our honeymoon. This time for us is so precious. I don't want to spend one moment on anything but our love. Now that we've eaten, what would you like to do?"

"I'm afraid to tell you." She slid off his lap to clean up their breakfast dishes.

Enrico got up and slid his arms around her waist from behind. "Don't ever be afraid to tell me you want to go back to bed. I've been waiting for our breakfast to be over so I could ravage you."

She wheeled around. "Is that the truth?"

He put her over his shoulder in a fireman's lift and took her to bed. After he covered her body possessively, he kissed her neck. "Do you need any more proof?"

Over the next week Enrico showed her what it meant to be loved while he took her to his favorite parts of the island, and they hiked and slept out under the stars.

The next day they drove to the Ionian Sea to swim and dive. But as they left a grotto for a morning snack, Enrico's phone rang. The sound filled Donetta with dread.

She sat frozen on the sand while he answered it. By the lines that appeared around his compelling mouth, she knew he'd received bad news.

"That was Giovanni," he explained after hanging up. "He says my father fell and is in bed with a broken arm. The doctor has been there and he's doing fine, but my mother is beside herself."

"Of course she is."

He nodded gravely. "My parents need me, so I'm afraid we have to go back when it's the last thing I want to do."

Their honeymoon had been cut short, but she didn't dare complain. The pain of knowing they had to leave was excruciating. Donetta was an ungrateful wretch when she knew her husband had taken off more time than he should have.

They drove back to the waterfall to pack up and leave the tent that had become their love nest. But while she was looking for a pair of shorts, he pulled her down on the bed.

"You're not going anywhere yet," he said in a fierce tone.

After kissing her with abandon, Enrico made love to her one more time. But she knew they needed to leave. Donetta draped her arms around his neck. "You know the only reason I can bear to leave here is because I'm going home to live with you."

"Tell me about it."

They carried their belongings to the car. His black eyes impaled her. "Being able to have you in my life forever is all I ever wanted. Loving you as I do, to wake up every day in your arms from now on makes me feel reborn."

The Land Rover reached the road that led to Saracene. Donetta looked back at the waterfall one more time. One memory after another swamped her with emotions that made it hard to breathe. By the way Enrico grasped her hand and never let go, she knew he was experiencing them, too.

It was strange coming back to civilization. They'd been in a world of inexpressible pleasure. Entering the suburbs of the city seemed an intrusion on her whole psyche.

"It's hard for me, too." They were so in tune with each other's thoughts that Enrico had no trouble reading hers. "I promise we're going to get away often, *amore mio*."

The lake shimmered in the afternoon sun. Rising above it was the palace, with a commanding view of the water and the landscape. After they reached the estate, he drove them to his private entrance.

Enrico parked the Land Rover and walked around to open her door. He leaned in and gave her a long, sensuous kiss. "Welcome home, *squisita*."

Donetta felt his eagerness to take her to his apartment. *Their* apartment now. She was excited, too, never having seen it before.

He reached for their bags and escorted her inside the doors. A guard nodded to both of them. "Welcome home, Your Highness."

"Grazie."

They walked up the staircase to the second floor, where another guard nodded. Donetta stayed close to Enrico as they walked down the hallway to a set of double doors. After he opened them, he put the bags down and turned to her. She knew what he was going to do before he picked her up and carried her over the threshold.

"You need to go to your parents."

"I will after I've shown you your new home."

Donetta had known his luxurious apartment would be fabulous. She loved it immediately, especially the view of the lake. He carried her around to every bedroom, the sitting room, study, dining room and kitchen.

"What do you think?"

"I know I'm going to be ecstatically happy here."

He let out a triumphant sound as his mouth closed over hers. They clung as if they'd never kissed before. When he eventually let her go he said, "I fear it's a man's domain, so I want you to decorate it any way you want."

"I love the light blue décor. The ambience is so *you*. The only thing I might change is to showcase all your riding trophies and pictures in a prominent place rather than a walk-in closet in one of the bedrooms. I remember your winning all of them."

"I'll agree to find a special spot as long as we ship your trophies here and display them together. They represent a big part of our lives."

She grasped his shoulders as she looked up at him. "Am I dreaming, or are we really standing in our own home?"

He lowered his mouth to kiss her again, but she finally pulled away from him. "You need to go."

"I promise I'll be back soon."

Donetta blew him a kiss, knowing he'd be gone a long time. By now the queen would know they'd returned.

She took the suitcases to Enrico's bedroom, which

also had a spectacular view of the lake. Taking advantage of the time, she took a long shower and washed her hair. While she dried it, she phoned her family to let them know she was back and happier than she'd ever been in her life. Fausta had gone to town. Donetta would call her later.

She found jeans and a short-sleeved soft orange top to wear and then walked back to the living room. Donetta was drawn to the three framed oil paintings of his horses artistically arranged on part of one wall. Their names had been engraved on brass plaques below each one.

Donetta immediately recognized Malik and Rajah, the two horses that had garnered Enrico international championships. But she didn't know about the third one, which was a pony named Osman. All were black and came from the Sanfratellano breed.

"Osman means warrior in Arabic."

She turned around to see Enrico had come into the bedroom. "Darling—"

He put an arm around her waist. "My father gave me that pony when I was five years old. I felt like a warrior riding him around until my tenth birthday. At that point I'd outgrown him and was presented with Malik."

At the *concorso* in England, Enrico had told Donetta that the name Malik meant king in Arabic.

"The artist of these magnificent oils has captured their living, breathing essence. I wish I'd had paintings done of my horses."

"It's not too late. You have pictures. We could hire an artist."

"You're right, but it's not like painting them from real life. These are treasures."

"You're *my* real, live treasure."

She hugged him. "How's your father?"

"It's difficult to tell. He's been given pain medication and has to keep his arm in a sling."

"Poor thing. I bet your mother is happy you're back."

"She is, but she's insistent that I send a letter to Valentina and her parents right away. I told her I'd already planned to do it." He drew Donetta to the bedroom and sat down on the bed with her. "Now enough said about that."

"I agree. It would have been wrong for both of us to marry people we don't love, but all that is in the past."

"Tonight you and I have been asked to join Mamma and Papà for dinner at six thirty. But if—"

She put a finger to his lips. "Of course we'll go. I intend to do everything I can to win her trust."

"Donetta —" He crushed her to him.

For the rest of the afternoon the world receded to a place where only Enrico could take her. They would have been late for dinner if his cell phone hadn't rung.

Her husband groaned in protest. "I'd better answer it."

He reached for his shirt on the floor and found his phone. It was Giovanni. Clicking on, he said, *"Ciao, amico."* Enrico eyed her. "It's hard for us to come back, you know?"

Whatever his cousin said next produced a frown, forcing him to leave the bed and head for his walk-in closet. After noticing the time, Donetta got up to take a quick shower.

By the time she'd dressed in a silky black-on-white printed short-sleeved dress and slipped into her white high heels, he'd reappeared in a navy robe.

His eyes played over her. "You look fabulous."

She eyed him anxiously. "Thank you, but I can tell something's wrong."

"Give me a minute to shower and change. Then we'll talk."

Enrico dressed in record time, putting on a casual light blue suit with an open-collared darker blue shirt. Ten minutes wouldn't give him much time for what he had to tell his wife, but he needed to prepare her after hearing Giovanni's latest news.

"Donetta?"

"I'm right here, enjoying the view." So she was. He joined her at the bedroom window. "There are a lot of sailboats out on the lake. Do you have one?"

He smiled. "I'm sure you know the answer to that. Have you done much sailing?"

"No. You'll have to teach me."

"I'll take you out this coming weekend. There's a resort on the other side where we'll have dinner and go dancing. Afterwards we'll sleep on the boat overnight."

"That sounds heavenly, but now I want to know what has produced those lines around that mouth I can't stop kissing."

He drew her over to the love seat and sat down with her, resting his arm on the frame behind her.

"As I told you when you first came to Vallefiore, our country has too much corruption causing serious trouble. My father did his best to deal with the problems. But just when he was gaining ground, he was stricken with Alzheimer's."

"I realize that's why you were so involved when you returned from England. But I had no idea how deeply you've had to contend with these problems."

"I'm glad you understand. The day Giovanni informed me you had arrived in Vallefiore, I'd been in one of the villages where I'd ordered some arrests. I had just left there to drive to Caserta, another village, to do an investigation. But when I knew you were at the hotel, I turned around and sped home."

He took a few minutes to explain the reason for the arrests. "But there are other problems cropping up. Because prosecutors have tried to break up certain strongholds, the criminals have been pushed back to their rural origins. Some of them have been operating their corrupt money laundering and drug business dealings here in Vallefiore for years.

"Let me give you an example of what has been happening on another part of our island. A family of wheat farmers have complained to the police that a huge herd of cows and horses have been invading their fields and destroying their entire wheat harvest."

"That's unconscionable, Enrico."

"Amen. Illegal grazing is the oldest form of intimidation. Six months ago a poisoned dog and half a dozen poisoned cow carcasses were delivered to the home of one of the farmers. A few months later the farmer's thresher had been destroyed."

She shook her head.

"All this has to be stopped, but it takes a lot of undercover investigating and difficult police infiltration work to produce the proof for the prosecutors. Since I've given our police full power to go after these people, we're getting a lot of pushback."

"You mean death threats." Donetta was a quick study. "Who's receiving them?"

"In the past, a police chief and several of the officials in my government."

"What about you?"

"I've had several. When Giovanni phoned me just now, he told me the latest threat against me personally came into the office by an anonymous phone call they couldn't trace. The timing coincides with those arrests I ordered in Avezzano on the day you flew here."

"I hope you've quadrupled the security surrounding you."

"Around all of us and now you. We've tried to shield my mother, but her palace spies keep her informed. If she brings any of this up during dinner, I wanted you to be prepared."

"Is this the news you didn't want to talk about when we left on our honeymoon?"

He nodded. "As you can see, I'm going to have my hands full cracking down on this criminal element. With you governing the normal areas of our government on a day-to-day basis from here on out, I'll be free to set up and follow through to trap these lowlifes and put them away for good."

"I know it's dangerous business, but if anyone can handle it and make a difference, you can."

"Thank heaven you have confidence in me. Tomorrow we'll go to my office and I'll walk you through my schedule of responsibilities, many of which you'll understand because you've been a close observer of your father all your life. There won't be anything you can't handle. I know in my gut you're going to be a great ruler."

She stared hard at him, as if mystified. "Why do you have so much faith in me?"

Because Giovanni had made him party to a very important secret and Enrico loved her enough to help her succeed at something she'd wanted all her life.

"I've observed your strength for years. You have a natural leadership ability along with a softness that sets you apart from everyone else. The way you've handled my mother so far has been masterful."

"In that case we'd better be on time."

His half smile melted her bones. "She knows we're still on our honeymoon and will forgive us if we're a few minutes late."

"But she'll like me better if I don't find ways to detain you when she wants your attention."

He chuckled. "You're sounding like an intuitive queen already. When I first saw you astride your horse Luna, you sat like a young queen. I was mesmerized by a ten-year-old girl who had an astounding bearing and command of her horse.

"During the jumping, your composure was flawless. You weren't like any other girl, Donetta, and my impression of you never changed that you were someone exceptional. I couldn't wait to see you again at the next *concorso*, and the next."

Her gaze didn't leave his. "You've left me speechless."

He kissed her and they clung before he pulled her to her feet and they left to walk to the small dining room in the other part of the palace. This time his mother was already seated at the table next to his father, waiting for them. King Nuncio's casted lower arm was in a sling. His caregiver was helping him eat. Enrico's heart went out to him.

"Your Majesty." Donetta curtsied to him and then bowed to the queen. "Your Majesty, I'm so sorry His Majesty fell. How hard that must've been for him and you. We came back the minute we learned what had happened."

"You were away much longer than I had anticipated." Her wintry tone couldn't have been more deflating.

"You're only given one honeymoon in life, Mamma. We wanted to make it last as long as possible."

Enrico kissed his parents before seating Donetta next to him. The staff served them dinner and poured coffee. He waited until they'd left the dining room to talk.

"To be honest, we had the honeymoon of a lifetime and couldn't bear to come back."

The queen's eyes riveted on him were closer to black than brown. "At least you *came* back. There's been another death threat on your life, *figlio mio*."

"Giovanni has already informed me, but it's nothing new."

"You're entirely too cavalier about it. When I learned the two of you have been camping out instead of flying to another country, I couldn't believe you'd left yourselves open as targets."

"I understand your fear, and I'm afraid that's my fault," Donetta spoke up. "Enrico asked me where I'd like to go. We share a lot of the same interests and love being in the mountains."

"But that's not the proper kind of honeymoon for you."

"It was what we both wanted, Mamma, and we've never been so happy. Just so you know, I'll be spending all day tomorrow and evening with Donetta. If there's anything I can do for you or Papà before morning, I'll be happy to do it now."

"As a matter of fact there are several things we need to discuss."

"I totally understand you two have missed each other and want to talk," Donetta spoke up. "I have some phone calls to make to my sisters, so why don't I leave you now. We'll see each other later, Enrico."

He loved this wife of his for her understanding. Giving her a kiss, he helped her to her feet.

"Thank you for the lovely welcome-home dinner, Your Majesty. *Buona notte.*"

Donetta sent her husband a silent message that she'd be waiting for him and then left to go back to his apartment. But some of their earlier conversation had given her the oddest feeling and she was anxious to talk it over with Fausta.

Once she reached the bedroom, she hung up her dress and brushed her teeth. After putting on a yellow cotton shorty nightgown, she sat up in the bed to talk to her.

Disappointed when her call went to voice mail, she left a message for her sister to phone her back when she could. Fausta was probably still out with Mia and her friends.

The next call to her sister Lanza went to voice mail, too. Donetta left the message that she and Enrico were back from their camping honeymoon and installed at the palace. She hoped to hear from her soon.

After sending her love, Donetta hung up and reached for the TV remote to watch the nightly news. She imagined Enrico would join his mother and talk to her while the caregiver put his father to bed. Enrico would probably be late returning to their apartment.

A half hour later, the phone rang. It was Fausta. "Thanks for calling me back."

"I've been hoping to hear from you. Is he still to die for?"

"Yes."

"Just yes? What kind of an answer is that?"

"I— It's an I-don't-know kind of answer," she said, her voice faltering.

"Donetta—what's wrong?"

She sucked in her breath. "Maybe nothing and I'm just being paranoid."

"About what?"

"Everything has been so divinely perfect until this afternoon."

"Go on."

"Today was the first time he talked about my running the country. He kept paying me all these compliments and telling me I was going to be a great leader. It sounded so odd when he doesn't know if I could do the job or not.

"When I asked him why he had such faith in me, he said that I'd seemed like a queen to him even when I was ten years old and he'd always admired my strength. Don't you find that strange? Bizarre even?"

"Are you kidding me? He's in love and letting you know how much! Before you got married, he said he wanted you to rule equally with him. How has that changed?"

"I don't know!" she cried. "You weren't there. Enrico was...different."

"Isn't this what you've always wanted? To be queen?"

Donetta gripped the phone tighter. "I thought I did once. But not like this..."

"Not like what?"

"What he said to me today didn't sound like the real Enrico. It was more like he was reading from a script. Oh—I realize I'm not explaining this right or making sense. All I know is, he didn't seem like the man I married. When he told me I'd been a close observer of my father all my life and there wouldn't be anything I couldn't handle, it disturbed me."

"Disturbed you? Am I talking to the real Donetta?"

"Don't make fun of me, Fausta."

"I'm not. I'm just surprised."

"Why does he think he knows so much about me? Something else is strange, too. He was supposed to be crowned king at his marriage, but because he married me instead of Valentina, his mother wouldn't allow the coronation to happen."

"You're kidding. I thought his father was incapacitated. Is Enrico upset about it?"

"I can't tell." Suddenly she heard a noise and knew Enrico had come back. "I'll have to call you another time, Fausta. Good night." She clicked off and put the phone on the side table just as he walked into the room. Thankfully, the TV was still on.

Those penetrating black eyes of his zeroed in on her. "There you are. Just where I want you to be and looking delightful in yellow." When he disappeared into the bathroom, she turned the TV off with the remote.

In a minute he'd changed out of his clothes and put on a robe. After turning out the lights, he slid into bed and pulled her against him. "Our first night in our own home. I hope it will feel that way to you soon."

"I'm with you forever. It's all that matters."

It *was* all that mattered.

Fausta had been right about Enrico wanting to show her how much he loved and believed in her. Donetta had been reading way too much into the earlier conversation with her husband. She loved him more than life itself. "Is your mother all right?" She kissed his hard jaw.

"No," he said honestly. "She can't let it go that I didn't marry Valentina, but in time she'll come around. You're wonderful to her. Please don't let her upset you too much. The day will come when she'll learn to love you."

"I want to believe that, too. Now tell me what else is wrong."

She heard his sharp intake of breath. "The truth is, she's afraid I'm going to be assassinated."

Donetta's fingers tightened in his hair. "You can't blame her for that. I think deep down that the wives and children of any sovereign harbor that same fear. If you want to know the truth, my sisters and I have always lived under that same worry where our father is concerned."

"But you can handle it."

Enrico was wrong. The thought of losing him to a sniper's bullet or the slash of a dagger terrified her.

He held her tighter. "The problem is, she's demanding I stop taking on the corrupt elements with so much force. Of course that's something I won't do."

"Doesn't she realize you're carrying out the same policies as your father?"

"Yes and no. In the last year I've been more aggressive than he ever was. These death threats prove I'm getting more results with every arrest. The progress we're making is vital for our country's welfare. My goal is to rid Vallefiore of this menace.

"Since college Giovanni has been helping me develop a massive internal structure of intelligence operatives. In time we're going to win this war. We can't back down now."

Donetta rose up on one elbow. "*That's* the reason she didn't allow the coronation to happen. Once you become king, with all the power, you'll be their target more than ever, and she's terrified of losing you."

"Trust my brilliant wife to figure it out, but we have the needed kind of security in place to ensure that you and I will reign for a long time, God willing."

They *were* in God's hands. She knew that.

CHAPTER NINE

"I ADMIRE YOU for your fearlessness and determination, Enrico. I promise I'll do everything I can to help."

"You already do that just being here in my arms."

The time for talk was over. With one kiss he swept her away. They gave in to their desire, which continued to grow with every passing minute, taking them far into the night. Donetta fell asleep nestled against him.

They slept in and enjoyed breakfast in the apartment. After both of them dressed in casual clothes, they left for the wing of the palace that housed the government. His staff resembled a small city of men and women officials.

When they saw Enrico, they all stood and clapped. Chief among them was Giovanni. His arms were folded. He wore a broad smile on his good-looking face.

Her husband put his arm around her waist. "Thank you for welcoming us this morning. Let me introduce you to my bride, Princess Donetta Rossiano of Domodossola. She will be working with all of us from here on out on a daily basis.

"You are to offer Her Highness the same help and

courtesy you offer me. There will be times when I'll be away on other business, but she will be here. Any matters that would come to me will now come to her. Let me make it clear that she'll speak with the same authority as I do."

Donetta marveled how quickly he was changing the dynamics of a system of male succession that had been in place for centuries. Already Enrico was preparing the staff for her to carry out the role he'd created for her.

Everyone continued to pay attention, but deep down she knew they didn't really believe he meant every word of that speech. But in time they'd find out and be in shock. Common sense told her they weren't going to like it.

He ushered her through massive, ornate floor-to-ceiling doors into his large, sumptuous office, where the king had worked until he'd become incapacitated. A framed picture of Enrico's father hung on the wall.

A stand placed in one corner held the flag of Valle-fiore and the individual flags of each province. There was also a grouping of leather couches and chairs around an octagonal coffee table with a fabulous Moorish pot overflowing with flowers.

Enrico pulled out his swivel armchair for her to be seated at his desk. He perched his hard-muscled body on a corner of the massive oak desk and buzzed one of the secretaries in the outer office. He asked that another matching chair, desk and lamp be brought in by the end of the day.

With that accomplished, he flashed his devastating

smile that sent her heartbeat skyrocketing. "Your Highness? Behold your kingdom. All that I have is yours."

Overcome by his generous heart, she felt her eyes prickle with salty tears. "Are you sure this is what you want?"

"Aren't you?"

He often answered a question with another one. This question gave her pause. As she was growing up, she'd always wanted to be queen by right of succession. At least that was what she'd told herself. But in time she could see that it had been nothing more than a child's pipe dream.

For Enrico to walk in here today and install her as a fait accompli in front of his subjects who answered to a king and no one else was an entirely different proposition.

For one thing, Enrico hadn't been crowned king officially yet. If his mother continued to feel so negatively over his choice of wife, maybe it wouldn't happen for several more years.

Donetta wasn't Enrico's queen in the legal sense that he could set her on the throne beside him. No matter what he'd promised her, for the time being she was Princess Donetta, wife of the crown prince. But she'd promised to help him and she would do everything in her power because she adored him.

"I'm ready to learn."

"I'm glad, because there's no time to waste. The first thing to do is get on the computer and we'll go over my daily routine. Later on, we'll take a look at my weekly and monthly agenda."

Finally she could see the world he'd been immersed in since college. He carried a huge load.

"In a minute I'll show you the list of our legislators, the cabinet and staff overseeing the military, housing and education, with names, phone numbers and job descriptions. However, the names of your bodyguards and mine won't be on any computer."

Of course not. Her father had security, but she couldn't remember him ever having to deal with a personal death threat.

"Another file will show you the entire floor plan and layout of the palace, plus the palace staff. We also run many businesses and some hospitals and organizations in the city and throughout the country. I'll show you how to access that list as well."

Donetta knew she'd be looking at it a lot until she had everything memorized.

"Giovanni is the head of security and that includes the country's police and fire departments. He also runs our Sanfratellano Horse Federation and will familiarize you with everything when you're ready. My sisters oversee many charities and will be available to you. Soon I'll discuss our treaties and immigration policies with you."

By midafternoon Donetta's head was too full of new information to learn any more and Enrico knew it. "We've done enough for today, *bellissima*. Let's eat lunch in our apartment, and then I have a surprise for you."

"You do too much for me."

"I'll never be able to do enough."

As they started to leave, Giovanni knocked before coming in. "Excuse me, Donetta. Can I talk to your husband for a minute?"

"You can," Donetta said with a smile. "I'll see you at the apartment, Enrico. Shall I call down to the kitchen?"

He nodded. "All you have to do is pick up the phone and give the order."

She walked down the hallway lined with glassed-in offices. Many curious eyes followed her progress. Not all looked that friendly and she understood why, but maybe she was letting her paranoia take over again. Donetta couldn't afford for that to happen.

Giovanni closed the door so no one could see or hear them. "When you introduced Donetta to everyone this morning, the part about her having the same power as you didn't go over well with anyone, especially you know who."

Enrico nodded. "Leopold. The man can't be trusted, but father appointed him to the cabinet and he's a good friend of Mamma's."

"Not to mention a titled member of the aristocracy. I saw him get on the phone immediately."

"That's no surprise, but the only way to make this change was to deal with it head on."

"You certainly did that," his cousin murmured. "I just wanted to give you a heads-up."

He clasped Giovanni's shoulder. "No one ever had a better friend."

"How's it going with Donetta?"

"I didn't know I could be this happy. This afternoon I'm giving her my wedding present."

"Does she know?"

"Not yet. How's the woman situation with you? Are you still seeing Celesta?"

"No. That's over."

"You sound like the old me. One of these days it'll be your turn, cousin."

"You think?"

"I know."

On his way out of the office he talked to several associates and then hurried to his apartment. He found Donetta on the phone with her sister. A minute later their lunch arrived and he carried the tray to the dining room table so they could eat.

She followed him and he helped her to sit. They were both hungry. "How are your parents?"

"Amazingly well. The news of Lanza's pregnancy seems to have given them a new lease on life."

"Don't you think that seeing you happy has made a difference, too?"

"Of course. They like you very much already."

"That's nice to hear." The baked cod with green beans and potatoes hit the spot. "Just think how thrilled they'll be when we can tell them the news that we're expecting our own baby."

She finished her coffee. "That's my greatest wish."

"And mine. In the meantime, let's take a short drive to the other end of the property. Everything is open to the public except the tennis courts and swimming pool."

* * *

Enrico had told her he had a surprise for her. Donetta had seen the map that showed the twelve-square-mile Montedoro estate. She was excited as they left the palace in his Jaguar. He drove them along a road behind the palace.

"The estate gardens are breathtaking."

"Mamma oversees their care and design. Every day she pushes Papà for a walk along the paths. She's an amazing gardener."

"I'd love to learn from her."

Soon she saw a cluster of buildings in the distance, among them a state-of-the-art stable that could probably house a dozen horses. She turned her head to look at him. *"Enrico?"*

"I see you've already guessed my surprise," he teased.

When he parked in front, she was out of the car in a flash. He caught up to her and took her inside to the fourth stall. Her eyes clapped on a gorgeous dark chocolate brown mare.

"My precious wife, meet Mahbouba. It means beloved in Arabic."

"I can't tell you what this means to me," she whispered and threw her arms around him. "Ever since you told me about the Sanfratellano horses, I've dreamed of owning one. In fact when I came for your *concorso*, I'd planned to arrange to buy one. But everything changed after our campout. I knew I couldn't trust myself to be with you any longer. She's really mine?"

"All yours."

Donetta approached her horse, talking softly to her while she rubbed her head and neck. The mare seemed to like the attention while Donetta inspected her legs and hooves. "You're beautiful, Mahbouba." She looked over at Enrico. "Can we go riding?"

"Let's go bareback. She's been broken in. I asked the trainer to get her ready for us. After I help you mount, we'll walk back to the end of the stable to get my stallion Quatan."

"Every day with you is a miracle."

She pressed a kiss to her husband's lips before he helped her on and handed her the reins. The mare pranced in place while Donetta let her get used to her weight. "Come on," she said in soothing tones. "Let's go for a ride."

Enrico started walking. Donetta directed the mare to follow him. It had been over a month since she'd ridden, and now she felt euphoric. When they reached his stallion's stall, both horses neighed. Enrico moved inside and mounted his steed with his usual masculine dexterity.

"That new black stallion is a prize. He's gorgeous."

"I didn't think I could replace Rajah, but Quatan is exceptional." He made a clicking sound and headed out of the stable to the field. Donetta was close behind, taking care not to startle the mare until she got used to her.

All the while they walked, she talked to her and patted her neck. "You're a real beauty. Did you know I saw your brothers and sisters running across the plain? I hope you don't miss them too much."

Enrico must have heard her. His smile lit up her universe. "Keep that up and you'll have her eating out of your hand before the day is out."

They walked for a good half hour and then returned to the stable. When they came to Mahbouba's stall, Donetta slid off to give her water and feed her. Then she reached for the currycomb hanging on a hook to brush her down. Enrico stalled his horse and came back to watch her.

Donetta turned to him. "She's as good as gold."

"So you think you'll keep her?"

She laughed. "This morning you presented your kingdom to me. Now you've presented me with this beautiful animal. You make me too happy." Her voice caught.

"We'll go riding every day, either morning or evening, and get you a saddle you can break in."

After giving her mare more love, they left the stable and got back in his car. As he drove them to the palace, she finally had an idea for a wedding present she could give him. Right away she would secretly find out the name of the artist who'd done Rajah's picture in oils. If he or she were available, Donetta would commission a painting of Quatan and have it hung on the wall of their bedroom.

But she wanted to do something for him right now. When they arrived and hurried to the apartment, she turned to him. "I'm going to cook our dinner tonight."

"I'm already salivating."

"Will it be all right if I call the kitchen for the ingredients I need?"

"Go ahead while I check my messages."

A half hour later they'd both showered and gotten comfortable in their robes while she cooked up a storm. Donetta ordered some red wine to go with their meal.

"I'll feed you." She stood next to him and gave him a heaping forkful of fried bruschetta.

He munched on it before reaching for her. "I've died and gone to heaven."

She chuckled. "I hope you'll like my *escalope de veau* with rice just as much."

Enrico devoured their meal in no time. "Promise me you'll cook our dinner every night."

They clinked their glasses of wine. "I plan to do whatever you want to keep you satisfied."

When they'd finished, he turned on the radio to some music and took her out on the patio off the dining room to dance with her. Their dance soon moved to the bedroom just as his cell phone rang.

"We're not home," he said aloud.

"You need to pick up," she urged.

"I'm still on my honeymoon, *esposa mia*."

"But it might be important."

"You're right, but I resent the intrusion." He reached for his phone before looking at her in surprise. "It's Lia."

Donetta got in bed and listened, but she only heard half of the conversation. Before long he turned to her with an almost forbidding expression.

"She's been with mother for the last two hours. Mamma's informant told her about my speech this morning. She's not only livid, but she called an emergency meeting of the most influential members of my cabinet."

Donetta got out of bed. "Why would she do such a thing?"

"She's asked them to gather the entire legislature in the next twenty-four hours for an emergency meeting. She's demanding they call for a vote that will bar you legally from having anything to do with my work as crown prince."

"Oh, no—" A shiver racked Donetta's body. "You warned me she would fight it, but to talk to your ministers behind your back…"

"Mamma has gone too far. I'm stymied by her behavior. It simply isn't like her to make this so ugly. Something's going on I don't know about. I've got to talk to Giovanni and find out what he knows."

"Wait, Enrico. You and I need to talk first. Before you do anything, I think you should go to your mother tonight and work things out with her even if it takes all night. This situation on top of her disappointment over Valentina has been too much for her."

Lines marred his handsome features. "I'm too upset to talk to her right now."

"But she's more upset than you and we know why. She's frightened for your life and is threatened by my presence. I'm sure she believes I'm influencing you to do things you would never do if you hadn't met me."

He shook his dark head. "She has no right to be this cruel to you."

"I agree. You warned me she would be difficult, but I didn't want to believe you. I don't understand it when she loves you so much. I'm positive she doesn't believe I'm worthy of you. Let's face it. She's not ready for a daughter-in-law like me. I'm a horsey person who loves to camp out. I arrived on your doorstep and upset her world in one day.

"Instead of a big wedding in the cathedral in front of your countrymen, we married quietly without anyone knowing. Her world has spun out of control. In her mind I'm a terrible person and the cause of her pain.

"You need to spend time with her and listen to her fears. She didn't know you and I have had a long history. It has shaken her. If she understood more, she'd see why we wanted to get married immediately.

"Help her understand that you'd like to be able to concentrate on the threat to your country if you're going to make a real difference. Let her see that you would like the woman you married and trust to run the daily affairs while you deal with the criminal elements. She has no idea how much I'd love to help you in any way I can. For both our sakes, please go to her tonight and explain. I'm begging you."

At first she didn't think she was getting through to him. But he eventually got up from the bed and started to get dressed. "I'll go, but I might not be back until morning. Besides talking to her, I've got phone calls to make. Don't wait up for me. I'm so sorry, Donetta."

"Don't worry about me, darling. You're the only person in the world who can fix this."

"I intend to," he ground out. "She had no right to hurt you this way. You're my wife!" he exploded in a savage voice.

"I'm not the one hurt," she cried even though she was dying inside. But for the first time since she'd flown in to Vallefiore, he wasn't listening. In the next breath he left the bedroom without holding or kissing her first. For him to do that revealed the depth of his torment.

No sooner had he gone than the landline phone rang. Donetta threw on her robe and rushed over to pick it up. "This is Donetta."

"Oh, Donetta. It's Lia. I'm so glad you answered. Are you alone?"

"Yes. Enrico has gone to talk to your mother."

"That's good, because I need to talk to you. Can I come to your apartment? I should be there in five minutes."

"Of course. I'll be right here waiting."

Donetta hung up and paced the living room floor until she heard a knock on the outer door.

"Come in, Lia."

"Forgive me for barging in, but I can't keep this to myself." Enrico's sister hurried inside and sat down on one of the couches, patting a spot so Donetta would sit by her.

"What's wrong?"

"I overheard my mother talking to our cabinet leader, Leopold, earlier in the small salon. She's talking about having your marriage annulled because it wasn't legal under our constitution. I don't know if she can really do that, but she's going to try to influence them. Out of respect for our father, they'll probably listen to her. If that doesn't work, then she wants Leo to begin divorce proceedings for the two of you."

Donetta got up from the couch. "Enrico warned me

she wouldn't want our marriage, but I never dreamed it could get this bad."

"Mamma has surprised me, too. I heard her say it's not too late because she knows Valentina will still marry him if he can be free. Since the whole world doesn't know about it yet, she's hoping your marriage can be undone and go away. But it has to happen right away."

"Oh, Lia. I don't know what to do."

"I wish I knew how to help you and my mother. I'm sure she's talking about a divorce with Enrico right now in the salon. I've never seen her in such a rage. This is so awful, because I think you and Enrico are perfect for each other."

Donetta's heart warmed to her new sister-in-law. "Thank you for saying that and defending us." She leaned over to give her a hug. "I owe you a debt of gratitude for everything, especially for that wedding dress and all the lovely things that went with it. You're wonderful."

"So are you. Enrico has never been so happy. I wish there were something I could do to calm my mother, but she's not listening to reason right now and Papà's fall didn't help."

"I agree she has more on her plate than a human should have to handle. I know deep down she's a wonderful person or she wouldn't have such marvelous children like Enrico and you girls. You don't know how much I appreciate your coming here to warn me. When Enrico comes back, I'll be prepared."

Lia nodded. "I'd better leave so he doesn't find me here."

"He said he'd probably be gone all night." Donetta followed her to the door. "We'll stay in close touch. Thank you again for being such a good friend to us."

After another hug, Lia hurried off. Donetta watched until she disappeared, but she couldn't stand to wait for Enrico. With no time to spare she left the apartment and hurried through the palace to the salon to find her husband. But as she approached the door, she heard his mother's voice. "It's better that she leave the country, Enrico. You shouldn't have married her in the first place."

Pierced to the heart with pain, that was all Donetta needed to hear. Once alone in the apartment again, she knew what she had to do. She refused to stand in Enrico's way. He must go on to be king. The country needed him. Though she would have loved to get behind him and manage by his side, it was better that he get the chance to rule, even if it meant she couldn't remain his wife.

Her beloved husband needed help. The one path open to her was to leave the country and give him the chance to handle this desperate situation without her. It was the only way he could take on the throne.

When she found her phone, she called the pilot of the Rossiano royal jet. Donetta asked him to fly to Vallefiore ASAP. She would be waiting on the tarmac.

At three in the morning, she slipped out of the apartment with her two suitcases, praying Enrico wouldn't catch her in the act of fleeing. The palace guard saw her leave in the taxi she'd called for. But she knew that by the time he would have reported her actions and someone tracked down Enrico to tell him, she'd be on her way to Domodossola.

So far, so good, she thought as she boarded the jet and they took off. She sat there during the flight absolutely devastated for Enrico and the trouble his mother was creating. In hindsight she realized that what he'd wanted just wasn't possible. His mother had lived a lifetime with her own set of principles and couldn't change now.

Donetta refused to hold him or his kingdom back by her selfishness. She wouldn't fight a divorce. All she could do was return home and help her own family.

Oh, Enrico... I love you so much.

An hour and a half later the plane landed. Enrico hadn't phoned her yet. Maybe he still hadn't heard that she'd left the palace. Hoping that he didn't have to cope with that worry yet, she undid her seat belt and phoned Fausta.

"You've left Enrico?" Fausta sounded aghast.

"It's not what you think. Can you come for me in the limo so we can talk?" It was six in the morning. "I don't dare phone the parents. They need their sleep." The last thing she wanted to do was bring them more grief, but under the circumstances she was afraid it was going to be inevitable.

"I agree. I'll be there within half an hour."

"Bless you."

CHAPTER TEN

AFTER LEAVING HIS parents' apartment, Enrico raced to his in the other part of the palace. He needed to talk to Donetta. On his way, he got a phone call from his cousin. He clicked on, trying to keep his emotions under control after the long, disturbing talk with his mother and Leopold.

"Giovanni? I presume you know everything."

"I'm afraid I know more than you do."

"What do you mean?"

"The guard outside the entrance to your wing of the palace phoned to let me know Donetta left the palace in the middle of the night in a taxi."

No! His body broke out in a cold sweat.

"Her bodyguards followed her to the airport and confirmed she flew out on the royal jet from Domodossola. I contacted their country's police to put a bodyguard on her the moment she landed. A few minutes ago they confirmed that she had arrived and was picked up by Princess Fausta, who also has security."

Enrico reeled. That was all he needed to hear. "Thank you for all you've done. I should never have left her while I tried to talk sense to Leopold and Mamma. It accomplished nothing."

"Hold on. I'm coming to your apartment now so we can talk without anyone listening in on our phone conversation."

By the time his cousin burst into the apartment, Enrico was in agony. The two stared at each other.

"I should never have told Donetta she could share the throne with me, Giovanni. After what I learned tonight, Leo said that the leaders of the cabinet would give me a no-confidence vote if I had her rule with me. It could be the end of my rule, too, and throw our country into utter chaos."

"You'll have to listen to them, Enrico. Our country needs you at the helm. The problem is, they're not ready for a modern world."

"Apparently not. It isn't as if I'd proposed changing the rules of succession!"

"The problem is, no wife of a sovereign of Vallefiore has ever shared the throne. It's never been done."

"Then something needs to change, Giovanni. We no longer live in the age of dinosaurs."

"Not changing the rules has kept the monarchy strong."

"So strong that the cabinet's rejection and Mamma's have done irreparable personal damage to my wife. Mamma's insisting on a divorce, which is out of the question. Donetta married me after I made her the promise that she would rule as queen in her own right.

"It's something she's wanted all her life. I thought I could make her dream a reality. As your informant once told you, Donetta stayed single all these years because she wanted to change the laws of Domodossola and be queen.

"When she realized she could never do away with the rules of succession in her country, she grabbed the chance I offered her. I believed I could work a miracle. Donetta trusted me enough that she walked out on Arnaud because of what I could do for her.

"I have to be honest with myself. It may have not been a lie, but my marriage proposal was made on shaky ground and now I'm paying for it. But I'm not about to lose her, because I love her too much. I told Mamma I would never divorce her."

"How can I help?"

"Giovanni, will you fly to Domodossola right now in the jet and bring her back? I know how her mind works. She'll tell me she'll agree to a divorce. Say whatever you have to in order to bring her back with you."

"I'm on my way, but don't you want to go?"

"I can't if I'm going to get everything ready in time. I've made plans that I pray will convince her I can't live without her. When you reach the airport, drive her as far as the road leading down to the waterfall where we had our honeymoon."

"Good news, cousin. The tent is still there, being guarded. I haven't had time to see about dismantling it yet. Now I'm glad I haven't."

"That makes two of us. I'll be there waiting."

"Now you're talking."

"When this is over, I'm going to repay you for being

the best friend a man could ever hope to have and give you the long vacation you deserve and anything else your heart desires."

When the limo reached the palace, Fausta asked the driver to take her around to the side entrance closest to her apartment. Donetta hurried inside with her and they closeted themselves in her bedroom. Before long their parents would hear that Donetta had arrived, but for the time being they were free to talk.

She checked her phone. By now Enrico had to know she'd flown here, but he hadn't phoned or texted her yet. Still, it was early in the day. All she could do was hope that by her leaving Vallefiore, he'd be free to do what he had to do as crown prince.

"Sit down and talk to me, Donetta. Was it really so terrible with his mother?"

"You can't imagine. She was unfriendly the first time I was introduced to her at the *concorso*. It grew worse from that time on. After Lia told me about his talk with her last night, I had to leave.

"I was afraid that the very sight of me was too much for his mother to handle. She was taken by surprise from the very beginning. I love Enrico so terribly and can't bear it that I've come between them."

"From what you've told me, she was already upset because he never wanted to marry Valentina."

"The whole thing's a nightmare, Fausta. I'll give him a divorce if that's what is needed." While Donetta stood there with tears gushing down her cheeks, her cell phone rang. "Maybe that's Enrico—"

She pulled it out of her purse and checked the caller ID. "It's Giovanni. At least *he's* calling me."

Fausta watched her as she answered. "Put it on speaker."

Donetta nodded. "Giovanni?"

"Can you talk?" He sounded so anxious her heart plunged to the floor.

"Yes! I guess you know I just arrived here in Domodossola. My sister Fausta is with me. Is Enrico all right? I love him so much and have been hoping, waiting for him to call."

She heard him expel a deep sigh. "I have a better idea. I'm on my way in the jet right now to bring you back on Enrico's orders. Then you can talk to him yourself. Be at the airport in an hour."

"But Giovanni—"

"There's no time to talk."

She heard the click and looked at Fausta.

Her sister was smiling. "You ran out on your husband and it didn't fix anything. Now he's searching for you. If I were you, I'd take a quick shower, grab a bite to eat and let me drive you back to the airport with your bags."

"I'm frightened, Fausta."

"Have a little faith, sister. I'm afraid if you don't show up with Giovanni, your husband will send reinforcements and it could get uglier than even *you* dreamed."

Enrico checked his watch. Eleven o'clock in the morning. He'd arrived at the camp behind the guys who'd trailed the horses and would take care of them. He waited on his stallion for the sight of Giovanni's car on the mountain road.

Donetta's saddled mare stood next to them with the reins in Enrico's hands. After Donetta arrived, they would ride down to the camp together. It would give him the chance he needed to tell her he would choose her above his kingdom. She was all he wanted.

Earlier this morning, with the help of his sisters, he'd prevailed on his mother to accept his marriage to Donetta, but there'd be no more talk of her ruling equally with him. In his heart Enrico planned that one day he could give Donetta the prize she'd always hoped for. That time would come.

His heart leaped when he saw the blue car round the bend. Giovanni pulled up to the side of the road where Enrico was waiting. Donetta got out of the car. The first thing he saw were those shimmering light green eyes clapped on him in stunned surprise.

"I don't blame you for wanting to run away, *amata*. Thank heaven you came back." He waved to Giovanni, who reciprocated before returning to the city. "Mahbouba is waiting for you."

"I can't believe you're here. Giovanni was so mysterious about where we were going."

"My cousin was only carrying out my wishes. I couldn't believe it when you weren't in our apartment earlier, but all our troubles are over now. Let's ride."

Enrico watched her mount with a grace that was thrilling to watch. They started to make their way through the trees. "Tell me something, *bellissima*. Why didn't you wait for me?"

His question stunned her. "Surely you must know! I wanted to ease the tension with your mother and decided that getting away from the palace was the only thing to do. I've come between you and her in the most terrible way possible and thought it best to give you the space to work things out with her."

A groan came out of him. "Lia told me what she told you. Don't you know I couldn't handle it if you ever left me?"

"But your mother despises me."

"My mother isn't your problem, Donetta. Our marriage is all we need to worry about."

She gripped the reins so tight it hurt her hand. "That's not true. She's been hurt so badly it's killing me."

"I think we're talking at cross-purposes here."

Donetta frowned. "I don't understand what you're saying."

"Answer me one question. *Why* did you marry me?"

"Do you really have to ask me that?" she cried.

"Just tell me."

"Because I loved you from the moment we met years ago. When you told me you were planning to get married, too, and then admitted that I was the woman, I almost died from happiness."

"So it didn't have anything to do with my telling you that I would make you queen in your own right after we were married?"

What? "Of course it didn't! I wanted to be your wife, period! That's the *only* reason I flew here the next day! Why would you say such a thing?"

"Because a friend of Giovanni's, who happens to be

friend of your sister Fausta's, told him that you never intended to marry. He said it was because you wanted to be queen of Domodossola one day and didn't want a husband."

Donetta let out a cry. "It wouldn't have been Mia Giancarlo, would it?"

"She's the one. After I saw you in Madrid, I told my cousin I was in love with you and wanted to marry you. He told me I was out of luck. He said that the only reason you were still single was because you wanted to be queen in your own right. You didn't want a husband. When I heard that, I loved you so much I didn't let that stop me and I vowed to find a way to get you to marry me."

Right now Donetta's heart was pounding so hard it actually hurt. "*That's* why you told me you would make me queen?"

"The *only* reason! But when I invited you to Vallefiore and you said you were going to marry Arnaud, I was devastated. Still, I refused to give up. When you were getting on the jet to fly home, I gave it one last stab, hoping you would be persuaded to marry me and not leave."

"I almost didn't!" she cried.

"After you flew off, I never dreamed you'd change your mind. I'm surprised I didn't go into cardiac arrest when Giovanni phoned and told me you'd returned to Vallefiore."

"Oh, Enrico—" Now she understood why he'd talked about what a great leader she would make. Fausta had been right. Enrico had been saying everything he could to show her he loved her!

"Tell me the truth, *amata*. Are you hurt because I can't make you a queen after all?"

They'd reached the camp. Donetta jumped off her horse and tied it to a tree before wheeling around. She looked at Enrico, who'd started to dismount.

"I gave up the dream of being a queen a long time ago. It was a foolish, stupid, unrealistic idea I developed as a girl that could never have happened. When you told me I could reign equally with you, I had trouble believing it. But I was so thrilled you wanted to marry me that I was happy to do anything I could to help you, if that's what you wanted."

Enrico let out a groan and hurried over to her, wrapping her in his arms. "This whole misunderstanding is my fault for believing the gossip about you, Donetta."

She shook her head. "If anyone is to blame, it's I. Fausta grew up with me and knew my feelings when I was young. She didn't mean to tell Mia. I'm the one who should never have said anything so foolish.

"But Mia has a brother who had a crush on me and knew I'd never give him the time of day. I know that's why she told her brother about my vow so he'd stop hoping for a chance with me."

"Donetta—" The revelations were flying fast and furious. "This news changes everything." He kissed her every feature. "Do you hear me, my love?"

"Yes. Oh, yes! But, darling, your mother needs to know that I've never tried to manipulate you. The only thing I plan to do is love you and our babies, if we're so lucky to have them. If she'll let me, I'll love her, too."

"You'll win her over, Donetta. I know you will."

"When I tell my parents that you tried to make my childhood dream come true, they'll love you all the more. But no one could love you the way I do. It's not possible."

Once again he picked her up in his arms and carried her inside the tent. For the next two hours they tried without success to assuage their desire, renewing their vows in the most elemental way.

He pulled her on top of him. "Promise me you'll never leave me again."

"I promise."

"Much as I want to have another long honeymoon with you, we need to get back to the palace. Mamma needs to know we have a solid marriage and nothing will hurt us."

"I love you so much, Enrico, and need to let her know how I feel."

Two hours later they were back in their apartment at the palace where she could shower and change into her pink suit. She wanted to look her best for Queen Teodora.

Enrico had arranged for them and Giovanni to eat an early dinner in the small dining room. He felt that the element of surprise when the three of them showed up would work in their favor.

The queen was already seated at the table, dressed in a lovely blue suit. Her dark brown eyes flashed in anger when she saw Donetta and Giovanni enter the room at Enrico's side. There was no sign of the king.

"Your Majesty." Donetta curtsied before Enrico helped her to a seat around the other side. "Is the king not well today?"

"He's never well and doesn't have his dinner until later."

"Zia Teodora?" Giovanni began. "We have something of vital importance to share with you. So does Princess Donetta."

Her jaw hardened. "I heard you'd flown to Domodossola during the night."

"I did."

"But I brought her back on the royal jet," Giovanni explained. "The drastic situation required drastic measures in order to restore peace and understanding."

Donetta was holding her breath. Enrico gripped her hand.

"Thank you for accommodating us, Zia. What I have to tell you will change your perspective on everything."

After they were served dinner and coffee, Giovanni began. "My story starts when Enrico confided that he'd been in love with Donetta ever since their first *concorso* in England seventeen years ago. He kept his secret until we came home from Madrid about six weeks ago. That's the first time I'd heard that he'd been wanting to marry her since college. But I'm afraid I said something to him that presented a challenge."

In the next instant Donetta listened while Giovanni laid everything out for his aunt so there could be no misunderstanding. "When Enrico made his speech to the cabinet, he was fulfilling his promise to Donetta, who never wanted to rule equally with him."

The queen's expression underwent a fundamental change. "I still don't understand."

Donetta broke in and told her about her childhood dream to be queen of Domodossola one day. "My sister knew how I felt and shared it with her friend, who happens to be a friend of Giovanni's."

He nodded. "I told Enrico he would never be able to marry Donetta because she didn't intend to marry. She wanted to be queen in her own right."

"It was a ridiculous, foolish dream I gave up on a long time ago," Donetta explained. "When Arnaud pursued me and wanted to marry me, I knew I didn't love him. But if we had children, I knew it would bring me happiness. The trouble was, I had always loved Enrico and had waited in vain for a proposal from him."

Enrico spoke up. "When she came to our *concorso*, she let me know she planned to go home and tell Arnaud she would marry him. I proposed anyway. To influence her even more, I told her she could rule equally with me. Until this morning when I told her the truth, Donetta had no idea I had ever heard the gossip about her."

"You can't imagine my joy that Enrico loved me, Your Majesty," Donetta cried. "I told Arnaud it was over with us. Even if Enrico changed his mind about me, I knew I would never love anyone but him."

The queen sat back in the chair, her eyes dim with thoughts. "This explains why you could never get interested in Valentina, my son. What I don't understand is why you didn't tell me and your father."

Donetta broke in. "I didn't tell my parents about him, either. I would have if he'd kept on writing and wanted to see me. But there was never a word. My sister Fausta knew how I felt, but she never said anything."

Enrico's mother looked at her with sadness. "My husband was struggling so much at the time. When Enrico came home and took over, it was like a godsend. I can see now that I leaned on him too much and had too many expectations that didn't give him any free time."

Donetta smiled at her. "I just want you to know that I would have done whatever he asked. But now that I know everything, I have no plan to run the government with him, even if you and the cabinet were to allow it. Please convey that message to them.

"The truth is, I'm just so happy to be Enrico's wife that it's all I want, except to hope that one day you will learn to accept me a little bit. He loves you and his father more than you know."

The queen sat straighter in her chair. "It's very evident he's found the love of his life. I hope that one day you'll be able to forgive me for the ungracious way I have treated you."

Donetta felt her eyes smart. "There's nothing to forgive. My biggest worry is that Enrico will not forgive me for leaving."

"You know I have." Enrico kissed her cheek. "And my gratitude to Giovanni for helping us knows no bounds."

Queen Teodora patted Giovanni's arm. "He's my second son and I love him like my own. When his parents lost their lives in a plane accident, he became one of the family and has been a blessing."

Donetta smiled. "I can believe that. I love him, too."

After they'd finished their meal, Enrico got up and walked over to his mother. "Why don't we go check on Papà?"

"I'd like that."

"Donetta? I'll see you back at our apartment in a little while."

"Take all the time you need." Both Giovanni and Donetta got to their feet. "Thank you for letting me talk to you, Your Majesty."

The queen actually smiled at her. "Call me Mamma."

Donetta left the dining room with Giovanni, who looked over at her. "I hope you realize my aunt just welcomed you to the family."

She nodded. "I'm still overcome that she has forgiven me."

"Beneath that exterior she has a heart of gold. But where Valentina was concerned, she had a soft spot. However, I'm afraid the princess no longer holds first place in her heart."

Donetta smiled at him. "Have you ever been interested in Valentina?"

"No, but there is one woman I've had my eye on for a couple of years. It's hopeless, of course."

"How can you say that?"

"Because it's your sister."

"Fausta?" she cried out in surprise.

"I met her in Paris. But I gave up on pursuing her

when I heard the gossip about her." He flashed Donetta a glance. "Is it possible that by now she has given up the dream of marrying a commoner?"

What she'd give to have Giovanni for a brother-in-law! "I'm afraid not, or I'd throw her at you." He laughed that rich laugh, sounding so much like Enrico her heart hurt. "We're going to have to find you a woman you can't live without."

"Please do."

It was her turn to laugh.

"Do you know my cousin went through a period where he wished he hadn't been born royal? He eventually got over it."

"He told me about that. Would it surprise you to know my brother-in-law Stefano disliked being royal and was legally exempt for a decade? But that changed when his brother died and he married Lanza."

"Are they happy?"

"Ecstatic. But Fausta is different. She likes being royal and believes that if she marries a commoner, they'll have such an unusual, interesting marriage they'll always be in love. It's that unknown element separating the classes she believes is missing from many marriages, royal or otherwise."

"Her mind is as fascinating as yours."

"Mine doesn't match hers. When we were little, Mamma would read fairy tales to us. After she turned out the light and left the room, the three of us would discuss them for hours.

"Lanza loved *Cinderella* the most, where life would

be perfect. Fausta loved *The Twelve Dancing Princesses*. She would speculate that instead of meeting a dumb prince, she would meet a commoner, which was much more exciting and dangerous."

He laughed. "What was your favorite?"

"I didn't have one because something was missing in all of them. So I wrote my own about a good queen who ran her country beautifully without any help."

"You're an original, Donetta Rossiano. So is Enrico."

She gave him a hug. "You're the best, Giovanni. Marrying Enrico, I've gained a brother. There isn't anything we wouldn't do for you."

"I'll remember that." He hugged her back.

They parted and went different ways. She returned to the apartment to wait for Enrico. He came in two minutes after.

"Donetta?" He swung her around. "We're going back to our camp. I need time alone with you away from the palace. Pack what you need and let's get going."

Life with Enrico was one of total excitement. She threw a few things together and they left in the Jaguar. She looked up at the sky. It was semi-cloudy and she could tell the clouds were gathering. Donetta wouldn't be surprised if there was a rainstorm by dark.

After they reached the mountains, there was still some sun. They changed into their swimming gear and walked out on the sandbar. So much had happened since the moment Enrico had left their apartment last evening that she could hardly believe it.

He leaned over her to give her a long, sensuous kiss. "This afternoon we achieved *détente*."

"Incredible, isn't it? She told me to call her Mamma."

"I knew she would in time."

"Did you honestly think that dangling the 'queen' carrot in front of me was what it took for me to say yes to you?"

Enrico let out a deep sigh. "I didn't know, but I wasn't about to take the chance of losing you if it would convince you to say yes to me."

"When you kissed me the first time, my sixteen-year-old heart knew I wanted to marry you. If you'd asked me to visit you at Cambridge, I would have been on the next plane and never gone home."

"Donetta—"

"It's true. Yesterday was a revelation to me when you introduced me to the leadership in your office. In my naivety growing up, I thought that changing the law of succession in Domodossola would be a snap and all I had to do was get my father to present it to the legislature.

"But with every word of that speech you gave your legislature, I saw their shock and consternation, not just your mother's. For the first time I understood for myself that you don't change a law that has run a country like yours or my family's for centuries without bringing on a civil war. That's what would have happened with your cabinet.

"Do you have any idea how much I love you for trying to do that for me? But I don't want to run your country with you. I never did! What I want to do is be there with you and for you when you need me.

"I'll always help you in any way I can, but you're the acting king. Your people love and respect you like I do. The only reason I married you is because I *love* you. Can we start over again, *amore mio*?"

At this point Enrico was having trouble taking this all in. He had no words, only love he needed to lavish on her. He took her inside and followed her down on the bed where he could devour her. His sweet, passionate wife showed him so much love that by the time they became aware of their surroundings hours later, the rain had started.

"It's a good thing we came in when we did and missed the cloudburst," he whispered against her throat.

She burrowed against him. "There's been another kind of burst in here. I'm so in love with you. There's no one like you in this whole world and I can't do enough to show you how I feel."

He crushed her to him. "I owe Giovanni for bringing us together so fast."

"I love him. We have to do something wonderful for him."

"Tomorrow we'll go back and free him of all responsibilities for a good month. We have an apartment in London where he can stay. He has friends there he enjoys."

"Girls, too, I hope."

"Of course. There was one I know he liked. What he needs is the chance to get something going with her."

"I agree."

"Right now I need the rest of the night to believe that you've come back to me. Give me a minute to raid the cooler. We need something to eat before I have my way with you again."

Her laughter was the most beautiful sound he'd ever heard.

Three months later

Donetta was in their apartment getting ready when Lanza and Fausta knocked on the door and came in.

"Oh— —" They both gasped in awe at the same time.

"Your coronation gown is perfection itself," Lanza cried out.

"It's the same gown I was married in. Enrico asked me to wear it, but we had it altered to add the train."

"You look like Cinderella at the ball."

The reference to Cinderella made her smile, reminding her of a certain conversation with Giovanni. "Do you have any idea how much I envy you? You look adorable pregnant. I bet Stefano can't keep his hands off you."

"Donetta—"

Fausta laughed. "I was just about to say the same thing. This is one exciting day." She turned to Donetta. "You do look incredible, sister dear. Enrico will be speechless when he sees you. Only a woman with your coloring and figure could possibly carry it off. Forgive me if I say you look like a queen?"

They all laughed at the insider joke. "Thank you, but I'm the one who'll lose it when we walk down the aisle and Enrico is crowned king. Honestly, he's so gorgeous in his ceremonial suit I die every time I look at him. I'm just thankful his mother decided the corona-tion could take place."

Lanza eyed her with concern. "Is his father worse?"

"He's slowly failing physically, but I believe she's trying to make up for the way she treated Enrico when we first got married."

Fausta smiled. "I take it all is well now."

"Things couldn't be better. Guess what? Giovanni told me a secret. He said Enrico made another speech to his cabinet that he was so in love with me that he'd wanted to impress me and give me power I didn't have. They all laughed, thinking it was a great joke. They'll never know what we've been through, but that's all right because everything is running beautifully."

Lanza opened the door of the apartment for her. "We'd better go downstairs to the limo, Donetta. Your husband will be waiting for you at the cathedral."

As the three of them left, Fausta said, "To think there was a time when you didn't want to get married."

"Don't remind me. I can't believe I was ever that stupid. While this subject is under discussion, maybe you should reexamine your desire to marry a commoner."

"Why did you just say that?"

"I don't know. Remember the old adage? *Be careful what you wish for.*"

"Donetta—"

"Don't mind me. I'm so happy I don't know what I'm saying."

"Shall we go?"

Within minutes the limo whisked them away to the cathedral.

Donetta was stunned by its beauty. She could hear the organ and choir as they entered the doors. While her sisters joined their mother inside, Donetta joined her father.

He wore his ceremonial dress suit and sash, looking kingly and splendid as always. She was afraid he was worn out, but he seemed to be handling all the festivities very well.

They walked arm in arm down the aisle toward the cardinal in his red robes. The grandeur of these surroundings made the experience surreal.

Their families were seated on carved chairs on one side, facing the aisle. Queen Teodora wore a cream-colored gown. Next to her, King Nuncio sat in his wheelchair. He was dressed in his ceremonial finery and no longer wore a cast. Enrico's sisters sat by him, along with their husbands and Prince Giovanni.

Donetta's mother wore blue chiffon. Her sisters were dressed in their lavender gowns. Lanza sat close to her handsome husband, Stefano. They all looked spectacular.

Holding on to her father, Donetta walked to the front, where King Victor helped her to sit in the carved chair next to the one Enrico would occupy. Then he took his seat next to her mother.

Enrico came in through a side door at the front to join her. He was dressed in his ceremonial navy blue suit with gold epaulets on the shoulders and his light blue sash. If Donetta were the type to swoon from such unmatchable male beauty—an old-fashioned word— she would have fallen at his feet in a white lace heap.

Today her husband was being proclaimed king. He looked so handsome and splendid she could hardly breathe. How blessed was she to be his wife and lover. No woman could be as insanely in love as she was.

Enrico's black eyes met hers and flashed. *He* knew exactly what was running through her private thoughts, and she blushed.

Like in everything he did, Enrico had been thoughtful, asking the cardinal to keep the coronation short enough to accommodate both their fathers, who shouldn't have to endure anything lengthy.

She'd learned that the cardinal was an old friend of their family, eager to comply with Enrico's wishes. The speech about anointing the king didn't take long. After his solemn talk, they were instructed to pray, and the choir sang a gorgeous piece of music.

Donetta was overjoyed when the cardinal picked up the crown and placed it on Enrico's head. No man in existence could match her husband for his striking presence or inner goodness.

Her heart turned over on itself when Enrico reached for her hand so she could stand next to him. "Just wait until later," he whispered in her ear, sending darts of awareness to the tips of her fingers.

The cardinal blessed both of them before the organ burst forth and they heard bells ringing. Donetta was excited beyond belief when they walked down the aisle to the enclosed carriage waiting outside. Their ride would end at the palace with a feast awaiting everyone in the main dining room.

Once he released her, they turned to their families.

To her everlasting gratitude, everyone showed a surfeit of love today. As for Enrico's mother, her decision to allow the coronation to proceed made Donetta love her more than ever.

Back at the palace, Enrico removed the crown and the festivities began. Their coronation dinner included champagne toasts from everyone, including Enrico's sisters. Donetta loved all the tributes, especially the ones from Fausta and Giovanni, who'd sat together and seemed to be enjoying each other's company. They stood at the same time and revealed secrets back and forth to everyone's amusement.

"To my cousin Enrico, whom I've never seen so happy in my life. Every time he had a date with a girl, I'd ask him if he was going to see her again, but he'd say he wasn't interested. I couldn't figure out what was wrong until he finally told me about Donetta. And then we planned the *concorso* here so she'd come."

"That explains everything," Fausta blurted. "To Donetta! If you've all noticed, she's glowing. When she returned home from that competition, I never saw anyone so happy. She told me Enrico had taken her on a picnic. I knew she was crazy about him.

"She reminds me of Lanza who came back from their last trip to Argentina and told us she and Stefano were expecting a baby."

Everyone laughed and clapped in delight. Knowing Lanza was going to have a son very soon made this coronation day extra special for Donetta.

Her father made the last toast. "To my beloved daughter Donetta. I couldn't agree with your sister more. I've never known you to be this happy, which means you've met the right man in Enrico. May you always feel this same joy through the years and know the contentment I've had with my bride."

His toast brought tears to Donetta's eyes and her mother's. She glanced at Enrico's mother. How hard this had to be for her because of her husband's illness. Enrico had to be thinking the same thing. He squeezed Donetta's hip before leaving her side to go hug his mother and father.

His devotion to them made Donetta love her new husband with a fierceness she didn't know herself capable of. Later in the day he stole her away and they hurried to their apartment where they could be alone at last.

He kissed her long and hard. "Let's hurry and get changed. I have a surprise for you."

"You do too much for me already," Donetta murmured against his lips.

"This is a small thing, but I know you'll enjoy it. Wear something casual."

"Life is always exciting with you."

She rushed to get out of the gown she'd worn to the coronation, wondering if he wanted to go on a horseback ride or some such thing.

In a few minutes they were both ready. He'd dressed in cargo pants and a sports shirt. From king to sailor, he was equally gorgeous.

Donetta smiled at him. "Before we leave, I have two surprises for you."

"You do?" He looked excited.

"One is in here. Come into the living room." She

reached for his hand and walked him out of their bedroom. "Look over on the far wall."

Those black eyes swerved in that direction. She felt his body quicken as he pulled her with him to the oil painting of his latest horse.

She knew she'd given him something he would cherish. He crushed her to him. "It's fabulous."

"Just like you."

"I adore you, *bellissima*."

After another lengthy kiss they left the apartment and hurried down the staircase to the entrance where he kept his Jaguar. Was he taking them back to their camp?

But her question was answered quickly when he drove down to the lake and parked at a pier, where she saw a gleaming white sailboat moored.

She squealed when she noticed the name on the side and turned to him. "You've named it the *Luna*!"

"That's right. When I decided to buy this sailboat, I had you in mind. But I didn't want to give away my secret and call it *Donetta*. Your horse's name was the next best choice.

"The day you won that championship on Luna was years ago, but I recognized there was something special about you even back then. You have no idea how excited I am to be sleeping on board with my wife who was once a girl with hair like a silvery gold waterfall."

She launched herself in his arms. This was love beyond imagining. He walked her down the pier and helped her onto the boat.

The sun was about to disappear below the horizon. She looked into his eyes. "Now it's time to tell you about my second gift. I haven't seen a doctor yet, but I did a home test and—"

"I've made you pregnant already?" he cried. The elation in his voice told her everything she wanted to know. *"Donetta!"*

"Won't it be fun to see if we have a boy with my color of hair or a girl with yours? You'll make the most wonderful father in the whole world."

Enrico rocked her in his arms, apparently too overcome to talk, and they lay together, looking forward to their wonderful future.

* * * * *

A FORTUNE'S
TEXAS REUNION

ALLISON LEIGH

In memory of my first
real-life hero.
I love you, D.O.D.

Chapter One

The car was upside down, resting on its crumpled hood.

Sheriff Paxton Price was out of his departmental SUV and running down the steep embankment toward the site of the crash before he was even able to discern that particular fact.

The only indication there'd been an accident at all was the way the guardrail on the side of the road had been mangled.

"Ambulance needed, Connie," he said into his shoulder mic, grabbing a spindly mesquite branch to keep it from slapping him in the face as his soles slid in the dirt. Twenty feet of prickly shrubs stood between him and the white car wedged against a gnarled snag.

If it wasn't for the dying tree, the car would have kept on going.

"Not just Charlie's wrecker. You got that, Connie? Send the ambulance, too."

"Ambulance is over in Amber Falls." Connie's response crackled badly, but in the two years since he'd come back to Paseo, he was used to the crappy transmissions by now.

"Call 'em, anyway," he barked. He wished to hell his brother Marshall didn't have the day off. He was a paramedic with the Amber Falls Fire Department. The town was the closest of any size, which didn't mean much when compared to tiny Paseo.

"On it…riff," Connie said through the crackling and Pax grabbed another shrub as he continued skidding his way down the embankment. He needed to slow his momentum before he shot beyond the wedged car and into the ravine.

Dust clouded when he went down on his side like a kid sliding into home plate. Only this time, he wasn't scoring a run for the Paseo High Panthers, but was avoiding slamming into the precariously perched sports car.

He succeeded, though barely. Adrenaline pumping, he tossed aside his cowboy hat and scrambled on his knees to the crumpled side of the car. The windshield was in the dirt and a dead tree branch bisected the back window. He'd seen too many vehicular fatalities back in Dallas, where there was emergency medical assistance available at the crook of a finger. Here in Paseo?

They had one ambulance covering an entire county. As Texas standards went, the county wasn't large, but still…

"Come on, come on." He ducked to look through the broken passenger-side window. It was the only one accessible. The driver's side was squarely jammed against the trunk of the decaying oak.

His gut clenched. The driver was hanging upside down, held in her seat by the safety belt. Her light brown hair was long and tangled in the spent airbags, and glittered with shards of glass. She was young. And her eyes, her terrified and very much alive blue eyes, fastened on his. "Help."

He read the word on her pallid lips more than heard

it, and lifted a staying hand when she started to reach out one of hers. "Don't move, honey. This big ol' snag is sturdy, but I don't want to take any chances. I'll get you out. Just hang tight, okay?"

Tears were caught in her dark lashes, but her lips lifted ever so slightly. "Fine time for puns," she whispered.

"Atta girl." There was no way the door would open. He didn't even bother trying. "Are you hurt?" Aside from the scrapes and scratches, he couldn't see any blood. But the deflated airbags were blocking most of his view. "Can you move your legs?"

"I can wiggle my feet."

"Excellent." He knew she couldn't have been hanging there for more than thirty minutes because he'd seen that guardrail perfectly intact when he'd cruised by it earlier. But thirty minutes or less was still thirty minutes or less too long.

And just because he couldn't see serious bleeding didn't mean there was none. She looked pale and limp and entirely helpless.

"Do you know how long you've been here like this?"

She made a sound that wasn't much of an answer. Her eyelids fluttered and closed.

"Stay with me, honey." With one sharp swipe of his Maglite, he cleared the rest of the window glass and tossed aside the jagged piece of dead tree branch that had shattered it. "Can you tell me what happened?"

She didn't respond at first and he reached in, grasping one of her hands. "Come on, honey. Try to stay awake here. Talk to me."

Her fingers moved. A slight squeeze. Enough to make him breathe a little easier. "I'm here." The words sighed out of her. She had a drawl, but not a Texas one. It was more Deep South with a twist. "You have a nice...voice. I don't know what happened." She opened her eyes again, blinking as if to clear her vision. "One minute I was singing along with Lady Gaga and the next—" She broke off, then pulled her slender fingers free, lifted her hand and fluttered it along the gray shoulder strap pinning her against expensive white leather. "My seat belt's stuck. I couldn't get it loose."

"Then it's doing its job." He pulled out of the window for a moment, grabbed his pocketknife and unbuckled his duty belt, letting it drop to the ground before he carefully reached through the window again with both arms and angled his shoulders so he could fit. "You from New Orleans?"

"Shows that much?"

The space wasn't exactly built for a guy his size, but he'd been in tighter spots. "Louisiana license plate." That and the distinct NOLA accent. "This your parents' car?"

She seemed to rouse herself a little. "No, but Daddy's gonna have a fit, anyway. He didn't want me driving out here in the first place. Wanted to double-check every safety system this car has before I started out."

There was a small R-Haz insignia on the dashboard. He hadn't gotten a notice from the telematics company that her car was involved in an accident, so at least one of those safety systems had failed to do its job.

"Protective, is he?" He gained another inch.

"And then some. Ever since Savannah's break-in he's been worse than ever."

"Who's Savannah?"

"My little sister. One of them, anyway."

"How many sisters do you have?" He'd managed to squeeze partially through the window but he still wasn't far enough to reach her well.

"Uh, two. And a, uh, a bunch of brothers. I'm smack in the middle."

"Middle-child syndrome?"

"Please."

He smiled at the way she rolled her eyes. She was making good sense, and he hoped that meant she didn't have a concussion. "I have three brothers myself," he offered conversationally. "No sisters, though, to my mother's everlasting disappointment." He stretched his arm across the interior of the vehicle and snagged the tips of his fingers around the headrest of her seat, so he could use it for leverage to heave himself halfway into the vehicle. He managed not to swear a blue streak when he got up close and personal with the gearshift as a result.

"I'm gonna cut the belt and catch you, okay?" His voice was rougher than he wanted. He was a pickup-truck sort of guy over sports cars and the nauseating throbbing in his groin cemented the fact. He turned gingerly onto his side, earning another inch of leverage.

She visibly trembled. "Maybe we should wait for more help."

"We could." He exhaled again, blowing out his own pain as he concentrated on the alarm sharpening her dazed eyes. "It might be a while before help gets here, though, and I'd just as soon get you outta this little beast now. Not real comfortable for you hanging upside down, I'll bet."

She shook her head slightly. "No," she whispered. "I was afraid nobody was coming."

She looked like she was going to cry. "I'm here now," he said steadily. "And I'll stay right here with you until more help gets here. Can't say I'm real comfortable with the position."

Understatement of the year.

He looked into her eyes, willing her to keep her focus on him. "I'm Pax, by the way. I'm the sheriff around these parts."

She gave him a barely perceptible smile. "Georgia," she murmured.

Savannah *and* Georgia. He'd have teased her a little at that if not for the way her eyes had fluttered closed again. "Don't pass out on me, Georgia." He wrapped his fingers around her dangling arm, sliding down to her wrist where her pulse was fluttering.

"I'm not gonna pass out." She managed to sound offended. "My head is pounding."

"Expect you'll have a lot of aches and pains. Considering everything, that's not a bad thing right now." It was awkward as hell, half inside the upside-down car and half out. At his angle, stretched the way he was against the headliner, the best he could do was let her land on him. The headrest of the passenger seat was digging into his ribs but at least it wasn't endangering his prospects of siring kids one day. "So, unless you really insist on hanging there until backup arrives, I'm gonna cut the shoulder belt first, and then the lap. That all right with you?"

"I'll fall."

"I'll catch you," he promised. "Just tell me when you're ready."

Her lips compressed. She closed her eyes again and gave a faint nod.

Good enough for him.

He reached up and slid the sharp knife between her snug purple T-shirt and the shoulder belt, then sliced through the belt.

She gasped and her hands shot out, knocking against his head and shoulder. Several cubes of broken glass rained down on him. "Sorry."

"Don't worry. You're good, Georgia. There isn't going to be anything graceful about this. I told you I'll catch you. Just keep your hand on my shoulder if you can, and—" He reached again and wedged his hand against the leather seat, snapping through the lap belt. The second he did, her body started to fall and he pressed his free palm against her stomach long enough to fold the knife safely out of the way.

Then she rolled down in a ball onto him, all long hair and trembling limbs.

The second she made contact with him, she burst into sobs and buried her face against his throat.

"It's okay, honey." He gently patted her back. She really was no bigger than a minute. "You're gonna be fine." He'd feel better about that assurance once she was actually checked out, but for now, she was lucid and showing the kind of normal reaction he'd expect. "Everything's going to be okay."

Eventually, her sobs quieted. Her trembling settled. She finally lifted her head, and her eyes met his. "You saved me."

Discomfort that had nothing to do with gearshifts and awkward positions chugged inside his gut. She was a looker. No amount of puffy, red eyes could disguise that fact. He hadn't felt such a visceral attraction to a woman since Whitney.

Which was a good reminder to keep his mind where it belonged.

"German engineering and advanced safety systems saved you," he said gruffly. "Think you can slide out the window?"

She angled her head, looking toward his legs still hanging outside from the knees on. She gave him a shaky smile. "In some places we'd need to be married before being this close. You'd better go first."

She didn't give him a chance to argue the matter, because she was busy wriggling to one side of him. Doing so meant pressing her hand against his chest to gain enough leverage and he hoped she blamed his thumping heartbeat on adrenaline.

He'd been a cop for eight years. A sheriff for nearly two. After what happened with Whitney in Dallas, he was too smart to let himself be derailed again by a pretty set of blue eyes.

Still, it was a relief when Georgia was finally curled alongside him rather than sprawled over him, and he worked his way back out the window. First his leather belt caught on something, and then his shirt tore as he awkwardly got one shoulder, then the other, through the bent window frame.

Finally, though, he was on his knees again in the dirt and he reached back in to her. "It might be easier for you if you come out headfirst."

She nodded and, far more deftly than he could have done, pivoted on the rear of her white shorts, then shimmied out the window. She was narrow. Slender. He had no trouble whatsoever catching her shoulders the second they cleared the metal and he lifted her free of the wreckage, moving her to the patch of dirt that had been scraped raw by the car.

She exhaled, and slowly fell backward until she was sprawled flat on her back. She pressed her hand to her chest and stared up at the sky. Tears slid from her eyes down into her hair.

He crouched beside her. "I'm just gonna check your arms and legs, Georgia. That all right with you?"

She sniffed wetly and nodded.

"You tell me if anything hurts."

"Everything hurts," she mumbled. "I've never been in an accident before."

"You started out with a doozy." He carefully worked his hands along her arms. She had a nasty scrape on her left shoulder and a small cut on her right wrist, but other than that, her skin was smooth and cool. A little too cool for the hot day, but she'd had a nasty shock. He moved to her feet and started at her ankles. More scrapes. More scratches. But no bones sticking out where they didn't belong. Nothing that was starting to swell.

He was doing his duty, but he'd have had to have been dead not to appreciate the way she felt. And because of that fact, he wondered if it was time he gave Mindy a call. She was a teacher in Amber Falls he'd seen off and on over the last six months. No more interested in anything serious than he was.

He realized he'd reached Georgia's knees and quickly moved his hands away, sitting back on his heels.

"You were lucky that snag caught your car and you were wearing your seat belt. You have some ID in the car?"

"Of course."

"How many fingers am I holding up?"

Her eyes followed his hand. "Three. I can see perfectly clearly," she promised tiredly.

"Do you think you lost consciousness at any point?"

"I don't think so. I wasn't even driving that fast."

"Wish I had a dollar for every time I've heard that." He'd be a wealthy man and his mom wouldn't have had to rent out the north section of land to an infamous billionaire just to keep the bank from taking it back.

"I wasn't," she insisted.

"Okay, NOLA girl," he soothed, because she was obviously going to get worked up. "Just rest there for a few minutes."

She didn't argue. Merely threaded her fingers through her hair and shook away pieces of glass still clinging there.

He left Georgia long enough to retrieve his duty belt and fastened it around his hips again. He fingered the tear in his uniform shirt as he attached his shoulder mic and called in their status to Connie. He had to provide his own uniforms and he didn't think there'd be any way to fix this particular tear.

"Ambulance freed up," Connie reported back. "Should be there soon."

"Thanks, Con." He looked away from Georgia, who was still lying on the ground. She'd spread her arms wide and was alternately lifting one leg, which looked just as perfect as it had felt, then the other, and flexing her bare feet around in circles.

Her toes were painted a brilliant purple that matched the T-shirt that had crept up her stomach to reveal the low-cut waistband of her white shorts. They were diminutive, those shorts. Revealing both the small, thin gold hoop piercing in her navel as well as the sleek muscles in her thighs as she worked her legs.

He scooped up his hat and slapped it against his thigh a few times to shake off the dirt, then slid it on his head as he walked around the vehicle, taking pictures with the small digital camera from his duty belt. The only angle he couldn't get to was the north side of the car, because he'd have to climb into the ravine to get it.

He went back up the hill, taking pictures of the path the car had taken as it rolled down. He took pictures of the spot it had left the road—obvious only because of the safety guard along the curve that had been torn away. He took a few measurements and made note of them to add to his report later, then returned to Georgia and handed her the sandals he'd found tossed clear of the car about twenty feet away. If she hadn't been wearing her seat belt, it could have been her body tossed aside, too.

"You were lucky all the way around," he told her. "Two feet to the right or left of the tree and we wouldn't be having this conversation at all." He watched her slide on the shoes as she sat up. They were patterned flip-flops with thick foamy-looking rubber soles that added a good three inches to her height when she gingerly rolled to her feet. They also had a designer label that even a good ol' boy like him could recognize.

The shoes didn't mean she had money. But the expensive car that cost more than what he earned in a year sure did suggest it.

"Going to need to take a report of what happened, if you're up to it."

She brushed the dirt off the seat of her shorts and raked her fingers through her long hair, pushing it behind her shoulders. "Happy to cooperate, if I could even *tell* you what happened." She looked up the embankment, where his SUV sat, red lights flashing, and he saw her sway.

He quickly caught her beneath her arm. "Steady there, ma'am."

She pressed her hand to her head. "I preferred 'NOLA girl,'" she murmured. "Doesn't remind me how close I am to my thirtieth birthday."

"And how close is that?"

She wrinkled her nose as she dropped her hand. "'Bout eighteen months."

At least he knew she wasn't a teenager.

He nodded toward the SUV. "Let's get you up to the truck and you can sit down and get outta the heat."

"Heat here is nothing compared to the hot soup we have back home." She looked over her shoulder at the wrecked vehicle. "Nothing about that looks fixable to me."

"No, ma'am."

Her lips turned down. "I just got it, too. Picked it up yesterday morning before I left town. It drove perfectly all the way to Shreveport. I stayed the night there, then started out again this morning." She sighed audibly, then turned toward the embankment, taking a first step. He let go of her, but hung behind to lend a hand the second she looked in need of it.

Unfortunately, that meant he had a close-up view of her hind end as they progressed up the steep hill.

Only a few sliding steps in those platform sandals, though, and Pax took her arm again. One rescue a day was enough.

Before they made it to the top, he saw Charlie Esparza pulling up in his wrecker. Pax waved at the skinny man when he nimbly hopped down from the truck. Without waiting, Charlie started skidding down the hill toward them. "Bad spot t'go off," he said breathlessly. "No skidding, either." He lifted his cap long enough to reveal his white hair, then took Georgia's other arm. He was barely taller than her. "Any more vics?"

Pax shook his head and soon the three of them were safely back on the roadside. He settled Georgia in the back seat of his SUV with the AC running and a fresh bottle of water. He left the door open, though, not wanting her to feel like he'd taken her into custody.

For one, she hadn't done anything wrong that he could determine. He'd smelled no alcohol on her. There was no evidence of drugs. In fact, there was no evidence of

anything to explain why she'd careened off the highway
without seeming to make any attempt at avoiding it.

As Charlie had observed, no skid. Meaning no brak-
ing.

While Charlie headed back down to the wreckage
dragging his long winch cable with him, Pax checked
in with Connie again. The ambulance was still en route.
He pulled out his metal clipboard and flipped it open to
fish a blank report from the contents inside, and leaned
against the side of the SUV next to the opened door.
He kept his focus on the form, even though the sight of
Georgia's bare legs beckoned. His fingers tingled and he
clicked his pen a few times.

"You say you just picked up the car yesterday? Is it a
rental?" If it was, it was a pretty specialized one.

"No, it's mine." Her fingers turned the water bottle
this way and that. "First sports car I've ever owned. My
purse is still in the car. My license. The registration. And
my suitcase—"

"We'll take care of that once Charlie pulls the car up.
Where were you heading? Paseo's not usually a person's
final destination. Too small. Not enough services. I can
help you get to Amber Falls, though. Is there someone I
can contact for you? Parents? Boyfriend?"

She bit her lip, looking in danger of crying again. "I
was heading for Paseo, though. In fact, I was looking
for the turnoff when—" She broke off, swallowing. She
pressed her fingers to her forehead. "My, uh, my oldest
brother, Austin, is the best one to contact. He's here with
Felicity. His girlfriend. She's lovely and actually is light-
ening up my brother. He's way too serious, and…" She
trailed off as if realizing she'd been rambling.

To a person, Pax knew everyone in town. The only
Austin he knew of didn't have a girlfriend and definitely

wasn't too serious. In fact, just last month he'd celebrated his third birthday with a party at Rosa's Mexican restaurant. Pax had stopped in to say hello because he'd been filling his gas tank at the pumps in front of the restaurant, which also doubled as a grocery store. "What's your brother's last name?"

Her blue eyes peered at him from behind her wrist. "Fortune."

Pax exhaled, stifling a curse.

Naturally, it would be Fortune.

He'd grown up in Paseo. Aside from the years he'd spent in Dallas, he'd lived here his entire life. And until a week ago, the only Fortunes he'd personally known were Jayden, Nathan and Grayson. And their mom, Deborah. Good, normal folk who'd had no connection at all to the famous Fortunes that made their homes elsewhere in the state.

Or so he'd thought.

Now, since Deborah was getting hitched to that eccentric billionaire who *was* connected and also happened to be the father of Deborah's three sons, the area was overrun with all manner of people bearing that particular name.

And his peaceful little town had been turned upside down as a result. They'd filled up the little motel. And when that wasn't enough, they'd set up a camp on his mom's piece of land.

People like his mom and Rosa Hernandez, who had her whole family helping her provide enough food to feed the crowd at the makeshift campground, were benefiting financially, but Pax found it all a headache.

He clicked his pen a few times. "I should've known when I saw the make of the car," he muttered. In the last few days, there'd been more luxury vehicles traveling this small stretch of highway than in the last decade. Before that, it had been semis and buses transporting all manner of things to his little spot of paradise.

What was usually his haven had turned into the worst kind of circus. Paseo. The newest playground for the rich and famous.

Which now included the NOLA girl.

Steeling himself against her appeal, he tapped the business end of his pen noisily against the form and its metal-backed board. "All right, then. Let's get to it. Full name and date of birth—"

Chapter Two

Georgia shivered as she stared at Pax, wondering where his gentle demeanor had disappeared to. The man who'd pulled her from the wreckage had made her feel safe. When he'd wrapped his arms around her, the blinding terror she'd felt had slid away.

A reaction to the situation? Undoubtedly. But she'd never ever forget that incalculable sense of pure and utter safety.

"Full name, ma'am," he repeated brusquely.

Her rescuer still looked exactly the same. Except his eyes were no longer a soft, mossy sort of green filled with warmth and kindness. They were more like hard chips of emerald. Had turned that way the second she'd said the name *Fortune*.

He was the sheriff. He'd told her so, even though it said the word plainly enough on the gold badge pinned to the front of his torn khaki shirt.

"Georgia Mae Fortune," she recited slowly.

"You're one of those Fortunes, then." The sheriff's tone was even, but there was no question that he didn't think very highly of "those Fortunes."

Her nerves were too raw and she couldn't help bristling. "I don't know which Fortunes you've got a beef with, but *my* family comes from New Orleans. We just learned this year that we have a tie with the folks from around here. Not that it's any of your business."

"From what I've heard, your family has more branches on its tree than Carter's got pills, and a scandal for every single one."

"What bothers you more? The branches or the scandals?"

"The money you toss around like confetti. Date of birth?" His voice was clipped, too.

"January 1. And *I* don't toss around money."

"You bought that fancy car, didn't you?" He didn't wait for an answer. "Year?" He arched an absurdly handsome eyebrow, considering how much dirt was caked on it. His hair had clumps on it, too, obscuring the dark strands. If he had any gray, she couldn't tell. Not that it would detract from his looks. Men were always lucky that way.

She, on the other hand, had discovered a gray hair earlier that year. She'd promptly visited her hairstylist, who'd laughed it off and masterfully hid the culprit in a subtle weave of lighter shades of blond among her brown.

"Still waiting, ma'am," the sheriff prompted.

She wanted to bare her teeth at him. She grudgingly supplied her birth year.

"Thirty's not the end of the world." He jerked his chin in the direction of the car, which was now being dragged up the hill by the heavy metal cable that the tow-truck driver had fastened to it. "Be glad that you're going to be alive to see it when the day actually rolls around in a *year and a half*," he reminded her flatly.

She shivered again, harder this time, and water spurted from the top of the bottle, splashing on her knee.

She felt his gaze follow and shivered even more.

Whether he disapproved of the Fortunes or not, she recognized interest in a man's eyes when she saw it.

He didn't wear a wedding ring. But then she knew plenty of men who didn't. She'd even dated one for a few weeks before discovering he had a wife *and* a newborn baby waiting devotedly back home.

When Georgia had found out, she'd given the guy a blistering earful, along with the boot. And been glad that she hadn't shared anything more intimate with him than crème brûlée. She certainly wasn't looking for a husband, but she still had her standards when it came to the occasional fling.

It just had been a while since she'd been...flung.

"Address?"

She rattled off the address of her town house in New Orleans.

How was she going to explain this to her parents? Neither Miles nor Sarah was a fan of her visit to Paseo. It was bad enough that her siblings were attending, too, but Georgia had traveled alone, and these days, her dad was feeling hypersensitive about things.

"You *are* here for this wedding business, I take it. Deb Fortune and Gerald Robinson?"

Her chin came up again at the sheriff's disapproving tone. She wondered what he'd think if she told him that Gerald was her newfound uncle. "What if I am? The wedding festivities run for the next two weeks. Instead of turning up your nose at the confetti, I'd think the people of Paseo would be grateful for all of the business being brought to the area!"

His lips twisted. "Area's done fine for years without all the hassle you beautiful people bring with you."

"I won't mistake that as a compliment."

"Smart. Not smart enough to keep that expensive car of yours on the road, though. Assuming you weren't *trying* to kill yourself, what had you so preoccupied? Looking at your phone? Taking a selfie to post on some social-media thing?"

Her jaw loosened. She wasn't ordinarily stuck for words, but she was now. Instead of telling him exactly what she thought of his judgmental attitude, all she could do was stare at him.

And he didn't even bat an emerald eye.

"Well? I'll know eventually what you were doing with your cell phone, honey, so it'd be better to tell me up front than try to lie."

"I wasn't doing *any*thing with my cell phone," she said through her teeth.

"Not checking directions, or calling your boyfriend—"

"I don't have a boyfriend. Not that *that's* any of your business, either."

"It's my business to understand why you went off the road in my county."

He glanced over as the tow truck's winch whined loudly and the cable went taut. Then he turned back and focused on his form.

She wasn't sure what grated on her nerves more—the squeal of her car being dragged up the hill, or the way the sheriff tapped the point of his pen against the metal clipboard.

"So you were distracted and looking for a turnoff—"

"I never said I was distracted," she snapped, which just made her head pound even more. "You did. But yes, I was keeping an eye out for a turnoff. Mile post twelve, as a matter of fact. It must be near here."

Those emerald chips drifted over her face. "About half a mile up the road. The highway curves here a little, but not sharply. It's easy to see approaching vehicles if you're paying attention."

"There weren't any other vehicles."

"Are you sure you were paying attention?"

"Yes! I have a perfect driving record."

His lips twisted. "Something that can easily be bought, particularly by those who can afford to trash a car like yours."

"I didn't intentionally trash it," she said through her teeth, "and I have never needed to buy my way out of anything!"

He wasn't moved. "No signs of skidding. You said you were singing with the radio?"

"Don't try and tell me that's against the law."

"If you were speeding—"

"I wasn't."

"—that might explain the distance the car seemed to travel aloft before it impacted the ground."

She felt her stomach suddenly lurch and she jumped down from the SUV, running through the weeds on the shoulder of the road until she reached the guardrail and lost her lunch over the other side.

When she was finished, she didn't have enough energy left to do anything but hang her arms over the hard, hot metal.

"Here."

She wanted the ground to swallow her up. Spinning anything to a positive slant was her stock-in-trade, but there was just no positive way to spin throwing up on the side of the road.

She took the bottle of water from Pax. Ignoring him, she took a swig, swirled it in her mouth and spit it out.

Several yards away, her car crested the edge of the road and the horrible whining finally came to a stop. The short tow-truck driver began pushing levers on the side of his truck and the back of it began tilting down toward the ground.

"I wasn't speeding," she told the sheriff when she thought she could speak without vomiting again. "I wasn't texting on my cell." She had no idea if her phone had remained inside the car. But he definitely hadn't found it when he'd been traipsing all over taking his pictures. She felt certain he'd be examining it for God knew what if he had.

"My whole life is on my phone," she said, more to herself than to him. "If it's not still in the car—" She broke off, shaking her head.

"Nobody's whole life should be on a cell phone," the sheriff said dismissively before he walked away from her, heading toward the wrecker. She could see him talking into that small speaker thing attached by a strap to his shoulder as he went.

She made a face at the back of him. It was childish but it still made her feel a tiny bit better. Leaning against the rail, she sipped the water and studied him as he spoke with the driver. Charlie, he'd called him.

Unlike Charlie, the sheriff was tall. Her brothers were tall, too, so it was easy enough to peg the man as several inches past six feet. Her brothers tended more toward wiry builds, though. The sheriff was stockier. Broader. Not heavy. More like a quarterback than a runner. All broad shoulders, narrow hips and muscular—

Her mouth felt cottony and she swished more water around, turning to spit it out again.

When she straightened, he was approaching her again. It was easier to focus on the tear in his shirt than it was his face, with its square jaw and slashing eyebrows.

"Here." He extended a small pink purse and she

snatched it greedily, flipping it open to find her wallet still tucked safely inside.

She extracted her driver's license and held it up. "Check me out," she challenged. "You'll learn I *do* have a perfect driving record. I have a respectable job with Fortune Investments as the director of public relations. I own my own home and I have never gotten so much as a ticket for jaywalking!" She slid a business card free as well and barely managed to keep from tossing it in his face. "My cell phone number is on there. You want to know what I was doing on my phone for the last twenty-four hours, feel free to contact my provider. I'll agree to whatever you need."

His fingers brushed hers as he took the license. "Charlie was able to get into your glove compartment, if I have your permission to look at the contents."

Oh, for crying out loud. She rubbed her aching temples. "Yes, you can look at the contents. I've been trying to tell you I don't have anything to hide."

He walked back to the wrecker again.

Her eyes burned and she swiped her nose. She was not going to cry again.

Her purse might have contained her wallet and a few business cards, but there was little else in it, and certainly not her phone. She closed her eyes, trying to remember where it had been in the car. Lying on the passenger seat with her sandals? Tucked in the console?

Her stomach churned as she tried to think. She'd taken one call that morning from her assistant, Julie, about the media campaign they were launching. After that, her phone had remained silent as she'd neared Paseo and the campground where the wedding guests were being lodged.

The campground was one of the selling points she'd used with her folks when she'd told them that she, too, wanted to attend the wedding, along with her siblings. In Georgia's case, not only was she attending the nuptials, but she was also actually going to stand up in the wedding party. Even though none of them had ever even met the bride or groom.

That fact was only one of the interesting aspects of this whole wedding business. It was Gerald and Deborah's desire to bring together all the branches of the overgrown Fortune tree. They were showing it again and again with the incredible task of mounting a large wedding in such a small town. Once they'd known Georgia and her brothers and sisters were coming—even though their father flatly refused—they'd asked if one of them would be part of the wedding party. They wanted someone from each family to be represented.

Georgia had basically drawn the short straw at that point because—as her sisters Savannah and Belle liked to point out—Georgia had the most practice at being a bridesmaid.

Nineteen times, in fact.

For her dad's sake, she'd pitched the whole thing as a lark. A summer getaway, camping under the Texas sky for a few weeks before the launch of the new campaign. For herself, she'd mostly thought it would be highly entertaining to be part of the wedding for a man who was actually her father's half brother.

Of course, her father didn't believe anything about the situation was the least bit entertaining. He certainly didn't appreciate the fact that he might be somewhat similar to his half brother. Gerald Robinson of Texas had been born Jerome Fortune of New York. It was only after his father, Julius, died that he'd remade himself as Gerald, far, far away from his true family. He'd even gone so far as to fake "Jerome's" death, presumably to be good and sure nobody came looking for him.

Georgia's father, Miles, on the other hand, had been born Miles Melton in Louisiana. He was just one of Julius's illegitimate sons with various women other than his wife. Aside from her father, there were at least three more that she knew of: Kenneth Fortunado, who hailed from Houston, David Fortune from Florida and Gary Fortune from New York. Other than those few details, she had no real knowledge of the relationships—or lack of—that they'd had with Julius while he'd been alive.

As for her dad, when he'd finally divulged the truth last Christmas to his family that they were, in fact, related to the famous Fortunes after all—something he had been denying all of Georgia's life—he'd admitted that he'd only taken on his father's name when he'd been a young college graduate as an "up yours" against the man who'd never acknowledged him.

The similarities between Miles and Julius ended there, though.

Miles had married Georgia's mom when he was only a year older than Georgia was now. They'd had seven children together and were the only truly happy couple Georgia had ever seen.

Gerald, on the other hand, had inherited Julius's penchant for infidelity. For the last few years especially, the scandal sheets had chronicled the tech mogul's indiscretions. How he'd cheated on his society wife, Charlotte. How he'd produced even more illegitimate children than Julius had.

Then, when the news had broken a couple years ago about Robinson's real identity, the media hounds had gone into a feeding frenzy. It would have died down eventually. When a fresher scandal hit the light of day. That's the way scandals always worked.

But the flames were fueled all over again by Gerald and Charlotte's highly acrimonious divorce when word got out that he'd actually dumped her in favor of marrying his first love, Deborah Fortune, who wasn't really a Fortune at all, but had assumed the name herself when she'd given birth to Gerald's triplet sons nearly forty years ago. Before Gerald had even married Charlotte.

It was either the worst of reality-television-style trashiness, or the most outlandishly romantic story in modern-day history.

Georgia, nineteen times a bridesmaid, didn't expect that Gerald's marriage to Deborah would be any more successful than his first one. But she definitely expected the whole scene to be pretty entertaining.

Particularly since she had a not-so-private fascination with reality TV.

Plus, she came from a family of seven kids but had never had cousins. Now that she knew that she did, she was unabashedly curious to meet them.

So, with a brand-new car she'd worked hard to buy and a chance for the first vacation she'd taken in years, what else was a girl to do but plan a road trip?

It was all perfect.

In planning, at least.

Reality had turned out to be something entirely different.

The winch was whining again and she realized her car—what was left of it—was being pulled onto the back of the tow truck.

She pushed away from the guardrail and hurried toward the two men standing beside the vehicle. "What about the rest of my stuff? My suitcase is in the trunk."

"Only thing I could get at was this, miss." The short man wiped a greasy hand on the front of his overalls before he handed her the small overnighter. "It'll take more equipment than I've got here to get that trunk open. Don't you worry none, though. Once I do, I'll get your stuff to you wherever you're at."

She clutched the overnighter against her. It held her toiletries and not much more. Except for the yoga gear she'd tossed in it that morning, all of her clothes were inside the suitcase.

She felt shaky all over again.

The sheriff must have noticed because he wrapped his hand around her arm. "You need to sit down again."

She preferred the weedy highway shoulder than the back of his SUV, but she never had the chance to tell him, because an ambulance pulled up then. The sheriff turned her over to the two people who hopped out of the boxy white vehicle. One male. One female. Both young and harried-looking, though they didn't act it as they took charge of Georgia and settled her on the wide back bumper. They introduced themselves. Sean and Sarah.

"My mother's name is Sarah," she told them faintly and closed her eyes again, resting her head on the vehicle behind her. She answered their questions while they tended to her cuts and scrapes and produced a cold pack that she pressed against her forehead.

She wasn't sure how much time had passed before she heard a familiar voice calling her name.

She looked up to see her brother Austin jogging toward her. He was the oldest of her siblings and she always teased him that he'd come out of the womb wearing a suit and tie.

But now, he wore a T-shirt and blue jeans, his dark hair looked like it had been combed with a garden rake and even from a distance she could see the concern in his brown eyes.

No amount of willpower kept her tears away then.

She dropped the ice pack and ran into his arms. It was comforting. Familiar. And if she'd never felt that utter sense of security in the sheriff's embrace, she never would have known it wasn't there in her own brother's.

"Damn," he muttered as he took in the mangled mess of her vehicle. "What the hell happened, Georgia?"

She shook her head. "I don't know. I don't know, Austin. I was driving along, everything was fine and then bam! Everything was out of my control. I couldn't steer, I couldn't brake and I was crashing through the guardrail and—" She closed her eyes against the terrifying memory of the engine suddenly screaming, then turning quiet as she soared over brush and through trees, turning in one long, slow somersault—

She realized she was sweating and dug the heels of her palms against her closed eyes until the images faded. "All I could think was that Daddy was right." She finally dropped her hands and looked up at him. "I should have gone on the family plane with the rest of you. I should have stuck with my old car—it was perfectly good—instead of spending a fortune on a sports car like that—"

He exhaled an oath and kissed her temple. "Stop. You'd been waiting months for that car. Accidents happen. I'm just glad you're okay."

"I want to get away from here."

"Felicity's waiting at the campground," he said. "She's making sure the travel trailer you'll be using is all set for you."

"How *did* you know what happened?" When she'd set up her emergency account with the car dealer, she'd listed him as the person to contact.

"The sheriff's office sent someone out to the campground to find me."

She rubbed her temples. "You didn't get a text or some automatic notice from R-Haz that my vehicle was in an accident?"

"Nope."

She looked around her brother at the man in question, only to see that he was heading their way. "Watch out," she warned Austin. "He might have rescued me from my car, but he's got a beef against 'those Fortunes.'" She air-quoted the term.

"What the hell's that supposed to mean?"

She spread her hands wordlessly.

Pax stopped a few feet away. "You're the brother? Austin?"

"I am." Austin kept an arm protectively around Georgia's shoulder but extended his other. "Austin Fortune. I appreciate what you did for my sister. She says you pulled her out of that." He nodded toward the mangled vehicle now fixed in place atop the flatbed. Charlie had a broom and a bucket and was sweeping up debris where she'd gone through the rail.

The dusty brim of the sheriff's hat cast most of his face in shadow, but Georgia still felt his gaze roving over her as he briefly shook her brother's hand. "Sheriff Price. I'm glad she wasn't hurt more badly than she was. And that nobody else was involved. I'm not issuing a citation, since she didn't commit any offenses—"

"Big of you."

He ignored her. "That could change if under the course of investigation new information comes to light." He was still holding his boxy metal clipboard and he slid a business card free, handing it to Georgia.

She automatically took it, annoyed with the way she shivered when her fingertips brushed his. "There isn't any new information," she assured him. She glanced down at the card.

"That's Charlie's card," he said, pointing out what she'd just realized.

Why had she thought he might want her to have his *number?*

Thankfully unaware of her thoughts, he was continuing. "You'll want to arrange things with him when it comes to getting the rest of your personal belongings. And you'll want to keep the accident report when you deal with your auto-insurance folks. If you want Charlie to contact them for you, I can tell him to go ahead. Don't know if they'll want to send someone to see the vehicle in person or not. It's a given it'll be totaled, though." He tore off a carbon copy of the report he'd made and folded it in thirds before extending it.

"Since my phone is MIA, I'd appreciate him making that call." She plucked the report from his grasp. No shivers, no way, no, ma'am.

"She can come with me now?" her brother asked.

"Address of the urgent care in Amber Falls is on the back of the report. Might want to get her checked out for good measure. But as long as she's got clearance from Sean and Sarah, I've got no reason to keep her."

At the mention of their names, Sean waved a thumbs-up. "She's good, Sheriff. Lucky as hell, that's for sure."

Which was what Georgia needed to remember.

"Let me get the air-conditioning going in the SUV," Austin told her. "Then we'll get you out of here." He squeezed her shoulder gently before jogging across the highway.

She looked toward the sheriff.

No matter how his attitude had changed when he'd learned she was a member of the Fortune family, he *had* saved her from the car.

She stuck out her own hand. "Thank you for your help,

Pax." She wasn't sure what devil made her use his name. Maybe the same devil that made her curious to see the circus that the coming wedding was sure to be.

But the devil got more than she bargained for when Pax tapped his thumb against his hat brim and pushed it up an inch before he slowly closed his hand around hers. His fingers were long, his palm warm. "Glad to be of service—" he waited half a beat "—*Georgia.*"

Something in her chest went tight. His emerald eyes were once again soft and warm and vaguely mossy.

She moistened her lips and slowly pulled her hand away.

It was probably a good thing that he was biased against people with her last name. Everything else about him would just make for complications.

She preferred short, simple and uncomplicated.

Moistening her lips again, she grabbed her little purse and overnighter from where they sat on the ground near the ambulance.

Aside from it, the tow truck and the sheriff's SUV, there was only one other vehicle sitting on the side of the road, and Georgia immediately started to cross the road toward it.

"Whoa, there." A hand grabbed her arm, hauling her up short, and she jerked, looking up at Pax.

Her heart simply thudded. That's all there was to it. And it had nothing to do with the car accident. It was all him.

"Better watch where you're going," he said mildly, and she realized that a fast-moving car was approaching.

It slowed only minimally as it passed them, and only when it was gone again did Pax let go of her arm.

She hugged her meager belongings to her chest. "You're right. I had better watch where I'm going." Then she finally managed to pull her eyes away from his and she jogged across the once-again empty two-lane highway to her brother's rented SUV.

Chapter Three

The only thing missing from the travel trailer was a big soaker tub.

Georgia turned away from the otherwise well-equipped bathroom and stared down the length of the so-new-it-sparkled trailer.

She knew it wasn't a concussion befuddling her brain, because Austin had insisted on taking her to the urgent care in Amber Falls for a proper exam. She had a lot of superficial abrasions and would be sore for a while, but a concussion had been definitively ruled out.

"I think there are nicer appliances in this thing than I have in my town house," she told Felicity.

The other woman grinned. Before becoming her brother's girlfriend, she'd been Austin's personal assistant. Georgia was hoping and praying that one day when they got down the aisle, they'd be one of the few to beat the odds. After the disaster of his first marriage, he deserved it.

"The trailer we have is a mirror image," Felicity told her. "And check this out. Even though Marcia—she's the wedding coordinator I was telling you about—has arranged group meals and activities every day until after the wedding, look what they still did."

Felicity walked around the granite-topped kitchen island and pulled open the door of the full-sized stainless-steel refrigerator. "Fridge is still fully stocked." She pulled out a bottle of beribboned champagne and waggled it. "Good stuff, too." She returned the bottle to the fridge and let the door close. "Can you just imagine how much all of this is costing Mr. Robinson?"

Georgia shook her head. "Truthfully, I can't imagine anything but fixing some tea, closing all the shades and collapsing in bed."

"Of course you can't," Felicity immediately agreed. "You just go on in and lie down. I'll get your tea."

"Felicity, you don't have to wait on me."

"You need some coddling. Lord, girl. While he was waiting for you at the urgent care, Austin sent me the pictures he'd taken of your car." She shuddered as she stuck a teapot beneath the faucet. "You must have been terrified."

"I was." Despite her claim of wanting a bed, Georgia sank down on one of the reclining chairs situated in front of the big, tinted picture window. She leaned back in the comfy chair and let out a deep sigh. "But Pax was so sweet and…" She trailed off.

"He's the sheriff, right?" Like magic, Felicity produced a cold pack that she tucked gently behind Georgia's neck.

"Heaven. Where'd you find—? Oh, never mind." Her brother's girlfriend had always been able to produce exactly what was needed in the moment it was needed.

"You were saying about the sheriff?"

"It doesn't matter." She swiveled her chair a few inches to look out the picture window. Her closest "neighbor" was an enormous cabin-style tent situated on top of a wooden deck about fifty yards away. Two bicycles were propped against the deck. Beyond that was an enormous RV that made Georgia's travel trailer look tiny. There were other trailers and tents, too. And more to come over the next few weeks. "I doubt I'll have any reason to see him again." Considering his attitude toward her family name, she couldn't imagine that he'd seek out any of them, either.

"You're frowning."

She pushed him out of her head. "Just longing for a soak in a big bath. Something that's not really possible until after the wedding." It wasn't entirely a lie, though she'd always been more of a shower person. And as soon as she had the energy, she was going to stand beneath the hot, pulsing spray of one.

She pushed a button on the side of the chair and the footrest slowly lifted while the back of the chair slowly lowered. "I may need one of these chairs in my place when we go back home." Her furnishings tended toward sleek and modern, and in her opinion that had never included an overstuffed, leather recliner.

"Your father would never let you live it down," Felicity said humorously. "He's always telling you to get some normal furniture for your place."

Georgia smiled slightly. "True."

"Speaking of your father." The other woman perched on the recliner's twin. "You don't think your accident was...well, not such an accident, do you? You know that's what Miles is going to think."

Georgia nudged the cold pack farther down until it was between her shoulder blades. "Only if he finds out I *had* an accident."

"You're not going to tell your parents about it? I know

he's busy speaking at that conference in Arizona this week, but—"

"But nothing. I'm not going to tell him and neither is anyone else. Including Austin."

Felicity snorted. "You know he is never going to agree to that."

"He already has." She gave Felicity a sly smile. "Helps when you know all the dirt about your siblings."

"Austin doesn't have any dirt."

Her chuckle made her wince at the ensuing ache in her ribs. "Love really does make y'all blind. Fortunately, that's an affliction I've avoided." She pulled out the ice pack from behind her and pressed it against her side. "Actually, all I had to do was beg a little. He's always been a sucker for his little sisters that way."

"Maybe so. He's also protective of his sisters," Felicity pointed out seriously. "And considering everything—"

"Like what? The fact that Savannah's apartment was ransacked a few months ago?" It didn't take a genius to know where Felicity was headed. "It's a big leap from ransacking someone's apartment to tampering with a vehicle." She gave Felicity the same argument she'd given Austin all the way back from the Amber Falls urgent care. "And Gerald's ex-wife hasn't been officially charged with orchestrating the break-in at Savannah's place, anyway. It's just a theory of Connor Fortunado's."

"Doesn't mean he's not right. It just means Charlotte's wily enough—or rich enough—to avoid charges."

"You sound like Daddy." And Pax, who seemed to think money paved a person's way out of all sorts of things.

She closed her eyes, then kicked off her sandals and imagined doing the same with thoughts of Pax.

It didn't really work. His image was still fixed firmly

in her mind. As firmly as that encompassing sense of security she'd felt.

Until he'd made it plain what he thought of "those Fortunes."

She opened her eyes to study Felicity. "If you're worried that Gerald's ex-wife really is out to wreak havoc on all persons Fortune, why did you agree to come with my brother to Texas at all? Could have stayed in New Orleans and far, far away from…what did Dad call it at dinner the other day?"

"The Great State of Trouble," Felicity answered.

Georgia adjusted the cold pack once more, pressing it flat against the bandage taped across the gash on her left arm. Miles had been fit to be tied at their united front concerning Gerald and Deborah's wedding invitation. "If there's any truth to Connor's claims, then coming to this wedding does kind of put us right in the thick of things. You could have talked Austin out of coming. He'd do backflips to keep you happy."

"Connor's a private investigator. He seems to know what he's doing."

"And I know he's put a lot of work into connecting the dots between the mishaps among Gerald's own family and the rest of his sibs by daddy-Julius. If he's right, Charlotte's at the center of the web. No pun intended. But if he is right, why *hasn't* she been caught? At the beginning of the year when we were all visiting Texas for Schuyler Mendoza's little meet-and-greet, Ben Robinson ended up in the hospital after their family estate went up in flames." Schuyler was one of Connor's sisters and had thrown the fete in order to bring together her family, Gerald's legitimate children based in Austin and their newfound New Orleans cousins. But the event hadn't turned out the way she'd hoped because of the fire.

"Nobody likes to be humiliated, I know," she went on. "But would any mother *really* put her own son in danger like that?"

"Depends on the mother," Felicity said pointedly. "Fortunately, Ben recovered, but it's pretty suspicious that Charlotte was absent for the whole ordeal, don't you think?"

"I think once he and his brothers and sisters found out their mother had been keeping tabs on their dad's illegitimate offspring all along, things have been strained between them."

"It is a strange story," Felicity agreed. The teapot started whistling and she rose to turn off the burner. She filled a tea ball with a deft pinch of loose-leaf tea.

Georgia frowned, looking a little harder. "That's my favorite tea. How did they know to stock my favorite tea?"

"If you ask me, it's almost creepy. The soap in our shower is the same brand I've been ordering from France for your brother since he first hired me, way back when. It's like someone's been investigating all of *us*."

"Gerald *is* the brains behind Robinson Tech. And you know what they say. All our devices are spying on us."

Felicity gave an exaggerated shudder. "An equally creepy idea."

"More like their wedding coordinator sent out a questionnaire to everyone asking for a couple of our personal likes or dislikes."

Georgia's youngest sister, Belle, slid the glass door open and stepped inside. She'd obviously overheard them. "And you're welcome for me filling it out for you all, since none of *you* gave it any attention." She was holding a sheet of paper, which she dropped on Georgia's lap. "Huh. I always thought you looked more like Mom, but you're the spitting image of Dad, sitting in his chair at home."

Georgia was too comfortable to muster offense. "I thought you were out with everyone on a horseback ride." That's what her brother had told her when they'd arrived at the campground.

"We're back, obviously." Belle pulled out one of the upholstered stools tucked beneath the small granite island. She ran her hand down her ponytail as she sat. "The trail ride was a lot of fun, actually. We had a picnic lunch near a pretty little pond and a windmill. There was plenty of eye candy around, too, of the hot-guy variety." She stretched out her sneaker-covered toe to push at the footrest of Georgia's chair. "Should have taken the plane along with the rest of us and you could've been out there checking out the prospects for a vacation fling. Instead, here you are, looking like death warmed over."

Felicity made a sound and pulled out her cell phone to hand to Belle. "You obviously didn't see the car," she chided. "Austin took that picture."

Belle paled as she looked at the image. "Are you serious?" When she looked at Georgia this time, there were tears in her eyes. "God, Georgia, I had no idea!"

Georgia waved her hand, hoping to allay her sister's alarm. "I'm fine and you'd better not go tattling to the folks, baby girl." The term usually never failed to annoy Belle. "And you'd also better not be looking for a vacation fling!"

Belle propped her fist on her hip, her tears already evaporating. "And why not? We're here for *two weeks*!" She made it sound like two years.

"Because this is a family event," Felicity told her. "Not a singles' resort."

"Easy for you," Belle grumbled. "Every time I turn around you and Austin are getting busy."

"They're also in a serious relationship and you can stop acting like little Miss Hotsy-Totsy," Georgia ordered. "And if you didn't want to come for the full two weeks, you needn't have. You could have chosen to stay home and had the house to yourself, what with Mom and Dad in Arizona." She lifted the paper Belle had put in her lap. "What is this, anyway?"

"The schedule for the week," Belle said, as if Georgia ought to have known already.

Georgia let the paper slip from her fingers to the little table that sat between the chairs. Before they'd come to Texas, the wedding coordinator in charge of all the activities had provided a broad idea of what to expect, so they'd know what to pack. She'd look at the finer details of the schedule later.

She returned the chair to its normal position and pushed herself stiffly out of it. "Meanwhile, I'm going to get out of these clothes. I still feel covered in dirt. Maybe try some yoga after. Want to join me?"

Belle crossed her eyes. She was only twenty-three and figured yoga was for old people. "Please." She headed to the glass door again. "Happy hour and a taco bar at the ramada in an hour. It's the huge gazebo thing at the center of everything here. I want to shower, too, before then." She made a face. "Not all of us were outfitted with private little trailers like this," she said over her shoulder as she left.

"Don't let her fool you." Felicity nudged the warm cup of tea into Georgia's hand. "The monster RV she's sharing with Draper and Beau is bigger than my first apartment. If I hadn't seen three others just like it, I'd have said they lucked out getting drawn for the Taj Mahal of the Fortune Campground."

Georgia had no intention of admitting it aloud, but she was glad her baby sister had agreed to share with their two brothers. Savannah had Chaz with her. Nolan had Lizzie and their baby girl, Stella. And of course, Austin had Felicity.

"If you're nervous about being alone, you can sleep in our trailer. We're just a few rows over."

"Mind reading isn't polite." Georgia sipped her tea. The fragrance was comforting. "But I'm *fine*."

"And I'm not as easily diverted as Belle," Felicity countered. "Regardless of how the accident occurred, you survived something ferociously serious today. That has an effect, Georgia. You don't have to pretend for my sake."

Her eyes felt hot and she gave Felicity's arm a quick squeeze with her free hand. "I'm not pretending. Much, anyway. The fastest way for me to really be fine is to get on with exactly what I came here to do. Jumping in to all the activities with both feet."

Felicity picked up the copy of the event schedule. "Tomorrow's activity is a day hike. Don't even try to pretend you're going to be up for that."

"Okay, so I'll give you that one. But one way or another, I'm going to be up and at 'em for the cocktail party the night after that." It was to be the first event actually hosted personally by the bride and groom. "Even if we hadn't learned Gerald is our uncle, I'd still want this chance to meet him." She spread her arms. "The man's a bazillionaire. There's not a one of us who doesn't have a Robinson Tech computer." She flipped her hand toward the kitchen. "His company probably even designed the chip that runs that microwave over there."

"Better that than the R-Haz system in your car," Felicity said darkly. "I still can't believe the emergency notification function totally failed. Isn't that their claim to fame?"

"Maybe I didn't get it set up right in the first place. Techie stuff like that is never my forte."

"Unless you can run it from an app on your phone," Felicity said on a laugh.

"Let's hope I get *that* back," Georgia muttered. "I'm going to have a hundred texts from Julie waiting for me."

"You're supposed to be on vacation."

"Yeah, well, I'm not in the office, am I? Let's hope I get my suitcase before the cocktail party, too. I'm pretty sure there's not a lot of handy dress shops in Paseo."

"I'd loan you a dress but you'd swim in it."

Georgia gave the woman a wry smile. Felicity was tall. Georgia was *so* not. As for Savannah, Felicity would never be able to cram her hips into one of Savannah's impossibly narrow dresses. She'd have better luck fitting her boobs into one of Belle's. So she'd have to prevail upon her youngest sister to have mercy on her. "For now, I'm going to finish my tea and stand under as hot a shower as this trailer can produce." She gave Felicity a close look. "It *does* have hot water, right?"

"An endless supply, pretty much, considering the temporary plumbing hookups that were put in. Hot and cold running water and flush toilets, even for the tenters. If you feel claustrophobic in the trailer shower like I do, there's a building with private showers and stuff. One for men and one for women. Laundry machines, even."

"A regular luxury campground."

Felicity nodded. "We might be in the middle of what is supposed to be a cornfield, but from what I've heard, we've got more comforts than the motel in town. It's astonishing, really, how much effort Gerald's taken. The man's from Austin, for heaven's sake. He and Deborah could've gotten married there and saved themselves a whole lot of work."

"Maybe he didn't want his ex-wife raining on his parade. And you've got to admit, he's not going to get the media interference way out here that he would have there."

"Maybe." Felicity propped her hands on her trim hips. "I suppose it's pretty romantic, when you think about it. Deborah and her sons are from Paseo. After all this time, she's getting what I assume is the wedding of her dreams." Her gaze sharpened on Georgia's face. "What?"

"It's nothing," Georgia dismissed. "Just seems like most of the weddings I've been in have been the bride's 'wedding of her dreams.' And the fancier the wedding, the faster the divorce." Only two of those nineteen were still intact.

"So if there's a wedding in Austin's and my future, we should make it bland?"

Georgia's shoulders slumped. "You know I think you and Austin are perfect for each other. As far as I'm concerned, there's no if about it. He's never been happier than he is with you. It's just my jaded—"

"Bridesmaid cynicism?" Felicity's lips curved. "Let's just get you through *this* wedding first. I'll bring by dinner for you later."

"You don't have to bring me anything," Georgia protested. "If I don't find my way to the taco bar, I've got a kitchen full of food. I'm sure I can fend for myself." She pushed Felicity toward the sliding door. "Go on back to Austin. I'm sure the two of you can find something to do besides worrying about me."

"I'm still going to look in on you later. If not tonight, then tomorrow for sure."

Resigned, Georgia gave a shrug and a wave, and headed into the small but well-appointed bedroom.

The second she heard the glass door slide closed, her shoulders sagged yet again.

She set the teacup on the built-in dresser with a hand that shook. Above the dresser was a wide mirror that reflected a beautifully made bed behind her.

Her eyes looked hollow. She had a long scratch on her forehead that was only partially covered with a bandage strip. She angled her chin, gingerly running her fingertips over the scrape on her neck. It wasn't deep enough to merit a bandage but it still stung like crazy.

She'd taken some over-the-counter pain relief at the urgent care. If they were doing their job, she didn't really want to think about how she'd feel when the medication wore off.

She started to pull off her purple T-shirt, but a laugh from outside the trailer stalled the motion. She went to the windows on either side of the bed and closed the blinds. Then, mindful of the easy way Belle had entered, she went back into the living area to lock the glass door and yank the tasteful gray drapes across it.

Privacy more assured, she went back into the bedroom and carefully peeled off her clothes. She did still want a shower, but now that she was alone, her energy was fading fast.

Wearing only her panties, she tossed aside the puffy comforter on the bed and slipped under the sheet. With the blinds drawn, the room was cool and dim.

She rolled onto her back and stared up at the ceiling. From outside, she could hear muffled voices and the occasional laugh. Maybe from the occupants of the tent across from her. Family members that she'd come here to meet.

A lump filled her throat.

"Thank you for not letting me die today," she whispered.

Then she turned her face into the pillow and closed her eyes.

Kindly leave your cell phones "at home" for this evening's event.

Georgia read the looping chalk writing on the rustic blackboard propped on a tripod at the entrance of the ramada.

"Cruel words," she muttered as she walked past it, heading under the large open-sided tent that seemed to be the heart of the campground. If the campground was a wagon wheel, the ramada was the hub. It was where the camp kitchen was situated, where there were a dozen picnic tables for those wanting to share common meals and where a bonfire was scheduled every night, complete with roasted marshmallows and cold drinks.

It seemed an odd combination to her, but then she wasn't from Texas. And she'd learned that even though the June days were hot, the evenings were not. The second the sun went down, the heat went with it.

Over the last two nights, she'd been grateful for that puffy comforter on her bed after all.

In every direction from the center hub were the trailers, RVs and tents, arranged in long lines, like spokes. Yesterday, when she'd finally dragged herself out of the bed to go exploring while most of the people were out on the day hike, she'd located Austin and Felicity's trailer on the opposite side of the campground. Savannah and

Chaz were in a tidy little motor home not too far from them. On another spoke was the "Taj Mahal" that Belle and the boys were occupying. On yet another row, Nolan and Lizzie had one of the wooden-platformed tents. They hadn't gone on the hike, either, but even though Georgia had suggested they should trade with her and take her trailer—they had baby Stella with them after all—they'd both emphatically refused.

Turned out, they loved their tent. Thought it was *trés romantique* the way they could roll back the roof of the canvas tent and watch the stars all night, snuggled together with their nine-month-old baby girl.

Georgia chalked it up to the fact that they were newlyweds. She'd told them when they changed their mind—and she was certain they would—to let her know.

Nolan had laughed in her face, accusing her of being her usual bossy self.

She spotted her siblings clustered together to one side of the ramada waiting for the bus that was going to transport them to the cocktail party. They were all there, except Nolan and Lizzie, who'd again chosen not to attend with a baby in tow, even though children had been specifically welcomed. Savannah and Chaz were missing, too—probably because they were busy trying to make a baby of their own, considering the way they couldn't keep their hands off each other.

She hoped, for their parents' sake at least, that they didn't succeed until after the "I do's." Even though her parents were overjoyed now with little Stella since Nathan and Liz had made things official, they had *not* been thrilled at first with what they'd considered Nolan's carelessness for not even knowing he'd created a child until several months after she'd been born.

"Thought we were going to have to send out a search

party," Beau said when he spotted her. While Nolan was two years younger than her, Beau was two years older. "Good thing the bus is late. What were you doing? Cutting your hair?"

Georgia gave him a look and adjusted the lightweight black wrap she'd borrowed from Felicity around her shoulders. She wasn't going to respond to the haircut comment. Using her manicure scissors, she'd snipped long, shaggy bangs to hide the scratch on her forehead, and if that made her vain, so be it.

Didn't mean she wanted to listen to her brother razz her about it, however.

"That dress looks better on you than it does on me," Belle complained.

At least some things felt normal.

"There's the bus."

She tugged at the short hem of the red dress that Belle had loaned her and turned to watch as the bus approached.

"Good thing your cell phone's not recovered yet from the accident," Austin told her humorously when the vehicle finally stopped in front of the crowd that had been growing beneath the ramada. "Since you're incapable of voluntarily leaving it out of reach, I'm not sure where you'd have hidden it."

That was true. The only thing tighter than the dress were the strappy sandals she'd borrowed from Savannah. What fabric the stretchy red dress did possess was fully occupied clinging to Georgia's figure. There wasn't an inch of it to spare. Which was one of the reasons why she had borrowed the wrap from Felicity. To cover some of the skin laid bare by the plunging, minuscule bodice.

The other reason was to cover the bruises that had darkened since the accident. She had one blotch on her chest that she assumed had come from the airbag. If she couldn't get the thing to fade before the wedding, the oyster-colored bridesmaid dress that she was supposed to wear was going to be a problem. All of the wedding wear was being arranged by a designer out of Red Rock named Charlene Dalton, who'd be delivering everything to Paseo a few days before the wedding.

"If I get my phone back," she told Austin under her breath, "I am *not* letting it out of my sight no matter *what* the chalkboard says."

A dark-haired woman had stepped out of the bus. She was carrying a clipboard that made Georgia immediately think of Pax.

Again.

The man had crept into her dreams for two nights in a row now. Between that and the nagging aches left from the accident, she hadn't exactly had much sleep.

She joined the throng lining up to board the bus. It was entirely ordinary. Bright yellow and, judging by the words printed on the side, on loan from the Paseo Panthers.

Marcia, the wedding coordinator, marched them all up onto the bus with efficient speed. And even though she wore a smile as she checked them off by name as they boarded, Georgia's impression of the woman was more one of security guard than wedding coordinator.

She found a seat beside Draper. "You think she'd frisk us if she doesn't believe that we don't have our phones with us?"

He grinned and gave the coordinator a long look as she boarded the bus. She was speaking to the driver as the vehicle started to slowly move. "Might be worth a try just to find out. She's not bad to look at."

Georgia rolled her eyes and shifted position again, trying to alleviate the persistent ache in her back.

"Thank you all for being here," Marcia said loudly above the din of voices and the engine. She was a tall, lanky brunette in a navy blazer and skirt, and was as different from the coordinator of the last wedding Georgia had participated in as night was from day. "I just want to send a thank-you to the school district here for lending us a hand at the last minute when the charter bus we'd arranged had some unexpected mechanical difficulties."

There was a round of cheers that made Georgia wonder if the cocktail party guests had started off with cocktails before even boarding.

"As you know, your host and hostess are thrilled that so many of you have taken time out of your lives to share in their celebrations, and it's my job to ensure all of you have a comfortable and enjoyable stay." Instead of remaining at the front of the bus, Marcia slowly made her way down the aisle as she spoke. "If you need anything at all while you're in Pasco, don't hesitate to let me know and I'll do my best to accommodate you."

"Sounds good to me," Draper murmured in Georgia's ear.

"A couple housekeeping items that may be new to some of you who've just joined us and a repeat to the others who arrived before today. As you know, Mr. Robinson values his privacy."

Georgia looked down at her hands to hide her expression. Personally, she figured that if Gerald really valued his privacy, he should have done a better job of avoiding his publicly romantic scandals.

"Even more important to him, though, is the privacy of his bride. It's his intention to shield her from unwanted scrutiny and public limelight as much as he possibly can.

The wedding is a private time for them and their families. It's for this reason, of course, that for some functions—like tonight's cocktail welcome—we're asking that you leave your cell phones behind. They want to limit exposure to social media and other publicity as much as possible. I'm sure you all can sympathize and appreciate this point."

Draper elbowed her side and Georgia winced.

"Oh, damn. Sorry," he apologized under his breath.

"If you encounter anyone who seems suspicious or doesn't seem to belong, please feel comfortable pointing them out to me or to any of the security who may be present at some of the functions. You'll know who they are by their black T-shirts with the word *staff* printed on them."

Georgia immediately thought of Charlotte and wondered if Gerald was less concerned with the media hounds than he was his ex-wife. From what Connor had told them, the woman had seemingly disappeared into thin air. Even her own children hadn't seen or heard from her.

Belle, sitting in front of them, turned around in her seat. "What do you bet that Dad is having heartburn right now and can't figure out why?"

"While a master schedule has been prepared and distributed to all of you, please remember to consult the board at the ramada every day. That's where I'll post any changes arising throughout our time here together in Paseo. Most importantly," Marcia concluded as she began making her way back to the front of the bus, "enjoy one another's company and have a good time!"

There were more hoots and hollers following her speech.

While the overall pulse among those present seemed

upbeat, glancing around the bus, Georgia couldn't help but notice that some expressions that were shy of exuberance. "Do you know who that older guy is across the way? Fifth row?"

Draper shook his head. "Kind of looks like Dad, though. The way he holds his head."

"The way he frowns," Georgia added. "Considering his expression, I wonder why he's here."

"Maybe he's one of Julius's bastards, too, but unlike Dad, decided to come despite his misgivings."

"Maybe." She bit back a groan when the bus hit a bump that rocked her spine. She shifted again, but finding a comfortable position eluded her and by the time the bus came to a stop again, she could have wept with relief. She actually felt worse now than she had the day before.

She stood so quickly, she was the first in line to get off the bus.

"Watch your step," Marcia warned with what Georgia was beginning to suspect was a perpetual smile as she went down the first two of three steep steps.

Each one brought a fresh spear of pain shooting up her spine and she couldn't help hesitating before she took the last step down to the ground.

Unfortunately, while *she* hesitated, the person behind her did not.

"Oof!" She felt herself being launched out of the bus and threw out her hand to grab at anything to keep from falling.

A strong arm caught her around her waist, causing as much pain as relief.

"Once again, not watching where you're going, I see."

Chapter Four

The woman in Pax's arms stared up at him, consternation plain in the snapping blue eyes peering from beneath a loose sweep of bangs that he hadn't noticed before.

"What're you doing here?"

"Keeping you from falling on your face, for one thing." Pax quickly set Georgia out of the way of the people disgorging from the school bus.

She shrugged off his touch and yanked the dark scarf that had trailed behind her off the ground. "I thought you hated all things Fortune."

"Not all things." He thumbed back his cowboy hat. "I've known Deb Fortune and her boys since I was a kid. I was invited, too."

The surprise she couldn't hide had his jaw tightening. He needed to remember she wasn't just any ordinary woman. When he'd finally gotten a chance to check her record after the accident, it was clean of any traffic violations. It had been pure curiosity, though, that had driven him to look more closely into her life.

She lived in an affluent area of New Orleans. She

worked for her father's investment firm—one of the most prestigious in her state—but since she also held an MBA, it didn't look as if she'd just been handed the job. And her father... Well, she could claim that her arm of the family was nothing like Gerald Robinson's ilk, but Miles Fortune wasn't without plenty of his own power and influence. The second Pax Googled them, he'd found a slew of articles, photos and videos of the man hobnobbing with governors and the like.

If he'd wanted to be attracted to a clone of Whitney, he couldn't have chosen better.

Knowing it nagged the hell out of him, too.

It meant he hadn't learned one damn thing from that disaster.

"Most of the town of Paseo is here tonight, honey. If that means there are too many hicks for your taste—"

Georgia made a face and flung her scarf around her shoulder, then turned on her heel and sashayed away from him.

"Smooth."

Pax grimaced at his brother Redford's comment and took the cold soda can that he was extending.

He hadn't exactly told Georgia the truth. Oh, he had been invited to the shindig that was being held at the ranch where Deb had raised her sons. His mom and brothers had also been invited.

But Pax was nevertheless there to make sure everyone present kept the peace. Thus the cola, when he would have much preferred a beer.

Particularly after seeing Georgia in that dress that was basically painted on her.

He popped the top on the can, pretending that he wasn't watching her cross the grassy expanse of tables and chairs. The sun had nearly set, but there were plenty of string lights suspended between the trees and the narrow pergola, where the bar had been set up. "Don't know what you're talkin' about."

Red laughed. At twenty-four, he was the youngest of Pax's brothers. He was also the tallest, topping Pax's six-three by several inches. And he had the annoying habit of propping his elbow on top of Pax's shoulder as if he was a piece of furniture to be leaned upon.

Like he was doing right now.

Pax shoved away his brother's arm. "Appreciate the soda, but go bother someone else."

"I've taken an oath to help, serve and protect," Red drawled. "And, brother, you really need some help when it comes to a girl like that."

"You took the oath over in Austin with their police department," Pax reminded him, even though he knew it was pointless. When Red got a bone between his teeth, he never let it go. "Not with my crew."

"That's 'cause you wouldn't let me," Red countered. "My own brother wouldn't hire me."

"I did you a favor. You'll be a better cop learning your way in Austin than you would starting out as a deputy in a dinky place like Paseo, where nothing ever happens."

Except for white sports cars taking flying leaps off the highway for no obvious reason.

"Like you became a better cop working in Dallas?"

Pax ignored the dig. During the eight years he'd been in Dallas, he *had* become a better cop. Worked his way up to detective, in fact, until everything had turned sideways on him.

"I could'a gone to Amber Falls PD like Jas."

"Could have," he agreed blandly, knowing it never would have happened. Their fourth brother, Jasper, was already a sworn officer with the small department. And Red had never liked following in Jasper's wake.

As if reading his thoughts, Red made a scoffing sound. "You're never gonna get her to hook up if you don't work on your delivery." Typically, he wasn't finished with the bone he thought he'd found.

Pax settled his hat more firmly on his head. "I'm not trying to hook up with Georgia Fortune," he said dismissively.

"Sure. That's why you're drooling all over your sad self. Keep up with the abstinence thing and you might as well look into the priesthood."

"Shut up," he muttered. "Better yet, go over and talk to our mother. She hasn't seen you yet and for some unfathomable reason, you're her favorite."

Red's grin widened. "I'll go talk to Ma, 'specially considering where she's sitting." He nodded his head in the direction of a round table partially occupied by a trio of laughing women. "Never would have expected the preacher's daughter to grow up quite so well. But little Dahlia Ramirez looks almost as good as your lady in red."

A red that was easy to find among the sea of little black dresses. "She's not my lady—" He broke off, feeling stupid for rising to Red's bait, but also because his brother was already striding away in the direction of their mother where she was sitting with, among others, her best friend, Marguerite Ramirez.

Despite himself, his focus zeroed in again on Georgia. She was sipping from a wineglass and laughing at something. Her head was tilted back and her thick, long, shining hair swung well past her shoulders and was caught up in some sort of loose braid down near the ends.

He looked away, not knowing what was worse. The memory of her glass-speckled hair tangling with the airbags, or the fact that tonight's braid only made him itch to undo it.

Then he shook himself as he spotted Grayson and his two brothers and started to head their way.

In the grand scheme of things, having to keep a clamp on his unwelcome interest where Georgia Fortune was concerned was a lot better than thinking about her accident. About how much worse for her it could have been.

As he neared Deborah's sons, who'd been the ones to ask him to keep an eye on things, Pax wondered again whether or not they'd cleared it with their mother and her intended groom first. Since he'd been elected sheriff, he'd had few occasions to see them. Social functions, town meetings and such.

Until then, though, Pax hadn't been all that close to them. The other men were nearly a decade older than he was. But as long as he'd known them, he'd never quite been able to tell Jayden apart from Nathan. Grayson was easier, just because the guy had started out rodeoing when Pax was a little kid, ultimately becoming so famous at it that he even had his own line of Western wear called Grayson Gear. Tonight he wore a belt with a prize buckle nearly as big as a dinner plate.

Other than that, the three men looked exactly alike, from the tops of their heads to the Castleton boots on their feet.

The cowboy hat on top of Pax's head was a Grayson Gear model. But the only Castletons he'd ever worn had been given to him by Whitney. The expensive gift had sparked just one of their many arguments over money.

She had it. He didn't.

Now, though, wasn't the time to dwell on the past and he stuck his hand out first to the rodeo rider. "Grayson. You've got yourselves a nice evening for a party."

The older man inclined his head and shook Pax's hand with a firm grip. "Sheriff. Glad to see you. Appreciate you keeping an eye on things for us."

"It's been pretty calm," Pax replied. "Only had to remind one person about the cell-phone deal. They took it back to their car with no argument."

"That's it?"

"So far." He glanced around at the gathering party-goers. The line at the bar was growing and the white-clothed tables were filling. There were also a handful of servers, dressed in black pants and white shirts, carrying trays among the tables. Below the amplified music coming from the live trio set up on the wide raised porch surrounding the house, the voices and laughter were getting louder, but not in an unruly way. "I'm not sure my presence is going to be all that necessary."

"Yeah, well, the main attraction hasn't made their first appearance yet," the triplet to Grayson's right interjected as he shook Pax's hand. "Expect that might ramp up people's excitability some."

A slim young woman wearing what looked like an ankle-length T-shirt joined them, sliding her arm around the man to Grayson's left. "EJ settled okay with Monica?" he asked her.

"With his headphones and the latest *Trace the Triceratops* episode, Otis on one side of the bed and Sugar on the other. He doesn't usually get to have the dogs on the bed, so needless to say, he's pretty happy. I told Monica that once he's asleep, she could come out and enjoy the party, but you know how she is. Given a chance, she'd rather have her nose in a book."

Pax didn't know what *Trace the Triceratops* was, but he did know EJ was Nate's stepson with his wife Bianca, which meant the guy to Grayson's right was Jayden.

Detective work at its finest. The wry thought circled in his head. "Do you know when that arrival might be, Jayden?"

"I'd think pretty soon." He glanced at his watch and frowned slightly. "Mom hates being late for anything."

"They're late only because of *him*," Grayson added.

"It's a cocktail party," Nate chided. "I don't know if there's an official definition of being late for something like this."

"Don't defend the man," Grayson said. He pushed back his cowboy hat, looking annoyed. But the expression smoothed right out when his wife, Billie, appeared from inside the house and began crossing toward them. She had a scarf thing that didn't look too different from the one that Georgia had, only on Billie it was wrapped in a crisscross fashion around her torso and held a dark-haired infant against her chest.

If Pax had gotten around to proposing to Whitney, like he'd intended before she'd ruined his career, they might have had a baby by now, too.

Probing the thought like a sore tooth, he knew he missed the idea of a baby a helluva lot more than he missed Whitney.

Billie had reached Grayson and slipped under his arm to curve against his side. "Your mom was just on the phone," she told them. "They'll be landing any minute."

Pax raised his eyebrows. "Landing?" The last plane to land in the area had had to do it on the highway and it had been a helluva headache. Of course, it had been carrying at least a dozen of the guests at this very party.

"Helicopter," Jayden explained. "No worries about closing the highway. Gerald got called back to Austin this morning for some meeting he had to take care of and Mom went with him."

"He snaps his fingers and off she goes. Nearly forty years of independence gone in the blink of an eye," Grayson muttered.

"Don't mind him," Nate said. "He's just sore because he's lost his manager now that Mom's marrying—"

"Don't call him *Dad*," Grayson warned in a low voice.

"I don't have to call him *Dad*," Nate returned mildly. "Like it or not, it doesn't change the fact that he's responsible for our existence."

"Mom is responsible for our existence," Grayson said tightly.

"She didn't get pregnant on her own," Jayden snapped. "And we promised her that we'd all behave tonight, remember? Not for *his* sake, but for hers."

Pax wondered if the peace he was going to have to keep would be among Deborah's own sons.

He gestured vaguely toward the grounds behind him. "If you need me, I'll be making my way around, keeping an eye on things." On the plausible excuse, he moved away from them and into the growing throng of guests.

While the bus had let off a dozen people from the campground, there were a lot of others present, too. Paseo people. And to a one, they all bore similar expressions of awe when—before Pax had even made a full circuit around the party area—the air filled with the distinct *whop whop whop* of a helicopter.

It settled smoothly, almost delicately, a fair distance off from the house, though the Robinson Tech logo on its side was still visible. The rotors hadn't stopped whirling when the couple emerged, ducking as they jogged hand in hand toward the party.

They were quickly surrounded by well-wishers, and Pax hung back on the periphery of the lighted area, watching the reception they received.

Deborah's sons were also hanging back.

Allowing the other guests first crack?

Or putting off the welcome to their father?

Pax had lost his father nine years ago. Not a day went by without feeling the loss.

There were several others who also didn't race right over to greet the couple. One of the older guys who'd come on the school bus. Pax had seen him already pound back a few drinks. And Georgia, who was still holding her wineglass with one hand and pressing the other to the middle of her back. Aftereffects of her accident, no doubt.

It wasn't concern over that, necessarily, that had him moving in her direction.

It was the fact that she happened to be standing near the table where his mother sat. And if the grinning look Red was shooting Pax's way was any indication, his baby brother had noticed.

God only knew what sort of outrageous things might come out of his mouth, especially since Dahlia Ramirez and her mother had vacated their seats, leaving Red and Cara Price alone at the table.

Pax moved a little faster, reaching the table just in time to clamp his hand over his brother's shoulder, effectively keeping him in his seat. He was well aware of the look Georgia cast his way, but ignored it.

"Honey!" Cara's still youthful face beamed at him as he kissed her cheek. She was wearing her go-to black sequined top that she always wore when she had to dress up fancy and she'd let her wavy red hair down from its usual bunch on top of her head. But that was as far as Cara went, because paired with the sequins were her usual blue jeans. Crisp and dark and fairly new, but still blue jeans.

You could take the girl out of the country, but you couldn't take the country out of the girl.

It was his mom's basic approach to life, and the fact that she never changed was just one of the things he loved about her.

"I was able to mend that tear in your shirt," she told him.

That was one of the other things he loved about her. Her handy way with a needle.

"Thought for sure I'd be buying another uniform shirt."

"Nobody'd ever know it's even mended, unless they're sticking their nose two inches from your pectoral muscle."

From the corner of his eye, he saw Georgia join her brother and several others.

"Unless he gets into a wrestling match again with a drunk-and-disorderly Deeter Hayes, there isn't anyone he's gonna be that up close and personal with," Red said with a goading laugh.

"Bet the reason you keep harping on my love life is to keep us from noticing the Death Valley of your own." He felt his eyes straying again, and shifted so that his back was turned toward Georgia. "Who's the last girl you dated?"

"I have plenty of action, don't you worry."

"Fortunately, I'm old enough to understand the difference between action and dating," Pax said. "I just hope you know better than to share the details with Mom sitting right here."

Cara looked amused. Her hands were resting atop the table and she was twirling the wedding ring she still wore on her finger. "I am well aware of most of my sons' activities," she said dryly. "It's the nature of small-town living. And," she added, lifting her hand to forestall Red, "just because you're living over in Austin now doesn't mean the tales don't make their way home, same as with Jasper and Marshall over in Amber Falls." She gave him a fond-looking, but none-too-gentle-sounding, tap on his cheek with the flat of her palm. "I *do* expect you to behave yourself when you're right here under my nose, however."

Red gave her an injured look. "What kind of man do you think I am?"

"I think you are your father's son," she said pertly. "Just like your brothers. But I saw the glint in your eyes over Dahlia and I don't need you messing with her. Marguerite is my best friend, Dahlia's her only daughter, and she's much too sweet a girl for you."

"Nice to know whose side you're on," Red grumbled.

Cara ignored him and patted the seat next to her. "Come on, Paxton. You look tired, sweetheart. Sit down for a few minutes."

He shook his head. "I'm fine." Thanks to the two domestic disturbances in Amber Falls that followed Georgia's accident, a poultry truck losing its load near the county line as well as the never-ending details he dealt with on a daily basis, he'd had only a couple hours of downtime in the last two days.

"You work too hard."

He smiled faintly as he drained the soda and set the empty can on the table. "Shouldn't have talked me into running for sheriff, then," he told her wryly.

"Don't blame that on me," she called after him. "That's your father's genes always driving you into law enforcement!"

True enough, Pax thought, as he circled around once more to the edge of the string lights near the gravel drive. A breeze had cropped up, making the lines of lights bounce slightly. The sun was down now, the large barn behind him a darker shadow against the sky.

He leaned his shoulder against a tree and rubbed his

hand wearily down his face. He hoped to hell the party didn't go on until dawn. But the folks around Paseo knew how to enjoy a good time, so he wasn't going to bet on it.

"Thought that was you." A scrape of a boot on gravel accompanied the voice and Charlie Esparza's white hair materialized in the dark.

Pax almost did a double take. "Didn't know you owned anything other than overalls, Charlie."

Charlie smiled broadly and ran his hand down the front of his pale shirt. The closer he got to the golden lights, the more Pax could see the white shirt was untucked, buttoned from neck to hem and still showed the folds from its packaging. "Got this bolo from my daddy after he died." Charlie flicked the turquoise-and-leather corded tie.

"Looks real fine."

Charlie smoothed his palm over his hair, which might have been slicked down when he started out, but now looked pretty much like it always did—in need of a hat covering it. "Well, Miz Deborah's always been nice to me. Figured I'd spiff it up a little for the occasion."

Nevertheless, the guy didn't seem to be in any undue hurry to join the throng still surrounding Deborah and her intended, particularly when he pulled out a cigarette and a book of matches. "Mind?"

"Your lungs, Charlie." He waited until the man had lit up and taken his first drag. "Anything unusual show up on the sports car yet?" He didn't need to say which one.

"Not yet. I finally got to it this morning. Been trying to get that tourist bus going again for these folks, too." He gestured with his cigarette. "I'm documenting it all with photographs like you asked." An exhale of smoke—fortunately angled away from Pax's face—accompanied Charlie's words. "Insurance company doesn't want me getting into the black box 'cause I might accidently damage the data." He snorted softly, shaking his head. "I figure they're gonna try 'n' minimize their losses if they can."

"Probably so." Short of Georgia deliberately crashing her own car, Pax hadn't been able to find a single thing to indicate she was at fault. He'd even gotten a terse email from someone named Julie at Fortune Investments that included a copy of Georgia's cell-phone activity. It proved her phone had been idle before the crash.

"Did talk to the dealership where she picked up the car, though," Charlie added. "Evidently, your Miz Georgia's daddy is good friends with the guy who owns it. Has eleven of 'em all throughout Louisiana. Dude's making a pretty penny on them, you can be sure."

"What's your point?"

More smoke streamed through Charlie's nose. "From what they tol' me, the owner had his top guys go over the car with a fine-tooth comb before she took delivery. Not just the cosmetics, but under the hood, too. Brand-new car, with every bell and whistle it could have, right off the assembly line, too."

Overly cautious?

Or not cautious enough?

"Did you get the idea they were looking for anything in particular?"

Charlie shook his head, then made a sound and suddenly stubbed out his cigarette on the bottom of his boot.

Georgia walked closer, barely acknowledging Pax at all. "I thought I recognized you, Mr. Esparza. How are you?"

"Real fine, miss. Bet you're still feeling mighty sore, though."

"Nothing a few more yoga practices won't cure," she said with a rueful smile. "At least that's what I keep telling myself." Her gaze flicked toward Pax, then away again. "I, um, I don't suppose you've managed to get my suitcase out of the car, have you? I know you said you'd be in touch, but—" she spread her palms "—I'm reduced to borrowing clothes right now."

"Cutting through the trunk's been a little touchy." Charlie's expression knotted at the dismayed look on Georgia's face. "Don't worry, Miz Georgia. I *will* get into it. I can promise you that."

"Charlie does a lot more than drive a tow truck," Pax told her. "If it has an engine in it, he can take it apart or build it back up again." The skinny old guy lived in a house that looked like a hovel, but his shop was a thing of beauty. People came from three states away for his work. And any insurance adjuster who was worried that Charlie Esparza would accidentally damage anything didn't know who they were dealing with at all.

"I think we all know there isn't going to be any building up my car again," she said. "My auto insurance—"

"Been in touch with 'em," Charlie said quickly. "Just like you requested. Sent 'em a bunch of pictures of the car like they asked, but they plan to send someone to Paseo to actually see it." He shuffled his feet. "Don't have to tell you, it was a pretty valuable piece a' machinery."

Georgia's lips turned down at the corners. "*Was* being the operative word. Did they say how long it might take for someone to get here? It's already been two days."

"No, ma'am. Sorry."

She tugged on her braid a few times, then tossed it over her shoulder and adjusted the scarf farther up her shoulders. "It's not your fault, Mr. Esparza."

"Jus' Charlie. In my experience, though, they don't tend to take too long before attending to situations like this. Bad for business and all. I'd expect they'll be showing up pretty soon."

"I hope you're right, Charlie." She gave him a small

smile that anyone with two eyes in their head could see was tired and forced. "If I have to wait for the suitcase, I have to wait. I don't suppose you noticed a cell phone rolling around inside the car, did you?"

"Oh, jeez." In the light from the strings bouncing overhead, Charlie's red cheeks were visible. "I did find that. Wedged way up in the steering column. Had a heck of a time getting it out and the glass is cracked on it, but it didn't look too damaged otherwise. Then I go and clean forget it in my truck. I figured you'd be here, but if you weren't, I was gonna drive it on out to Cara's field to give it to you." He gestured behind them with a hand missing half a forefinger. Beyond the lights from the party, it was inky dark. "I'm parked down the road a bit. Lot of cars already here. I'll go get it."

Before Georgia could get a word in, Charlie had turned and was trotting into the night.

Leaving Pax and Georgia just standing there, eyeing each other silently.

"You know, there is a no-cell-phone policy here tonight," he finally said.

"Trust me. I've heard all about it." She lifted her palm. "I solemnly swear not to post anything about this little fais do-do on the internet." She dropped her hand. "Battery's going to be dead, anyway, after this long, but if you feel so compelled, you can confiscate it for as long as I am here tonight."

"I think that'd be taking it a little far."

The corners of her lips twitched. "Why, Sheriff. How very trusting of you."

He couldn't help but smile and after a moment that went on long enough to become awkward, she adjusted her scarf again. "Cara's field?" The question in her voice was a little bright.

Forced.

"The woman who owns the land where your…accommodations have been set up." He wasn't sure why he didn't just admit that the woman happened to be his mother.

"Ah." She looked around, not saying anything for another too-long moment. Then she tugged at her braid again. With the breeze, the loose weave looked in danger of coming apart altogether.

And it just made her seem even more appealing.

"I'd better get back to my family, I guess. We still haven't had a chance to greet our hosts." She suddenly took a step backward. She'd have bumped right into one of the white-shirted servers if not for the evasive action the other woman took.

Unfortunately, that resulted in her tray tipping to one side, dumping a dozen filled wineglasses onto the ground.

"Oh," Georgia gasped. "I'm so sorry."

"It's okay," the server started. "Oh, no, ma'am, you don't—"

But Georgia was already crouching down to help pick up the glasses. "I don't think any of them broke." She finished emptying the contents of two glasses onto the grass and handed them to the server, quickly following up with two more before the woman could stop her. "If they did, it's entirely my fault."

They were drawing attention now and Pax leaned over to pick up the glass that had rolled near his boot.

"No harm, no foul," he said, handing the glass to the server. He didn't recognize her, which meant she'd probably driven in from Amber Falls or somewhere else for the job. But this close, he could see the embroidered name on her white shirt. "Right, Kimmie?"

Kimmie's tray was filled once again, albeit with empty glasses. "Yes, sir," she assured him. "I'll just get these changed out and bring you fresh pours." She was gone before he could say a word.

Georgia was still crouched and her scarf had fallen to the ground.

"Dress too tight to stand?"

She made a face at him. "Just because it's close-fitting doesn't mean it's too tight." But she stuck out her hand toward him. "A gentleman would offer assistance without making a lady ask for it."

"You think I'm a gentleman?" He took her hand and pulled her to her feet.

She landed on her impractical high-heeled sandals only a few inches from him. Her nose could have, quite literally, brushed against his pectoral muscles.

Only this shirt had no mended tear to study.

"Don't forget your scarf." His voice was a little too gruff as he bent down and swiped it off the ground.

"I don't know about a gentleman, but you're definitely one of those rescuer types." She sounded a little breathless as she took the scarf from him.

"You're bruised." He hadn't noticed until then just how badly.

"And stiff and sore as the devil, but—" she flipped the scarf around her shoulders, covering the marks "—I'm grateful to have that problem. As everyone, including you, keeps reminding me, it could have been a lot worse." She smiled tightly and started to move away again, but he caught her arm.

Gently, because the last thing he wanted to do was cause her more bruises. "Wait."

Chapter Five

*W*ait.

Such a simple word to make Georgia's mouth so dry.

His fingers were still curved gently around her upper arm. She could feel their warmth burning against her skin, despite the thin scarf. Could feel her breasts tightening beneath the scanty triangles of red dress barely covering them.

Could feel a yearning inside her she wasn't used to feeling.

Forcing a blitheness she didn't feel, she raised an inquiring eyebrow. "Wait, for...?"

He drew back his hand. "Have you remembered anything else about the accident?"

Naturally.

Silly of her to have imagined his eyes all soft and mossy again.

Focusing on his uniform helped her maintain her blitheness. "I've told you everything. Which was, regrettably, nothing helpful."

"You said you left New Orleans the day before the accident?"

"On Monday. Yes. I'd just picked up the car from the dealer—"

"Right. And there were no problems driving it? Brakes okay? Steering?"

She exhaled. "No. No problems."

"You stopped in Shreveport. What'd it take you? About five hours?"

"A little more. I made a few stops along the way. Stopped in to some boutiques. A few roadside stands."

"Buy anything?"

"As a matter of fact, no. Except some fresh strawberries that I ate on the road."

"Pick up any strangers?"

She exhaled her impatience. "No. And the car ran fine the whole while."

"Where'd you stay in Shreveport?"

"At a quaint little B and B near the river. My parents stayed there once before I was born, when they were celebrating their anniversary." There had even been a photograph of them, smiling and looking painfully young, fashioned into an entire mosaic of similar photos covering one of the walls. Sarah had been pregnant with Austin at the time—

"Anything unusual happen there?"

Georgia crossed her arms. "Unusual like what?" She didn't wait for an answer. "There were three other guests. A couple on their honeymoon and an older woman traveling alone. Same as me. We all had dinner together on the porch—it had a nice view, just as lovely as my mom described even after all these years—and we went our separate ways."

"Did you have a nice view of your car overnight?"

She didn't like talking about her car. It made her nerves feel frayed and her stomach tight. "It was parked in front of the B and B, the same as everyone else's vehicle."

"Out in the open?"

She flexed her jaw. "You think someone messed with my vehicle overnight?"

"You don't think that's possible?"

She managed a dismissive laugh, and raised her palms. "But why?"

"You tell me. Is there any reason to believe someone would want to tamper with your vehicle? Anyone with a grudge against you?"

"No!" She almost, *almost* considered bringing up her sister's break-in and the ongoing suspicions about Charlotte Robinson being at the root of it, but controlled herself.

Coincidences *did* happen in life and were far more plausible than a woman actually plotting against them. What on earth would be the point? Charlotte didn't know Georgia's immediate family. It wasn't as if they'd had any involvement in the demise of Charlotte's marriage.

That wasn't even attributed to Gerald's publicly known peccadillos, since Charlotte had always turned a blind eye to them. No, the only reason Charlotte had lost Gerald was because Gerald had decided he wanted to marry Deborah. And Deborah had obviously said yes.

Television-type drama at its very best.

"Are you *sure*?" Pax persisted.

The sheriff had been appealing when he'd been covered in dirt with a torn shirt from rescuing her from her car. Now, in another sharp uniform, and definitely *not* covered in dirt, he was the most attractive man she'd ever met.

But the way he was watching her closely—too closely—was not at all appealing.

She lifted her chin. "Absolutely."

His jaw flexed. "How'd the car drive when you left the B and B?"

"Oh, my God. You're the perfect sheriff, do you know that? Suspicion must run in your veins. My car drove the same as it drove before I arrived! The car was perfect, Sheriff. It was perfect when I visited the yoga studio the owner of the B and B recommended." She'd left the yoga practice feeling totally and thoroughly relaxed for probably the first time in two years—since before she'd become the PR director for her father's firm. "And it was perfect two hours later, when I left there and stopped at a little hole-in-the-wall for lunch, and perfect *still* when I hit the state line!" Her voice was rising and she didn't care one bit. "It was perfect until—"

"It wasn't," he said flatly.

Chills ran up her spine. She took a breath and let it out slowly.

"Until it wasn't," she agreed more quietly. "I think I liked it better when you were accusing me of distracted driving."

His shoulders moved, looking restless beneath the khaki shirt. "It's not my intention to upset you, Georgia."

"Too late." She pulled in another breath and let it out on measured beats. She rolled her head around on her neck, feeling an ache all the way down her spine. "I don't suppose there are any yoga studios in the area, are there?"

"Maybe in Amber Falls. Not entirely sure."

"What about massage therapists?" She tossed out the question even knowing it was probably unlikely.

He shrugged.

"Don't keep your finger on the pulse of every single person and their occupation in your parish, do you?"

"County."

"Of course." She knew that. She was just tired, sore and increasingly hungry. Never a good combination.

She looked behind her and Austin caught her eye from where he and the others were standing. With Gerald Robinson and Deborah. "Shoot, I need to go meet my uncle and his intended."

"Uncle?"

"Didn't I tell you that?"

"You know damn well you didn't."

"Well, I have now. Excuse me." Without waiting for a response, she hurried to join her family as quickly as she could, considering the way her spiky heels kept sinking into the soft grass.

"Finally," Draper said under his breath when she reached them. "You making a new conquest over there with the sheriff?"

She ignored him and smiled brightly when Austin, who'd been in the middle of introductions, drew her in with his extended arm.

"This is Georgia," he said. "She's our middle one."

She found her hands caught and held by Deborah. "My dear girl. We've heard about your terrible accident! We're so relieved you weren't hurt."

"Thank you." Georgia offered a wry smile. "I'm pretty relieved, too." It had been easy enough to know ahead of time what Deborah looked like. She'd managed her son's rodeo career and he'd gotten famous enough for people to know him as just "Grayson." Pictures of Deborah hadn't been anywhere near as widespread on the internet as those of Gerald, but there'd been enough to know she was slender and dark-haired with a penchant for wearing Western-cut shirts and cowboy boots.

In person, though, her no-nonsense demeanor seemed softer. Gentler. Her long brown hair had a few strands of silver sparkling in her thick braid, and beneath her snug leather jacket, she was wearing a decidedly funky leopard-print tunic dress that showed off enviable legs tucked into cowboy boots.

Georgia looked from Deborah's smiling face to Gerald.

In person, his face seemed familiar, though she honestly didn't know whether to attribute that to the widespread media coverage of his life she'd studied since she'd learned he was their uncle, or because his looks reminded her of her dad.

He had the same salt-and-pepper hair. The same prominent eyebrows that had made women swoon through the decades when they gazed at Gable, Connery or Clooney. She'd read descriptions like "brilliant and eccentric" with as much frequency as "cold and ruthless."

And because she, herself, was in public relations, she knew enough to believe only half of what she read.

"So," she began, dredging up a presentable amount of cheerfulness. "Now that we finally meet, do we call you Uncle or what?"

His eyes brightened and he let out a laugh. "Little lady, you and your brothers and sisters can call me whatever you like, as long as it isn't a cab."

"Oh…" Deborah rolled her eyes, her own laugh mixed with a tsk.

"I'm just glad you and your brothers and sisters wanted to join us," he said.

"You've certainly gone out of your way to make us all comfortable," Felicity said. "The setup at the campground is remarkable."

Deborah smiled. "We definitely lucked out finding a place large enough once we received such an amazing response to the wedding invitations. If it wasn't for Cara Price's field—"

"Price?" Georgia couldn't help herself. "Any relation to the sheriff?" If so, why hadn't he just admitted it?

"Cara is Pax's mother," Deborah said easily. "She's always been lovely, and I was so happy that our needs happened to coincide. We could have tried putting everyone up on our own property—" she extended her hand and the diamonds on her engagement ring glittered like big chunks of ice beneath the overhead lights "—but our land is much rougher and less conducive—"

"She means more filled with cow pies," Gerald said dryly.

"That, too," she agreed with a chuckle. "We raise cattle here," she explained. "Not corn, like Cara." She brushed her head against Gerald's shoulder. "I warned this one that he was going overboard once we really set the plan in motion. But there's just no stopping him when he puts his mind to something."

He slid his arm around her shoulder. "Don't forget it. We have a lot of years to make up for."

Even being nineteen times a cynic, as Georgia was, she had to admit to feeling a tightness in her chest at the way the woman beamed up at her man as she slid her arm around his waist and fit herself close against his side.

It was the same way her mother often stood next to her dad.

Like two halves of one whole.

She was glad, then, for the interruption when one of Deborah's sons—she'd met them earlier but felt hopeless at telling the dark-haired men apart—joined them.

"Oh, Nathan." Deborah wrapped her free arm around his. "Have you had a chance to meet—"

"Sure have." His smile took in all of them and he

lightly tugged on his mother's hair where it hung over the shoulder of her caramel-colored leather jacket. "Had to tease Georgia there a bit about the braid. Two of you could be twins tonight."

Deborah laughed. "Flattering to me, son, but maybe not so much to your young cousin."

"You're both beautiful," Nathan assured her gallantly.

Georgia hoped she would look as good as Deborah did when she reached her age. "I'm going to need to take up stock in Kate Fortune's famous youth serum if I have any chance at all." The founder of the renowned Fortune Cosmetics was also part of their widespread lineage, but Georgia had given up trying to figure out how.

Deborah looked at Gerald. "Didn't we hear from Kate that she and Sterling plan to be here for the wedding?"

Gerald looked vaguely chagrined. "She called me up and gave me what-for for not getting the invitation to them quickly enough to suit her." His intense gaze encompassed Georgia and her siblings. "Just to forewarn you, if you haven't met her yet, Kate considers herself the matriarch of all things Fortune. Whether you're her first cousin or second or fifth, when she says jump, we're all supposed to ask how high. She does want her family unified, though, no matter how much of a challenge that might present."

"Like you?" Georgia asked.

He chuckled. "Maybe."

"Kate's definitely a force," Deborah added. "And she's just as beautiful as the rumors say. Woman is in her nineties and has better skin than I do."

"You look exactly the same now as you did when I fell in love with you nearly forty years ago." Gerald touched her hair lightly. "You had on that dark blue dress. And a white ribbon in your hair."

Deborah laughed, though her smile was tremulous. "Still sweet-talking me."

"Well, while you're all making me want to cut off my ears with the lovey-dovey stuff," Nathan drawled, "I came over to tell you that EJ is *still* awake, and says he can't sleep without a story and a g'night kiss from his grandma."

"Okay, then." Deborah gave Gerald a quick wink. "If there's a man to steal a little piece of my heart away from you, it's my grandson." She excused herself and strode away with Nathan toward the house.

Georgia, however, was more focused on Gerald and the look in his eyes as he watched her go.

Had he felt that…*longing*, for nearly forty years?

It hardly seemed fathomable, but considering the way his expression cleared the second he noticed her watching, she couldn't help but think it had been genuine.

She was quite sure no man had ever longed for her. And heaven knew she'd never felt that way herself about a man.

Would she ever?

She didn't know what was more disturbing —the question itself, or the fact that she was even considering the question. But it was still circling in her mind hours later when the motley passengers once more boarded the school bus under Marcia's ever-present smile.

Georgia was halfway to the back of the bus before she found an empty seat, and she collapsed onto it next to a blonde already sitting in the row who looked about Georgia's age.

She held up the bottle of water that she'd switched to after her limit of two glasses of wine. "Quite the party, wasn't it? I'm Georgia. New Orleans." Over the course of the evening, introductions had become nearly short-hand. "You?"

The other woman grinned. "Delaney. Horseback Hollow."

Georgia tried to concentrate, but it was no good. She leaned back against the headrest. "I know someone told me tonight, but I am too stuffed with food to think straight. Horseback Hollow is where?"

"There definitely was a lot of food." Delaney chuckled. "And booze. Near Lubbock."

It clicked then. "Oh, sure. Cowboy Country USA is located there, right?" Georgia had never visited the Western-themed amusement park, but she knew plenty of people who had.

"Yes, indeed."

"And you're related to all this how?" She waved her hand, indicating the passengers still boarding. Some looked as exhausted as she felt, while some looked as though they could go on for hours yet.

"My mother is a Fortune. Jeanne Marie. Second cousins twice removed. Or third cousins once removed?" She shrugged. "I can't keep it straight. Mama didn't even discover she was a Fortune until she was an adult because she was adopted. She's one of triplets, actually—"

"Good God. Multiples definitely run in the Fortune gene pool. I assume you met our hosts' sons?"

Delaney laughed. "Right?" She leaned her head closer. "And I know we're all distantly related, but Lordy, talk about some good-lookin' men. Not that I'm looking, mind you. Cisco is more than enough man for me to handle." She grinned again.

The name Cisco made Georgia wake up a little. "Cisco *Mendoza*?"

Delaney grinned. "None other."

"Any relation to Chaz Mendoza? He's dating my sister Savannah."

Delaney's eyes brightened even more. "They're cousins!" Her brow knit. "How did I not know they were here?"

"They didn't come tonight, but they're at the campground." She knew her sister was going to be delighted when she found out, too. "Aren't there, ah, Mendozas who married into Gerald's immediate family, too? One of his daughters, or—"

"Oh, yeah." Delaney shrugged easily. "Two of my husband's brothers. Matteo's married to Rachel and Joaquin's married to Zoe. But they're not here, either. None of Gerald and Charlotte's kids are."

"A little awkward for them?"

"Maybe. I think the jury's still out on who they're siding with in their parents' divorce. If they're choosing sides, of course. It's hard to tell with that group. You know, Ben and Wes—the two oldest? They're twins, too."

"Better warn my sister so she's prepared once the babies start coming," Georgia said dryly. "You look like you're solo here, though."

"Cisco couldn't make it for the wedding," Delaney explained. "There's some big thing going on where he works at the Fortune Foundation. If he can get away for the ceremony itself, he will. Is it true that Deborah's wedding dress is *blue*?"

"Haven't seen it myself, but that's the rumor," Georgia admitted. Only now did she understand the significance. Deborah had worn blue the day she and Gerald met. She drained her water bottle and peered toward the front of the bus, anxious for them to be on their way. She wanted to pee, shower and sleep. In that order.

The other woman continued chatting away, talking

about her brothers and sisters, and something about Galen in particular, but Georgia's attention was drifting.

"Oh, hey!" She felt Delaney shift and give her another look. "You're the one who had the car accident, aren't you?"

It was nice to be remembered, but oh, how Georgia wished it wasn't because of that.

She nodded.

"Yikes. I heard it was really bad."

"Bad enough to make me appreciate walking away from it." She closed her eyes, but was treated to an image on the back of her eyelids of her white car crumpled into a tree, and she opened them right back up again. "What kind of accommodations do you have at the campground?"

"Tent. I was a little worried about it at first, knowing we were all putting our names in a hat when it came to the assignment of tents and trailers and stuff. But I'll tell you, if we'd ever had a tent like it when I was a kid, I wouldn't have hated the thought of camping quite so much. I've got an honest-to-goodness bed! Not some cot or a sleeping bag on the ground. With fine sheets and blankets and everything. It's actually pretty cool. If Cisco makes it, he'll think it's a hoot."

"I've never camped in my life," Georgia admitted. Though she wasn't completely unfamiliar with the great outdoors. There'd been lots of times her grandmother Marjorie had pulled their Sunday dinner from the bayou near her house, and she'd often dragged her only son's kids along for the fun. Georgia had learned early on that if she wanted to enjoy that crawfish boil, she had to keep up with her older brothers pulling the nets.

Dinners with her grandparents on her mom's side hadn't been anywhere near as fun. She loved them, but the Barringtons had always been more about proper be-havior and elbows-off-the-table than her dad's mom had been.

Her attention rolled back down the aisle to the front of the bus again, and she blinked twice, clearing her vision.

But it really was Pax, hunched a little to keep the hat on his head clear of the roof. And he was heading her way.

"There you are." He stopped next to her and held out his hand.

Her nerves skittered around like bubbles on a frying beignet. She settled her hand on his, only to feel like a mammoth fool when she encountered the rectangular edges of her cell phone.

She curled her fingers around it, snatching it away. "I never did see Charlie return with it. Figured the phone police had kept him from letting it see the light of day."

She heard Delaney's muffled laughter.

"I guess I was the phone police on-site, so…" He shrugged.

"Surprised you're handing it over so easily." She stud-ied the cracked screen on the phone and pushed the power button. A light blinked on. So, not quite dead yet. "Have you searched it for proof I wasn't texting and driving or was the phone bill I had my assistant send you enough?"

His eyes roved over her face, making her feel a little flushed. "You do text a lot," he said after a moment. "But not before or during your accident. Whatever happened that day, it wasn't because of that."

"Told you."

His lips stretched slightly. "Yes, you did." He stuck his hand in his front pocket.

She blamed exhaustion for her tardiness in realizing

her gaze had followed his hand and then proceeded to linger there.

"Here." He pulled his hand back out, a business card between his index and middle finger. "Found the number of a massage therapist in Amber Falls. Only listing and I don't know anything about the person, so caveat emptor."

Feeling hot inside, she slowly drew the card away from his fingers. Whether or not obtaining the information had been a simple matter for him, it was still unexpected. "Thank you."

"Wouldn't want you to leave Paseo at the end of your stay thinking badly of our service here."

"I'm not going to think badly of Paseo."

"Good."

Then, like her, he seemed to realize they'd become the focus of everyone on the bus.

"Well," he drawled as he thumbed the brim of his hat in a charmingly Texas sort of way, "g'night."

"Good night," she returned, feeling much too bemused and much too attracted.

He smiled faintly and turned, still hunched slightly to make his way to the front of the bus. He tipped his hat to Marcia, who was standing there as neat as a pin, as if only five minutes had passed since she'd delivered them to the party. "Appreciate you holding the bus for me, ma'am." Considering how strangely quiet it had gotten, his polite comment could be heard all the way to the back of the bus.

The second he stepped off, though, and the bus doors slid closed, the silence ended.

"Whoo, doggie," Delaney murmured beside her. "Sexual tension, anyone?"

Georgia jerked, giving her a look. "What? Oh, no. No, no, gracious, no." It was a blatant lie.

Draper, across the aisle and up two rows, hung his head out into the aisle and looked back at her. "Yes, yes, oh, *gracious*, yes."

She threw her empty water bottle at his head. He caught it handily, laughing.

The Paseo Panthers' bus rumbled into life and Georgia's head fell back.

There she was.

Turning thirty in eighteen months, and still feeling like she belonged on an elementary-school bus.

The last time Pax had been out to the campground burgeoning to life on his mother's fallow cornfield, there had been a bunch of workers putting in temporary plumbing lines and framing up a huge ramada.

Now it was a small city filled with luxury RVs and fancy-ass tents bigger than the apartment he'd had in Dallas.

There were people sitting out in Adirondack chairs, their arms and legs gleaming as they baked under the summer sun, kids kicking a ball around in the open field, more people tossing a Frisbee. Radios were blasting, competing with one another for supremacy. He couldn't tell which was winning. Country or rock.

It could have been a day at the beach, he thought, as he slowly cruised between the trailers and vehicles with license plates from all over.

Yet they were here, on a section of land on a little bit of nowhere Texas that he should have been able to provide free and clear to his mother two years ago. If he had, the field would be green with rows of corn now and Gerald Robinson would have had to figure out some other lodging solution for his wedding guests. Pax's town would still be its peaceful little self and he would have finally fulfilled the promise he'd made to his dad a long time ago.

Instead of taking care of his mother, though, he'd let himself get distracted by the career he'd ended up chasing in a futile goal of being good enough for a senator's daughter.

Fortunately, Pax did have his head on straight these days.

Georgia Fortune wasn't the daughter of a senator, but she might as well be.

He'd be smart to remember that fact.

He had expected it would be a quick and simple matter to deliver to her the suitcase he'd picked up when he'd stopped in at Charlie's shop that morning. Nothing he wouldn't have done for anyone who'd experienced something nasty while visiting his town.

Five minutes in and out, he'd promised himself, and he'd be on his way to the only weekend he'd had off in months.

Five minutes had gone by and he was still traveling up and down the damn rows of the damn campground, kicking himself for offering to do the job for Charlie in the first place.

When he once again came near the big ramada at the center of the campground without spotting either Georgia or the travel trailer that she was supposed to be using, he sighed and turned up the air-conditioning in his truck a notch.

There were a few people sitting under the shade of the ramada and he rolled down his window, hailing their attention. "Any of you know where I can find Georgia Fortune?"

"Sure." A young woman bouncing a cute flush-cheeked baby on her hip rose from one of the picnic tables and walked closer. She tilted her head to one side, giving him a close look. "You're the sheriff, right?"

He'd never had a problem acknowledging that particular fact. He'd gone after the job willingly after all.

But for some reason, he felt his neck getting hot. "Yes."

She didn't really look old enough to have the baby, but the smile she gave him was definitely knowing. She pointed behind her. "She's down that row between the Lincoln with the New York plates and that pop-up trailer with the three-wheeler parked next to it. Last trailer on the right."

"Thanks." He rolled up the window and waited for her to back away from his truck before setting off.

It was hot and had been dry for too long without a rain, so he drove even more slowly than he ordinarily would have, not wanting to kick up too much dust from his wheels.

He found the last travel trailer on the right and just parked there in the improvised road and got out, tucking the suitcase under his arm as he aimed toward the sliding glass door that was obviously the entry to the trailer. It was closed, and he started to lift his hand to knock on it, but the sight of Georgia through the tinted glass stopped him cold.

At first, he thought she was naked, before he realized that the sports bra and body-hugging shorts she wore were nearly the same shade as her skin.

The next thing he thought was that for someone who'd been banged around inside a car only four days earlier, she was remarkably...flexible.

He realized he was angling his head, studying her contorted position. She was sitting on the floor, one leg stretched straight out to the side and one bent sharply at the knee. Her upper torso was lying on the extended leg, but was sort of twisted so her shoulders faced up. Her arms were above her head and her hands were cupping her foot.

And then he realized that she had seen him and was watching him watch her.

He straightened his head and rapped his knuckles against the glass.

"It's not locked." He could hear her voice through the door. She didn't uncontort herself.

He had the day off work, he reminded himself. And plans to spend it at the lake. So he would just deliver the damn suitcase and move his ass on out of there.

He slid open the glass door and stepped into the hotbox that was her trailer. He placed the suitcase on the floor inside the door before pulling off his hat. "Would have thought a trailer like this would have air-conditioning."

"It does."

"Don't know how to turn it on?"

"I know how. Mind closing the door? You're letting out my heat."

Hell, why not? The sight of her already had him feeling ten degrees too hot on the inside. He slid the door closed.

She slowly untwisted her torso, rolling forward until her nose was two inches from the ground in front of her, then smoothly straightened her spine upward, groaning a little as she did so. "I see my suitcase has at last been freed." She looked up at him, drawing in a deep breath that stretched the opaque fabric nearly blending into her flesh and straightened her bent leg until both were spread apart, high-school-cheerleader wide. "I should probably be glad it only has a broken handle and a few dents in it, right?"

He looked down at the somewhat battered suitcase that

had likely cost what he earned in a month and nodded silently, because if he tried to get a word past the constriction in his throat, he'd sound like a croaking frog.

"It was nice of you to bring it." She lifted her arms out to her sides, then above her head, crossing her wrists and pressing her palms flat together. She arched to the right. "I hope it didn't take you out of your way." Then she arched to the left, not as deeply and, judging by her expression, more painfully. "You're, ah, you're not in uniform."

He cleared his throat. It was hard not to look at her, but he did his level best by pretending an interest he didn't feel in the tiled backsplash of the little kitchen behind her. He was still seriously—painfully—aware of the smooth, strong and utterly feminine body on display right in front of him. The only things marring the perfection were the bruises. Darker today than they'd been the night before last at the cocktail party. "Day off."

She finally sat straight again and lowered her arms. The hair that had been bundled on top of her head came down with the single pluck she gave it and she roughly rubbed her fingers through it, shaking out the thick brown strands until it streamed messily past her beautiful, bare shoulders. She swiped the overlong bangs out of her eyes. "Is it against the law to tell you that 'day off' looks good on you?"

He felt the back of his neck heat again. He was wearing a plain white T-shirt and blue jeans because everything else he owned, pretty much, had been accumulating in his laundry basket for too damn long.

His mom might mend his uniforms for him and keep him supplied with homemade leftover meals, but he drew the line at her doing any of his laundry.

"If you're off, who's minding the shop in your absence?"

"I've got a couple deputies and a dispatcher-slash-everything-else."

"Really?"

"Did you think Paseo was so small it could get by with just me?"

"Maybe. So with this huge staff of yours, do you have every Saturday off?"

"Not even close," he said while she pushed to her feet and plucked a fluffy white towel off the chair beside him and tossed it around her neck.

Thankfully, it did a good job of covering her breasts, which were so lovingly outlined by the sports bra.

When she turned to walk barefoot into the kitchen area, however, that towel didn't do a damn thing where the perfection of her rear end was concerned. The beige shorts she wore were cut more modestly than the white ones she'd been wearing the day of her accident, but they still bore a close resemblance to underwear.

He tapped his hat against his thigh, dragging his eyes away as she pulled a chilled bottle of water from the refrigerator and pressed the side of it to her throat.

"Today's the first time in months," he muttered, more or less clearly. "I've got the whole weekend."

"Glory be." She gave him a considering look. "Then I really owe you my thanks. Would you like some water?"

Only if it had a whiskey chaser, and here it wasn't even noon yet. He thumped his hat against his leg again and pretended he didn't feel like a ten-year-old boy who'd just discovered girls. "I'm fine."

"Are you sure? It *is* pretty hot in here and you look a tad—"

He waved his Grayson Gear hat in the air between them. "I'm fine," he repeated. He cleared his throat again. "Thank you all the same."

She let the refrigerator door close and rounded the island to prop her hip against one of the stools. She shoved her hair away from her face and stretched out one leg, pointing and flexing her purple-painted toes in an absent sort of way as she twisted open the sealed plastic cap of the water bottle.

He had the sense that she recognized his discomfort and was enjoying it.

Typical woman.

"I called that number you gave me at the party," she said. "For the massage therapist."

"Hope it helps."

"It might have, if the person was still in business. All I received was a message saying they had closed up shop and moved on." She took the ends of her towel in her hands and stretched it wide. The scrapes on her neck were already healing but the bruised scratch on her forehead still looked tender where she'd pushed aside her hair.

But she'd lost the tired look she'd had the night of the party and her eyes were bright and sparkling. She didn't have a lick of makeup on her face and everything about her—except for the bruises and scrapes—seemed bright and sparkling.

"I'm left with yoga and my yearning for a long soak in a big, deep tub." Her lips curved up at the corners and a faint dimple appeared in her cheek. "Dear Uncle Gerald arranged a lot of conveniences and niceties for us all, but even he didn't have the foresight to bring in a soaker tub for travelers who couldn't keep their cars on the road."

"You could go home." It was easy to imagine her sunk chin-deep in bubbles. Fortunately, imagining wasn't the worst crime he could think of.

"And miss the wedding of the year? No thank you. I've

come all this way and I intend to see it through whether my back is killing me or not."

"Don't know many people who can turn themselves into a pretzel like you were doing if their back is killing them."

"I should be able to do that pretzel on both sides." She leaned to her left, grimaced and straightened again. "Tight as all get out." She dabbed one end of the towel at her chin. "So what does a sheriff do when he's got his first weekend off in months?"

"He goes fishing."

Her smile widened and that faint dimple flashed again. "Why am I not surprised to hear that?"

He turned up his palms. "Better than some vices I could name."

"No doubt," she drawled, eyes alight with amusement. "I, myself, could name some vices, too. Every single one more entertaining than the last."

"We can't all spend a couple weeks frolicking around at a rich man's playground. I've also got laundry to catch up on and dinner at my mom's house tomorrow afternoon."

"Aren't you the good son?" She took a sip of her water and a drip of condensation fell off the bottle, landing with slow precision on her thigh.

Not particularly. "And you? Besides playing pretzel in an oven, what's on the agenda for you today?"

"Ah. You say that lightly, but there is, in fact, an agenda for this particular playground." She lifted a sheet of paper that had been sitting on the island. "Voilà." Her bright gaze moved from him to the paper. "Hot dogs and water-balloon fights for the kid in all of us this afternoon. Steaks and stargazing tonight."

"You'll have a good view of the sky here. No bright lights to speak of for miles and miles."

"Yeah. Marcia says the area is a two or three on the Bortle scale."

"Do you even know what the Bortle scale is?"

She spread her hands. "Please. What do I look like?"

The laugh came out of him from nowhere. "Oh, darlin'. You really don't want me to answer that, do you?"

Chapter Six

Did she?

Georgia's skin prickled. Her mouth was dry. She tucked her tongue against the back of her teeth for a moment, watching those warm mossy eyes grow even warmer. "Well, I don't know," she said huskily. "Am I going to want to throw a pan or something else at your head, if you do?" Something like herself?

He chuckled and she didn't quite know how to explain away the strange feeling inside her that sort of rippled in response. It was as unfamiliar as that sense of safety he'd given her, the memory of which still nagged at her.

Attraction was one thing. This was…lagniappe. Definitely a little something extra.

She swallowed. Then took a drink of water because her mouth still felt dry.

Faint lines formed at the corners of his eyes as his smile widened slightly.

It was the first time she'd seen him wearing something other than the khaki-and-brown uniform. He'd looked both imposing and comforting in that uniform. Now he just looked—

Like a complication?

She ignored the taunting voice inside her head and set aside the bottle. She tugged on the ends of the towel still draped around her neck and straightened away from the stool. Until now, she'd marveled over how spacious her trailer was. Now, with him standing there so tall in front of the glass door, his shoulders so broad and defined in his plain white T-shirt as he nearly blocked the sight of the tent across from her, the space felt like it was shrinking by the second.

She didn't dislike that, either.

Would a little vacation dalliance with the sheriff really be so bad? She wasn't as naive as Belle. Her little sister might act as if she had the world by the tail, but Georgia knew better. While she, on the other hand, specialized in short-term, meaningless dalliances, since it described every attempted relationship she'd ever had.

Things didn't *have* to get complicated with Pax after all. Not if she kept her head.

"Okay." She shifted her weight from one foot to the other. "So what *is* the Bartle scale?"

"Bortle."

She gestured, the towel still bunched in her fist. "Whatevuh," she said, deliberately emphasizing her Southern drawl. "Bortle."

He chuckled again and the sound was low and male and delicious in a way that whetted Georgia's appetite as it hadn't been in, well, forever.

"It's a measurement that basically ranks from one to nine how dark the sky is in any particular location accounting for light pollution. Or lack of it. The darker the sky—and the lower the score according to Bortle—the brighter everything up there is. Bright stars are good. Bright skies are not."

"That hardly takes a genius to understand. More stars are visible outside of a city than inside of one."

"Yeah, well, when it comes to viewing celestial…stuff, Bortle is a good way to figure out how light pollution affects the view. Of course, there are more ways to measure sky brightness. SQMs and photographic evidence—" He broke off when she started to smile. "If you were an amateur astronomer you'd probably appreciate all that."

"I'm taking it that *you* are an amateur astronomer."

He frowned darkly, as if she'd just called him the biggest nerd of nerds. "Not even close."

She stepped closer. "Are you sure? You seem to know a lot of details about this Bortle business."

He actually backed up a step, which—shameful as it was—delighted her no end.

He couldn't go far, though, because the closed glass door was at his back.

"We've had a number of people visit the area specifically because of our dark night skies." His voice seemed a little gruff to her. "We're not as dark as Big Bend Ranch State Park down by the Mexico border—they're a class one—but we're right up there with any of the state parks that are ranked as a two. Couple folks here are trying to get Paseo designated as an International Dark Sky Park."

Heaven help her, she was positively charmed by the tough-guy sheriff with a hidden nerdy center. "Is this common-knowledge kind of stuff or should I be suitably impressed?" She realized she'd moved even closer to him than she'd intended when her knuckles actually grazed against that black cowboy hat that he'd suddenly moved between him.

Even with the hat acting as a barrier, she could feel the heat radiating off of him.

"Don't think you'll have to ask the question when you're

lying flat on your back staring up at the sky and you see the Milky Way rising above you." His voice was even gruffer.

Her imagination immediately conjured images of him rising above her, and her entire body warmed deliciously. "Sounds...amazing."

His shoulders moved, stretching against the white cotton even more. "Georgia—"

"Not just mossy green," she murmured. There were flecks of amber and blue between those thick black lashes of his.

"Pardon?"

She inched closer and couldn't help but smile a little at the sound of him bumping the glass door. "You have a girlfriend, Sheriff? A wife?" It was one thing to indulge in a little fantasy and another entirely to take action.

His eyebrows pulled down and annoyance cooled those eyes. "If I did, you think I'd be—" He broke off, his jaw clenching.

"Be what?"

He just swore, though, pushing her gently but firmly to one side while he reached behind him.

A moment later, he'd produced a phone that she realized must have been vibrating, because he held it to his ear. "What?" He slid open the glass door and stepped outside, closing the door behind him.

She dropped down onto one of the recliners and exhaled, pulling the towel from behind her neck to press it to her perspiring throat while she watched Pax pace outside as he held the phone to his ear.

She wasn't embarrassed. Not exactly.

But the interruption did offer a timely moment for caution. For hesitation.

Nineteen times a bridesmaid, she had plenty of experience with the whole hookup thing that occurred during the frenzy of a wedding. Bride's attendants sleeping with groomsmen. Or, in two separate cases that she knew for certain, the groom. She could use up all of her fingers and toes counting the dalliances she'd witnessed. Some ended easily, both participants on the same page. Some added more and more drama to an already ripe-for-drama situation.

Georgia had just never been one of them.

She'd been doing PR for investment firms during some of the most volatile economic times in generations.

Drama was never something she deliberately sought out.

And just because she specialized in short-term didn't mean there'd been all that many who'd actually made it to "term." She didn't even need all the fingers on one hand to count the number of men she'd actually allowed into her bed.

She looked out the window at Pax.

He was facing away from her, one hand raised to squeeze the back of his neck. The action only accentuated the spread of his shoulders and tugged up the T-shirt enough that she could see a wedge of skin above the edge of his jeans. It was just as tanned as the arms showing beneath the short-sleeved shirt, and she was immediately beset with images of him sans shirt altogether.

Of course, Pax was not part of the wedding folderol. He was the local sheriff.

And she was just trying to justify.

"Georgia, Georgia, Georgia," she muttered to herself. "It really *has* been too long since you've been flung."

She pushed off the chair and went to the small cupboard, which she'd discovered hid a fancy little Robinson Tech R-tab that automated all of the controls for the travel trailer, then tapped an icon on the screen, turning on the air-conditioning unit. She'd deliberately kept the trailer as hot as she could while she'd practiced her yoga in hopes that it would help her muscles loosen. Now, though, she just wanted things to cool off.

With the AC rumbling comfortably to life and Pax still pacing around outside while he spoke on the phone, she closed herself into the bathroom, tossed her yoga togs onto the floor and stepped into the narrow shower.

The sun was shining through the skylight overhead as she washed and rinsed her hair.

What would it be like to watch the stars with Pax?

Pretty amazing.

She turned up the cold water and turned her face into it, blindly reaching for her lavender-scented bar of soap.

It popped right out of her hand, though, when she heard a thump on the bathroom door. "You going to be a while in there?" Pax's voice was perfectly audible above the water.

She leaned over and grabbed the soap, quickly running it over herself. "Do you want me to be?" She rolled her eyes at herself. Obvious much?

The beat of silence that followed was enough to make her shiver even without the encouragement of the cold shower.

She leaned her head against the crystal clear shower enclosure. "Pax?"

She heard a soft thump and then his voice. "That was Charlie on the phone." His voice sounded flat. "The insurance adjusters came to see the car."

She had her phone now. It had been sitting on the charger all morning. The screen might be cracked, but she knew the thing was working just fine because she'd been answering texts and emails from the office that had been piling up since the accident. "Without even trying to contact me first?"

"I don't know. I need to get over there."

"Wait!" She shoved the bar of soap back on the little ledge designed for it and shut off the water. "Just hold on a sec." She grabbed one of the fluffy towels from the stack of them and twisted it around her head. Then she took another, wrapping it around her torso, and shoved open the bathroom pocket door to face him. "What's going on? Why the hurry?"

His eyes raked over her and even though she was more covered now than she had been the night of the party in that scrap of a dress from Belle, it felt like he was seeing right through the thick white cotton.

"I want to get over there before they screw up my evidence."

She clutched the knot over her breasts, feeling her stomach fall. "E-evidence? What is that supposed to mean?"

He leaned over her. "I asked you the other night if there was anyone who might want to tamper with your car and you denied it. Too vehemently. I thought it at the time, and I think it now. So why don't I ask the question again? Who have you pissed off?"

She tightened the knot on her towel. "I haven't pissed off anyone! And why are you talking to me like I've done something wrong? Last I recall, I was the one behind the wheel when my car decided it preferred air travel over road, so—"

"You're pissing *me* off because I can tell you're not being entirely forthright!"

They both startled when the sliding door to the trailer opened and her brother Nolan stood there, frowning at them both. He was holding little Stella in his arms. "What the he…eck is going on in here? Could hear the two of you shouting from across the campground."

"Save me from men who exaggerate," Georgia muttered. She pointed at her brother. "Aren't you supposed to be playing horseshoes?" A tournament was planned, with Marcia driving the schedule with the precision of a military general.

Nolan pointed his finger back at her. "Don't you ever get tired of bossing me around?" He nuzzled his daughter's velvety soft-looking cheek. "Auntie Georgia is being a *B-I-T*—"

"I don't have time for this." As enchantingly nerdy-macho as Pax had been before, he looked equally annoyed and impatient now. He stepped around Nolan and Stella with a terse "'Scuse me," as he left the trailer.

Georgia didn't give her little brother a glance as she hightailed it after the sheriff. "Hold on! It's my car. I want to go with you."

He turned and his emerald gaze raked her from head to toe. "I get that you're comfortable parading around in front of people nearly naked, but folks around here are a little more conservative than that."

"Seriously? First you accuse me of—of, I don't know what, and now this?" The dirt under her bare feet was scorched from the sun, making her practically dance from one foot to the other. As a general rule, she didn't have a hot temper, but he had the ability to bring it out of her in spades. "You want to see what naked really is, Sheriff?" She reached for the knot holding her towel in place.

"Whoa, sis." Nolan's arm suddenly surrounded her shoulder as he wheeled her around so she was facing the door to her trailer rather than Pax's truck. "No Lady Godiva tricks here. You've got an audience."

She jerked out from beneath his arm. "Don't you leave without me," she warned Pax.

"Or what?" He yanked open the truck door. "You'll chase after me in your towel?" He climbed inside. Then he gestured impatiently. "Make it quick, then. I told you, I don't want to lose my evidence."

Evidence. ·

The mere word sent chills through Georgia.

She darted inside, nearly tripping over the dented suitcase he'd delivered. Clothes! That's right, she had her own stuff.

She grabbed up the suitcase in her arms and tossed it on the bed in the bedroom. She had a frustrating time with the zipper, made worse because she was almost certain that Pax would drive off without her. When she finally succeeded, she blindly grabbed the first thing off the top and pulled the cotton maxi sundress over her head. When she heard an impatient horn honk, she shoved the panties she'd finally found into her pocket with one hand and grabbed her brush with the other hand. She stuffed her feet into her sandals as she ran back outside.

The truck was still there, its engine running.

"Close up for me," she said as trotted past Nolan and Stella to yank open the passenger door of Pax's truck. She practically threw herself into the seat.

Breathless, she yanked the door closed and raised an eyebrow at him as if she wasn't sitting there with nothing separating the upholstered seat from her bare bottom except for a cotton, tropical print dress. "Well?"

His jaw slid from one side to the other.

Then he put the truck in gear and they drove off.

Chapter Seven

By the time Pax pulled off the highway and turned up a narrow, roughly paved road, Georgia had detangled the mess of her wet hair, cursed the fact that she'd actually forgotten her cell phone back at her trailer and decided that enduring Pax's fulminating silence for the past twenty minutes had been worse than enduring any number of infuriating words from him.

When he stopped next to a chain-link fence surrounding a shack of a house, she really wished she had her cell phone in her pocket. But instead of feeling the phone's familiar hard edges against her palm—a symbol of civilization being just a call away—all she felt was a hank of stretchy lace that should have been covering her rear instead of bunched up in her pocket.

And she was left with that same feeling she'd had as a girl, trying to keep up with Austin, Draper and Beau when their grandmother sent them out crawfishing. If Georgia wanted to do what they were doing—and she usually did—she'd better get over the bugs and the snakes.

Now, instead of bugs and snakes, she needed to get over the snarling fangs of a huge, pinkish-white dog.

On the other side of the fence, the vicious-looking animal ran back and forth, barking wildly. The only portion of yard not congested with weeds was the track of raw dirt the dog had obviously worn bare.

She really and truly did not want to get out of the truck next to that dog. "I thought we were going to see about my car." She had to raise her voice to be heard above the canine racket.

"We are." He got out of the truck and slammed the door shut. "Quiet, Betsy."

Instead of being cowed, the dog's barking just grew even more frenzied.

Georgia's door was a foot away from the fence, but the dog still managed to shake the drool from its bared teeth across the distance and it landed with a splat against the window.

"Crud on a cracker," she muttered, jerking back instinctively. She so did not want to get out of the truck.

Pax took the matter out of her hands when he yanked open her door. "Don't have all day, Georgia."

She swallowed her misgivings. He was the sheriff. It wasn't as if he was leading her to Paseo's very own house of horrors.

"Right." She slid off the seat, being careful to keep the folds of her dress down where they belonged. The sleeveless V-neck tunic reached all the way down to her ankles, but there were still slits on the sides that reached up to her knees, and despite her hotheadedness with her bath towel, she really was not in the habit of parading around naked.

The second her soles hit the ground, the dog's triangular head loomed even closer, its teeth showing and big paws clawing at the fence as if she was desperate to climb right over it.

"Ah, Betsy, calm down." Pax reached out and scrubbed his fingertips over the dog's head between her floppy ears. "You're gonna scare the lady out of her knickers."

Georgia wasn't one who blushed easily. But she felt her cheeks get hot, as if Pax knew exactly what was bunched in the fist she was hiding in her dress pocket.

"She's a noisy thing, but she wouldn't hurt a fly," Pax assured her. He gave the dog's head another pat. "Only had one treat with me today, Betsy, and you gobbled it up the first time I was out here."

Georgia realized then that the dog's abbreviated excuse of a tail—it wasn't exactly docked, nor did it seem fully sized—was wagging like crazy.

And if she looked beyond the wicked incisors, the dog looked like she was actually smiling.

"This is where Charlie works on cars?" She tried hard to keep the skepticism from her voice as she looked past the dog to the run-down house standing among the weeds.

"That's where he lives. He has a shop 'round back for work. Betsy, *down*."

The dog whined, but finally lowered her paws from the top of the fence. She plopped down on her rump and looked positively pathetic.

"Next time I'll bring two treats," Pax promised and the dog's stumpy tail thumped the dirt, sending a wave of dust up and over her already dusty white coat. As soon as he started walking away, Betsy turned her eyes on Georgia and gave a hopeful *woof.*

"Sorry, Betsy. I'm just with him." Georgia poked her thumb in the direction of Pax.

Betsy let out a huge sigh and stretched out on the

ground. She yawned and laid her huge, triangular head on her paws. Her light brown eyes blinked up at Georgia.

Pax started walking farther up the narrow road and Georgia skipped several times to catch up to him. As soon as she did, she immediately saw why he had chosen to park by the house.

Beyond it was the garage, large enough to hold several houses the size of the little weed palace, with half a dozen garage doors that looked two stories high. Vehicles of every size and condition were parked nose-to-bumper in the parking area in front of it. There was even a speedboat on a trailer among them.

"Is this a junkyard or a repair shop?"

"Right now it looks like both." He scanned the mélange with what seemed a practiced eye and his lips compressed with displeasure.

"What's wrong?"

"No strange cars." He angled his shoulders as he walked between a commercial tour bus and a tractor, clearly aiming for one of the opened doors.

"How can you tell?" She saw plenty of strange cars. "Does Charlie have the only repair shop around?"

"No, but he's the best in a 150-mile radius." He made it through the logjam and walked into the cavernous space.

She followed and immediately spotted her vehicle, despite its dismantled state.

It had been several days since Pax had cut her out of the vehicle, and the sight of it was a blow.

Wrapping her arms around her middle, she looked away, shivering despite the warmth of the day. "Is there a…um, a restroom here?"

"Through the office." He pointed at an enormous structure filled with rows upon rows of tires. "Other side of the rack. I'm going to find Charlie."

She nodded. Took another glance at the car.

A cloying wave of heat crawled over her.

Her legs felt shaky as she walked past the car and then past the tires. The strong odor of rubber added to the churning in her stomach and she quickened her pace, entering the office through a swinging door. The restroom was across the room, easily identified by the metal sculpture of a toilet on the door.

Despite the number of vehicles that had clogged the parking area, there wasn't another soul in the office. All of the black-and-white checkered chairs lined up against the wall were empty. She went into the bathroom and closed the door behind her.

The room was neat. Scrupulously clean.

She stared at herself in the spotless mirror over the pedestal sink. The bruise on her forehead had already begun yellowing, but it stood out against her pale face. As did the shadows under her eyes.

She heaved out a breath, trying to heave the memories of the accident from her mind, as well.

From outside the door, she heard muffled voices and quickly turned on the water, running her wrists beneath the chilly stream as the sickening heat inside her subsided.

She added some soap and properly washed and dried her hands before she pushed back through the door into the office. She stopped midway, mentally slapping herself for not emptying her pocket properly as well, and started to back up.

But Pax had already spotted her. "Good. There you are." He gestured toward Charlie. "Go ahead and tell her."

She swallowed, her nerves ratcheting tighter all over again. She looked from Pax to Charlie's weathered face and let the door swing closed behind her. "Tell her what?"

"I tried to keep those insurance fellas here, but they

were in a damn hurry once they got wind o' what I'd discovered. Pardon my language, miss."

"What did you discover?"

"You know cars these days are full of microprocessors. Computers running this thing and that thing."

"I...yes, I guess I do. I know I can start my car with an app on my cell phone." Which she'd left sitting on the charger back at her trailer. "Or at least I could until... you know."

"Right." Charlie was nodding. "And cars these days have an EDR. An event data recorder."

"Okay."

"A black box," Pax explained. "Like on airplanes."

She sank down onto the edge of one of the checked chairs. "Sure. Whatever."

"Your insurance folks didn't want me to remove it or access the data—they usually don't. Nothing unusual in that. But after what I found doing the autopsy—"

"Autopsy!"

"Just my bad sense o' humor, Miz Georgia." Charlie rubbed the white whiskers on his jaw. "When I'm pulling apart things trying to figure out what went wrong, kinda seems a little like one."

"Just cut to the chase, Charlie," Pax interjected. "Tell her what you think."

"I think the electronic systems on your car were hacked. It's the only thing that makes sense of the way everything was malfunctioning."

"Hacked." Her stomach was tightening again. She stopped worrying about her uncharacteristic forgetfulness where her phone was concerned and started worrying instead about what Charlie was actually saying. "You're not talking about a bad wire or crossed connection. You mean like *computer* hacked."

"Yeah. There were crossed connections all right." Charlie sat behind a metal desk that held nothing on top. Not even a phone. He opened a drawer and pulled out a manila file folder, spreading it open. "But nothing mechanical in nature. And nothing that leads me to believe it's a manufacturing defect. That's what your insurance folks are claiming, so better prepare yourself for a long wait on getting your insurance settlement ironed out." He knocked his knuckles lightly against the sheets of paper inside his folder. "Seen it before. They'll blame the car maker. Rather than cop to a lemon, the car maker blames the driver. It's a nasty cycle and you're the one caught in the middle."

"Mr. Esparza—Charlie—I'm less concerned about the insurance settlement than I am this *hacking* business." She'd bought the car outright, so there was no lender who'd be anxious to recoup their loss. It was only her severely dented savings that would need to recover.

She looked toward Pax. "I've been hacked before. Earlier this year, but it was work-related." And a mighty huge pain it had been, too, involving computer replacements and even her cell phone. It had set her back nearly a month on the promotional plan consuming her department. "He's telling me someone really did tamper with my car? By hacking? It's not just a theory. He can prove it?"

"Can't prove jack since they took the EDR to preserve the crash data," Charlie said, looking peeved. "Which is only gonna show them that instead of slowing through that mild curve on the highway, you accelerated and steered straight into the guardrail."

"But I didn't! I know I wasn't accelerating!" She looked toward Pax, but his expression was unreadable.

"And I believe you." Charlie nodded.

"If this EDR thing says otherwise, though, what else makes you think—"

"I've written it all out here for you." Charlie slid a sheet of paper toward her. "It's kinda technical, so…"

She could see that for herself as she picked it up and scanned it. The page was covered with lines and lines of typing, which ought to have been easy to read, but was instead just a long series of what looked like scientific equations.

"I don't read foreign languages like this," she murmured. She slid the paper back onto the desk, looking from Charlie to Pax again.

"You couldn't have stopped the car from going off the embankment if you'd tried," Pax said.

"If it hadn't happened there," Charlie said, "it would have happened somewhere else. That much seems clear."

Georgia exhaled shakily. She pushed her fingers through her damp hair, then pulled it away from her face. "Nothing seems clear about this."

"Thanks, Charlie," Pax said.

As if the mechanic had been waiting for the signal, he closed the file folder and hopped out of his chair. "I'm real sorry about this, Miz Georgia," he said as he headed to the door back into the garage area. "I wish I'd had better news for ya." His gaze went to Pax. "Need anything else, I'll be out back in the boneyard." He went through the door and Georgia saw him pull on the ball cap that had been shoved into the back pocket of his overalls.

Pax moved into her line of vision, arms crossed over his wide chest. "Now. Want to tell me who has it in for you? Or should I just start investigating on my own? When you had the accident, you mentioned your sister having a break-in. Is it related?"

"I don't know! This is all crazy," she muttered. She stood up and spread her hands. "Connor warned us, but I didn't want to believe—"

"Who is Connor?"

She started to rub her forehead, then remembered the tender bruise and satisfied herself with the press of her fingertip against the pain between her eyebrows. "Connor Fortunado. He's a cousin."

She explained how the private investigator had approached her family—all of Julius Fortune's progeny, Connor's family included—with his suspicions about Charlotte Robinson. He'd warned them all to take care because he believed that she was bent on exacting revenge on anyone connected to her ex-husband, Gerald—even his illegitimate siblings and their families.

Alarming her father for no good reason, she'd always thought.

"Nothing has ever been proven," she concluded. "And the woman has never even met any of us, so I just don't understand what possible satisfaction she'd have for targeting us like this."

"Where is she?"

She spread her hands. "That's kind of the problem. No one seems to know."

"She's the ex-wife of a Texas billionaire. She can probably go anywhere she wants in this world and ensure their silence just by greasing the right palms. As for her satisfaction? From what you've said, you have the right name."

Her lips twisted. "You know, my dad didn't even know he was a Fortune until he graduated from college. Up until then, he'd been Miles Melton. Only reason why he took the Fortune name as his own was because of the doors it opened. Because he took perverse satisfaction in succeeding all while bearing the name that had been deliberately withheld from him by his father."

"I want to speak to him."

"My father?" She shook her head. "Not a good idea."

"I meant Connor, but why isn't it a good idea to speak with your father?"

"First of all, he's the keynote at a big conference in Arizona right now. And secondly, because he'll want all of us to run back home to New Orleans! We were all safely removed there from this Charlotte business."

"Are you sure about that?"

"Of course." Her mouth dried a little as she looked at him. "Shouldn't I be?"

"This was a lot more than a simple break-in. It takes more than a simple swipe with a magnet for your car systems to be remotely controlled the way they were. It would have taken planning. Deliberate, premeditated planning. It's more likely that occurred in a location you were expected to be. Or where your car was at least expected to be."

"What do you mean? Like the dealership? Come on. How likely is that? Charlotte wouldn't have any way of knowing about the vehicle I'd ordered. I didn't even do it at the dealer." She'd done it online one night after another fizzled date and learning that her little sister had found herself a hero to fall in love with.

Instead of admitting that to her family, though, she had made a big deal about how excited she was to finally treat herself to the exorbitant luxury.

"It took two months to be delivered to the dealer! You're just trying to scare me, and I don't much appreciate it!"

His expression darkened. "Dammit, Georgia, you *should* be scared. You could have been killed!"

Her eyes felt hot. "So what am I supposed to do? Run home to New Orleans with my tail tucked between my legs?"

He raked his fingers through his hair, leaving the short, dark strands sticking up. "Until we know where

Charlotte Robinson is, I'd like to say the whole lot of you should head to your homes far away from—"

She cut him off. "You know how much planning has gone into the whole lot of us *coming* to Paseo?" She shoved her fists into her pockets and paced around the office. "You know, I didn't feel any particular loyalty to Gerald Robinson up until now. I was more curious about the rest of the family we've discovered. But now?"

She threw her hands wide, feeling anger balling hot and tight in her chest. "Let's say, circumstantial or not, that Connor has been right about everything. That he's been right about Charlotte. If that's the case, there's no way I'm gonna back down. She wants to wage war against my family? I'm not tucking my tail and running!" She pointed her finger at him. "And I can guarantee you that every one of my brothers and sisters is gonna feel the same way."

"I said I'd *like* to say you'd all be safer elsewhere. But when someone can pull off something as treacherous as this? Frankly, honey, I don't think any place is all that safe. One thing I can say positively is that y'all need to be taking better precautions." He leaned over and scooped something off the ground. He turned his palm up to expose the hank of stretchy white lace. "And carrying a spare pair of panties around isn't the kind of precaution I'm talking about."

She snatched them off his palm and pushed them back into her pocket. "So what kind of precautions are you talking about?"

He leaned his hip against the edge of the metal desk and folded his arms across his wide, wide chest. "Don't do anything alone, for one thing. Avoid following any sort of routine. Watch out for strangers."

"Half the people around the campground are still strangers!"

"They're Fortunes, aren't they?"

"That's what I've been told. They just keep arriving so it's hard to keep up." She paced the room, then turned around again. "Now you're making me suspicious of every unfamiliar face. How on earth are we going to keep this from reaching my father? He doesn't know anything about my accident."

"Damnation, Georgia! It needs to reach your father. The man needs to know that his faith in his car-dealer buddy may be misplaced. Doesn't matter how you ordered it, sweetheart. Someone, somewhere along the line, had direct access to your vehicle. I can make some calls. Do some inquiries. But now the data that could have conceivably been used to trace down anything useful is in the hands of your insurance company."

"Wouldn't they rather be able to blame a single person than an entire automobile manufacturer?"

"Whatever brings the biggest payoff is what they'll want." He grimaced. "That's always been my experience, anyway."

She couldn't help wondering if the tight expression on his face was from one specific experience, or a sum total of them.

"Is this Fortunado guy here for the wedding?"

She shook her head. "Not yet."

"Do you have his contact information?"

"Not with me." She spread her hands. "All I brought with me was my brush."

He waited a beat. "And spare panties."

She smiled weakly. "Sure."

He raised an eyebrow. "They're not spare?"

Earth, just swallow me up now.

Speculation and amusement filled his eyes at her lack of response. "Interesting."

She huffed. "You were rushing me!" She twisted around, intent on entering the bathroom to rectify the mortifying situation, but the sharp catch shooting down her spine froze her for a moment.

"What's wrong?"

"My QL." She exhaled as the pain subsided, then finished shoving open the bathroom door. Inside the room, she donned her underwear and glared at her reflection in the wall mirror. "Should've left them in the suitcase, Georgia," she muttered to herself. "He'd have never known you were going commando."

Pulling her dress back into place, she straightened her shoulders and went out to face him.

Amusement was still rife on his face.

"Not one word," she warned.

He spread his palms. "I wouldn't know what one word to choose."

She rolled her eyes and walked out of the office. Even though she hadn't planned to, she stopped when she reached her car. The doors had been cut off, and the wheels and hood had been removed, as well as the seats from inside.

Charlie had called it an autopsy and she could see why.

Pax stopped next to her.

"Can I borrow your phone?"

He handed her his cell phone. "What's a QL?"

"Quadratus lumborum."

"Sounds like a curse out of *Harry Potter*."

Despite everything, she smiled. "It's a muscle in the lower back on either side of the spine." She ran her thumb across the small device he'd given her. "I haven't seen one of these kinds of phones in years."

"It does what I need it to do. Make and take phone calls. Anything more than that is overkill around these parts.

We didn't even have cell service until the last few years, and then it was spotty at best. And don't even mention internet." He slid the phone from her hand and flipped it open, then handed it back to her. "You can thank your uncle Gerald for beefing up those particular situations."

"Why do I get the feeling you're not very thankful for it?"

"Paseo used to be pretty much off the grid. It was one of the last places in Texas—hell, probably half the US—where you could disconnect, for the simple reason there were no ways *to* connect in the first place. Damn straight I'm not very thankful."

"Inconceivable," she muttered as she punched in Austin's number. "I manage everything on my smartphone, from my calendar at work to brainstorming presentations with my department."

When her brother didn't answer after three rings, she disconnected. If he hadn't answered by then, he wasn't likely to. "I suppose it doesn't send a text message."

"It's not quite that antiquated." He took the phone from her and pushed a few buttons, then gave it back once again.

She quickly sent a brief message to her brother asking him to forward Connor's information to Pax's phone, then handed it back again.

He folded the phone in the palm of his hand. "You use your smartphone for anything *not* work-related?"

She peered inside the doorless car. "Everything in my life for the past few years has been work-related. Right up until last week, anyway." Without the seats inside the car, the seat belts that he'd cut to free her were hanging loose and limp.

Her chest felt tight and it had nothing whatsoever to do with any muscular trauma.

She stepped back. "Did I ever properly thank you for saving me from the car?"

"Depends on what you consider proper."

She looked at him for a moment, then stretched up on the toes of her platform sandals to wrap her arms around his neck. "Thank you," she whispered thickly. "And if you say you were just doing your job, I may hit you."

After a brief hesitation, his hands lightly circled her waist. She could feel the warm imprint of every single fingertip. "I *was* doing my job."

She blinked hard until the heat surging behind her eyes was under control again. Then she balled her fist and lightly punched his shoulder with it. "Warned you." She lifted her head to smile at him.

Those green eyes were soft. Mossy.

And focused on her lips.

She couldn't help it. What else could a woman do when her mouth ran dry like hers had? Not moistening them was impossible.

She felt his fingers flex against her hips. "Georgia."

Just that. One word. Her name. Said in his low, husky voice.

Flutters erupted in her veins. Nerve endings sparked. She took a deep breath, feeling the solid wall of his chest against her breasts.

She had never felt so thoroughly flung as she did in that moment.

And all it took was him saying her name.

Her breath eked out of her as she leaned closer, watching his eyes come nearer to her, lips hovering mere inches above hers.

"Yo, Charlie!"

They froze at the shouted greeting.

"You in here somewh— Oh, hey there, Sheriff."

Pax had straightened, his hands falling away from her, and it was such a loss, she wanted to wail in protest. Instead, she crossed her arms over her chest and stared at her toes while she struggled for composure.

"Deeter," Pax replied. "Didn't know you were back in town."

"Ma dropped me off so's I could get my truck." The intruder shuffled through the wedge of sunlight angling through the tall, open bay. He had an affable grin on his face, a paunch on his waist and flimsy pink thongs on his feet. "S'prised your brother didn't give you warning. He's the one drove me back to Ma's from my fine accommodations in Amber Falls. Who's your friend here?"

Pax looked resigned. "Deeter Hayes. Georgia Fortune."

"Pleased to meet you, Miz Fortune."

She managed a polite smile. There was nothing wrong with the other man, except his timing. "Mr. Hayes."

Deeter elbowed Pax, his grin widening. "Went to school with this ol' boy," Deeter told her. "You in town with all those other folks camped outside a' town?"

She nodded.

"Charlie's out back at the boneyard," Pax said a little abruptly.

As if he'd needed a reminder for the reason he came, Deeter snapped his fingers. "Oh, yeah. Right." He tipped the nonexistent hat on his dirty-blond head. "Maybe I'll see you around, Miz Fortune."

"Maybe."

Then he turned with a tuneless whistle between his teeth and walked back out into the sunlight.

"You don't want to see Deeter Hayes around anywhere," Pax said once they were alone. "He's friendly enough until he gets drunk and then he's an ornery son of a…gun."

"Is he ornery a lot?"

"Often enough. That's why I tossed him in the Amber Falls jailhouse." He stepped away from the car. And her.

Talk about the moment being broken.

And he obviously had no desire to recapture it, considering the way he aimed toward the wedge of sunlight.

She followed him. "What does your brother do?"

"Jasper is a police officer in Amber Falls."

"And your other brothers?" She distinctly remembered him telling her he had three.

"Redford's a cop with Austin PD. Marshall is a paramedic for Amber Falls." He gestured. "Watch out for the wheel chocks."

She dutifully stepped over the two chunks of rough wood tossed haphazardly on the ground. "And your mom farms corn. Deborah mentioned it at the party," she said at the surprised look he gave her.

"She farms corn." He skirted the tour bus. "Not as much corn as she could."

"Is that some reference to the field where we're camping?"

His shoulders moved restively.

"Why didn't you just tell me from the start the field was hers?"

"Why didn't you just tell me from the start that Gerald Robinson was your uncle?" He looked back at her.

She shrugged. "I don't know. It just didn't really seem relevant."

He lifted a hand. "There you go."

They rounded the run-down house again and Betsy immediately hurled herself toward her chain-link enclosure. Even though Georgia had seen for herself the dog's friendly nature behind all that barking, she still gave the fence a wider-than-normal berth. "Does she ever succeed in getting over the fence?"

"Oh, yeah. Usually because she's on a tear playing with another dog. She's a lot of noise so she makes a good alarm system for Charlie. But she'd lick an intruder to death before she'd ever hurt one." They'd arrived at his truck and he reached over the fence to the panting dog. "Isn't that right, girl?"

Betsy slathered his hand with sloppy kisses.

"See?" He wiped his hand on his jeans and opened the passenger door for Georgia. "Let's get you back to the campground."

She slipped between him and the door. "Do we have to?"

His gaze settled on hers. "Sooner or later, yes."

There was that grade-school feeling again.

But she wasn't in grade school. She was a grown woman who, if the suspicions were to be believed, had been the target of a crazy, spurned woman. And time— particularly Georgia's remaining time in Texas—was precious.

So she let her gaze linger on his lips. "I vote for later."

Chapter Eight

*L*ater.

Pax pulled himself out of the depths of Georgia's blue eyes. He brushed the tousled bangs away from her fore-head. They'd dried, but the rest of her hair was still damp and it swirled and curled around her long neck. Her bare shoulders.

He looked at the bruise on her forehead. "You can't avoid it forever." It was as much a reminder to himself as for her. "We need to tell everyone the truth about your accident."

"I won't avoid it forever. Just…for a while." Her fingers fluttered against his chest, her touch there, then gone just as quickly. "I'll even tell my father about it. Please?"

He was weakening, and she knew it.

"I haven't been fishing in a long time," she said, "but—"

"*You* fish?"

The corners of her lips curved. Her dimple appeared. "Don't sound so aghast. Yes, I've fished a time or two."

"For *fish*?"

She let out a breathless chuckle. "What do you expect me to say? For men?"

"Frankly? Yes."

"I don't usually have to cast a line for men, darling."

"I'll bet you don't."

Her smile widened. "I'm going to choose to take that as a compliment, whether you meant it as one or not. But as it happens, I'm more than a little choosy. Most get tossed back before getting close to the net."

"Heartening," he said dryly. It was either take the humor route or kiss her.

For the moment, humor was safer.

"All right, then." He lifted her right off her feet and set her up on the truck seat. "Fasten your seat belt. It's a bumpy ride out to the lake. And if you expect me to bait your hook, you're in for disappointment."

Her smile was so brilliant it was almost enough to eclipse his misgivings that he was heading down a road he shouldn't be traveling.

"Do I need a fishing license? Or does the sheriff get special privileges?"

"He does not." He shook his head. "But as it happens, we don't need a license where we're going."

"And where's that?"

"Martell Lake. It's on property my grandparents owned. My mom's folks."

"Your family has its own lake?"

"*They* did. When they died, the land was sold to pay debts, but it still carried the stipulation that their descendants would always be able to fish the lake." He chose not to mention that the section on which she and her relatives were staying had also been part of that land. Land that he'd promised his dad he'd finish paying off so the deed would finally be Cara's, free and clear. It had been his dad's final admission to Pax before he'd died. That he felt he'd failed his wife on that one thing.

And Pax, in turn, had failed to finish his father's work.

The bank still owned more of the land than the Prices' did.

"What did your grandparents do?" Georgia's light voice nudged into the dark mood descending on him.

"Farmed."

"And your dad? Did he grow up on a farm like your mom?"

"He was a cop from Dallas. From a long line of them. But he gave up the city when he met and married my mom and worked for the Amber Falls PD after that, until he died of a heart attack."

"I'm sorry."

"So am I."

"Was it expected that you follow in your father's footsteps? Or did you grow up knowing it was what you wanted to do?"

Joseph Price had been Pax's hero. His best friend. "I didn't intend to be a cop at all." The admission surprised him more than it ever would her. "When I went to college, it was on a baseball scholarship."

"Really!" She shifted sideways in her seat to face him and the vibrantly patterned dress parted like the sea, giving way to a lithe leg.

His fingers tightened on the steering wheel. They already knew how supple that smooth, tanned skin felt and wanted a repeat.

"Yeah, really."

"What position?"

"Shortstop."

"Like Jeter."

He gave a short laugh. "The same position. Beyond that, all comparisons to Derek Jeter leave me way back in the weeds."

She chuckled. "What were you studying?" She lifted her hand the second she finished the question. "No, wait. Let me guess. Astronomy or astrophysics or something like that."

"Honey, you're crediting me with way more brains than I really have."

"Okay, then what?"

"Poli-sci and law."

He expected the surprised silence.

"Wow," she said after a moment. "That's, um, unexpected. And not without a need for brainpower. Thinking about a political run sometime in the future?"

"Some would consider becoming sheriff to be a political run. I *did* have to be elected."

"Was anyone running against you?"

He smiled wryly. "No. But after eight years on the force in Dallas, I figured I was more qualified for the job than Harvey Kavanagh. He owns the hardware store in Paseo and was reluctantly going to put his name on the ballot if nobody else stepped up." He turned off the highway again, heading up the dirt road leading to the lake.

"So how does a political-science-and-law student end up becoming a police officer?"

"Idealism is fine until you see how the world really works."

"And how is that?"

"Money rules all."

Her eyes narrowed, more in study than displeasure. "That's not realism. That's cynicism."

"So says the woman from money. People who have it control the *Monopoly* board. End of story."

She made a soft "hmm."

"What's that supposed to mean?"

Her shoulders moved. She shifted again and a couple

more inches of leg were exposed. "Whoever she was must have really made an impression."

He gave her a quick frown. "What's *that* supposed to mean?"

"Nothing," she assured him blithely.

He glared at her for a moment longer with no apparent effect before the bumpy road took his attention again. "I didn't quit school because of a woman," he said after a while. "I quit because my dad had a massive heart attack when he was way too young to die."

"How old were you?"

"Twenty-one. I learned real quick then that life is precious. And short." It propelled him to follow in his dad's footsteps. It made him acknowledge what he wanted out of life. A home. A family.

"When I was twenty-one," she said as she flicked her fingers against the folds of her dress and her knee once again went undercover, "I was just starting my MBA."

"Did you always have an eye to public relations?"

She smiled and shook her head. "That was my father's suggestion. I had in mind being his next great financial analyst."

"What happened?"

"Besides sucking at it?" She rolled her eyes. "At first I was infuriated when he plopped me in the marketing department. He'd made his first million before Austin was born. I wanted to be like him. And I wanted to be better than my brothers in the worst way. I might have had the education—I was good enough at it to manage my own money pretty well—but I just didn't have the knack for managing anyone else's. You know that knack that elevates you from being the paint-by-numbers type in some pursuit to achieving true artistry? My dad has it. My brothers have it. Even Nolan, and he's more of a musician at heart.

"So there I was, sitting in the marketing department, annoyed and frustrated because I wasn't measuring up to what I thought I needed to measure up to and my mom—a woman who I'd always considered the pinnacle of propriety when it comes to family honor and duty—tells me to quit working for my dad and make my mark somewhere else." She smiled, her eyes looking distant with memory. "Nothing my mother had ever done or said shocked me, but that did. Ever since I could remember, we've had the importance of our family obligations impressed upon us. Yet she was telling me to chuck all that and take my own road."

"Did you?"

"For three years. I worked doing everything under the sun at first, but somehow everything kept heading back to marketing. When I took a job with a direct competitor of Fortune Investments and edged them out for the first time ever in media exposure, my dad came to me and actually pleaded with me to come back and work at FI. Offered me PR director and since then I've never looked back. He knew where my skills were best served all along, but I needed to figure that out for myself."

Their stories weren't entirely dissimilar. "I didn't know I could be a good cop, either. Until I was actually in the trenches becoming one."

"And now you're a sheriff. Bet your dad would be proud of you."

"My mom seems to think so." He gunned the engine as they passed over the rise before the lake. He wasn't so convinced.

Georgia suddenly sat forward in the seat, her expression eager. "It's beautiful!"

"Yeah." He coasted the vehicle down the hill, not coming to a stop until his front tires were inches from the water's edge. He turned off the engine and got out of the truck. Then he pulled out his tackle box from the truck bed and grabbed a couple of poles from the collection of them. "You sure about this?" he asked Georgia when she came up next to him.

"Absolutely."

"Okay. But remember, I'm not—"

"Baiting my hook for me. I know." She took one of the poles from him and turned toward the lake with a flip of her hair. "What's biting?"

"Crappie. You know what that is?"

She gave him a look. "I know *we* don't pronounce the *a* like in apple. It's *ah*. Like in crop."

He chuckled. "Says you, NOLA girl."

"Says everyone," she retorted on a laugh.

Two hours later, there were twice as many fish on the stringer from her line than there were from his.

"Fished a *time or two*?" He tossed the line of fish into the ice cooler he'd loaded into his truck bed that morning and turned to take the tackle box from her. "Remind me to never play poker with you."

She grinned. The afternoon sun hadn't only gotten too hot to produce any bites on their lines, but it had also put a shine of pink across her face. Her nose was pink. Her cheeks were pink. Even her forehead was pink, the bruise seeming less noticeable beneath the color. She'd twisted up her long hair with a length of fishing line and tied the long folds of her dress into knots around her knees with no more regard for the garment than if it was a rag.

"You need to crawfish with me someday." She stood on her toes in the designer sandals that were caked with mud and didn't seem to care as she placed their fishing poles into the truck bed. "Then I'd *really* impress you."

He was afraid he was already getting pretty damn

impressed. Whitney had always turned up her nose at fishing. And she had never looked less than magazine-perfect.

Until he'd gotten involved with her, he'd never thought "perfect" was all that desirable.

Looking at Georgia now was a reminder of what was. *Real*.

She wasn't any less beautiful than Whitney. She just seemed a whole lot more human.

Which made her a whole lot more dangerous.

She didn't seem to notice his silence as she scratched a bug bite on her arm. "What're you going to do with the catch?"

"What else? Cook it up for supper. It's getting to be that time." He swiped a fly from the pink skin on top of her shoulder and had to force his hand not to linger there. "Suppose I should invite you."

She raised her eyebrows at him as she moved to open the passenger door. "I suppose you should, seeing how I caught more than half of them." She bent down and a moment later had tossed her shoes—designer label, mud and all—into the truck bed. "Please don't tell me you're going to bake them or something equally dreadful."

"Hell, no. Little flour. Little cornmeal, salt and pepper." He got behind the wheel. "And fried in a couple inches of seriously hot oil."

Her eyes fluttered dramatically. "Pardon me while I drool on myself a little."

"Tell me about it," he muttered under his breath as he backed away from the lake and turned the truck around to head back to the highway.

"You ever cook up your fish right by the lake?"

"Lots of times. Too hot today, though." He slid another look in her direction. "And you're already sunburned."

"Don't forget mosquito-bitten." She scratched her arm again.

"You've earned an injury of one sort or another nearly every day since you arrived."

"I wish it was a simple matter of being accident-prone. Trouble doesn't usually follow me around." She tipped her head back against the seat rest and looked at him. "Thank you for allowing me to procrastinate, though. You know—about bringing all the suspicions about Charlotte back to everyone at the campground. It still makes no sense to me why *I'd* be targeted. I mean, the person who done her wrong is her ex-husband. You'd think he'd be the one she'd want to tar and feather."

"Guy like Robinson? Pretty hard to get close to, I'm guessing, even for an ex-wife. Maybe particularly for an ex-wife."

"Well, he was right out in the open the other night at the cocktail party, wasn't he? Wasn't surrounded by any sort of entourage or security. Aside from arriving in a helicopter, he was just a man who seemed genuinely besotted with his bride-to-be."

"Deborah's sons asked me to keep an eye on things."

Her eyebrows went up. "You mean you were pulling more than phone-police duty?"

"They wanted to make sure there was no trouble."

"I think it's more likely that any trouble cropping up is going to be between Gerald and his half brothers than Charlotte. I don't mean my dad. Not Connor's dad, either. One thing Miles Fortune and Kenneth Fortunado seem to have in common is their ongoing practice of distancing themselves from being a son of Julius Fortune. But the others? David and Gary? They came to Paseo, but it doesn't seem to me that they're any happier about things than my dad is." She shook her head. "Biologically, he's my grandfather, but I can't imagine what kind of man Julius must have been. Gerald made an entirely new identity for himself to get away from his parents. That's pretty drastic stuff. Then he goes and marries Charlotte. And she just seems more diabolical by the day."

She fell silent as he drove past the spot where she'd gone through the guardrail. The damaged portion had been removed by a road crew and a temporary barricade was in its place.

"What do you know about her?" Pax asked.

"Factually? Only what Connor Fortunado has told us. Charlotte was married to Gerald for something like thirty-seven, thirty-eight years. Put up with his infidelities even though it was pretty much common knowledge. I'm guessing the perks of being a mogul's wife were greater than the embarrassment. I don't know. Anyway, Connor's theory is that she snapped when Gerald started divorce proceedings. That she's behind some of the misfortunes—his word—that have occurred among the various Fortunes."

"Your accident was intended to be a helluva lot more than *misfortune*."

She made a sound that he took for agreement. She exhaled noisily and pulled the fishing line out of her hair, which then tumbled around her shoulders. "Do you like being sheriff?"

"Tired of talking about Charlotte?"

She smiled ruefully. "Tired of talking about all things Fortune. Tell me about all things Price."

"Everything has one."

She looked blank for a moment. Then rolled her eyes. "Ha ha. I get it. Everything has a price."

He smiled. "Yeah. I like being sheriff, but only because it's for *this* county. Any bigger an area and it'd end up being too political for my tastes."

"Such an admission for a former poli-sci student. What was it like growing up here?"

"Have you driven through town yet?"

"When my brother took me to Amber Falls to the urgent-care place there."

"Then you've seen how small it is. Nothing much has changed since I was a kid."

"And you like it that way."

"Should I deny it? Yeah, I like it that way. It's reliable. The people here care about each other in a way you don't find in the city. They've had to."

"Were you sheriff here when that tornado came through a couple years ago?"

"I was elected shortly after it."

"I read about it. Ariana... Jayden's wife? She wrote an article about a family here who'd lost everything in the storm. I read it online not too long ago."

"The Ybarras. They were at the party the other night, too. Paloma's good friends with Deborah."

"It was a wonderful story," she murmured. "The way the community all pitched in to help them rebuild."

"That's Paseo. I know disasters can bring huge communities together. But Paseo doesn't need the disaster. It's that way all the time."

"There's your town slogan." Her eyes sparkled as she ran her hand across an imaginary banner in the sky. "'Paseo. That way all the time.'"

He chuckled and turned off the highway onto the dirt road leading to his place and they fell silent for the remaining mile. "It's not much," he said when he pulled up in front of his small house. He parked on the grass that surrounded it because he had no such thing as a drive-way, or even a garage for that matter. "But it's home."

Home was an unexpectedly charming stone cottage surrounded by green grass and tall leafy trees.

Georgia smiled as she pushed open her door, and slipped out onto the grass. It felt springy under her bare feet. "It reminds me of my grandma's old house," she told him. "The one she had when I was little. I always loved visiting her there."

"Where does she live now?" He reached into the back of the truck to retrieve the ice chest and his T-shirt rode up a few inches.

It was a feast for one's eyes, that's for sure.

"Somewhere more befitting the mother of Miles Fortune," she answered dryly. She followed him around the small cottage. It was stone almost all the way around except for some pale green painted siding and white trim. "My father bought her a new house, and by God, she'd better like it."

He dumped the chest on the grass next to an iron patio table that was vaguely rusty and flipped open the gas grill sitting next to it that wasn't.

"Door's open," he told her, "if you want to get outta the sun. Bathroom's in the hall next to the kitchen. I'll be in, soon as I get the fish cleaned and the fire going."

"I'll help clean the fish."

He raised his eyebrows. "You?"

Indignant, she propped her hand on her hip. "Hey there, honey, I know how to get a reasonable fillet off the bone. I caught most of those fish, if you'll remember."

"True." One corner of his lips deepened. "Guess you *should* do most of the cleaning."

She grabbed a handful of the ice he'd exposed and flipped it at him, then laughed and darted through the

back door of the house when he made a move to recip-
rocate.

"Think you'll be safe in there?" he called.

Finding herself standing in his quaint little kitchen,
she pressed her hand to the fluttery sensation in her belly.
"You're the sheriff," she called back. "It should be your
duty to keep your visitors safe."

His laugh was deep and rich. "Keep telling yourself
that, darlin'."

The flutters got even flutterier and she hurried through
the kitchen. It was easy enough to find the bathroom right
where he'd said—in the hallway next to the kitchen.

What he hadn't said was that it was also next to a
bedroom.

His bedroom, if the basket full of rumpled clothes sitting on the foot of the wide bed was anything to go by.

She tiptoed closer to the room, peering through the
doorway. A quilt covered the bed. It was blue and gray
and green and faded, which made her think it was probably handmade. Maybe handed down from generation
to generation, because she simply couldn't imagine him
paying extra for that really authentic look the way so
many people did. Three pillows in white pillowcases were
at the head of the bed, bunched up against the industrial
metal headboard. No photographs on the nightstand. Just
a lamp and a… She took another step to see around the
edge of the doorway better—a holstered gun.

It made her realize that even though he'd always been
in uniform up until today, she hadn't ever noticed he'd
been armed.

A noise from the kitchen had her nearly jumping out
of her skin and she darted into the bathroom, closing the
door quietly.

The small exterior footprint of the house had been

warning enough that Pax's home didn't contain a lot of extra space. The bathroom where she now stood was probably the only one it possessed. There was a shower with a striped shower curtain, a sink with a cordless electric razor sitting on the edge and a toilet. Lid down.

Nothing fancy.

But aside from the faint smear of green toothpaste on the edge of the sink, it was as clean as Charlie's had been at the repair shop.

Georgia had grown up with four brothers and two sisters. None of them had ever been this tidy. She knew, because one of her chores growing up was cleaning the two bathrooms the siblings shared.

Even though Sarah Fortune had had a cleaning service, Miles had made certain his kids grew up knowing what real work actually was.

She supposed it was possible that Pax had someone come in to clean his place. Maybe even the same person who took care of Charlie's office and restroom. Maybe it was cleaning day for both places and Georgia just happened to catch them at the right moment.

For some reason, she hoped otherwise.

She liked thinking that Pax was responsible for the admirable state of his personal surroundings.

She used the toilet and washed her hands and tried to finger some order into her messy hair, but gave up and just wound it into a braid. She'd find something to fasten it with, even if it was another hank of fishing twine.

Mostly, she tried to wipe away the goofy smile that seemed permanently etched on her reflection in the mirror over the sink.

But it was pointless, and when she heard more clattering in the kitchen, she gave up altogether and left the bathroom. "Have to tell you, Sheriff, you really do get extra points for the clean— Oh!" She stopped short at the sight of the shapely redhead rummaging in the refrigerator, and felt her stomach plummeting. "Sorry, I thought—"

The woman straightened with a shallow pan in her hand and looked over at her. Unlike Georgia, she didn't seem surprised at all. She also was older than that hourglass figure had at first suggested. "Don't be sorry." She closed the refrigerator with her hip and moved to the sink to rinse whatever stuff was clinging to the inner corners of it. "I just stopped by to retrieve this pan from my son. He's always grateful when I have leftovers for him, but he's just terrible returning my dishes." Her mossy green eyes sparkled and she stuck out her hand. "I'm Cara Price."

The speed of recovery from plummeting to soaring should have alarmed Georgia. "You're Pax's mother." He had her eyes.

"I am indeed. And you are—"

"Georgia Fortune." She shook the woman's hand. It was slender and strong and slightly calloused.

Cara tucked her hair behind one ear and the pan under one arm. "You're the one whose car went off the highway."

"Guilty as charged."

Cara chuckled. "From what Pax told me about it, lucky as sin would be more like it."

"That, too."

If Pax's mother thought anything about Georgia's presence in her son's house, she was hiding it well.

Maybe Pax had women at his house all the time. How was Georgia to know? He'd said he didn't have a girlfriend, but that certainly didn't mean he had no interactions with women at all.

Gnawing at that particular thought, Georgia followed his mom back outside.

Pax had set a big white cutting board on the patio table and was deftly wielding a long thin knife as he filleted the fish in just a few strokes. Then he flipped it over again on his board and slid the knife once more, and the meat came away perfectly from the skin in a way that Georgia had never been able to master. He rinsed the fillet under the slow stream of water coming from the hose he'd rigged up next to the table, then tossed it in a bowl of clean water.

"You do that even better than your daddy used to," Cara said as she walked around him, studying the pile of fish already prepped and sitting in the bowl. "He never left the tail attached before removing the skin."

"Thought you were going to leave some of that work to me," Georgia commented.

His knife paused as he looked over at her. "Would have if you hadn't been taking forever inside."

She managed to keep her smile in place even though she felt her cheeks heat.

"Now, don't tease the girl," Cara chided. "Georgia, first thing you need t' learn when it comes to one of my boys—any boy, really—is to hush up and let the man work when he's actually inclined to do so. Joe Price was the love of my life, but Lord, that man did not know what to do in the way of cooking 'less he pulled it out of water on a hook."

Pax snorted. "Dad might have gotten away with it, but when did you ever let *us* sit around on our butts?" He tossed the carcass into a bucket on the other side of the table and pointed the tip of his knife at the ice chest sitting next Georgia's feet. "Hand me another, would you, please?"

Without thinking, she leaned to her left to pluck a fresh fish from the ice and sucked in air through her teeth when pain shot through her.

"Still hurting, I see."

"Mmm-hmm." She set the chilly fish down on the board and wiggled her fingers in the cold water coming from the hose. "It was feeling pretty good when we were fishing, but…" She dried her fingers with a piece of paper towel she pulled off the roll sitting on the patio table. "Just going to take time."

"Time in a hot bath if you ask me," Cara said with a nod.

"I don't disagree," Georgia said with a chuckle. She instinctively liked Pax's mother. "Unfortunately, my access to a bathtub at the moment is somewhat limited."

"Bring her to dinner tomorrow," Cara told Pax and before Georgia could properly digest that, his mom was looking back at her. "I'll get you set up with a bath to end all baths."

Then, in the vaguely awkward silence that followed, she patted Pax's shoulder and headed around the house on foot, a smile on her face.

"Did, uh, did she drive here?"

"No need." He jerked his chin. "Lives about a half mile up that way. Still in the same house where my brothers and I grew up."

"Oh." Georgia twiddled with the ends of her hair, pulling the braid tighter.

"She wasn't joking." Pax sliced the fish down the back. "About dinner. Or the bath." He didn't look at her as he shrugged. His T-shirt was still white, but sometime during the afternoon it had garnered several smudges of dirt. His sharp jaw, which had been clean-shaven earlier, was now blurred slightly by whiskers, and his dark hair had a hat ring from the cowboy hat that he'd discarded on the drive from the lake.

She'd never been more attracted to a man. "How, uh, how do *you* feel about that?"

He glanced up, one eyebrow raised.

She realized she was fiddling with her hair again and tossed the braid over her shoulder. "I don't want to intrude."

His lips twitched then. "Darlin', you're going to be an intrusion on tomorrow afternoon whether you're there in person or not."

She wasn't quite sure how to take that, but he didn't give her an opportunity to comment, anyway.

"Don't see any reason why you shouldn't at least benefit by soaking in my mama's big ol' iron tub," he continued. "Unless you've got some other wedding thing on your agenda."

She couldn't recall for the life of her what was on the schedule for the following afternoon.

And frankly, she didn't really care.

"Mind if I think about it?"

"Can think about it all the way up until dinnertime," he said, looking amused. "Mom always fixes enough to feed a crowd because she never knows for sure how many of us will make it in time for grub. If Redford—he's the youngest—can't get here from Austin, it means I have a lot more leftovers to see me through the week." He grinned and tossed the denuded carcass in the bucket before pointing with his knife again. "Still more in there?"

She looked down into the ice chest. "Quite a few." Being more careful this time with the way she leaned, she pulled another out and handed it to him.

"Good." His wet fingers brushed over hers as he took

the fish. His eyes were warm. Mossy. "'Cause I have an appetite it'll take a while to fill."

It was a wonder she didn't dissolve into a puddle right then and there.

"Anything I can do to help?"

"Just sit there looking pretty, NOLA girl, and relax."

She smiled and sat.

But it was going to take a lot of work to relax.

Chapter Nine

Hours later, still replete from the feast of delicately sweet, tenderly fried fish, Georgia had relaxed.

How could she not, stretched out the way she was on a blanket with Pax's darkened house fifty yards away while a million stars burst in the sky overhead? The earth was cool beneath the blanket and Pax was warm. He was patiently pointing out the names of the stars and the planets with an ease that delighted her.

She stretched out her arm, pointing to yet another pattern of stars. "And that one?"

"Cygnus." He wasn't lying beside her anymore. He'd only done so for a few thrillingly brief minutes before he'd moved to sit on the corner of the blanket, where he still was. In the starlight, she could see his arms resting on his drawn-up knees, a beer in his hand. "Now look back at Cassiopeia there." He pointed lower in the sky, closer to the horizon. "The last star on the left. Go up from that to the bright star."

"Polaris."

"Yep."

She sketched the brilliant shapes above her. "The Little Dipper and the Big."

"Follow Polaris downward and to the west, you'll pass Lynx—" He leaned some and gestured again, his finger drawing a line in the sky. "And there is Cancer, just above the shadow of that tree, there."

She thought she was following along, but she was honest enough to admit to herself, at least, that she was more fascinated with him than she was the night sky glittering above them.

"Another hour or so and you won't be able to see Cancer anymore. By midnight, Ursa Major's nose will be diving into the barn over there and looking like she's running across the horizon for a little bit."

With the absence of the sun, she was glad for the flannel shirt he'd given her. It warmed her and smelled of him, and she knew without a doubt that if he gave the slightest crook of his finger, she'd go straight into his arms.

She didn't even need the glass of pinot noir she'd been sipping to feel that way, either.

She rolled onto her side, propping her head on her hand. "It is a magnificent view."

He was looking up at the sky. The only lights on the horizon came from the direction of his mom's house and opposite that, from an occasional flicker from what she figured must be the highway.

"It's better after midnight."

"And with a telescope, it's probably even more amazing. How many do you have?"

He laughed softly. "Just one."

She squinted at him. "I think I'm surprised."

"It was my dad's. There's a little ridge of land not far from here where we used to go hunt stars. He told me once that he'd never been even remotely interested until he met my mom and moved here from Dallas and saw what a sky was really supposed to look like." She heard his faint sigh. "I haven't gotten it out in a while."

She would lay odds not since his dad died. "You must miss him a lot."

He just nodded once and she decided it was better not to probe too far. "Are your brothers into astronomy, too?"

At that, he laughed again, shaking his head. "Nah, that was pretty much just me and my old man." He pointed again. "See that really bright one? Moving fast?"

She caught her breath. "A shooting star?"

"A jetliner."

She stretched out her bare foot and shoved lightly at his knee. "Smarty."

He chuckled and the sound rippled along her nerve endings. "When you get back to the campground, you can check your phone's app store. There are dozens of them that help navigate the stars. Doesn't even have to be dark outside for some to work. The maps show you the stars are still there whether you can see 'em or not." Then he lifted his beer and upended the last bit of liquid the bottle contained onto the grass beside them. "It's late. Probably should get you back to the campground."

"Mmm." She didn't waste the pinot by pouring it out. It was too delicious and it was helping keep her warm. But she did roll to her feet, holding the soft flannel shirt together at her neck with one hand while she finished the wine and he picked up the blanket. She'd hosed the mud off her sandals hours ago, but they still felt a little cold and damp when she slipped her feet into them. "Just so you know, when it comes to putting off an unpleasant task, you're pretty good at aiding and abetting."

"Just so you know," he returned softly, "you make aiding and abetting a pretty appealing thing." He lightly took her elbow and started walking back toward the house.

While she'd gorged herself on fried fish and grilled corn on the cob, he'd told her the house had been the first house his parents lived in after getting married. Then, when his mom got pregnant with Paxton, they'd built the larger one, where Cara still lived.

Before long, she was sitting in the passenger seat of Pax's pickup truck again and they were bumping along the unpaved road to the highway. He hadn't turned on the radio and the only sounds were his tires on the earth.

She'd never realized how intimate that could feel.

Just two souls, sitting alone together as they drove.

She almost laughed at herself. She usually saved the poetic images for her media campaigns.

Instead, she looked out the side window and peered out at the shadows of the cornfields they passed once he turned onto the highway.

He'd told her that most of their land produced field corn. Harvested long after sweet corn would be, it was sold to be used primarily as livestock feed.

The corn they'd had that evening with their fish, though, had been sweet corn. The sweetest, most tender corn she'd ever tasted.

Maybe because he'd just picked it from the one patch his mom grew only yards away from his house, or maybe because of the company.

Didn't matter to Georgia. Either way, she couldn't recall a time when she'd enjoyed herself more. She hadn't even thought about her phone, or work or car accidents once he'd started frying up their day's catch.

She'd only thought about him.

"Despite the way things started out today, this has

been a nice day, Pax. A really nice day. I have to thank you for that."

"Just a regular summer day in Paseo, Texas." He turned off the highway again at mile marker twelve and began bumping their way once more on the uneven ground of the camp.

There wasn't much in the way of formal lighting at the campground except for around the ramada. Other illumination mostly came from the fire pits sprinkled around the wagon-wheel layout, or from the lanterns near the tents, or light coming from the windows of the RVs and trailers.

Tonight, though, even those were at a minimum and she assumed that meant the stargazing was still going strong despite the late hour.

Pax obviously recognized it, too, because he turned off his headlights and crept along with only the aid of his dimmer parking lights. And he avoided the ramada area altogether.

She couldn't say that she was sorry. She still wasn't looking forward to the task of telling her family about her car's sabotage. She didn't look forward to putting any sort of pall over their time together and she knew it was bound to happen.

When they reached her trailer, he turned off the engine.

From a distance she could hear voices and the faint music from someone's radio. She swallowed past the knot growing inside her chest. "Do you want—"

"Maybe I should—"

They both broke off.

"You first," he offered, sounding a little gruff. When they'd been out in his yard staring up at the stars, his expression had been visible courtesy of the overhead brilliance. But now, in the dark cab of his truck, she could only make out the shape of him. Imagined that she felt the warmth of him.

"I just was going to ask if you wanted to come in. Have some, uh, coffee or something."

"I'll come in, but not for coffee."

Her nerve endings whizzed straight to ninety miles an hour. It felt like the wind was whipping through her veins. "Okay," she breathed.

"I'll just check around and make sure everything is the way you expect. There're plenty of places an enterprising person could hide in a trailer like yours."

Instead of feeling alarmed at that notion, everything inside her slumped in dejection.

"Right." She fumbled with the door latch and quickly hopped out. "Very diligent of you."

She waited while he came around to her side of the truck before stepping up onto the metal step and sliding open the glass door.

"Start locking it." His voice was flat.

And this time her shiver *wasn't* from anticipation.

He stopped her with a hand on her arm when she would have gone inside. "Wait." He entered the dark interior before she could.

"You're creeping me out," she whispered and followed close on his heels. "In the movies, you know it's the girl who waits outside who's always the one to get attacked by the zombies."

"Give me a zombie over a spurned ex-wife with an ax to grind."

She bumped into him when he stopped. "Sorry."

His hand brushed past her shoulder. "Got a light switch in here?"

"Yeah." She felt along the wall until she found it and the lamp between the two recliners snapped to life.

It was more direct light than they'd had for two solid hours and she winced.

He didn't seem affected at all, though, as he opened the storage closet, glanced inside, then closed the door again. When he turned and bumped into her, he thumbed back his hat an inch. "This would be quicker without you on my heels."

She looked up at him through her lashes. "But it wouldn't be nearly as fun."

The look he gave her was stern and obviously not at all affected by the fact that their bodies were about two inches apart. "This is supposed to be serious business, Georgia."

She snapped a salute as she stepped back. "Yes, sir."

His lips twitched at that. "What am I gonna do about you?" he murmured as he brushed past her to go into the bedroom and then the bathroom, where her yoga togs were still bunched on the floor from that morning.

It seemed a lot longer ago.

"I take it nobody was hiding under the bed," she said when he came back out to the living area.

"There is no 'under the bed.' But I did look in the clothes closet."

"A ten-year-old child couldn't fit in the clothes closet. That's why there are drawers in every nook and cranny in there." It was easier to play it off than really think about someone actually lying in wait.

"All right, then." He resettled his cowboy hat. But when he didn't take a step toward the door, her nerves starting zipping around again.

"This is silly," she muttered, not sure whom she was

more exasperated with. Herself for her inward roller coaster, or him for causing it in the first place.

"What—"

He broke off, though, when she took matters in her own hands and pulled his head down toward hers.

"This," she said and pressed her lips to his.

Her instantaneous feeling of "oh, my" wasn't cowed in the least by the way he stiffened at first. Not when his hands went immediately to her waist the way they did, his fingertips pressing her toward him. And not even when he pulled his mouth away. "I'm not sure this is a good idea."

She tightened her hand around the back of his neck, her fingers sliding into his hair. "I am." She brushed her lips lightly over his. "Just kiss me," she whispered. "Nothing was ever harmed by a single kiss."

"Not so sure about that, either." But his fingers tightened.

He was going to kiss her. Really kiss her. She knew it with every cell in her body and oh, those cells were so ready, so full of anticipation.

"This looks cozy."

The amused comment was a dousing from an ice-cold bucket, particularly when Pax lifted his head and stepped back from her.

She took comfort in the fact that he left one hand behind her waist, then she turned her glare on Austin where he stood just outside the opened door. "What do you want?"

"Saw you were finally back. Just checking on you."

He was crushing the mood, and she could tell by the glint in his eyes that he knew it. She gave him a pointed look. "As you can see, I'm in good hands."

"It's good that you stopped by," Pax said. His hand

nudged her to one side as he stepped toward the door and her brother. "Need to fill you in on the latest where your sister's accident is concerned."

"Wouldn't have anything to do with the couple of drive-bys we had this afternoon from the sheriff's department, would it?"

Georgia looked at Pax. "You sent someone out here?"

"A couple of someones," Austin said. "Guy named Ladd and a woman named Colette. Neither one of them was particularly forthcoming about what they were really doing cruising through the campground. 'Standard procedure' doesn't really cut it for me. It feels either invasive— we're just a big family reunion more or less gathering for a wedding—or it feels precautionary. So which is it?"

"Yes, I told my deputies to keep an eye on everyone," Pax said, answering Georgia first.

"When?"

"When you were busy hogging all the fish in the lake." His gaze turned to her brother. "Invasive and precautionary aren't mutually exclusive, either."

Her brother's eyes narrowed. Sharpened. "Meaning?"

Georgia stepped between the two men, exiting the trailer. "I'd just as soon we only have to tell this once. I'm assuming most everyone is still gathered for the stargazing?"

"There's a bonfire out behind the ramada. Everyone was there a few minutes ago, except Nolan and Liz. I was getting a sweater for Felicity when I saw the truck here."

"Grab the sweater and Nolan, too. He's going to want to know, as well."

"Georgia." Austin caught her arm. "Cut to the chase. Know *what*?"

"Her accident wasn't an accident at all," Pax answered. "Her car was sabotaged. And from what she's told me about the other little mishaps—" he air-quoted the words "—that have been occurring and the working theory regarding the person responsible, I think every one of you with the name of Fortune needs to get a lot more serious about watching your backs."

Austin's lips thinned. "Charlotte Robinson?"

Georgia looked up at her brother. "Don't suppose you've gotten word this afternoon that she's been located?"

His expression told her all she needed to know.

"Get Nolan and the sweater," she said again. "We'll meet you at the ramada."

He nodded and, without another word, strode off into the dark.

Georgia rubbed her itching mosquito bite through the flannel shirt she still wore and eyed Pax. "That was nice of you. Having your people check in here today."

"Nice has nothing to do with it. Last thing I need is something bad happening in my jurisdiction." He gave her a quick wink that was wholly unexpected. "Paperwork is a pain in the ass." He knocked his knuckles against the sliding door. "Got the key to this?"

She went back inside and found the set of keys that were in the same cupboard as the control panel. "I have no idea which does what."

He took the small ring from her and selected one of the three keys. "This one." He handed it back to her and she stepped out of the trailer again, waiting for him.

When he joined her, he held out his hand. "And start remembering this thing, too."

Her phone sat on his palm.

Once again, she hadn't given it a thought.

She took it from him and slid it into the pocket of her

dress. "Are you going to write me a permission slip for Marcia at her next little soiree if phones are disinvited again?"

"Whatever it takes, darlin'." He closed the door. "Now practice."

She sighed faintly and fit the key in the lock and turned it.

Then, with Pax at her side, she walked back toward the ramada so she could be the rain on everyone's parade.

"So what're we supposed to do about it?"

More than an hour later, the flames of the bonfire had died down to a hot glow, but the debate was still going strong.

"I mean it." The latest man who held the floor looked angry. Georgia wasn't sure if he was Adam or Kane, but she knew he was one of Gary-from-New York's sons. "Karma's a bitch, as they say, and it's come around to even the score for all of the Fortune misdeeds."

That got Draper out of the Adirondack chair where he'd been sprawled. His shadow loomed across the fire. "Neither one of *my* sisters have misdeeds that are shaping their fate," he spit out.

Austin patted the air. "Calm down, Draper. Nobody's blaming anyone for any of this."

"I am," David, the other one of Julius's sons, from Florida, said curtly. "This is just proof that none of us should be here!"

"It's not proof of anything," Georgia said wearily. She moved toward the fire, too. "And even though we think it might be Charlotte behind my accident and Savannah's break-in—"

"And the problems at Fortunado Real Estate," someone called out.

"And the fire at the Robinson estate," Delaney Mendoza added. "Don't forget that, either."

Georgia nodded. "Right. All that stuff that's happened, well, in the last year, I guess, does seem to add up to something sinister, just like Connor has warned us all. And maybe Charlotte is responsible and maybe she isn't. We can't go around smearing someone's reputation without absolute proof! And bickering among ourselves and casting blame isn't going to solve anything."

She spread her arms wide. "We've been given a unique opportunity here, people. Let's not forget that. We're all family now. We're all in the same boat. Instead of getting mired in the negative aspects of how some of us came to be related, think about all the positive things Fortunes all over the place have accomplished. And let's remember what we came here to do. Celebrate the fact that we *are* family. And celebrate Gerald and Deborah's wedding!"

Her statement was greeted with a couple of cheers and an equal number of jeers.

No matter how long they debated things, she had the feeling that nothing was going to change on that score.

She looked toward Pax, who was standing away from the firelight. "Sheriff, do you have anything you want to add?"

He stepped forward into the light. With his black cowboy hat pulled low over his brow and the dark jacket he'd retrieved from his truck hanging loose over his white T-shirt, he seemed particularly imposing.

And authoritative.

"While y'all have been hashing this out, I've made a few inquiries of my own. The FBI and state agencies have all been alerted. But I want to reiterate the importance of what's already been said tonight." His steady gaze fell on everyone there. "Practice the buddy system.

Stay with a group. Watch out for strangers. Report anything that seems odd, no matter how inconsequential it may seem to you."

"How're we supposed to watch out for strangers when all of us are strangers?" someone called out.

"Yeah! Want us to confine ourselves to this campground for the duration?"

"What about the rodeo in town next weekend?"

Pax raised his hand. "I'm not telling you that you have to sequester yourselves. I'm telling you to use your common sense."

"If you see something, say something," yet another voice said, mocking.

"You can joke if you want, but that's exactly right." Pax's voice hardened enough that the rumblings around the fire died off into silence. "If you see something," he repeated, "say something."

"I don't know about y'all, but I need some hot chocolate, with a hefty shot of alcohol in it," Delaney said, finally breaking the hush. "Who wants to come with me?"

A half-dozen hands went up and soon, the area around the fire pit was vacated. Some headed to the kitchen area of the ramada. Some headed off into the dark.

But none of them went alone.

Hugging her arms to herself, Georgia stopped next to Pax. "Would you like some cocoa, spiked or otherwise? I had some last night and I can wholeheartedly recommend it."

"I need to be getting back."

"Sure." She moistened her lips. "Or you could drive me back to my trailer." He'd moved his truck while all the arguing had been going on.

He was silent for a heart-pounding moment that was accompanied by a too-shrill burst of laughter from the ramada. "I'll take you back," he said, "but I won't be staying." He waited another beat. "In case you were asking."

She had been. "Too forward for you?"

He exhaled a soundless laugh. "Too tempting." He reached out and touched her hair. Slipped it slowly behind her shoulder. "And I am tempted, NOLA girl. More 'n you'd want to know." His hand moved and the pad of his thumb brushed over her lower lip, dragging ever so maddeningly before it fell away. "Still want me to see you safely to your door?"

She could hardly breathe for the tightness growing in her chest. "I think I'll have some hot chocolate after all. One of my brothers will walk me home, I'm sure."

The corners of his lips tilted. "Then I'll say g'night now." He pulled off his hat, lowered his head and pressed a kiss to her lips.

Gentle.

Impossibly brief.

Entirely unforgettable.

"Good night," she whispered shakily.

But he'd already pulled on his hat again, and was striding toward his truck.

She let out a long breath. Then remembered. "Pax, wait." She took a jogging step after him. "Your shirt." She started to pull it off.

"Keep it. I'll get it from you next time." He swung up into the truck and started the engine.

When she could no longer see his taillights, she walked back to the ramada. She passed the schedule board sitting on the easel and stopped to study it.

A sunrise horseback ride complete with cookout breakfast—prepared by none other than their host and hostess. A midday mud-pie contest and mobile massages. A hot-air balloon glow rounded out the evening.

"Here." Felicity nudged her arm. She was holding a cup with a cardboard sleeve around it. "Extra shot in it to keep you warm."

"Thanks." Georgia took the cup with one hand and toyed with the edges of the phone in her pocket with the other. But she didn't need the extra helping of liquor mixed into the hot cocoa to keep her warm.

"Next time" had accomplished that.

"You interested in any of the activities tomorrow? Maybe a massage would help soothe the pain in your back."

"Actually, I have other plans tomorrow afternoon."

Felicity raised her eyebrows. "With the sheriff?"

Georgia laughed softly and pulled out her phone. "With a bath."

Chapter Ten

Cara Price's bathtub wasn't just any bathtub.

"All I have to say is wow," Georgia told the woman the next afternoon as they stood in the doorway of the pretty blue-and-white bathroom.

"I know," Cara said with a smile. "I did tell you it would be a bath to end all baths."

It was a claw-foot. At least six feet long and situated next to an oversize window overlooking a pond surrounded on one side by tall, waving cattails and by glorious wildflowers on the other.

The tub was also nearly full to the brim with downy swirls of white lather. Sitting on a small table next to it was a stack of thick, folded towels. On another table, a teapot and a pretty cup and saucer.

"Only things missing are these." Cara set a small plate that matched the cup and saucer next to the teapot. On it were stacked several delicate-looking cookies and three gold foil-wrapped balls. "Can't have a bath to end all baths without something sweet."

"This whole thing is sweet," Georgia said huskily. "This is really too kind of you."

"Don't be silly. It's my pleasure to help a friend of Paxton's. And goodness knows I never had a daughter to pass on the appreciation for a really good bath." She stood in the middle of the room, looking around. "My husband built this room just for me. Did all this wainscoting himself. I've had to repaint it a couple times over the years, but every time I look at it, I remember him working so hard on it." Cara's eyes sparkled. "The man was *not* a natural do-it-yourselfer when it came to building things. I was the one handier with a saw. But he was determined. And I loved him for it."

"He sounds like quite a man. You must miss him a great deal."

"He was quite a man. And I do miss him, every single day. But he's still here." She touched her chest. "Some days I hear his voice as clear as if he was standing right beside me." Cara gave her a conspiratorial smile. "Pax thinks I'm nuts when I say such things."

Georgia's eyes felt a little damp. "What does he know?" She said it lightly. Huskily.

"I love all of my sons, but I have to say that he is the most like Joe. I wish he'd let himself still hear his father's voice. I know he could if he'd allow himself." She shook her head slightly. "Big, strong men, you know? When it comes to protecting what they care for, they'll crush mountains. But some people are surprised at how close to their heart they can take things. How tender they are inside. I never felt as safe as I did when Joseph Price held me in his arms."

Georgia shifted suddenly.

"Listen to me prattle on." Cara waved Georgia into the room. "Now, you take as long as you like. That bath'll hold the water hot for a long time, but if it gets too cool for you, don't you hesitate to add more. I mean it. When you're finished, you come on downstairs for dinner. Oh, and don't worry about the window. Nobody can see in from the outside." She started to pull the door closed as she stepped out of the room.

"Mrs. Price—"

"Cara."

"My back is hardly even hurting today." Honesty made her admit it. "I think it finally calmed down after I was lying on the ground watching the stars last night because when I woke up this morning it felt much better."

"Should I bar you from the bath now?" Cara winked. "A girl doesn't need a sore back in order to enjoy a fine bath. Lock the door. Just in case. All my boys know when this door is closed, it means stay out. But if Redford comes home for dinner and gets wind that his brother's lady friend is here, he's liable to pester the life out of you. He's just that way."

"But I'm not—" She broke off when Cara simply closed the door on her.

"Paxton's lady friend," she said softly.

She exhaled in a whoosh and turned to look at the tub again as she slowly undressed.

It was an awkward feeling.

Getting naked in the bathroom of a woman she'd met only the day before.

That's not what feels awkward.

It was getting naked in one room and knowing Pax was so close by in another room.

She scooted the little table with the teapot closer to the tub and carefully stepped into the water, not wanting to send a wave of bubbles cascading over the side, and even more cautiously sat and stretched out.

"Oh, Goldilocks," she murmured, feeling the curving edge of the bath just right against the back of her neck.

The water wasn't too hot.

The water wasn't too cold.

The water was *just* right.

And even if she'd thought her back was feeling pretty decent, the absolute and total comfort of being submerged in that water seemed to point out just how many sore spots she did still possess.

She'd soak for ten minutes, she told herself. That would be plenty.

After all, the bath really had been the excuse to see the sheriff. Maybe he'd known when she'd called him. Maybe he hadn't.

She wasn't sure it mattered. He'd told her he'd pick her up that afternoon and he had, albeit a few hours late because he'd had to help his deputies deal with some situation. He hadn't said what that situation was, so she'd figured it was none of her business. His dispatcher, Connie, had called Georgia to let her know about the delay.

Georgia'd had plenty of experience with guys who didn't make that effort at all and would just show up late, expecting her to drop whatever she was doing and toddle along with them. Or not show up at all, then wonder why she said "no thank you" the next time they called or came around.

Not Pax, though. He'd made sure she knew. Then he'd even apologized for it again once he'd picked her up.

Even though Georgia certainly understood the demands of a person's job, both of her grandmothers would have heartily approved.

She gently swished her toes in the water. Bubbles tickled her chin as she inhaled the scents of lavender and peppermint and something else she couldn't quite put her finger on. She unwrapped one of the gold foil balls and popped the chocolate truffle in her mouth, sighing a little in pleasure as it melted on her tongue.

From somewhere in the house she heard a slam of a door. The sound of heavy footsteps on the staircase, then down the hall, moving past the bathroom door without so much as a hesitation. Another door. More footsteps.

Whatever bit of awkwardness that had been left after she'd sunk into this bubbly heaven dissipated with the sounds surrounding her. Ordinary. Homey. Lulling.

She reached out again, bubbles dripping down her arm as she lifted the pretty flowered teapot and tipped it over the teacup.

Then she giggled, because it wasn't tea coming out of the spout at all.

It was wine.

She set down the pot and picked up the cup, sipping at the rich red elixir.

Another thing her Granny Melton, at least, would have approved of.

She closed her eyes, imagining Pax still downstairs where she and his mother had left him. Leaning against the butcher-block island, hat mark on his hair where his cowboy hat had sat, sipping on a glass of lemonade and sneaking a corner off the brownies stacked on a plate beside him.

Brownies that Cara had expressly warned him were not to be touched until after dinner.

He'd given Georgia a quick wink behind his mom's back and done it, anyway.

She wondered if he knew that his mother sipped her wine from a teacup.

Cradling the cup high against her chest to keep the

bubbles out, she tipped back her head again and smiled to herself.

A woman could fall in love with a man who had a mama like Cara.

Pax looked at his watch for about the fifth time in as many minutes, though it felt like more. "Maybe you should go 'n' check on her. She's been up there more than an hour."

His mother didn't even look at him. She just continued standing at the stove, tending her chicken-fried steak. "She's fine."

"But—"

"If you are so worried, you go check on her." She finally looked back at him. "Relax, Paxton. Your girlfriend is fine."

He slapped down a playing card on the solitaire game spread out in front of him on the kitchen table. "She's not my girlfriend."

"Then why did you take her fishing? You never take anyone fishing." She looked amused. "Not even me."

"He took her 'cause he's sweet on her," Red said, strolling into the kitchen. "Question is whether or not that feeling is reciprocated. Gotta say, though—" he pulled out one of the chairs at the table with a scrape "—the bath thing's a pretty nice touch. Red eight, black nine."

"I see it," Pax said grouchily and moved the card.

"The bath was my idea," Cara corrected. "And not because I'm trying to hurry along your brother into a romance. But I know how comforting a bath is after a car accident."

"You believe that?" Marshall looked at Jasper as they walked in. They'd arrived within minutes of each other and all of them had been surprised that dinner wasn't already on the table.

"She's a visitor in town," Pax said.

Red snorted. "A visitor you were mooning for the other night over at the Fortune ranch. Have to give you credit, though. You've made more progress than I expected. The girl's upstairs wearing nothing but bubbles."

As if Pax needed that image underscored in his brain.

He slapped down more cards.

"He must like her better than Mindy from Amber Falls," Marsh observed. "He's never brought her home to Mom's."

"Never brought Whitney home, either."

"The only way Whitney would have come here was if it made good optics for her dad the senator," Jasper said flatly. He'd disliked Whitney most of all.

"I don't want to talk about Whitney." Pax gathered the cards in one hand and squared them up with a sharp tap against the table. "Old news."

"I hope so," Cara murmured. She set a stack of plates on the table near Red's elbow. "She was never right for you. You got involved with her much too fast."

Pax gave her a look. "Calling the kettle black, aren't you, Mom?"

"Yeah." Jasper nodded. "How long was it from the time you met dad until you married him?"

"That was different," Cara assured loftily, which earned a round of hoots from Pax's brothers.

Then Marshall gestured at Pax, who was still toying with the cards in his hand. "Deal 'em out. If we've gotta wait for supper, might as well win some money from you."

And maybe it would help distract him from thinking about the woman upstairs in his mother's bathtub. Not that Pax had any intention of losing money to any one of his kid brothers.

He shuffled the cards one last time and set the deck down on the table for Red to cut. "Stud or draw?"

"Draw," Jasper said, squaring his chair up to the table while Marshall grabbed the ever-useful box of kitchen matches and doled a handful out to everyone. The common value of each matchstick was a buck and they all had to settle up afterward.

No exceptions.

Not even for their mother, who was the biggest card sharp of them all.

"Ma?" Red looked to their mother. "You want in?"

"Every time I beat you boys, y'all pout." She dropped a stack of cloth napkins on top of the plates. "Which means you pout a lot," she added dryly. "I'll pass." She began refilling lemonade glasses and they all anted up a matchstick.

"What happened to Whitney, anyway?"

"Shoot, Red," Marshall muttered. "Does it matter?"

"Nothing happened to her." Pax's voice was even as he dealt the cards, then set the rest of the deck facedown on the table while he studied his own hand. He arranged them. Pulled out two. His brothers were doing similar things. "We had different goals in mind."

"Yeah, Whitney's goal was marrying someone with money. Enough to keep the senator in office and woe to anyone who stood in the way," Jasper said. "Two." He tossed in two matchsticks.

"Feeling lucky today, eh?" Marshall tossed in two sticks, then another. "People with money are always the same. Money wants money."

At the faint sound from the doorway, they all went silent, turning to look.

Georgia stood there wearing the silky blue halter and thigh-skimming white skirt she'd been wearing when Pax had picked her up at the campground. Her hair was piled on top of her head but there were damp strands clinging to her neck. Her skin was rosy and Pax would have given his right arm to be certain she hadn't overheard Marshall's comment.

Thank God his mother had more presence of mind than her stupid sons, who all seemed as dumbstruck as Pax.

Cara smiled and gestured Georgia into the room. "Just in time," she greeted. "Dinner's almost ready. Did you enjoy the bath?"

Pax realized Georgia was holding his mom's prized teapot in her hands when she set it carefully on the counter. "I did. Thank you very much."

"Enjoy the tea?"

Georgia's blue eyes skated over Pax, warming him inside. "I did. It was, um, very—"

"Soothing?"

Her lips curved. "Yes."

Whatever the hell secret signals were passing between the two women, Pax couldn't decipher them. He chalked it up to the mystery of females and scooted his chair slightly toward Jasper and grabbed the spare that always sat against the wall under an ancient cuckoo clock that his parents had bought on some long-ago trip. "Come on in and sit."

He didn't see any signs of hesitation in her expression as she slid onto the chair next to him. She smelled warm and fragrant and he had to bury his nose in his lemonade to keep from reacting too obviously when her thigh brushed against his as she adjusted her chair slightly.

"Georgia, these are Pax's brothers," Cara said and he

looked up in time to catch the look she bestowed on him for having failed to make the introductions right away. "Marshall, Jasper and Redford in order of appearance."

"Nice t'meet you all," Georgia murmured, looking a little shy.

Which was a hell of a thing, Pax figured, for the director of public relations for a big, important investment firm.

"One round," Cara warned them. "Dinner's going to be on in five minutes whether you finish the hand or not."

Georgia scooted her chair another inch, away from the table this time, and her thigh tormented him with another slight brush. "Is there something I can help you with?"

"Nope." His mother moved around the kitchen with her typical ease. "I have it all under control today." She sent an arch look toward the table. "Next time, I'll put you straight to work, though."

Red tossed three matchsticks onto the pot. "She's not joking," he said. "Around this place, anyone who eats eventually has to work for their grub."

"Says the guy who has always managed to do the least amount of work," Jas said, needling him.

Pax added his own matchsticks to the pile and gave Jasper two cards when his brother tossed down two. His dad had taught him to play poker as soon as he'd been able to identify the suits. He could play it in his sleep. Yet he had to force himself to concentrate on what he was doing as he went around the table, doling out the draws. When he got to his own hand, he replaced only one, which didn't gain him diddly. "You play?" he asked Georgia.

"Only a time or two."

"Well, deal her on in, then," Red said, obviously scenting fresh blood.

"Watch out for that 'time or two' of hers," Pax warned and caught the smile Georgia didn't really try to hide.

"No one is dealing anyone in right now." Cara reached to the center of the table to push aside the matchsticks and set a platter of crispy golden slabs in their place. She followed it up with a bowl of mashed potatoes, the creamed corn that had been a requisite for Sunday dinners since Pax was a kid and another bowl of green salad.

Then she pulled up a chair for herself between Jasper and Marshall and took one of the plates from the stack that Red was dealing out like cards. "Keep your elbows tucked around this crew," she advised Georgia humorously. "Food and hungry Price men should require danger-zone signs."

"She's exaggerating," Pax said, although he had to move fast with his own fork to snag the piece he was eyeing before Marsh did.

"I come from a family of seven kids," Georgia said dryly.

She didn't have to fight for her share of food, Pax noticed, because she simply chose to fill her plate from the untouched bowl of salad.

"That must have been quite something, growing up with so many siblings." Cara patted Marshall's arm. "Both Joe and I knew we wanted lots of kids but after four boys—" there was laughter in her voice "—I had to cry mercy. A woman can only take being surrounded by so much testosterone."

Pax looked at Georgia. "Mom trying to convince anyone that she was overwhelmed by a house of men is about like you saying you've only done something a time or two."

"Bubbles and tea have miraculous healing properties," Georgia commented, apropos of nothing. "That's for sure."

Then both his mom and the woman beside him giggled.

Giggled!

And Pax had to face facts.

Whatever was lying at the end of the road where Georgia Fortune was concerned, he'd already traveled too far down it to escape unscathed.

"Here." He forked up the last piece of steak a moment before Red and his bottomless stomach went in for seconds and plopped it on Georgia's plate. "Salad in this house is mostly for appearance's sake, anyway," he said gruffly.

Her smile widened and that dimple he'd begun wanting to see all the damn time appeared. "My hero," she said lightly.

"Oh, he's sunk now," Red said wryly. "Nobody has a bigger hero complex than Paxton Price."

"Your father was the same way," Cara said with a smile. "And he got me, didn't he?"

Pax exhaled. He slid a look toward Georgia. "Should've left the last piece of meat for him," he told her. "He doesn't know how to behave unless he's been properly fed."

Red tossed a biscuit at his head that Pax caught easily without even looking away from the woman at his side.

"Boys," Cara chided.

Pax raised his eyebrows, "See?"

Georgia laughed outright. "The only thing that I see is that you're all wonderful."

Then she shocked the life out of him when she planted a smacking kiss on his cheek right there in front of God and country and Pax's whole damn family, then sat back in her chair, still laughing as she dumped his mama's gravy all over her chicken-fried steak and cut off a chunk. "Positively wonderful."

"I still have a steak-and-gravy coma," Georgia complained two hours later when she climbed up in the passenger seat of his truck. "I can't *believe* I ate that whole thing."

"I can't believe you wiped out all of us, including my mother, at poker."

"Oh, that." She plucked the five twenty-dollar bills out of her skirt pocket and fanned them in front of her face. "I maybe felt a little bad about your mother since she did give me that wonderful bath and…tea." She knew she had a silly grin on her face but couldn't seem to help it. She folded the money away in her pocket and would have leaned over and kissed Pax right then and there, except she could see the faces of his brothers peering at them through the back windows of Cara's house. "Your brothers are watching, you know."

His lips quirked. "That's because they have no lives of their own." He shut the door and rounded the front of the truck to climb behind the wheel. "You were a good sport with them. Not everybody puts up with their BS quite so well."

Georgia pressed the tip of her tongue against the back of her teeth for a moment while he started the engine. "Was Whitney one of them?"

She saw his slight hesitation before he put the truck in gear. "You *did* overhear."

"Who was she?"

"Nobody important."

"Didn't sound that way to me."

"All right," he said after a moment. His voice was

even. "For a while, I thought she was important. I was wrong."

"What happened?"

He gave her a sidelong look. "Does it matter?"

"Only if you're comparing me to her. I like to know what I'm being measured against."

His lips twisted. "Trust me, darlin'. Any measuring I might have done between you and Whitney Jefferson got tossed out yesterday along with a bucket of fish guts."

Whitney Jefferson? There was no way that Georgia could fail to recognize the name. She was a United States senator's daughter who would probably succeed one day in getting her daddy to the White House. "Who was in the guts? Me or her?"

His gaze met hers. "You have to ask?"

"I just want to be clear," she said huskily.

"Be clear. Probably not the most romantic thing you've ever heard. But if you want pretty words, darlin', I'm not the guy. Sorry."

"Don't be. I'll take honest over pretty every day of the week." They were nearing his sweet stone house with the single bedroom and its ocean-sized bed and three pillows, and she threw caution to the wind, leaning over the console separating them. "Nobody's expecting me back at the camp for a while."

The truck slowed and her heart gave a quick skip. When the wheels rolled to a stop completely, it did a full-on somersault.

He put the truck in Park and unclipped his seat belt, turning toward her. "What do you want in this life, Georgia?"

"Right now?" She pressed her lips against his, reveling in the shape of them. The warmth of them. The way they moved against hers and turned her bones into warm, melting honey. "Right now, the only thing I want in this life is your body," she whispered throatily.

He made a low, rough sound that scraped deliciously along her nerves, and hauled her right across the console onto his lap. His hands cupped her face and he kissed her again. Slow and deep and intoxicating.

Then he swore slightly and lifted her right back across the console and dumped her in her seat, leaving her there trying to unscramble brains that might never unscramble. "Pax—"

"See all that out there?" He flicked his hand toward the windshield.

"The cornfields?" They waved slightly in the evening sunlight, thick green stalks with big leathery leaves undulating in a slow, sweeping ballet.

"The fields. My house. My mom's. I want it all. I want what it means."

She swallowed. Her mouth was already dry, but now it turned as arid as the Arizona desert her folks were visiting. "I—I don't—"

"I want a wife. Kids. I want *you* right now so much that I ache to my back teeth with it. But I'm not interested in a one-night stand."

Twice now, she'd made her interest in him plain, and twice now, he was turning her down. "I'm in Paseo for more than one night."

"Are you in Paseo for a lifetime of them?"

She exhaled. "Wow." She sat back in her seat. "I don't know what to make of you, Pax."

"I don't want casual sex with you."

She hadn't been feeling very casual about it, but she wasn't going to admit that now. "How long ago did you break up with the senator's daughter? Before you became sheriff, I'm guessing?"

He gave a single, brief nod.

"So you haven't, uh, casually…" She waved her hand, finding the possibility that he hadn't slept with a woman in at least two years positively inconceivable.

"I'm not dead," he said, sounding impatient.

"Then if you've slept with other women, why not me?"

He slid his hand around her neck, pulling her close again. "Because they didn't matter." His thumb rubbed over her cheek, the touch tender and fierce all at the same time. "And you do."

Her eyes suddenly burned way deep inside her head. "New, ah, New Orleans isn't so far away from here. When I go back home, we could still—"

"No." His lips curved slightly. Not a smile. Not amusement. But something else. Something sweetly bittersweet that made her feel an entirely different sort of alarm. One that she couldn't even put a name to.

"It wouldn't be enough. I want more than that. You can't even say what you do want."

"You said I wasn't like Whitney."

"You're not. Darlin', you are not. And that's how I know I couldn't stand the cost."

"The cost of what?" Her heartbeat pounded in her head as the silence lengthened.

"Loving you."

She inhaled a streak of panic. "You don't love me. You—you can't." She certainly couldn't love him!

"Because?"

She flapped her hands. "Because we hardly know each other!"

"Why? Because we haven't been on the requisite number of dates?"

"We haven't been on *any* dates."

"I *dated* Whitney for two years. Not once did she ever

sit down in the kitchen where I grew up with my family. She claimed to love me, claimed to support my career in Dallas. But she tossed me right under the bus without a second's hesitation when it came to the choice of doing what was right and doing what was expedient to save her father's reputation. One call is all it took. Her father's right-hand man walked away from a righteous assault charge and I lost my job over it. I learned real quick to recognize what is real and what is not and, NOLA girl, you are real."

She stared at him, feeling like she'd been tossed in a tailspin. "I—I don't know what to say to that. To you."

"I know you don't, Georgia." He put the truck in gear again. "I know you don't."

Then he drove her back to the campground in silence. And despite everything, he made her wait in the truck while he unlocked her trailer and went inside to assure himself that everything was perfectly safe before he gestured her inside.

Her chest was aching inside as she looked up at him. "Pax."

He rubbed his thumb slowly over her lip. And she still thought for a moment, a quick moment, that maybe he would stay.

But his hand fell away. He stepped out of the trailer and slid the door closed. "Lock it," he said.

Her hand shook, but she locked it.

Only then did he get in his truck and drive away.

Chapter Eleven

"And there you have it, ladies and gentlemen!" The announcer's deep Southern drawl was distorted through the crackling loudspeaker. "The winner of the Amber Days bull-riding event is none other than our own Harley H-a-a-aayes! Let's give Harley and all the others a big round o' love."

Sitting on the metal bleachers lining the fairground's grandstand arena, Georgia looked up from her cell phone and clapped along with everyone else.

It had been four days since her bath at Cara Price's home.

Four days since she'd offered herself to Paxton Price for the second time. And been rejected for reasons she was still struggling to believe.

Thanks to his conscientiousness when it came to his job, though, she'd seen him exactly seven times in the days since. Each time it had been more stilted and strained than the last.

"What do you keep looking at on your phone?" Belle, sitting beside Georgia, nudged her in the ribs. "Everything's fine with the media campaign."

Better for her sister to assume it was work than that she'd been trying to figure out the star app she'd downloaded on her phone.

Belle nudged her again. "Look. That's Max Vargas down there."

"Okay," Georgia said, not knowing nor really caring who Max Vargas was.

"He is *so* hot," Belle said.

Georgia made herself put away her phone. "Who?"

"Max Vargas." Her sister pointed to the end of the arena not far from where they were sitting. A group of tall men, most wearing chaps with their jeans and cowboy hats, were milling around. "The one with the brown cowboy hat and the superfine butt."

Deborah, sitting in front of them, looked back at Belle and grinned. "He does have a superfine butt."

"Hey." Gerald gave her a nudge. He looked almost unrecognizable in a cowboy hat, dark glasses and a smile.

"Well, he does," Deborah insisted with a laugh and looked back at Belle. "He got married not too long ago. Has a brand-new little baby. Hasn't stopped him from steer wrestling at all, though. Since Grayson's scaled back and is mostly focusing on Grayson Gear and ranching, they don't compete so much anymore. But here in his own hometown? Doesn't matter that it's just a good-time rodeo. Grayson's on the roster and you can bet he's going to give Max a run for his money."

"Looking forward to seeing that," Georgia said and smiled as if it was actually true. She was forcing herself to go through the motions, participating in every event Marcia scheduled just to keep her mind off of Pax. The wedding was in three days. On the day after that, following the wedding brunch, she would head home with the rest of her family and bury herself right back in work.

It was, at least, something she understood.

Deborah had turned back around and was cheering on a bunch of girls in fancy Western shirts and tight blue jeans as they raced into the arena on horses. Georgia had seen all manner of bling in her life, but the sparkles and shine on the women's shirts was something to behold.

Feeling restless, she stood. "I'm going to find something to drink." She worked her way past Belle on the bleachers. "You want anything?"

"A guy with a fine tush like Max Vargas?" Her sister grinned, then made a face and wrapped her hand around Georgia's, wiggling it. "Come on, Georgia. You've been acting in the dumps since last week."

"Sorry." She made herself smile. "You want me to bring you something besides a hot guy?"

"I'll take one of those cherry ices I keep seeing. I should go with you, though."

"The concession stand is ten yards away. I'll be fine for ten minutes." Georgia pressed her sister back down when she started to rise. "Besides, you get up, we'll lose those seats." She didn't care how powerful Gerald was in the tech world—it counted for nothing when the sun was hot and not a foot of seating space in the grandstand was empty. "I'll be right back." Her scrapes and bruises were mostly healed and she was no longer sore from the accident, but she had no desire to keep wandering around the fairgrounds.

They'd done that all day so far, and all day so far, the only thing Georgia had done was keep watching out for Pax. With this large of a crowd, she was certain he'd be around somewhere.

Keeping braced for that tormenting bit of heaven and hell had gotten worse than being constantly on the watch for some Charlotte-driven disaster.

She skipped down the metal steps at the end of the bleachers and made her way through the surprisingly large crowd that had gathered for the rodeo. Not only were the bleachers crammed full, but there were also people queued up around all the carnival booths and games lining the fairway. Beyond the fairway, she could hear the screams and laughter from the spinning zero-gravity ride, and see the Ferris wheel turning high above the fairway. Everywhere she looked, kids played with balloons and lassos, teenaged girls in short shorts and cowboy boots sneaked glances at teenaged boys in jeans and cowboy hats. The sweet scent of caramel corn vied with the deep aroma of smoking ribs and over it all was the sound of both country music and rock 'n' roll on the loudspeaker, occasionally overridden by the rodeo announcer, who seemed to possess an endless spiel of local lore and rodeo trivia.

She crossed the fairway, dancing around a little boy chasing after a squealing pink pig, and nearly peed her pants when an arm scooped around her waist and lifted her right off the ground. She rounded her fist, and glared at Draper. "Oh, my God!" She punched him in the arm. "You nearly gave me a heart attack!"

He laughed and set her back on her feet. "Where's Belle? Thought you two were on the buddy system today."

"This buddy system is going to drive me to drink." She turned again to make her way across the fairway.

"It's not the buddy system doing that." Draper followed on her heels. "That's your unrequited *love* for Prince Price." His voice was mocking.

If they hadn't been surrounded by another hoard of kids chasing after the boy and his pig, Georgia would have happily blistered his ears. "I'm not in *love*," she said, mimicking his deep, stupid drawl, and quickened her step again, finally slipping in line at the boxy white concession stand.

Draper leaned down over her shoulder. "Not what Savannah says."

She bent her arm and poked her elbow into his gut, happy to hear his "oof." "She hasn't told you anything of the sort." Her sister might have caught Georgia in a weak moment when she'd told her everything that had happened between her and Pax, but Savannah had promised not to say anything. Draper was just fishing, because that's what Draper did.

The broad-shouldered man in front of her moved to one of the three concession windows to place his order, leaving Georgia next in line. She gulped a little when she realized the tall man in the blue T-shirt with *Paramedic* emblazoned on the back at the middle window was Marshall Price. And that there was no way to avoid him seeing her when he turned away from the window, cradling a soda in one hand and a cardboard boat of French fries in the other.

His eyes lit. "Hey there, poker lady."

"Marshall." He looked so darned much like Pax it hurt. "You on duty here today?"

He set the French fries on a ledge and plucked the front of his *AFFD* shirt before grabbing a big red squeeze bottle. "Yeah. Grabbing a bite while I have a chance."

Draper hung his head down over Georgia's shoulder again. "Friend of yours?"

She gave him that warning elbow again as she made the introductions. "Marshall Price. This is my brother Draper."

Draper's arm stretched out next to Georgia's head and he shook the paramedic's hand. "You're related to the sheriff?"

"Brothers." Marshall picked up his fries again and moved out of the way so Georgia could order.

"Two cherry ices, please."

"Three," Draper said.

"Three," she amended, pulling some cash out of the pocket of her white shorts.

She'd been wearing the same shorts the day of the accident.

She flipped her braid behind her shoulder and sighed faintly as she counted out some bills to hand to the concessionaire, who looked about twelve years old.

Marshall plucked a long fry from the boat with his teeth and sucked it into his mouth. "You got the whole group here to watch the rodeo and see the fair?"

"Pretty much." The school bus had been retired now that the commercial tour bus was back in service, and it had been joined by a second tour bus to transport all of the guests now staying at the campground. "A bunch of us are near the stairs over there with Deborah and Gerald." She gestured. "The rest are spread out all over."

"You'll have a good view of the team roping there. Coming up next after the rodeo-queen deal. Heard bulldogging is going to be last, because of Grayson's draw and all."

The only thing that Georgia knew about the rodeo was that Grayson had gotten pretty famous at it. She didn't know what team roping was, or bulldogging. She took the cold, slushy drinks the child behind the counter handed her and turned to move out of the way, as well.

Draper slid one of the drinks out of her grasp and jabbed a straw through the lid. "Rodeo queens?" He'd perked right up at that since he'd had no luck making any impression on Marcia. "We're talking pretty women, right?"

"Pretty women who can whip your hide if you get outta line," Marshall warned with a laugh.

"Sounds like all the women in my life," Draper said, giving Georgia a look. "You know any of these queens?"

Marshall shrugged. "Grew up with a lot of 'em." He jerked his chin toward the end of the arena. "They'll all be coming out over there if you want to meet 'em."

She rolled her eyes and left them to slip her way through the herd of people, aiming toward the bleachers again while trying not to spill the drinks on herself. White shorts and white tank were not the safest of choices while bearing artificially brilliant red drinks.

"Whoa there, darlin'." A grinning man stepped across her path. "Nice to see you again."

He'd switched his pink flip-flops for cowboy boots. He already smelled of alcohol and had an enormous plastic cup of beer in his big paw. "Deeter. Was that a relative of yours who won the, uh, the—"

"Bull riding? Sure was. My baby brother. Toughest little guy I know." He guffawed as if he'd made a hilarious joke.

"Proud moment, I'm sure." She smiled politely, remembering Pax's warning about the man. She tried stepping around him. "Excuse me. I want to get these to my sister."

But he sidled along with her. "You ever find out what happened to your car?"

She pressed her lips together, shaking her head, and tried once again to get past him.

But he sidled yet again. "That was a damn shame. Fine vehicle like that."

He was making her nervous. "Yes."

"You must make a lot of money t'afford something like that."

"It took a lot of saving to afford it," she corrected. She gave him the firm smile she usually reserved for annoying vendors trying to garner her business. "You enjoy your afternoon, now." Instead of trying to go around him again, she moved in the other direction, toward the rodeo queen's exit. She could see Draper's head above the crowd between them and felt a little steadier.

But she still quickened her step until she caught up with him. Belle was just going to have to wait a few more minutes for her cherry ice. "Hey." She stopped next to him, then went quiet.

Near the big opened gate at the end of the rodeo arena, at least a dozen men on horseback were waiting. And in an instant she gained a full, visceral understanding of the whole appeal of a man on horseback. Before she even realized what she was doing, she'd juggled the drinks, pulled out her cell phone and snapped a picture.

As if he knew it, the rider closest to the chute where the calves and whatnot were loaded looked her way.

Warm. Mossy.

Seven times in the past few days, she thought again. Each time more painful than the last.

Him driving through the campground, doing his rounds to check on everyone's well-being. Even hers. Stopping to say that he hoped her QL was coming along, but if it wasn't, to call his mother since Cara had extended the offer of her bathtub whenever Georgia needed it. Pitching in to set up a volleyball net that someone had produced and helping to shuck the big bins of sweet corn he'd delivered. Hanging around yet another time to pitch horseshoes and talk baseball with her brothers.

She'd even caught him holding Stella once while Nolan and Liz were losing badly in a three-legged race. The sight had her needing to race back to her trailer on some stupid pretext about a message from Julie at work.

It was then that Savannah had discovered her sitting on the floor in a corner bawling her eyes out.

Georgia wasn't even really aware of moving toward Pax, until the smell of horse was strong in her nostrils and the reddish-brown one he was on jangled its head, seemingly interested in the cherry ices she held.

"Sally's got a sweet tooth," Pax warned. "Better watch out she doesn't try to steal your drinks."

Instead of his usual black cowboy hat, he was wearing a light straw one that looked as if it'd seen better days. In place of the sheriff's uniform, he wore a plaid long-sleeved shirt tucked into faded blue jeans that hugged his muscular thighs. He even had a big, oval buckle on his belt with an engraving on it that she tried to read but couldn't.

Then she flushed, because she was basically staring up at his crotch, and hoped he'd blame it on the heat of the day. "You ride a horse," she said rather stupidly, she realized. "You didn't tell me that."

"I told you the important stuff."

Her chest ached at that. She moistened her lips and tried to act nonchalant, but it was impossible. "You're not on duty?"

"Crowd like this, you never know what'll happen. Town police have it covered, but being sheriff doesn't end just because I'm on a horse." Sally nickered softly and shifted beneath him as she butted her nose against Georgia's arm. He clucked under his breath, moving the reins slightly in his hand. "She won't hurt you."

"I'm not worried about the horse," Georgia admitted. "I saw Marshall a few minutes ago."

"Jasper is here somewhere, too. And my mother. You

hanging around for the party after the rodeo? Heard Robinson Tech's sponsoring it. Got some musical group from Austin coming in for it. Supposed to be good."

She raised her shoulders. "I'm here until the bus loads up to take us back."

"Yo. You ready to do this?" Red trotted up on horseback, too. His horse was darker and slightly bigger than Pax's and he had a coiled rope hanging over the shoulder of his dark blue shirt. "Hey there, Georgia."

"Red." She looked from him back to Pax, realizing then that he had a number pinned to the back of his shirt. And his coiled rope was hanging on the opposite side from her. "You're *competing*?"

"Team roping," Red said with a cocky grin. "And if you don't want t' miss it, you'd better find a spot by the rail. Things move fast once they start moving and they just announced the rodeo queen."

Georgia had to drag her eyes away from Pax. "They did?"

"Dahlia Ramirez," Red said with a distinct gleam in his eyes. With a barely discernible flick of his wrist, he moved his horse around to the other side of the wide gate, leaving the chute area between him and Pax.

The line of women on horseback was trotting out of the arena and Pax gestured. "You'd better move out of the way. Maybe I'll see you later." His gaze felt like a caress, which she knew had to be her imagination.

"Maybe," she muttered, and with the line of horses heading toward them, she quickly scooted well off to the other side.

The rodeo announcer was jabbering on about something, but Georgia barely heard as she maneuvered her way through the people crowded around the rail surrounding the arena. She saw two horses' tails streaking across the dirt after a steer and pushed more insistently, afraid she was already missing Pax and Red.

"That there is a no time as we kick off the team roping event here in Amber Falls," the voice said over the loudspeaker. "Let's give a little appreciation to Team O'Neill, anyway. John and Terry, there, they traveled all the way here from Albuquerque and you know us folks from the Falls and Paseo area. We don't want to send anyone away not feeling the *love*." His voice dropped an octave on the last word, and the audience cheered.

She squeezed between two different groups of teenagers and finally reached the rail. Above her and to the right, she could see Belle and Deborah and Gerald, so she waved, but they didn't notice her among the throng below. In front of her and to the left, she saw Pax, his horse backed up in a boxed area smaller than the side where Red was. They were both adjusting their ropes, leaving a big loop in one gloved hand and smaller coils in the other.

"And next up, ladies and gentleman, is our own sheriff Paxton Price and his brother Red," the announcer drawled. "Y'all remember Red and his daddy, Joe Price, taking the trophy three years running back when Red was just a teenager. Pax there, he's no slouch, either. Used to compete in tie-down back when, didn't you, Sheriff?"

She saw Pax lift his arm in acknowledgment.

"They're lining up and waiting for the nod—yo, doggie, there they go! Red heading and Pax heeling just like always and oh, nicely done at five and six-te-e-een and we're off to the races with a real competition. Nicely done, boys, nice-uh-lee done."

The crowd was cheering and Georgia did, too, though she hardly even knew what she'd just seen. Red had lassoed the steer around its horns and a second later, Pax had somehow caught both the animal's rear feet in his loop.

She couldn't help but smile, though, seeing the grins on their faces as they shook off the ropes and the animal hopped to his feet, obviously unharmed and used to the whole event as another rider on a horse led it away. There was already another steer in the chute and she realized there was a whole line of them waiting.

Pax trotted around in a wide circle, heading back toward the gate, and his gaze fell on her and held, leaving her feeling breathless and wobbly inside. Then he gave her a quick wink and trotted out of the ring, and no matter what she did then, she lost sight of him.

Four more teams rode after that before she finally made it back to her small space on the bleachers.

"You were gone long enough," Belle said. "I was getting worried. Did you see the sheriff?"

"I saw." She sounded as breathless as she felt as she handed her sister one of the cups. "I was watching from down there," she said as she gestured, "but you obviously didn't see me."

Deborah turned around again. "Sheriff did us proud yet again. Not sure when he and Red have the time to practice. Team roping takes a heck of a lot of coordination. Two riders. Two horses. One steer."

"Not much different than bulldogging," Gerald commented. "Except going after a steer with ropes seems a helluva lot brighter to me than going after a steer with your bare hands, like Grayson does. He must take after my side. Not as many brain cells."

Deborah chuckled and rolled her eyes. "He takes after you in stubbornness, that's for sure. They all do."

"Yeah, well, at least they're willing to come to our wedding," Gerald muttered. "Unlike the rest of my children. Even knowing what their mother did, they're still holding out. Wedding's going to happen whether they show or not, though. I can tell you that."

Deborah pressed her head against his shoulder. "Don't give up, Jerome," she murmured quietly, and Georgia overheard. "We still have three days before the wedding. They may surprise you, yet,"

Belle obviously overheard as well and gave Georgia a look. *Sad*, she mouthed silently.

Gerald had slid his arm around Deborah's shoulders and turned his attention back to the rodeo ring below them.

Even though everyone knew now that Gerald was really Jerome Fortune, Georgia had never heard anyone actually address him as such. It was just one more reminder of how long the two had waited to be together.

"You know what?" She stood suddenly, and set her cup on the center of her seat. "I've got to hit the ladies'." It was an easier explanation for her sudden need to move than admitting she'd realized she didn't want to witness the wedding of Deborah and Gerald because it would prove entertaining.

She wanted to participate in their wedding because she'd begun believing the two of them really loved each other. And had for a very, very long time.

"I'll go with you." Gerald rose, giving Deborah's shoulder a squeeze. He couldn't have any way of knowing that Georgia had only wanted to escape.

"Don't take too long," Deborah warned. "Barrel racing's next and then steer wrestling, and judging by how fast team roping is going—"

"I'll be back," he assured her. "I want to see Grayson toss a steer on the ground as much as you."

"Good Lord, don't say 'toss' to Grayson," Deborah said with a laugh. "He *throws* a steer."

Gerald gestured for Georgia to go ahead of him. "God forbid I get the terminology wrong," he said wryly as he followed her down the steps.

Feeling a little self-conscious, Georgia aimed toward the animal barns, where she knew there were restrooms. When they passed the pens that held a row of cows, some with colorful award ribbons pinned on their halters, Gerald paused.

"They are kind of pretty," she offered. Soulful brown eyes blinked at them from the one sporting a big blue ribbon.

"They are." In the shade of the barn, he'd pulled off his sunglasses. "Never spent much time around livestock. Too busy making mistakes everywhere else in my life."

"Can't build a company like Robinson Tech without spending time on it."

He looked amused and they passed a pen holding three enormous pigs. "There's the positive spin. Have you heard from your father?"

Ah. There it was. "Routinely." She wasn't going to lie. "Tries to convince us all to go back home every time we speak."

"Can't blame the man. Wants to protect his family." He squinted at her. "He's doing a better job than I ever did."

"I'm sorry." They passed in front of the noisy, bleating goats. "I don't think his absence here is as much about you as it is about—"

"Julius," Gerald interrupted. "I know. Least that's what Deborah reminds me to believe." They stopped in front of a pen holding two llamas and an alpaca. "None of us are our father's keeper, but if you feel inclined next time you speak, you can tell him that I admire what he's done in his life. He's a good man, your dad."

She gave him a spontaneous hug. "He is. And he'll come around. He just needs time."

"I understand that, too." He patted her shoulder, then stepped away, gesturing toward the llamas as he started back in the direction they'd come. Clearly, he'd said what he'd wanted to say. "Weird-looking things, aren't they?"

The animals made her think of her Granny Melton, who'd had a two-headed stuffed llama in a box of toys when Georgia was a child. She'd loved that toy. She hadn't thought about it in years, but she found herself wondering if it was still around. If Stella would want to play with it.

If her own children would...

It was such a distracting thought, wholly entwined with that image of Pax holding her little niece with such ease, that she nearly backed into the woman behind her.

The woman just glared from beneath her bad dye-job and shoved past her.

"Pardon me," Georgia called after her and continued into the restroom, only to stop in surprise at the sight of Paxton's mother washing her hands at the sink.

Cara's eyes met Georgia's in the mirror and she quickly realized that the woman had been crying. "Cara!" She hurried over to her. "What's wrong?"

The other woman shook her head, looking up as she dabbed beneath her eyes with a ball of rough paper towel. "Nothing," she insisted with a sad laugh. "I always get like this when the boys rope. Just reminds me so much of Joe." She sniffed and swiped her cheeks again. "Did I tell you that I met him at this very rodeo? Thirty years ago now. Dallas boy, all duded up with his friends, visitin' a little ol' rodeo in a little ol' town and thinking they were some seriously hot stuff."

For one, Georgia could hardly believe that the town had produced the rodeo for as long as thirty years. It was impressive to say the least. For another, she knew that Pax was thirty. Which meant that Cara and Joe certainly hadn't wasted any time.

"I raced barrels then," Cara said. "I was good at it, too. So good that I just laughed at first when Joe came up to me at the dance they still hold after the rodeo and asked me to two-step. I had more boyfriends than we had ears of corn growing in our backyard garden and I just laughed and laughed. But he kept coming back, and by the end of the evening, we were dancing the two-step all right." She took another determined sniff and tossed the paper towel in the trash. "Married that man two weeks later on the Fourth of July and never once regretted it." Her voice had gone husky again.

Georgia's eyes burned. "That's quite a history."

"Yes, it is." Cara turned on the water and washed her hands. "My parents always said it was good to learn from history. Pretty common thinking, of course." She snapped off another piece of brown crinkly towel and wiped her hands. "You've heard it yourself, I'm sure."

Georgia nodded. Her throat felt almost too tight to speak. "My grandmother Melton always says we're doomed to repeat history unless we learn from it."

"Another angle of the same thing." Cara tossed the towel in the trash and turned to face her. "Pax won't like me saying anything, but he told me about what he said. How he scared you off—"

"Scared *me*?" Georgia's voice echoed a little in the tiled space. "He's the one who—" She broke off, shaking her head.

"Do you care about my son?"

Georgia opened her mouth but nothing came out, and Cara looked a little impatient then and a whole lot like her son. "Stop editing the details inside your head," she said. "Forget about how short the time's been since you met. Do you care about him?"

"I...yes." Georgia pressed her shaking fingertips to her forehead. It still felt tender, but if the fading bruise wasn't completely gone by the wedding, she knew she'd be able to hide it well enough with cosmetics. "He talked about the cost, but I'm the one who's put herself out there and gotten turned down. Twice."

"What were you offering?"

She was *not* seriously talking about this with the man's mother, was she? "Ah..."

Cara just nodded, with a knowing look. She tucked her red hair behind one ear. "Maybe you weren't offering the right thing," she said quietly. Then she gave Georgia's arm a quick squeeze and left the room.

Chapter Twelve

The sun was going down when the first tour bus started loading up to return to the campground. The other bus would remain to take back the second load later in the evening.

After the dance.

Nolan nudged her from behind, where she stood near the two buses. "You going or you staying?" He and Liz were going, wanting to get Stella to bed. The baby's routine had been suffering, thanks to their time in Texas.

"Going," she decided abruptly, and stepped up onto the bus, giving Marcia a nod where she was sitting temporarily in the driver's seat, making notes on her ever-present R-tab.

"Oh, Georgia." Marcia gestured. "I wanted to ask what you preferred for lunch at tomorrow's spa day with the bride. You have a choice of a citrus quinoa bowl, chicken Waldorf lettuce cups, or locally caught crappie and—"

"I changed my mind," Georgia said abruptly and turned on her heel, brushing past Nolan and Lizzie and the baby as they boarded. "I'll have the fish," she called over her shoulder as she hopped out.

Delaney Mendoza caught her hand as she jogged past her. "Hey, girl. Bunch of us are getting together in the morning to try and work off some of this fair food before we join the bride for the spa day. You want to join us?"

"Um, sure." Georgia pulled on her hand. "I'll see you later, though, okay? I'm heading over to the pavilion."

"Isn't Belle your buddy today?"

"She's already at the dance," Georgia assured her. "And I have my phone." She pulled it out of her pocket.

"Refreshing, right?" Delaney showed that she had her phone, too. "Guess Gerald can't very well expect to control them at a place like this." She headed toward the waiting bus. "I'd go, too, except Cisco called to say he's on his way. Have fun!"

Georgia didn't know about fun. But she did intend to see Pax.

If she'd thought the fairgrounds were crowded in the middle of the afternoon during the rodeo, it seemed even more so as she made her way down the fairway again. The booths were lit up now in every color of the rainbow. The Ferris wheel, still spinning over it all, was blinking red, then blue, then white. There was no rodeo announcer on the loudspeaker now, but the music had gotten even louder.

When she found the pavilion entrance well beyond the arena and the animal barns in the opposite direction, she presented the ticket Marcia had provided earlier that day and slipped through the turnstile.

The pavilion turned out to be an open-sided structure that reminded her of the ramada back at the campground, although it was considerably larger, and constructed over a grass field, versus one of dirt.

Her nerves bounced around in her stomach as she kept her eyes peeled for Pax. She saw a lot of faces from the campground, even the newcomers from Red Rock she'd met the day before, Wyatt and Shane Fortune and their wives. One of the wives was named Sarah-Jane. Georgia remembered that only because of the Sarah part. She spotted Savannah and Chaz. Not surprisingly, the two of them were already swaying in each other's arms. Draper was chatting up one of the rodeo-queen girls and Beau was drinking a beer with Schuyler and Carlo Mendoza.

She saw a lot of strangers, too.

But she didn't see Pax.

Didn't see any of his brothers, or even his mother.

She pulled out her cell phone, checking the time. It was still fairly early and the dance was expected to go on for several more hours yet. She breathed out, forcing her shoulders to relax, and stopped by one of the bars that were set up around the edges of the grassy area.

With a fortifying plastic cup filled with red wine, she made her way over to Beau.

Schuyler's face brightened when she spotted her and she darted over, pulling Georgia in for an exuberant hug. "Darlin'! Don't you look cute as a little star up in the sky."

Georgia chuckled. Trust Schuyler Fortunado Mendoza to lay on the compliments with enthusiasm. "You look great, too. I haven't seen you since your party. How are you?"

"Fine." Schuyler had a serious Texas drawl that seemed to come and go, depending on her mood. She propped a hand on her slender, shapely hip. "Little worried about fitting into that bridesmaid dress Charlene's designed for me considering how fat and happy my husband is making me." She gave Carlo an arch look.

"I'm worried about some bruises that haven't quite faded," Georgia admitted. "I sent her a message about it a few days ago, but she said not to worry. If she has to make any alterations to cover them up, she can do it on the fly."

"Oh, my goodness, that's right." Schuyler frowned. "Though how I could forget you had that accident considering the way my own brother has been hunting high and low to find that lunatic—" She broke off, shaking her head, as if there were simply no words left.

Georgia sipped her wine, not wanting to think too much about the accident or Charlotte Robinson. "Is Connor going to make it for the wedding?"

"Oh, yeah." Schuyler waved an indolent hand. "All my family will be here. Even our parents. Though I can tell you, it's taken some convincing for Mr. Kenneth Fortunado to change his mind and come to Paseo. My daddy's got some serious stubborn running in his veins."

Georgia chuckled as she met Beau's gaze. "I think we all can appreciate that trait."

"Your parents?"

She shook her head. "My dad still has no interest in meeting his half brothers at all. He would've come to Paseo if we'd told him about my car tampering, but he'd have only tried talking all of us into leaving if he knew. And I just am not ready to go."

"You mean that in a general sense, or just until all this wedding business is done?"

Georgia spun around at the sound of Pax's voice and her wine sloshed out of her cup, splashing on her and on him. "Hi. Uh, sorry." She swiped her hand over the droplets on his wrist. "I don't have a napkin."

"Think I'll live." The sleeves of his plaid shirt were rolled up his forearms now and his usual black hat was back on his head. His gaze flicked past her, taking in the others. "Mind if I steal her away?"

He didn't really wait for an answer, but simply lifted

away the cup she was crushing in her nervous grip and handed it off to Beau, then folded his hand around hers and pulled her along with him.

Her heart was climbing up into her throat when he stopped and smoothly twirled her into his arms. Her nose nearly hit his chest and she swallowed hard, looking up at him.

He took her hand and put it on his shoulder. Clasped her other one in his, keeping her at a perfectly respectable distance, and danced.

She didn't know why her eyes went damp, but they did. To hide it, she stared hard off into the distance. She saw the lady with the bad dye-job and the little boy who'd lost his pig. And she saw Pax's mother then, standing on the sidelines talking with a group of women. She swallowed again. "Your mom told me she met your dad at this thing thirty years ago."

"Yep." His hand gave a little pressure on her shoulder blade and she felt herself swinging out, twirling under their upheld hands, then close again.

"They got two married two weeks later," she added huskily.

"Yep." Another twirl, then close again. A little closer this time.

She took heart in that fact.

He danced smoothly. Easily. Made it easy to follow his lead as he maneuvered through the crowd on the grassy dance floor.

"You've done this before."

"Yep."

She sank her teeth into the inside of her lip. Obviously, the man didn't want to talk. That was fine with her. She—the supposed expert in communications—didn't really know what to say, either. "C-congratulations on winning the belt buckle," she finally said. "Second place in team roping? Seems pretty impressive to me." And only when he and Red had received their buckles had she realized it wasn't the first time he'd earned one. "How many do you have?"

"A few. You gonna answer my question or talk about everything else under the sun?"

She realized he'd danced her right out from beneath the protection of the pavilion. The sky overhead was black, but the grandstand lights were blazing. No stars were visible at all.

"Well?" He stopped moving but his hands still held her close.

Her heart was beating so fast she felt dizzy from it. "I c-can't just agree to stay in Paseo, Pax. I have a job. Responsibilities."

"A job you've been managing from here all along, even though you claim to be on vacation."

"I *am* on vacation."

He reached into her pocket and pulled out her phone. "How many emails and text messages have you answered for work in the last day?"

She snatched the phone and pushed it back in her pocket. "I hardly think that's relevant. It's okay for you to be constantly on duty because you're the sheriff, but I have to shut things off outside of nine-to-five?"

"What do you want in this life, Georgia?"

She frowned, confusion swamping her. "How many times are you going to ask me that?"

"Until you figure out your answer!"

"Well, maybe I'm more like Whitney than you want to believe." She couldn't understand the words coming out of her. Couldn't understand the absolute and utter frustration she felt, when all she'd wanted to do was *see* him. And now that she was, she just wanted to kick the man. "Obviously, you have a type and I fit it!"

"Hey, Sheriff. Looked good out there this afternoon." A couple passing by them greeted him and he lifted a hand in response.

"John. Rebecca. Having a good time, I hope." He waited until they'd passed. Then he sighed. Pulled off his cowboy hat and raked his fingers through his hair before resettling the hat once more. "How is it that I can see who you are more clearly than you can?"

The words shook her. "You know how many times I've been a bridesmaid?"

"Always a bridesmaid, never a bride? Is that how it goes?"

"Nineteen times. Twenty, including Deborah and Gerald's. And believe me, by the time I'd done it nine times I knew I didn't want to be the bride." She realized she was fiddling with her braid and made herself stop. "Every one of those marriages but two have already failed."

"That doesn't mean all marriages fail."

"I know that!" She rubbed her chest, where the bruise that was nearly healed seemed to be hurting all over again. "But the odds stink."

"You're afraid."

"Of course I'm afraid!" Her words rang out, earning several startled glances their way.

She ignored them and moistened her lips, lowering her voice. "Anyone in their right mind should be afraid. Including you."

"I am. I told you that already. I'm just not afraid of failing."

"Then what—"

"I'm with you, and I'm all in, sweetheart. All the way. If you fall, I will catch you. Always. What I'm afraid of is knowing that you're not right there with *me*. And I'm not talking about geography. About Paseo versus New Orleans or anywhere else in the world, for that matter. I'm talking about what's in your heart. In your head. Together? There's no failing. But if you're not all in?"

He lowered his head and took her mouth, catching her around the waist as he pulled her up. In. So close she could feel every hard ridge of him. Fireworks shot through her veins, and she groaned, clinging even when the kiss ended too soon and he was setting her back on her feet again. Still holding her when her knees were like rubber and she swayed.

He pressed his forehead to hers and his hat fell to the ground. She could feel his heart racing, pounding against her hands that clutched his chest. "If sex is all you want, NOLA girl, it is not enough. There's no timeline on love. And life can change in an instant. Just ask my mama that." His voice went rough. "I want your heart, Georgia. Your soul. I want your future and I want you to want mine. And I don't need thirty-two damn dates with you to know it." His shoulders moved and he raised his head. His eyes were dark. Intense. "What do you want in this life, Georgia?"

Tears were squeezing out of her eyes. "You terrify me," she whispered.

He closed his eyes, his wide shoulders moving with a deep exhale. Then he nodded once. "Right." He leaned over to grab his hat and scooped it back in place. He looked around, then called a name and a young woman in a police uniform trotted over. "Georgia, this is Lana with the Amber Falls PD. She's going to walk you back to your family." He pointed across the darkened area to the far side of the pavilion. "Okay, Lana?"

"Sure thing, Sheriff."

Georgia hadn't even realized they'd moved so far.

"Until Charlotte Robinson is found," Pax said quietly, "you shouldn't be alone." Then he gave the young officer a nod.

And he walked away.

The rumor was true.

The bride's gown *was* blue.

Not just baby blue. Some pretty, pastel shade that Georgia's mother would deem appropriate for an older bride.

No. The gown that Charlene Dalton created for Deborah Fortune was a rich, deep, beautiful blue. Every eye in the house was going to be on her.

"I had my doubts about the bridesmaids being in such a light color," Schuyler whispered to Georgia as they stood in the rear of the church, preparing to walk down the aisle, "but after seeing Deborah?" She blew out a soft whistle. "When the photos get out, it'll start a whole new trend, mark my words."

Emily Fortune Allen, who was the third bridesmaid and had come from Red Rock, the same as Charlene, leaned her head in, too. "Speaking of photos, I nearly forgot to leave my cell phone at the camp," she admitted. "I swear, that's what mommy brain does."

Georgia smiled weakly, ready to admit that she'd done worse. Her phone was tucked in the hidden pocket of her dress—designed cleverly by Charlene to hold a few discreet items. That's what Pax brain did.

Since he'd walked away from her at the rodeo dance, she wasn't sure her brain had been functioning at all.

"Ladies." Marcia hurried to them, fussing and fluffing their coordinating gowns. They were all made of layers and layers of oyster chiffon with tea-length asymmetrical hems and deep cowl backs. But after that point, the styles differed. The front of Emily's dress swept over one shoulder in a look that suited her tall, Nordic beauty. Schuyler's bodice was strapless and seemed to stay up out of sheer will. Either that or there was some invisible string between the top and the dozens of pearls circling her neck. Georgia's halter-style was still as deeply cut as ever, nearly reaching her navel, though Charlene had taken a little mercy on her the day before at their fittings and added a touch of embroidered illusion between her breasts. Not to hide any bruises. The external ones had fully disappeared.

The only ones left now were on the inside. And they hurt in a way that Georgia feared might never heal.

"The groom hasn't arrived just yet," Marcia said. "This rain is delaying everything a little bit." She fussed some more with Georgia's hem. "This doesn't look like it's hanging right."

"It's perfect." Charlene Dalton swept into the vestibule. "And the groom *is* here. I just saw him entering through the back." She was a tall, thin brunette dressed in a black sheath from neck to knee, and she practically vibrated with energy. She gave a quick tug on one of the strands of pearls around Schuyler's neck and adjusted the drape of the cowl sweeping just above Emily's rear. "Get the flowers, Marcia."

Up until then, Marcia had been the one issuing the orders, but she disappeared willingly enough and returned with the simple eucalyptus and peony bouquets. She doled them out, looking at her watch every few seconds.

"It's such a shame that none of the Robinson kids showed," Schuyler whispered again. "I can't believe they're holding out this way, can you?"

"Nothing's going to stop the wedding, though." Georgia thought about what she'd overheard between the bridal couple the afternoon at the rodeo. She startled a little at the sudden sound of the organ from inside the church.

"Guess they're ready," Emily whispered.

"I know I am," Deborah said, appearing in the doorway of the bride's room behind them. She looked luminous and was surrounded by her tall, crazily handsome sons. Instead of a bouquet, she held an old bible with a white ribbon hanging from it. "Let's get this show on the road, shall we?"

"Yes." Marcia clapped her hands softly, gesturing for the bridesmaids to line up as they'd practiced the day before during the rehearsal. She was waiting for a certain passage in the organ music, and then she'd open the double doors leading into the church, where the guests had already assembled. "Smiles, everyone. Yes? And—" She reached to open the sanctuary doors but gaped instead when the outer doors opened and the sound of rain accompanied the group of people rushing in.

"Sorry," Ben Robinson said, dashing water droplets off his dark head. "Rain delayed the helicopter." He held the door open while his wife and the rest of his siblings all darted inside.

Soon the vestibule was crammed with people and Deborah had a trail of tears running down her cheek. "You all came." She reached out and gave each a kiss, before gesturing for Marcia to let them enter the sanctuary.

The second they began filing in, a collective gasp filled the air. There was Ben and Wes, the two twins who now ran Robinson Tech and their wives. Kieran and Graham and their's. And the girls. Rachel and Zoe. Olivia and Sophie, handsome men accompanying them all. Georgia recognized them even though she hadn't even met them all, and she caught a glimpse of Gerald's stunned face where he stood at the altar in the moment before Marcia pushed the door closed again and waved them back into their positions.

"I have to wipe my face," Deborah said with a laugh. "I'm not marrying that man with mascara running down my cheeks."

"That man wouldn't care if you wore a burlap bag," Grayson said, not entirely begrudgingly. "Or whether any of us were here to witness it or not. Even I can see he's not letting one more sun set on a day when you're not his wife."

Deborah's eyes gleamed all over again. She stretched her arms around her sons for a moment. "Mascara is one thing. But a runny nose is quite another. Marcia, get started. I'll be just a second." She disappeared into the bride's room in a flash of brilliant blue.

"All right, then." Marcia clasped her R-tab to her chest and, staying out of sight behind it, opened the sanctuary door wide.

The organ music swelled. The procession began. There was no plan to their order. Neither Deborah nor Gerald had wanted to choose a best man or a maid of honor. Instead, they'd simply drawn numbers the day before to decide. Emily went first. Schuyler. Then Georgia. Nineteen times a bridesmaid, she'd never shed a tear. But today she did. But she wasn't the only one, which made it easy to pretend they were out of happiness for the couple and not sheer misery for herself.

She reached the altar and took her place on the carpeted step, turning to watch Deborah, her mascara perfect and her smile brilliant, take her long-awaited walk down the aisle.

And then the moment was there. The organ ceased.

The rustling in the pews went quiet. Deborah handed off her bible to Georgia and the minister spoke.

"We're gathered here today to witness the union of Deborah Fortune and Gerald Robinson."

"Wait." Gerald lifted his hand, earning a ripple of sound from the pews. He took Deborah's hands in his. "I want us to do this the way we started," he said gruffly. "As Jerome Fortune and Deborah Ralston. Who we were when we first met. Who we really are."

Georgia's throat tightened. And this time it *was* for the bridal couple.

The minister was smiling. "Very well. We're here today to witness the union of Deborah Ralston and Jerome Fortune." He looked toward the congregation. "Is there any reason why these two should not be wed?" He didn't wait for an answer, because, of course, there was never an answer, and focused on the bride. "Deborah, will you have—"

"I can think of eight!" The shriek came from the side of the church, earning startled gasps from all corners. "I bore you eight children and you *threw* our life away like it was nothing!"

"Charlotte?" Gerald shoved Deborah behind him protectively. His face had gone white with horror as he stared at the unrecognizable person rushing toward them.

The society wife's expensively coiffed hair and designer clothes were gone. In their place was a bad dye-job and a stained T-shirt hanging over dirty blue jeans. Ben, who'd stepped in for Galen in the best-man position, tried to catch his mother, but she darted around him.

And when she waved a gun in the air, they all froze.

Someone in the congregation was crying.

"Mother," Ben said urgently, but she was beyond listening as she fired a shot into the glorious flowers near the organ. Glass and peonies exploded. Georgia saw people diving under the pews. Scrambling toward the exit.

Panic streaking through her, Georgia wanted to do the same. But Charlotte was waving the gun in front of her, seeming to take aim at the entire bridal party. The flowers in her hands were shaking and she accidently dropped the bible, earning the hateful focus of Charlotte.

"You." The sound was guttural.

"Mother!" One of Charlotte's daughters was running up the aisle toward her and Charlotte whirled on her heel.

Georgia shoved her hand in her pocket and fumbled with the cell phone, wishing, longing for one like Pax's. A simple thing, she thought, trying not to hyperventilate, or pass out like the minister had just done. One that did what it was supposed to do. Make and take phone calls. She didn't know if she was calling 911 or taking a picture of the inside of her pocket, for God's sake.

"Get back," Charlotte shrieked at her daughter. "Your father was your favorite, Zoe. Don't pretend you care about me!"

Zoe paled even more, not seeming to notice the man who swept her aside, shielding her to the front of the church.

Schuyler had darted around Georgia to cradle the minister's head in her lap. Galen had grabbed Emily and the organist and pulled them away.

Charlotte seemed oblivious to all of it.

"Charlotte." Gerald's voice was tight. "If you—"

Charlotte whirled again, gun still outstretched. "Don't *speak* to me," she screamed and dashed forward, reaching. But she didn't reach for Deborah, whose face was frozen in horror behind Gerald as his arm kept her in place.

Instead, Charlotte sank her claws into Georgia's braid

and yanked her nearly to the ground. "I should kill you right here," she cried and kicked her in the ribs. "Deborah. Precious, precious *Deborah*. It's what you deserve."

Pain, red and hot, shattered through Georgia, making her vision blur and her stomach heave. She tried to loosen Charlotte's grip on her hair, but the woman only yanked harder, dragging Georgia right off the carpeted step of the altar. She shouldn't be so strong, Georgia thought, frantically struggling to free herself. "But I'm not Deb—"

Another deafening gunshot exploded and the stained-glass window behind the pulpit shattered. "Another word out of you, whore, and I start shooting those pretty sons of yours."

Dear Lord, the woman thought she really was Deborah.

Pax. His name screamed through Georgia's mind as she abandoned the phone to cradle her side. Her hair streamed over her face, but she could see Charlotte's aim switching to Deborah's sons, all sitting in the front pew.

Shielding their wives. Their little boy. The baby.

One twitch of the woman's finger, and any one of them—all of them—could be hit.

"Wait," she cried, desperate to get the gun pointing anywhere else. To slow the frenzy. To buy time.

Pax.

She swallowed hard. "I'm sorry, Charlotte. I never meant to hurt you."

"Well, you did!" Charlotte gave another vicious yank, so hard that Georgia couldn't understand why her scalp didn't simply tear free. "Get up!" Charlotte screamed in her ear.

Georgia got up. She could fight the woman. She was younger. Stronger. But not here. Not in the church. Not with so many people so close. The pews in the back of the church were already cleared as people raced out of the sanctuary. "I'm up," she gasped. "See?" She raised her hands, casting a pleading look toward Ben, who looked ready to rush his mother again, no matter the danger. "I'll do whatever you want. You can hurt me, but you don't really want to hurt your own children. I know you don't, Charlotte."

Charlotte's eyebrows pulled together. "I'd never hurt *my* children. Ben—" She looked toward him. "The fire. You weren't supposed to be at the estate. You weren't supposed to be there!"

He lifted his hands peaceably. "I know, Mother. I know. It's all right. Just put down the gun. Please."

"I'll put the gun down." Charlotte lowered it, but only as far as Georgia's ribs. "Everything I did to keep you away. Stop this wedding." She jabbed hard with the gun. "Stop you from stealing my life. You know how hard that was?" Another jab. Harder this time.

Any second, Georgia knew it, any second, Charlotte was going to squeeze the trigger. "I'm sorry!"

It infuriated the mad woman more. "All those years. Keeping him from ever knowin' about all those damn kids. But you were the *worst*," she screamed, and yanked Georgia so hard she fell again. "It was always *you*," she spat out. "No matter what I did, you were in his head. In *our* bed. Every minute of every day of every year." Fist still anchored in her hair, Charlotte dragged her on her knees across the front of the church. "You can't *have* my life!"

Georgia grabbed her hair, too, futilely trying to relieve the pressure. Another yard, she thought frantically. Another yard, and Charlotte would have dragged her out the side door. After that, she'd fight. Help would be coming. Pax would come.

She knew it with every fiber of her being.

She saw her brothers poised to help and caught Austin's eye. "Stay," she breathed, "Please, just…stay."

"I'll stay with you, all right," Charlotte growled, sounding more animal than human. "I'll stay with you until you rot. Precious *Deborah*. Get up." She threatened to kick her again.

"I'm up." Georgia scrambled to her feet. One of her heels had broken off. "I'm up." She gestured sharply at her brothers, warning them back.

And then they were through the door.

Into the rain.

She gathered herself, ready to launch against the woman, but Charlotte just laughed like the crazed woman she'd become and swung the gun, catching Georgia across the head.

And everything went black.

Chapter Thirteen

She woke and her wrists were tied. Her dress muddy. Her hair wet. Her ribs on fire.

They were driving, she realized. She was on the floor of a motor home. Like the one that Savannah and Chaz had. The crazy woman was behind the wheel, still swearing, still screaming. And swerving.

Georgia rolled over and got to her knees.

Charlotte didn't notice.

A reprieve.

Georgia closed her eyes, trying not to cry. Not to just lose her mind right then and there. They were out of the church. That's what she'd wanted. Away from hurting anyone else. She pulled herself up onto the seat. High enough to see out the window.

She nearly chewed off her tongue to keep silent when she saw the SUV in the distance. No flashing lights.

But she still knew.

Pax.

She pressed her forehead against the window. *Thank You, God.*

"Should have stayed out of our life," Charlotte kept repeating. "Should have stayed out." She suddenly looked over her shoulder at Georgia.

"I'm sorry," Georgia said, feeling the tears slide down her face. "I never intended to hurt you." She was speaking through the window. Speaking to Pax.

"You should be sorry," Charlotte snarled. "He's just *weak*. All men are weak. You tossed Jerome away. But *I* made Gerald into the man he is. And he's *still* weak. You deserve each other!" The RV swerved again. Hit the guardrail and sent sparks flying.

Oh, God, she really didn't want to go over the road again.

The SUV was pulling closer.

Pax. Her lips formed his name. She didn't dare speak.

He'd told her life was short. She didn't want him to feel the pain of that proof all over again. "I'm sorry," she said again. "You're right about me. About everything. If I can make it right, I will. I promise." She twisted her wrists against the plastic ties. Charlotte hadn't tied her ankles. She was smart enough to do a lot of damage but crazy enough to forget something so critical. If only Georgia could think how to use it to her advantage.

She leaned down with her tied hands and unfastened the broken sandal, then slid out of its mate.

"You can't make anything right," Charlotte screeched. She was weaving all over the road now. "I'm ruined. My life is gone."

They sideswiped the guardrail again. More sparks. More screaming.

A second SUV had joined the chase. A third. She spotted a helicopter against the rainy sky bearing down on them fast. A fourth vehicle. A car this time. Coming up

along the side of the RV. She recognized Deeter Hayes behind the wheel and wondered if she'd truly lost her mind.

The SUV behind them had gained ground.

She could see him now.

Pax.

Through the windshield of his SUV she could make
out his face. The deadly expression. He couldn't see her,
though. The RV windows were tinted, like the ones on
her trailer.

She felt the RV skid, wheels sliding, and fell onto the
floor again. Still Charlotte didn't notice. She was in her
own mad, mad world.

Georgia crawled along the floor toward the door there,
next to the couch that turned into a bed. She could feel
the vibrations of the straining engine, the bumps in the
road as the RV swerved wildly, Charlotte suddenly curs-
ing at the top of her lungs and turning off the highway.
They were now running through a field of corn. Green
stalks smacked the sides of the RV, ears and leaves flying against the windows.

She made it to the door. The field was better than the
highway. Above the engine and Charlotte's screeching,
she heard the helicopter. Close above.

Then Charlotte screamed in such rage that Georgia
just reached for the door and shoved it open. She threw
herself out, tucking her head, her limbs, and flew into
the cornfield. She landed hard and tried to roll because
some cell in her brain told her that was the thing to do
when you jumped out of a moving vehicle.

She heard the violent slam of metal on metal and cried
out, finally coming to a stop on the muddy ground, covering her head with her hands.

And then just lay there, waiting, waiting for the world
to crash down on her.

Sirens screamed now. Voices shouted.

And arms found her.

Lifted her.

She opened her eyes. Looked at Pax. His face was white. His eyes nearly black. His hands were shaking as he pulled her against him, cradling her. Holding her safe.

Purely. Utterly. Safe.

She cried then, her face against his throat, and inhaled the scent of him. The warmth of him as the rain fell. "You got my call, then?"

He gave a choked laugh and pulled out a pocketknife to cut the ties on her wrists.

As soon as her hands were freed, she wrapped her arms around him. "I'm sorry. So sorry."

"Shh." His lips touched her cheek. Her mouth. "You're okay. We're all going to be okay." She felt him lift an arm and wave to someone. "Over here," he called out. Then he held her again. Held her against his heart, which was pounding harder than her own.

And she understood.

"Charlotte?"

Pax looked over to the RV where it had crashed against Deeter Hayes's car. The woman was sitting on the ground, hands cuffed together. Her shoulders were rounded, all the fight seemingly worn out of her. His deputies weren't taking any chances, though. They had their weapons trained on her while the helicopter settled in the field. Better them than Pax. It was going to be a while before he could gain some perspective where the woman was concerned. If he ever could.

"She's not going to hurt anyone again," he promised. "Especially you."

"She's delusional. She thought I was Deborah. I

don't—" She broke off, shuddering. "You saved me. Again."

He'd aged ten years in the last thirty minutes. "You saved yourself," he corrected roughly, cradling her face. "I should have been at the wedding. Should have been prepared."

"Who can prepare against that kind of madness?" Her makeup was smeared around her eyes, her hair soaked and hanging in her face. She was still the most beautiful woman he'd ever seen.

The only woman he was going to love for the rest of his days, whether she liked it or not.

He rolled to his feet and helped her up. Her feet were bare. The dress was ruined.

She wrapped her arms around his waist and clung.

It was okay with him. Now that she was safe, he wasn't letting her go. Even if she still wasn't sure about them. He would wait. Forever, if he had to.

"You're wearing your gun. You never wear your gun."

He kissed the side of her neck. Inhaled the scent of her. "I do when everything that matters to me is kidnapped by a psychotic." One day, maybe, he'd be able to recount the murderous rage he'd felt when Connie had patched the 911 call to him. The sounds at first were too muffled to make out, but the phone number that had made the call was unmistakable. As had been the sound of gunfire.

He cleared the knot lodged in his throat. "I need to get you out of the rain. Get you to the doctor."

"Wait." Her blue eyes searched his. "Love doesn't have a timeline."

It wasn't a question and his chest tightened even more. "No, it doesn't."

"And if I fall, you'll catch me."

His eyes burned. "Always." He could hear the others

crashing through the cornstalks, running toward them. Even Deeter, who Pax was going to owe now for the rest of his life. He'd been at the station when Pax heard Georgia's call. "And if I fall?"

"I'll catch you," she said thickly. "Always."

He cupped her face. Stared into her eyes and saw it all. Everything he'd ever wanted.

"What do you want in this life, NOLA girl?"

She pressed her hands against his. "Your heart. Your future. Your everything."

It was good enough for him. "I love you, Georgia Mae Fortune."

Her drenched eyes overflowed. "I love you, too, Paxton Price." She sniffed hard. "I think I'm going to have to marry you, you know."

The choked laugh came out of nowhere. He wasn't going to argue. He'd had his first inkling that she was the woman for him when she'd threatened to shuck her towel and show him what naked really was. "Why's that?" He lifted her into his arms and started walking out of the decimated cornfield.

She wrapped her arms around him and her head found its way to the spot between his shoulder and his neck that he was pretty sure God had designed for just this purpose. "This is my last stint as a bridesmaid," she said fervently. "It's bride only from here on out."

He pressed his mouth against her temple. That was something he could definitely get on board with. "Darlin', as long as I'm the husband, you won't get any argument from me."

"It's not as fancy as those deals Gerald arranged at the campground, but it'll do the job."

Pax stood back to survey his handiwork with the tent

he'd put up and Georgia slipped beneath his arm, fitting herself to his side. "I think it's magnificent." She pointed toward the valley below. "Are those fireworks from Amber Falls?"

"Paseo." He slid his hand down her arm, adjusting her angle slightly. "Amber Falls is there." His hand kept going until his fingers slid through hers. Even though it was already dark, she could see the gleam of the wedding ring she'd placed on his finger that afternoon. "You sure this is what you want for our wedding night? A tent?"

"A night under the stars." She wrapped her arms around his back. "You've even promised me a meteor shower. What's more romantic than that?"

He touched her hair. It was shorter now. The first thing she'd done after getting the all-clear from the doctor at the urgent care in Amber Falls where Pax had taken her that awful day two weeks ago, was to cut off the long braid. She'd done it right then and there, using a pair of scissors one of the nurses had produced. Now her hair swung around her shoulders and neck, feeling light and flirty. Especially flirty with Pax running his fingers through it the way he was. "That hotel in Austin where Gerald wanted to set us up was a pretty nice place."

"Jerome now, I think. And nice has its place in the world." She trailed her hands up his spine and slipped them beneath his shirt. "But this is so much better than nice." She brushed her lips against his neck. He'd changed out of the suit he'd worn earlier. Now, he wore a T-shirt and blue jeans. Same thing she'd changed into from her ecru lace dress.

Their wedding had been perfect. Simple. Entirely without drama and entirely filled with love. Just her family and his, standing alongside the pond outside his mother's house, saying their vows on the same day that Cara had once said them to Joe.

Georgia had carried wildflowers and cattails and her dad had given her way. Her parents had tried to talk them into having the wedding in New Orleans. But when Georgia remained steadfast, they'd come to Paseo. Her mom had cried a little and her dad's voice had been more than a little choked up as he gave her away.

Utterly, utterly perfect.

She kissed her way along Pax's jaw. "Are you going to set up the telescope?" She knew he'd brought it, packed it carefully in the back of his truck along with their tent and camping equipment.

"Eventually." His hands molded to her back, then slid downward to sneak beneath her T-shirt.

She felt gooseflesh rise on her skin as his warm fingertips walked up her spine, bringing the shirt with them. She lifted her arms and he pulled it off over her head and tossed it aside.

She shivered.

"Are you cold?" His hands swept around her again, pulling her close. "It'll be warm in the tent."

"I don't want the tent yet." He'd set up an inflatable mattress that filled the tent nearly from side to side. They had lanterns, sleeping bags zipped together, camp chairs and an ice chest full of provisions. Not to mention the fishing poles that were always in the bed of his truck.

They had an entire week to spend together out here on the ridge overlooking his county before they returned and began the beautiful task of married life. One of his deputies had a vacation scheduled, which meant he'd be shorthanded at the office for a few days. She had to begin coordinating her public-relations department from Paseo. She couldn't wait to begin it all.

But first, they had this night. Their wedding night. Their *first* night.

And she was aching everywhere for his touch.

She drew his hands to her breasts. "I just want you. I feel like we've waited forever."

His thumbs slowly rubbed over her tight nipples. "You were the one who wanted to wait until our wedding night," he reminded her. "Once I knew you didn't have any cracked ribs, I was all set—"

She boldly reached between them and he broke off with a laugh that made everything inside her sing a little. She twined her arms around his shoulders, holding tight because her legs were turning to mush. "Waiting seemed like the right thing to do," she said throatily. Not that he'd made it easy. Every time she'd turned around, it seemed, her sheriff had been right there, tempting her. She pulled at his shirt. "Take this off."

He obliged, then pulled her back against him and she melted a little more. "Did you see Gerald—Jerome... whatever—talking with your dad this afternoon?"

"I saw my father didn't look entirely thrilled." He wanted to blame Jerome for the danger they'd faced at Charlotte's hands. But he also knew that it was Jerome's helicopter that had been instrumental in forcing Charlotte to veer into that cornfield two weeks ago. "He'll, ah, get over it." She sucked in a needy breath when he kissed her shoulder and began working his way down from there. He kissed her breasts, leaving her nipples damp and so exquisitely sensitive that she could hardly breathe when he went down on his knees and kissed the plane of her stomach. Toyed with her pierced navel. Gently stroked the bruise still showing on her rib cage where Charlotte had kicked her.

"Does it hurt?"

"What hurts is you stopping to talk." She dropped to her knees and clasped his face. She knew he still blamed himself for not getting to the church quicker. "Charlotte won't hurt anyone ever again," she reminded him. "Remember?" He'd promised it to her that day in the cornfield.

"She's gotten more mercy than she deserves." His voice turned flat. "She paid to set fire to the Robinson estate. Even sabotaged things at Robinson Tech despite the fortune she stood to lose. She terrified Savannah with the ransacking of her apartment. Damaged the Fortunados' real-estate reputation. Maneuvered the hacking at your work long before you came to Paseo. Hell, the woman was hiding in plain sight in that motor home. It was only a matter of time before she'd have succeeded in slipping into the campground the way she'd planned."

"I know," she soothed. "But she didn't succeed." It was that initial hacking at Fortune Investments that had enabled Charlotte to keep track of everything going on in Miles Fortune's world. Including Georgia ordering her sports car. After that, it had been a simple matter to take control of the vehicle. From its basic mechanics right down to the R-Haz system, designed by Robinson Tech.

She'd wanted the entire affair to come home to roost at the doorway of the man she claimed she'd made. By the time she'd seen Georgia and Gerald together in the animal barns at the rodeo, she'd unraveled to such a degree that she couldn't distinguish reality at all.

"She's a sick woman." When Charlotte began confessing, they'd all been shocked at the lengths she'd gone to. None more so than her own children. "At least the hacker she hired is going to jail for a long time."

"And Charlotte will live out her days in a high-priced institution, paid for by Gerald."

"Everything has a price," she murmured. "The man's paying for his sins." She was still glad that he had Deborah at his side. The two of them had married the day after their aborted wedding. Deborah had been adamant. After Charlotte was finally found out, she wasn't going to let the woman steal yet another day from them.

"Now…" She reached between them and slipped his belt buckle free. "Are we going to keep talking about her, or are we going to do what we came up here to do?"

His hands nudged hers aside, making quicker work of the task than she could. "Watch the fireworks?"

"I have fireworks in mind," she whispered, shaking a little as she wriggled out of her jeans. "Not necessarily the ones they're setting off down in Paseo."

"That's good." He reached inside the tent and, with a hard tug, yanked the mattress out of the tent.

She laughed breathlessly. "I just watched you spend twenty minutes getting that thing situated *inside* the tent."

"Yeah, well, I'm inspired." He pulled her to him and pressed his mouth to hers. Overhead, flashes of light sped across the sky, a pale imitation of the glory speeding through her veins. His hands raced over her. Molding her to him. Fitting every indentation against him as if she'd been created for this purpose and this purpose alone. "And I've waited a long damn time for this night, so I'll just promise you now, we'll take things slow the next time."

"Next time," she breathed as he lowered her to the air mattress. It felt springy and soft against her spine. "I do like that phrase." She pulled him close, wrapping her arms, her legs, her everything around him and then he was there.

At last, oh, at last he was there. Reaching into her so deeply she couldn't tell where she ended and he began.

Tears leaked from her eyes as she stared up at him. This man she'd never expected. This man she never wanted to live without.

"Don't ever stop loving me," she whispered.

He caught her hands in his. Slid his fingers through hers and surged inside her. "I couldn't. I love you." He kissed the tears on her face. "Everything may have a price, but this price has its fortune. And I will treasure her for all the days of my life."

And then he pressed his lips to hers and they flew.

* * * * *

COMING SOON!

We really hope you enjoyed reading this book. If you're looking for more romance, be sure to head to the shops when new books are available on

Thursday 13th June

To see which titles are coming soon, please visit
millsandboon.co.uk/nextmonth

MILLS & BOON

Coming next month

A WEEK WITH THE BEST MAN
Ally Blake

Harper turned to Cormac and held his gaze, despite the fluttering inside her belly. 'Where *is* my sister?'

'Catering check. Wedding dress fitting. Final song choices. None of which could be moved despite how excited she was that you were finally coming home.'

Harper bristled, but managed to hold her tongue.

She was well aware of how many appointments she'd already missed. That video-chatting while wedding-dress-hunting wasn't the same as being in the room, sipping champagne, while Lola stood in front of a wall of mirrors and twirled. That with their parents long gone from their lives she was all Lola had.

Lola had assured her it was fine. That Gray was *such* a help. That she understood Harper's calendar was too congested for her to have committed to arriving any earlier.

After all, it was Harper's job in corporate mediation that had allowed Lola to stay on in the wealthy coastal playground of Blue Moon Bay, to finish high school with her friends, to be in a position to meet someone like Grayson Chadwick in the first place.

And yet as Cormac watched her, those deep brown eyes of his unexpectedly direct, the tiny fissure he'd opened in Harper's defences cracked wider.

If she was to get through the next five minutes, much less the next week, Cormac Wharton needed to know she wasn't the same bleeding-heart she'd been at school.

'You sure know a lot about planning a wedding, Cormac,' she crooned, watching for his reaction.

Harper played chicken for a living. And never flinched.

There! The tic of a muscle in his jaw. Though it was fast swallowed by a deep groove as he offered up a close-mouthed smile. 'They don't call me the Best Man around here for nothing. And since the Maid of Honour has been AWOL, it's been my honour to make sure Lola is looked after too.'

Oh, he was *good*.

But she was better.

She extended a smile of her own as she said, 'Then please accept my gratitude and thanks for playing cheerleader, leaning post, party planner, and girlfriend until I was able to take up the mantle in person.'

Cormac's mouth kicked into a deeper smile, the kind that came with eye crinkles.

That pesky little flutter flared in her belly. She clutched every muscle she could to suffocate it before it even had a chance to take a breath.

Continue reading
A WEEK WITH THE BEST MAN
Ally Blake

Available next month
www.millsandboon.co.uk

LET'S TALK
Romance

For exclusive extracts, competitions
and special offers, find us online: